The

"The best part about ... and Jason Hough understands that like no other. Full of compelling characters and thick with tension, *The Darwin Elevator* delivers both despair and hope, along with a gigantic dose of wonder. It's a brilliant debut, and Hough can take my money whenever he writes anything from now on."

—KEVIN HEARNE, *New York Times* bestselling author of The Iron Druid Chronicles

"Claustrophobic, intense, and satisfying . . . I couldn't put this book down. *The Darwin Elevator* depicts a terrifying world, suspends it from a delicate thread, and forces you to read with held breath as you anticipate the inevitable fall."

—HUGH HOWEY,
New York Times bestselling author of *Wool*

"Jason Hough writes with irresistible energy and gritty realism. He puts his characters through hell, blending a convincing plot with heart-stopping action and moments of raw terror as the world goes crazy in the shadow of unfathomable alien intentions."

—SARA CREASY, author of the Philip K. Dick Award–nominated *Song of Scarabaeus*

"A thrilling story right from the first page. This book plugs straight into the fight-or-flight part of your brain."

—TED KOSMATKA, author of *The Games*

"Get this book as soon as you can. . . . Jason is going places and *The Darwin Elevator* is sweetened-condensed proof."

—Dustwrites

The Darwin Elevator

The Dire Earth Cycle: One

Jason M. Hough

BALLANTINE BOOKS • NEW YORK

A Del Rey Mass Market Original

Copyright © 2013 by Jason Hough
Maps copyright © 2013 by Robert Bull
Excerpt from *The Exodus Towers* by Jason M. Hough copyright © 2013 by Jason Hough

Published in the United States by Del Rey, an imprint of The Random House Publishing Group, a division of Random House, Inc., New York.

DEL REY and the HOUSE colophon are registered trademarks of Random House, Inc.

This book contains an excerpt from the forthcoming book *The Exodus Towers* by Jason M. Hough. This excerpt has been set for this edition only and may not reflect the final content of the forthcoming edition.

ISBN: 978-0-345-53712-6
eBook ISBN: 978-0-345-53713-3

Printed in the United States of America

www.delreybooks.com

9 8 7 6 5 4 3 2 1

Del Rey mass market edition: August 2013

For my wife, Nancy,
and her confidence in this crazy dream.

For my sons, Nathan and Ian.
May they never stop exploring.

For my friend Kevin,
and all the stories he left us with.
Rage on, brother.

THE CLEAR

AURA'S EDGE
(No Man's Land)

THE AURA

LYONS

THE MAZE

Stadium

THE DARWIN
SPACE ELEVATOR

Rancid Creek

NIGHTCLIFF
FORTRESS

Clarke's Café

PLATZ
DESALINATION
PLANTS

Temple Sulam

EAST POINT

Skyler's Hangar

THE GARDENS

OLD
AIRPORT

Prumble's
Garage

THE
NARROWS

OLD
DOWNTOWN

HIDDEN
VALLEY

DARWIN, AUSTRALIA
circa 2283

0   2 km.

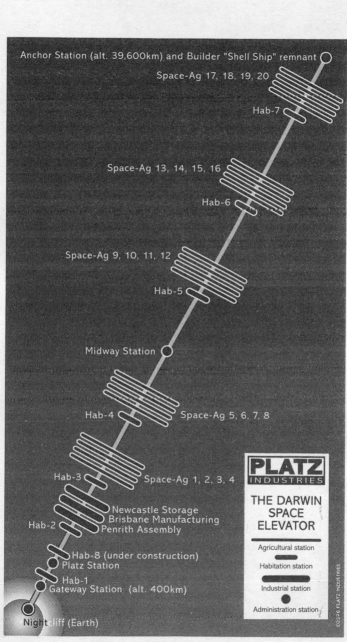

Anchor Station (alt. 39,600km) and Builder "Shell Ship" remnant

Space-Ag 17, 18, 19, 20

Hab-7

Space-Ag 13, 14, 15, 16

Hab-6

Space-Ag 9, 10, 11, 12

Hab-5

Midway Station

Space-Ag 5, 6, 7, 8

Hab-4

Space-Ag 1, 2, 3, 4

Hab-3

Newcastle Storage
Brisbane Manufacturing
Penrith Assembly

Hab-2

Hab-8 (under construction)
Platz Station

Hab-1
Gateway Station (alt. 400km)

Night Cliff (Earth)

PLATZ
INDUSTRIES

THE DARWIN
SPACE
ELEVATOR

Agricultural station

Habitation station

Industrial station

Administration station

©2236 PLATZ INDUSTRIES

Humanity is trapped. A blind newborn dangling from the umbilical cord of an unknown mother.

She sets the world afire, even as she swaddles us in the flames.

—a verse from the Jacobite *Testament of the Ladder*

They said "The meek shall inherit the Earth" like it would be a good thing.

Thanks a lot, assholes.

—Skadz, 2279

The
Darwin
Elevator

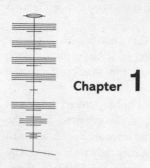

Chapter **1**

BLOOD STREAMED DOWN the inside of the tiny vial and pooled at the bottom. A finger, the source of the fluid, knocked against the glass with a dull thud.

Skyler turned the vessel over again. Fresh from its temperature-controlled sleeve, the vial felt cool against his skin. A small refreshment in the otherwise balmy cockpit.

The scene replayed again in his mind. The dead subhuman, half its scrawny body still smoldering, the scent of burned hair so strong that Skyler had retched. Then Samantha, always acting, never thinking, stood triumphant over the corpse. In one swift motion her dark combat knife flashed from a sheath on her calf, flashed again as she brought it down on the poor creature's hand. Two fingers and half of a thumb skittered away. "Before it all burns," she'd said.

"We only need one," Skyler had replied when his nerves allowed.

Hair would have been simpler, cleaner, but the hair had all singed away. A messy piece of work, though the end result was all that mattered, or so he kept reminding himself.

"Visual on the Elevator," Angus said from the pilot's chair.

Skyler grunted acknowledgment and flipped the vial over again. The muscular digit was caked with dirt and ended in a yellow, cracked fingernail chewed to uneven

length. It almost defied belief that it had been shorn from a
once-human hand. Almost.

Even by subhuman standards, this creature had been ex-
traordinarily aggressive. And part of a large pack, twice
the typical "family." Strange, yes, but thankfully in the
past now.

He glanced up. Ahead, a series of lights marked the line of
the Elevator cord. Eight climbers, Skyler counted, from the
peaks of the clouds all the way to the stars above. He watched
them long enough to discern which way they were going. Up,
at the moment. Air and water then, for the Orbitals. Some
spare parts, maybe. A little contraband thrown in for good
measure.

He pictured the contents of his cargo bay, flush with spoils
from a decaying Malay air force base outside Kuala Lumpur. Tomorrow, maybe the day after, one of those climbers
would lift the items stowed back there. Paid for first, of
course.

Skyler grinned. Success felt good. He'd almost forgotten
the sensation. The finger alone would cover the mission's
cost, if the DNA matched.

"Do you want the stick back?" Angus asked.

The grim, hypnotic spell of watching blood slide down
the glass tube vanished with the question. He slipped the
vial back into its sleeve and sealed it. Out of pure habit he
reached for the flight stick, then stopped himself. Old habits
die hard. He balled his fist and pulled his hand away. "You
handle it this time."

"Sure?"

"You're ready. Just take it slow."

Angus turned in the pilot's seat, trying to see Skyler over
his shoulder and failing. A few seconds passed before the
kid flashed a halfhearted A-Okay.

The *Melville* tilted forward and began to descend. Skyler
leaned to his left and looked down, watching mountainous
clouds rise toward them. Lightning danced beneath the purple morass, which grew and grew until finally the aircraft
slipped into the thick haze.

A ghostly fog roiled around the cockpit window for less

than ten seconds and then they were through. Once below the storm, monsoon rain pelted the cockpit window and hammered against the fuselage.

Another minute went by before they passed under the storm. Over Darwin itself the sky was clear, such a rare thing in wet season. A nice welcome to their return.

"Aura's Edge," Angus said. "In ten, nine . . ."

Skyler closed his eyes. Some small part of him wanted to *feel* it, wanted to know the Elevator's strange aura on a physical level. The invisible field emanated roughly nine kilometers out from the space elevator before abruptly ending. It protected those within from the alien disease that had laid waste to the rest of the planet. How, or why, the aura did this was as much a mystery as the Elevator itself.

". . . five, four . . ."

The shifting, rippling effect ended in a zone coined Aura's Edge. A no-man's-land where the protection faded.

Skyler leaned his head back against the copilot's seat. He would feel nothing. He never did; nor did the rest of his crew. The disease had no effect on them.

They were immune, an inescapable fact. A blessing and curse, a trait few others shared. Very few.

". . . three . . ."

Though immunity allowed him to leave the city at will, there remained that small part of him that wanted to be normal, to be trapped like all of the rest of them. He didn't want to be special. Or sought after. Truth be told he'd rather be back in the Netherlands, flying mundane patrols for the air force, living a good life. But that was a long time ago, in a different world.

". . . two, one . . . *mark*."

The aircraft bucked.

Not much, but Skyler felt it. *Damn fine timing for a spell of turbulence,* he thought. An embarrassed laugh escaped his lips.

Below, out the window, trash fires dotted the city's edge. Small crowds huddled around the flames for protection more than warmth. The worst-off lived here, so far out from the Elevator, so close to the Clear. Skyler thought it must be like living on the edge of a cliff.

"Weird. Did you feel that bounce?" Angus asked. Then, "Oh, shit. Look at this."

Skyler glanced up. The kid's voice had shifted from wonder to fear.

Something had changed, ahead of them. Skyler couldn't decide what—

"Where'd the climbers go?" Angus asked.

The lights on the cord were gone. "What in the world?"

The wireless crackled. "*Melville,* this is Nightcliff control," a panicked voice said over a hiss of static. "What the *hell* did you do?"

Skyler's throat went dry. He could only stare at the thin strip of sky where the climbers had been.

"*Melville!* Answer or be shot down!"

"Angus," Skyler said, ignoring the radio. "Hover here."

The kid nodded and tilted the aircraft back, switching to vertical thrust.

"Think, think," Skyler whispered to himself. He leaned forward in his seat, as if a few extra centimeters would give him a better view. Squinting, Skyler traced a line from the tip of Nightcliff's tower.

There, against the dim clouds, he saw the black shape of a climber, motionless on the cord. Not vanished, then, just dead.

Loss of power? he thought. It shouldn't be possible. Something about friction with the atmosphere, he remembered. The Elevator couldn't help but generate power. In the five years since he first came to the city, he'd never seen Darwin's skyline without the awe-inspiring sight of climber vehicles gliding their way along the cord, taking fresh air and water up to the Orbitals, or bringing food back down.

"*Melville,*" came the garbled voice again. "Last warning."

Skyler absently tapped the transmit button. "Nightcliff, this is the *Melville.* Don't fire. We're holding position. What happened?"

Even as he waited for a response, Skyler saw the beacon lights on the climber cars flicker, then come back on at full brightness.

A few seconds later they turned off again. One by one this time, in perfect sequence from space down to the fortress.

Minutes passed. Skyler felt a trickle of sweat run down the side of his face and he mopped it away with the back of his hand.

A blast of static from the tiny speaker preceded the controller's voice. "You will reroute to Nightcliff and submit to inspection. Failure to comply will result in the destruction of your vessel. Any delay will result in the destruction of your vessel. You have thirty seconds to acknowledge."

The order rattled Skyler like a sick joke. The mission had been flawless, a masterpiece, until this. *Inspection.* He shook his head. All their hard work, dashed with that loaded word.

"What do I say?" Angus asked. He strained against his harness to glance over his shoulder at Skyler.

The young man's brown eyes pleaded for reassurance. Skyler could only shrug. "Stall," he said. "I'm thinking."

He tried to conjure a memory of the last inspection. It must have been two years ago. More than that. They'd claimed fear of a flu epidemic on that occasion. A case of vodka had settled the matter, if he remembered right. He'd been the pilot then, stuck in the cockpit, uninvolved. This time it would be his neck on the chopping block.

The first successful mission in months, since Skyler took over the captain's chair.

And now this. *Inspection. Goddammit.*

They probably just wanted a handout. The pick of the litter from a returning scavenger ship. Maybe they'd blinked the climbers' lights on purpose, now that he thought about it. A clever ploy, really.

He ran through a mental tally of the *Melville*'s cargo bay. For two days they'd rummaged through the abandoned complex, and they'd packed the old girl full. There'd be no shortage of goods to bribe Nightcliff with. The trick would be steering them away from the high-value items. The specific requests.

The neoprene sleeve hanging from the back of the pilot's seat caught Skyler's eye. He thought of the morbid contents within, and the commune that had pooled their money to have the evidence recovered. A lot of money, in fact, along with the promise of six crates of fresh food. Even after Prumble's cut, it was too tempting a reward to pass up. "All we want is to know the fate of our father. Bring us something, anything, that we can give a proper burial."

Like a finger. Skyler yanked the container from its cord and slipped it into his inner jacket pocket.

He activated the intercom. "Sam, Jake, I need you to bury that welder."

A few seconds passed before Samantha replied. "We could toss it overboard. Pick it up later."

"Negative. We're over the Maze."

"You're not going to land, are you? Call their bluff," she said. "They won't waste a missile on us."

Skyler bit back an urge to argue. The welder, a special model suitable for work aboard a space station, had a large reward associated with it. The highest out of everything they carried. Trying to wrestle it back from the occupants of the slum below them would be difficult, and very dangerous.

Angus interrupted the thought. "Five seconds. We'd better answer them."

Unhappy with the alternative, Skyler sighed. "Acknowledge it. Change course for Nightcliff, and drop to two hundred meters."

Within seconds the aircraft began to turn and descend. The fortress of Nightcliff, which surrounded the Elevator's base, came into view.

Samantha's voice crackled over the speaker. "I guess we're playing along then?"

"We can't risk our lift privs, Sam. Can you and Jake go through the crates and put anything valuable at the bottom?"

With a frustrated groan, she said, "Aye, aye," and clicked off.

Skyler grunted. He thought of placing a few choice items near the door—an unspoken bribe—but that might backfire.

Through the rain-streaked canopy, Darwin looked like it had for years: a nearly perfect circle of chaotic slums and dense shanty neighborhoods, graduating to taller buildings toward the center. Gardens flourished on the more defensible roofs.

At the heart of it all, perched on the coastline, the fortress of Nightcliff surrounded the space elevator.

A flotilla of derelict barges and rusting cargo ships radiated out into the ocean beyond. The sea, a garden in its own right, provided a haul of fish that shrank a little every day.

"The climbers aren't moving," Angus said.

Skyler looked from the tower at Nightcliff all the way up to the clouds. Sure enough, the climbers were frozen in place.

"Very strange," he said. He kept deeper concerns to himself. No traffic on the Elevator meant no trade. No way to move the goods they'd plucked from Malaysia.

Damn the luck, he thought.

Angus did another half turn in his seat. "Should I ask Nightcliff about it?"

"Don't bother," he said. "We'll know soon enough."

Angus guided the *Melville* in a wide arc to approach the fortress from the east, as instructed, handling the gusting winds with quiet precision.

"Mind your altitude," Skyler said. The kid flew with natural skill, and giving him the pilot's seat, even for brief periods like this, built confidence. Yet even as the *Melville* leveled off for her approach to Nightcliff, Skyler caught himself mimicking the pilot's actions. He loved to fly, to feel the bond between man and machine. The desire flowed deep within his psyche. Passing on the flight duties felt like the end of a lifelong friendship.

Someone has to lead, he reminded himself. With a smirk he contemplated putting Angus in the captain's chair. The thought of returning to the simple pleasure of flying would almost make it worthwhile.

The sun, now set, left only a thin red smear along the

western horizon. Darwin hid mostly in shadows. It looked almost peaceful from above—a cruel deception.

Few structures had electricity this far from the Elevator. Those that did were fueled by miniature thorium reactors buried deep underground. Based on the large payments offered to Skyler for finding spare parts—breakers, insulated wire, and the like—he knew such buildings were prized among the citizens. Electricity meant power, in every sense of the word. The ability to run lights, an air conditioner, or even spool capacitors could make all the difference in laying claim to a neighborhood.

Closer to Nightcliff, the buildings became taller. Gardens blanketed every rooftop, giving the skyline an eerie, forest-like silhouette in the waning light. The gardens were defended even more jealously than power sources. The wealthy, if they could be called that, barricaded themselves into the upper floors in order to protect their private food supply, their cisterns of water. Garden owners did not have to squabble over rationed food sent down from orbit. They could live in relative ease, trading any surplus for whatever goods and services they required. Like the recovery of the bodily remains of some left-behind patriarch. Skyler patted the vial inside his jacket.

These rooftop denizens could not, however, leave their penthouse enclaves. Not without a healthy, trusted escort. The price of success.

Darwin's poorest lived at street level, cut off from the rooftops. They were wholly reliant on food grown in orbit for their survival, and they fought for every scrap. Some had informal jobs, running errands for the garden owners or extracting protection fees from the neighborhood street vendors. Swagmen, pickers, thieves. A skill of any sort all but guaranteed a life in modest comfort. Bicycle repairmen were cherished as much as midwives.

To be a scavenger, like Skyler, brought with it a celebrity status and all the problems that entailed. Everyone needed something from the outside, but few could pay.

The thrum of the *Melville*'s engines changed as Angus shifted power to the vertical thrusters. Glancing forward over his pilot's shoulder, Skyler could see the wall of Night-cliff clearly now. They'd fly over the massive barrier in less than a minute.

He felt a trickle of sweat run down his back. "Sam, Jake, how's it going back there?"

"We need more time," Samantha said over the speaker. "One crate to go."

Skyler cursed.

"Should I hover here?" Angus asked.

"No, it'll just look suspicious." He tapped the intercom. "There's no more time, Sam. Hurry it up."

"And if we find something truly offensive?"

At that Skyler paused. He knew what she really meant: *Should we hide it?* Her preference, of course, would be to do just that.

"Captain, take a look at this," Angus said.

Skyler leaned forward to get a better view over Angus's shoulder.

A knot formed in his gut at the sight ahead.

Outside Nightcliff's southern gate, in Ryland Square, a massive crowd churned and roiled. People streamed in from every adjacent alley.

A riot, Skyler realized.

Enforcers formed a line in front of the gate. Their black batons rose and fell like a millipede's legs. Pockets of white tear gas obscured the center of the square. Through the haze Skyler could just make out a large cargo container lying on its side. Ragged citizens, clutching bits of cloth over their faces, swarmed over the contents like ants. On the edge of the crowd, Skyler could see children throwing bits of debris toward the fortress.

"What the hell is going on?" Angus asked, shades of hysterics in his voice.

"Just relax," Skyler said. "Breathe, nice and deep. Stay on course."

The intercom crackled, and Samantha spoke. "Skyler? What do you want us to do? There's some one-rope back here."

Octanitrocubane cord. He recalled it from his military

training and winced. High explosive shaped in the form of a rope. Nasty stuff, perfect for precise explosions. Just the type of thing Nightcliff wanted as far away as possible. The fortress had one mandate above all else: Keep the Elevator safe. Such weapons were seen as a threat to the alien-built device.

Stunned by the view of the riot, and the dark, frozen climbers on the Elevator, Skyler muttered, "I don't know, Sam. I don't know."

"We either hide it or throw it overboard," she said. "You pick, *Captain*."

He doubted that the third option, to let Nightcliff have it, even occurred to her. She just didn't think that way. Skyler did, and he judged that such a prize might keep the inspectors from taking too much else. Assuming they believed it hadn't been fetched on purpose.

"We're over the wall," Angus said.

"Sam," Skyler said, "we're inside. We can't toss it."

As he watched, the huge fortress wall passed under them, obscuring the view of the riot. He had a vague awareness of Angus negotiating a landing pad with the controllers in the fortress tower. The aircraft lurched as the young man adjusted their course.

"Easy, Angus," Skyler said. "Deep breaths."

"Sorry."

"Can you handle this? I'm going in back."

"I'll try," Angus said.

Skyler tapped the intercom again. "Leave the explosives where they are, Sam. If they're found, so be it."

"I knew you'd say that," she replied.

In the cargo bay, Samantha and Jake crouched over a green hard-shell case with white block letters painted on the top and sides. They were sorting clips of ammunition. A storage locker on the wall next to them stood open, already half-full.

"We can say it's ours," Jake said, "not from the mission."

Insurance against a total confiscation of the cargo, Skyler translated, and he couldn't blame them. Bullets served as currency in much of Darwin. And they certainly had their use beyond Aura's Edge. Skyler nodded agreement and continued on.

Samantha stood and blocked his path. Well over two meters tall, she stooped slightly in the crowded compartment. Upright she'd tower over him, but when she was hunched over, their gaze met. Her long blond hair had been tucked under a camouflage cap, accentuating already sharp features. "You're letting Angus land?"

"Sam . . . not now."

He skirted by her and worked his way to the rear loading ramp. The aircraft banked steeply as Angus guided her down, forcing Skyler to grasp frayed nylon straps hanging from the wall for support.

The items recovered on the mission filled six large wooden crates arranged in a line down the center of the bay, held in place by yellow plastic nets anchored to hooks on the floor. Despite the hurried search, the crates still looked secure.

"Good work," Skyler said. "Like you never touched it."

A dull thud from below marked the *Melville*'s landing, followed by a rapid decline in the hum from her engines.

"Nicely done, Angus," Skyler said into the intercom.

"Thanks. There's . . . ah . . . a bunch of soldiers waiting outside."

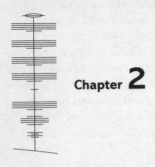

Chapter 2

UNSURE WHAT ELSE to do, Skyler pressed his palm against the ramp control button.

A buzzer sounded from the ceiling, matched by a spinning amber warning light. The bulb flickered as if reminding him to replace it, a task he'd put off many times. Months without a successful mission meant necessities slipped by the wayside. *Sorry, old girl,* he thought. *You deserve better.*

Hydraulics below the floor whirred to life, and he stepped back from the ramp as it began to rotate down.

Rainwater from the earlier storm, whipped up by residual thrust from the *Melville*'s dwindling engines, sprayed in through the opening and lashed across Skyler's face. He squinted as he wiped the water away with his sleeve.

As the ramp lowered, the sprawling compound of Nightcliff came into view. To Skyler's left, the Elevator tower rose more than two hundred meters toward a dark purple sky. On any other night a string of climber car beacons would mark the actual Elevator cord, like a vertical strand of holiday lights stretching all the way to space.

But not tonight. With the climbers dark, the thin strand was all but invisible.

Skyler wondered if the stalled cars alone had driven the crowd outside to violence. Perhaps something had led to the shutdown. A spat with the Orbital Council, or striking water haulers. Rumors like that would spread like fire. The whiff of trouble, of a serious change to their already bleak situation, might spur such a desperate, violent action.

A group of tall buildings clustered around the base of the tower, obscuring from view the crater left behind when the cord punctured the earth. Climber vehicles were loaded and queued within the structures, behind massive rolling doors. A series of cranes, each more than fifty meters tall, ringed the area. Here cargo containers were attached to, or detached from, the climbers. Skyler noted an empty climber dangling from one crane. The spiderlike vehicles consisted of a central shaft that housed electric motors, inversion plates, and billions of tiny arms that gripped the incredibly thin cord. Attached to the top and bottom of the shaft were eight scaffold arms where cargo could be attached. A stack of the long steel boxes waited on the asphalt, idle workers huddled nearby.

To his right, toward the ocean-facing wall of the fortress, Skyler saw a jumble of barracks and other support buildings, including the old Platz family mansion, boarded up long ago. Someone told him once that the lavish home now served as storage. Such a waste.

The fortress at Nightcliff had been constructed out of pure necessity, to surround and defend the alien-built Elevator. Why the Builders placed the Elevator here thirty-two years ago, no one knew. Few cared anymore. The aliens never presented themselves, never said hello. No explanation, just an automated construction vessel settling into orbit and firing its thread to the ground like a fishing line.

Skyler subscribed to the "blind luck" theory. The cord had come down out of the sky, led by a dart-shaped black mass, and implanted itself deep below this small spit of land.

Almost overnight Darwin transformed from sleepy beach town to bustling metropolis: the center of the world. Skyler remembered the footage shown in school; before-and-after comparisons astounded his young mind. Such a time of progress and wonder. A time of hope.

It didn't last.

Almost twelve years after the Elevator arrived, the disease

appeared and spread across the globe. Why the Elevator negated it, or even how, remained a mystery. The two were linked, that much was obvious, but in that time of worldwide panic only one thing mattered: *Get to Darwin. Darwin is safe.* The city as it was collapsed under the onslaught of refugees, Skyler among them. Memory of that journey made him shiver even now. Amazing what humans could do to one another when their survival instinct kicked in.

The *Melville*'s ramp met concrete with a deep crunch, forcing Skyler's attention away from the view.

Russell Blackfield, prefect of Nightcliff, waited on the landing pad. His presence dashed any hope Skyler had for a cursory inspection.

Flanking the powerful man were four guards, two on each side. They wore maroon combat helmets, the only common piece of gear among them. The rest of their clothing came from a variety of pre-disease military uniforms. Skyler saw mostly Australian army fatigues, of varying condition. One wore an ill-fitting Chinese officer's coat.

Their weapons were trained on Skyler—sleek black machine guns, to a man. The uniforms might not match, but the guns did.

Russell stepped forward. "Come out of there. Your crew as well. Hands where we can see them."

The man wore a simple white T-shirt, soaked. His closely cropped blond hair lay in wet clumps. Black cargo pants and military boots completed the outfit. He carried no weapon that Skyler could see.

Skyler glanced back to see that Jake and Samantha were already coming. "Jake, get Angus, would you?"

His sniper nodded and turned back.

Samantha walked between them, down the ramp to the tarmac. Russell followed her with a lecherous gaze, the conversation suddenly forgotten.

Skyler leaned into the prefect's view. "What's this all about?"

"Sabotage," Russell muttered, craning his neck to see past Skyler.

Jake emerged from the ship a few seconds later, with

Angus in tow. They took positions next to Samantha, hands outstretched.

"Right, then," Russell said. "What the hell did you do to my Elevator?"

Silence fell over the yard.

With the *Melville*'s engines fully off, only the distant sound of the riotous crowd beyond the south gate could be heard.

Skyler saw genuine concern behind Russell's dictator façade. "You think we caused that?"

The brusque man stepped in close. His eyes narrowed. "Power failed the exact moment you hit the bloody Aura. *Exact.* Play stupid all you want, scavenger, but we'll get to the bottom of this."

Russell gestured. Three of the guards jogged up the ramp and began to remove the yellow nets from the cargo bins. The fourth remained steadfast, his rifle pointed at the ground between himself and the crew.

Skyler could only watch, helpless. "Look, we were surprised to see the climbers go dark, just as you were. We're not carrying anything that could cause that. I don't even know how that could happen."

Russell strode halfway up the ramp, his focus on the contents of the ship rather than on Skyler. "You're the crew of *immunes,* right?"

"That's right. In from a spec run up north."

If Russell heard, or cared, he made no indication of it. His interest remained firmly on the crates of cargo. "Immunity. Must be nice to leave the city without a suit. To travel freely."

"It's no Eden out there," Skyler said.

"Still, you have the choice."

Skyler kept quiet. He rarely told people of his immunity to the disease, because of the questions that followed. They always asked the same things: Do you feel different? Do you think the Builders *chose* you? Could you search for my wife, or my child, or the earthly remains of a commune leader left behind?

And ultimately: Why do you bother coming back?

He had no answers that would satisfy them.

Most of all, he hated describing the world outside. *The Clear,* people called it. "What's it like?" they would ask. No one wanted to hear that the world had fallen to shit, that all the great cities of man were now home to weeds, rats, crows, and worse. No, they wanted to believe that the world had recovered from the sins of man. They wanted a silver lining after everything that had happened.

Such questions from Russell Blackfield, the tyrant of Nightcliff, would have their own surreal flavor. Though he'd never admit it, Skyler wished he'd taken Samantha's advice and ignored the call to land.

To his surprise, Russell skipped the topic. He seemed wholly uninterested. "Define 'north,'" he said.

"Malaysia," Skyler said. "An air force base."

"Run into subs?"

"Not on this trip," Skyler lied. He could feel the weight of the subhuman finger in his jacket pocket.

Russell stared into the cargo bay as if he expected a subhuman to leap out. "That's smart," he said, "hitting military bases. Plenty of spare parts and ration stores to pick through?"

"That's the idea," Skyler said.

"And weapons, too?"

Skyler shrugged at the rhetorical question.

"Like an EMP bomb, maybe?"

Which would knock out my own aircraft, and every other gadget in the city, moron. "I see where this is going," Skyler said. "I'm telling you, we didn't sabotage the Elevator. It's our lifeblood, after all."

"It's everyone's lifeblood," Russell said.

"Even more to the point."

The prefect walked farther up the ramp, to the lip of the cargo bay. His men were yanking everything out of the crates and tossing the items aside after a cursory glance. "Anything for the Orbitals in here?" Russell asked.

"I have no idea," Skyler said. "Our agent provides a list, and we try to fill it. Who he sells to is his business."

"Keeps your hands clean, eh? Deniability. I like it."

Skyler shook his head. "I'd just rather focus on the mission."

"Who's your agent?" Russell asked. "Grillo?"

"Prumble."

"Ah," Russell said. He raised his voice, speaking to all of them. "A petty middleman like that is wasted on a squad like you. You should work directly for me. For Nightcliff."

Skyler shot a glance at his crew. Samantha had folded her arms across her chest, her eyes brimming with defiance. Jake, unreadable as always. The young pilot, Angus, was staring at Skyler, craving a role model it seemed, from the look on his face.

"I could use a group like you," Russell added. "There's plenty of things we need here in Nightcliff to keep you busy, and you won't have to deal with the rabble out *there*." He gave a casual gesture toward the south gate, where the riot now raged, judging by the sound carrying over the high wall.

No one spoke. Skyler searched for something to say, a clever response to assert himself as the decision maker. But words eluded him, and the moment passed.

"Think about it," Russell said as he strode up the ramp into the cargo bay.

They went through the entire ship, front to back, for almost thirty minutes.

At one point Skyler saw Russell speak into a handheld radio. A short time later another Nightcliff crew approached the ship. Not guards, but ordinary workers dressed in greasy overalls. They pulled a pallet mounted on a hand truck with them.

Under Russell's orders, the men began to load select items onto the pallet.

Another failure, Skyler thought, dismayed. The fourth in a row. He doubted they could afford a fifth.

"Told you not to land," Samantha said, just loud enough for Skyler to hear.

He shook his head, frustration brimming inside him. She never missed an I-told-you-so.

Russell then stomped down the ramp, his face grim, the

case of onc-rope cradled in his arms. "You know I can't allow shit like this in the city. I've stated this *many* times."

"Packed it by accident," Skyler said.

"We'll be taking some things, as penalty."

Skyler assessed the items being loaded on the cart. Three boxes of ammo, a case of whiskey, and a welding kit. The welder irritated him most. Prumble, likely on behalf of an Orbital, had specifically requested the device. A substantial payment would vanish along with it.

It could be worse. They could take it all, and he couldn't stop them. Once again he kept his mouth shut.

A booming explosion shook the yard.

Distant, from the direction of the riot. Skyscrapers beyond Nightcliff's wall lit up in the sudden flash. A fireball rolled into the air before dissipating.

The ground shook and rattled the *Melville*'s wings, sending a shower of fine droplets into the air. Skyler dropped to a crouch on instinct, and closed his eyes against the sudden spray. The sound of the blast echoed through the compound like rolling thunder.

Everyone flinched. Everyone except Russell Blackfield.

"See what I mean about explosives here?" He held the radio to his mouth again. "I want second battalion at the gate, full gear, in five minutes. Time to crush these lunatics."

Skyler watched the plume of smoke rise into the sky. When he looked down, Russell stood only centimeters away. Their eyes met.

"I get it," Russell said. "You provide a cherished service, I get it. But the contraband stops, *right bloody now.*"

"No EMP bombs aboard, though, right?"

"Don't fuck with me, Skyler," he said. Then he smiled. "You're off the hook, for now. Just remember I control your only access to our betters up above. I can lock it down just as easily."

Skyler glanced upward, along the empty path of the hair-thin cord. "Point taken."

"You're wasting your time fetching junk for that rabble out there. Or the bloody Orbitals," Russell said. He paused, and sized Skyler up. "Consider my offer. Before I take it off the table."

"I will," Skyler said.

Russell turned to the larger group. "I hate to cut our visit short, but I've got an adoring public to address."

With that he walked away. A casual pace, as if nothing had happened. The guards and workers followed, prize cart in tow.

"Angus," Skyler said.

"Yeah?"

"Let's go home."

The pilot needed no further prompting and jogged up the ramp.

Jake went next, quiet as always, his hard face impossible to read. The man kept his head clean shaven, and a vein bulged near his temple, the closest thing to a display of emotion he would likely show. In the years since they'd met, Skyler had never seen the man lose his composure. A good trait for a sniper, perhaps not so good for squad cohesion. Still, he got along with Samantha, which Skyler realized probably took a sniper's patience.

The thought made him grin.

"Is this funny to you?" Samantha asked. She waited on the landing pad, arms folded.

"No, it's just . . . C'mon Sam, it's not a total loss. They didn't take everything."

"They took plenty," she said. "Another cock-up."

She stalked up the ramp, her combat boots pounding on the steel surface.

Skyler lingered, trying to think of something—anything— he could say to her that might win her support. He thought back to the crew as it had been, before Skadz walked away. The former captain had no problems handling Sam, somehow always turning her concerns into jokes.

He thought of kicking her out but dismissed the idea as quickly as it arose. He needed her, and not just because she had the immunity. There were precious few immunes in the world, sure, but Samantha could also *fight*.

Footsteps from the direction of the Elevator tower scattered his thoughts.

A pale man, and thin. Sickly, Skyler decided. Stringy gray hair hung in wet clumps around the man's bony face. He wore a long, dark blue overcoat, which clung to him like a wet blanket. Both hands were shoved deep into the front pockets. Another Nightcliff official, looking for a bribe.

"You're Skyler, yes?" he asked. "The immune?"

Not another special request, Skyler thought. "Maybe. Who's asking?"

"You work through Prumble?"

"I do," Skyler said.

The man paused, brow furrowed as if making a decision. "Would you deliver a letter to him? I can't leave on account of the lockdown."

Before Skyler could respond, the man produced a thin memory card from his overcoat. He pressed it into Skyler's hand. "Thanks," he said, and turned to go.

"Wait."

"Yes?"

"What happened to the climbers?"

The sickly man cast his gaze upward. "Some kind of malfunction," he said. "Power went away, then came back."

A malfunction. The idea that the Elevator could fail sent a sharp ripple of fear through him. That would be the end, he thought, for everyone except himself and a handful of other immunes. "If power came back, why are they still not running?"

"Carpe diem on Blackfield's part. It's a game of chicken, now," he said, and began to walk away.

Skyler didn't know what that meant. He decided not to press. "Who should I say it's from? The letter, I mean."

The man in the overcoat kept walking. "Kip!" he shouted over his shoulder. "He'll know. See that he gets it."

As the stranger ambled off, Skyler pocketed the card.

Back in the cockpit, Skyler requested clearance to depart and the tower granted it. Angus did not wait for an order before he spun up the verticals.

On the short flight to the old airport, Skyler strained his eyes to find the Elevator thread, a difficult exercise without the beacon lights.

Eventually he spotted the dark climbers, still stalled on the cord. Bloated mechanical spiders clinging on for dear life.

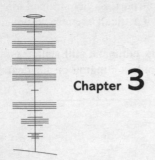

Chapter 3

TANIA SHARMA WATCHED with keen interest as a swarm of tiny black ants carried away the remnants of a fallen avocado. The fruit, dark and rotten, lay discarded on the white tile floor.

Above her, the huge tree that had dropped it grew in a chaotic sprawl, gray branches flush with green leaves. It extended out in all directions from a central tube filled with a nutrient-rich synthetic soil. A gentle breeze stirred the leaves into a sporadic dance, taken up in sequence by the entire orchard. The gusts came every three minutes, exactly on schedule. Each time the wind blew Tania inhaled deeply, trying to identify all the smells carried by it—a fun exercise, hopeless as it may be.

The "sky" above dimmed, then brightened, as the station adjusted to keep sunlight pouring in. Articulated mirrors directed the beams in through expansive borosilicate windows. Tania had memorized the layout and programming of the farms as a child, fascinated. She'd studied the crops grown, their genetic modifications, and their ideal soil composition. Everything she could find, her young mind insatiable. Even now, at twenty-six, the orbiting farms gripped her imagination.

"Missed one, did we?"

She turned at the familiar voice.

Neil Platz bounded toward her in the low artificial gravity, a childlike movement that belied his mane of silver-gray hair. For her own part, Tania preferred full Earth gravity, which most stations maintained, but she knew the agriculture platforms were configured for optimal plant growth, not human comfort. Each ring of the station rotated at a different speed, depending on the crops grown. Apples grew best in a fraction of Earth norm, while potatoes hit their optimal yield in a pull slightly more than Mother Nature's. That always struck Tania as particularly curious.

The grin on Neil's face told of his joy at being here, light on his feet. Despite his age, he exhibited more zest for life than anyone she knew. He'd dressed casually today, black slacks and a simple white sweater. A fresh pair of running shoes adorned his feet.

She smiled at the sight of him. "Missed one what?"

Neil landed in a graceful stance in front of her, dropping to a knee to study the avocado. "This little bugger. The ants don't seem to mind."

"The ants just follow their genes."

"Cheapest cleanup crew I ever hired," he said. "Marvelous efficiency."

Tania smoothed her plain blue jumpsuit and folded her hands across her lap. "You wanted to see me?"

"Indeed," he said. "Thanks for coming all this way."

"I love it here, the air is so . . . it's delicious, really."

He drew in a deep breath, and nodded. "I've missed you, dear girl. You look radiant, the very image of your mother."

"I like the beard," she said. "It suits you."

He scratched at the gray stubble covering his chin. "Ran out of bloody shaving cream. I hope the scavengers will find more." He spoke with an Australian accent, as strong as ever, despite his time living in orbit. Tania found it charming.

"Did Zane come with you? I haven't seen him in so long."

"My brother is on Gateway, keeping the council at bay."

"Four months is a long time between visits," she said, enunciating the words so that Neil would catch her chastising.

He broke away from the insect parade and moved to sit next to her on the bench. "I've been preoccupied. But now, this climber blockade . . ."

Tania knew then why he'd called, why he wanted a personal meeting in a tranquil place. A shift in priorities, an end to pet projects. Four months had passed since she'd made her request, four months of silence, and now he'd kill it officially.

She bit her tongue, allowing her disappointment to fade. "The power fluctuation on the cord. It's that serious, is it?"

"Hah!" he barked. "Some sure want it to be. The self-styled king in Nightcliff has grasped the opportunity with both hands and shut everything down. Just the excuse he needed."

"Shut down until when?"

Neil looked up as another waft of air stirred the branches. "Until he gets a satisfactory explanation."

"Well," she said carefully, "it *is* unprecedented. We should have a team look into it."

He waved off her remark. "Relax, dear. I'm assigning Greg and Marcus to study that. You've got a more important project to work on."

A rush of excitement coursed through her, a feeling quickly dashed by anxiety. Neil swore her to secrecy every time the theory came up. She glanced over her shoulder toward the entrance.

"We're alone, dear. I gave the staff a few hours off. Except the ants, that is."

She took a long breath of the fragrant air, willing herself to be calm. "I thought perhaps you'd forgotten about it."

"Just the opposite. I can't get the idea out of my head."

"I'd nearly given up on the theory, Neil," she said, conscious of how meek her voice sounded. "You could have told me. Why wait so long?"

He grimaced.

Tania studied him closely, looking for any subtext in his expression, and as usual found little. She knew his face better than her own dad's. Sometimes when she dreamt of her father, rest his soul, he wore Neil's face.

"Sorry about that," he said. "I had preparations to make."

"Preparations?"

He leaned back on the bench, tilting his face to the reflected sunlight, and closed his eyes. "Tania, you're a brilliant scientist. The best I've got. But there's politics to consider. If your theory is correct, the world is going to change. Again."

"Maybe. Until I've been able to analyze—"

"I need to be ready for what happens if you're right," he said. His voice took on a full, sonorous tone, one Tania knew only from his speeches to the Orbitals, or the citizens of Darwin in times past. He'd never spoken that way to her before, not when they were alone.

Since she first voiced the theory three years ago they'd discussed it often. Sometimes over hot tea in his opulent office on Platz Station, sometimes over terse interstation messages. Neil gave her the original spark, an offhand comment that the Builders "probably weren't done," though he maintained he'd said no such thing. Tania took the idea and ran with it, theorizing that they might be on a specific schedule. The disease had come almost twelve years after the Elevator, 11.7 to be precise, and it made sense to her that if they were to return it would be after a similar time period.

"Maybe they'll get lazy, take longer," Neil had said in a message four months ago.

Tania's tunnel vision fell away with that remark. *Or . . . what if they come sooner? What if they're here and we missed it?* She'd called Neil in a mild panic, asking him to find the data she needed right away. He'd said he would look into it, and avoided the topic since.

"It's just . . ." She paused. "Granted, we might have years, if they're even coming back at all. But we could just as easily be too late already. Without data, it's impossible to know."

"I know," he said. "I know."

"Plus, the analysis may take ages. If my assistant, Natalie, could help . . . She's brilliant—"

"Forget it," Neil said. "Secrecy is paramount. You must do this alone."

The breeze picked up again, rustling the leaves along the line of trees.

"It reminds me of the ocean, that sound," Neil said. His

voice now fatherly, again. "Waves on the shore of Nightcliff, before the disease came."

"I barely remember it," Tania said. "Bits and pieces. My home has always been up here."

He smiled. "I used to walk with your parents along the rocks, discussing their research of the Elevator. Your father and I took turns carrying you. You hated to get your feet wet."

The mirth drained from his face then. Tania knew this expression well—an inevitable outcome when her parents became the topic of conversation. He'd be thinking now of how they died, and she hoped he wouldn't talk about it.

She was twenty-one at the time, in the first days of the disease. Her mother, a doctor, had rushed back to India, hoping to find a way to stop SUBS. A fool's errand, in hindsight. Tania never heard from her again.

At the same time, Neil had sent her father to one of the older space stations the company ran, one far from the Elevator. But a freak accident destroyed the place. Her father had been the only person aboard.

Neil felt responsible for them, despite Tania's assurances otherwise. They were gone, along with almost everyone else. She found it hard to mourn her parents with so many dead.

She changed the subject. "You were saying, about preparations?"

"Yes," he replied. "You know we've spent years trying to complete another habitat station. Hab-Eight." When she nodded, he continued. "Well, it's much closer to completion than the council realizes. It's better if you don't know more. Point is, I've been stocking it like a bomb shelter, just in case."

"In case . . . what?"

"*What,* exactly," Neil said. "The unknown, one of my least favorite things. Which is where you come in."

"There may be nothing to it. It's only a theory."

"A brilliant theory," he said, a hint of annoyance in his voice. "There's something to it, Tania. I know it. Call it a gut feeling, I don't care."

She nodded, slowly, despite her disagreement. She couldn't make that kind of mental leap, not without evidence. "Without the data—"

"That's why I wanted to see you today. The data."

Excitement rippled through her again, and she couldn't suppress it now. The anticipation of discovery was too strong. "You have it!"

"Not yet," he said, then noted her disappointment. "Soon, I hope. It's a difficult thing you're asking. Any venture beyond Aura's Edge is risky as hell, and your data is quite far from Darwin. It's going to cost me a small fortune."

She said nothing. Neil's concern about spending a fortune, however small, depressed her.

He'd become the richest man in the world when the space elevator connected to Earth on land he owned, some seventeen years ago. Platz Industries dominated the ensuing renaissance in space activity. Neil ran the company with ruthless efficiency, Tania's father always nearby as his chief scientist.

She caught glimpses of that Neil, the business tycoon, too often. From her perspective none of that mattered anymore. Wealth should no longer have a place in society, and yet it remained—ingrained in the psyche.

Neil went on. "They'll have to take their own air and water. Put their lives in the hands of environment suits made decades ago. One little puncture, Tania, and that's it."

Tania knew all this. She'd studied SUBS, as much as one could. Little had been learned before the bulk of the human brain trust perished. It bore some similarity to Alzheimer's, a disease cured almost a century earlier. Only one detail mattered: Outside Aura's Edge, the disease killed most people in less than four agonizing hours. Around 10 percent survived only to be left in an animalistic state, "devolved," their primal urges and emotions amplified beyond what the sane mind could handle. Entering Darwin would not help them. The Aura did not cure SUBS; it only put the virus in stasis. Leave its relative safety, and once the inactive cells contacted active ones, they'd wake and grow again.

A microscopically small percentage was totally unaffected.

"Point being," Neil said, "I've set things in motion. Today, in fact."

"Then we'll have it soon?"

"Patience, dear. Even if the data is out there, they have to find it, bring it to Darwin, and get it up here. All difficult tasks."

Her mind raced. She knew of the scavenger crews in Darwin; their adventures beyond the Aura were often talked about. The romance of danger and adventure in forbidden places. Tania assumed the stories to be greatly exaggerated by the time she heard them. "Who did you hire? Someone trustworthy, I hope?"

"I have no idea." He patted her arm. "Nothing to tie me to it, should things go awry."

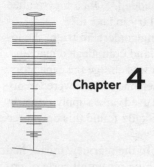

Chapter 4

THE ARMORED TRUCK hummed through Darwin's old warehouse district, crushing rock and garbage alike beneath its thick, knobby tires.

"Where is everyone?"

Skyler emerged from a daydream at the sound of the voice. He'd slumped into the deep cushions of the passenger seat and let the warmth of the day and the motion of the ride lull his senses. He looked across the wide cab at Angus, and noted the tense manner in which he gripped the steering wheel. "Hiding. Watching from inside."

Angus nodded, but his brow creased. "Why?"

The innocence in his voice made Skyler grin. Angus had lived a privileged life by Darwin standards. He'd grown up inside a sky crane, sitting beside his pilot father, flying water shipments from East Point up to Nightcliff. At age six, his dad let him take the stick for the first time, or so Angus told it. He was seventeen now, all gangly limbs and shaggy black hair, and already a better pilot than Skyler.

If only he had some street smarts, Skyler thought. "A working vehicle, this far from the Elevator, means nothing but trouble to these people."

Angus eased back into his seat. "Right. Makes sense."

They drove past a lone bicyclist, wearing a scarf across his face and an AK-47 on his back. Saddlebags were strapped to a frame over the wobbly back tire. A courier.

"Don't fool yourself," Skyler added. "Once they realize we're not from Nightcliff, they'll try to take it."

A white lie, but he wanted Angus alert. In truth, the locals had no use for such a large and complicated machine. They couldn't maintain it, much less charge the capacitors. And even if it were stolen, Skyler knew there were twenty more just like it waiting, never used, at a supply depot in Russia. The same place he and Skadz found this one, three years ago.

No, the bicyclist disappearing in the rearview mirror had much more reason to worry. A bike meant all sorts of opportunity.

Skyler turned to face the window, watching with vague interest as a light drizzle rearranged the dirt on it.

Looking up, beyond the rooftops, he could see the cord of the Elevator. Morning sunlight glinted off the thin thread. It looked like a strand of spider silk, stretching to infinity. After all these years the sight still filled him with awe.

Lifeline to Earth, they say. Yet everything of value goes up.

He strained his neck to look higher, tracing the slightly skewed line until it faded into the sky.

"Any climbers?" Angus asked.

"Not a damn one," Skyler said. He frowned. Ten hours ago, Skyler had stood on the roof of his hangar and watched with growing concern as the stuck climbers began to move again. Instead of continuing their journey up to Gateway Station, the vehicles had come down. Since then, nothing. The cord, for the first time Skyler could remember, was vacant.

If the situation went on much longer, he feared, a full-fledged revolution would ensue. As nasty as Blackfield was, Skyler didn't like the alternatives. Ambitious crime lords, or even zealous Jacobites, would try to fill that void.

The truck slowed. Skyler turned his attention forward and saw a shanty building that had collapsed into the road. Laborers young and old, of varying ethnicities, scrambled over the rubble, picking it clean of useful items. Bits of copper pipe, electrical wiring, insulation. They worked under the watch of two Asian men armed with machetes, enforcers for whatever local gang claimed this stretch of road. They shared a cigarette between them, and one swatted a resting worker, using the flat of his blade to urge the sullen youngster back to his task.

The laborers would be paid with a meal, perhaps two. A hell of a way to put food on the table, Skyler thought. The city teemed with such unskilled workers. Those who'd fled to Darwin as the disease raged across the planet, with nothing but the clothes they wore and no goal other than survival. Few had the skills humanity needed, and they found little opportunity to better themselves. To learn a trade here meant moving up into a wholly different caste. The ability to stitch a wound or a sweater, fix a bike, cultivate a seed— such knowledge made all the difference.

Several lean-tos, made from bits of tarp and plastic trash bags, clustered around the base of the debris pile. A Middle Eastern family huddled within one, wrapped in threadbare silk scarves and thin blankets. One child among them was racked with a violent cough.

"Go around," Skyler said. Though he was immune to the disease beyond the city limit, earthly ailments were another matter. "Not too slow."

Angus complied, jerking the vehicle hard to the right and accelerating. He squeezed the truck between the rubble and a concrete wall across the street, a scant few centimeters separating them from the hard surface.

"Nice piece of driving," Skyler said.

At the next corner, a small crowd gathered around a man clad in improvised white robes. A Jacobite preacher. He stood atop a wooden box, his face contorted as he spewed a sermon. A woman paced back and forth in front of him. She hoisted a tattered flag, blood-red with their emblem handpainted in white: the Christian cross, with a ladder forming the vertical part.

Skyler had no stomach for the sect, who believed the space elevator to be Jacob's Ladder. They preyed on the bored and desperate rabble of Darwin's outer districts and in Skyler's view were little more than a criminal gang. Worse than that, a criminal gang with devout followers.

"Give this freak a wide berth, Angus," Skyler said.

"Gladly," he replied.

Skyler scanned the crowd and the buildings all around them. Jacobites usually traveled in groups, often armed.

The sermon halted at the approach of the vehicle. As the truck rolled by, the preacher stared at Skyler with an unflinching gaze full of simmering hatred.

He must think we're from Nightcliff, Skyler thought. *And if he has friends around . . .*

"Quickly now, Angus."

The kid steered back into the center of the road and pushed the accelerator. The electric motors whined from the surge of power, and Skyler felt himself pressed into his seat as they picked up speed.

Through the side mirror, Skyler watched the preacher and his crowd fade from view.

After a few blocks, he told Angus to ease up. The streets were clear here, and safe, in relative terms. One of the rare neighborhoods that banded together for the collective good. Such places were easy to spot from above, with gardens flourishing on every roof. Maintaining a grove of papaya or banana trees wasn't easy with thieves or jealous vandals next door.

He wondered, not for the first time, how much food Darwin would really need from orbit if the populace would stop living like prisoners in a gulag.

Crumbling warehouses passed by, each one a relic of Darwin's boom years after the Elevator arrived. Skyler tallied the faded logos of aerospace companies and construction firms.

More than a few bore the Platz Industries name. On one, a likeness of Neil Platz had been painted to resemble Stalin. Skyler smirked at that; the drawing was rather good.

"Turn in here," he said, pointing at a nondescript parking garage.

Angus swerved the vehicle into the open maw of the multilevel structure. Darkness swallowed them. Inside he stepped hard on the brakes, just centimeters from an interior iron gate. "What now?"

"Just wait," Skyler said.

A thick exterior barricade rolled closed behind them, sandwiching the vehicle. Angus began to drum his fingers on the steering wheel.

With a loud creak, the gate in front lurched and rotated out of the way.

"Take the downward path," Skyler said. "Nice and easy."

The vehicle spiraled down a decrepit concrete ramp, descending three levels before reaching the bottom. They rolled to a stop in front of a rusty chain-link fence, illuminated only by the truck's headlights.

"Engine off please," Skyler said. "Lights, too."

Devoid of enthusiasm, Angus complied. The whine of electricity from the motors faded to a stop, leaving them in a silence broken occasionally by dripping water. The only light came from the gauge cluster on the dash.

"Thought there'd be guards," Angus said.

"Who said there aren't?" Skyler removed his pistol from its shoulder holster and placed the weapon deliberately on the dash in front of his seat. He turned to his right, nodding calmly at Angus. "Shouldn't take long," he said. "Keep your wits about you, eh?"

Angus kept his eyes forward, studying the layout of the room. "You're going in there alone? Unarmed?"

Skyler nodded and pushed open the passenger door. "Relax. Prumble and I go way back."

His worn combat boots thumped against the floor as he dropped from the vehicle. Without another word, he slammed the door shut.

Two floodlights mounted high on the walls blinked on, filling the space with a sodium-yellow pall. They hummed like swarms of insects, electricity stressing the antique wiring. Skyler kept his head down, letting his baseball cap shield his eyes from the jarring brightness.

He approached the fence with his arms spread wide, palms open. A narrow gate in the center unlocked with a dull click, and Skyler pushed through it. On the opposite side, he waited. The sodium spotlights clicked off, plunging the area into darkness again.

He heard the slightest scrape of metal and saw a tiny yellow dot on the wall in front of him as a peephole opened.

"What's your business here?" came a voice.

Skyler fought the urge to laugh. Prumble's theatrics grew with each visit. "I'm expected. Skyler Luiken."

"Luke Skywalker?"

"That never gets old," Skyler growled.

"Ah, sarcasm! The lowest form of wit."

Skyler smirked, despite himself, and shook his head. "Open the bloody door, Prumble."

The peephole snapped shut. Skyler looked back at Angus, whose face was drawn in red by the dashboard lights. The kid gripped the steering wheel with one hand, drummed it with the other.

Nearly a minute passed before a brief commotion from beyond the door, as many locks were undone.

Finally the door opened. "Leave your weapons outside."

Prumble was already snickering when the door slammed shut. "How's the new guy?" he asked between laughs.

Skyler grinned. "On pins and needles, thanks to you."

The fat man wore a constant, jovial smile. Despite the cold of the garage, beads of sweat dotted his bald head, and he dabbed them with a white handkerchief. He motioned for Skyler to follow him. "You have a keen eye for people, Skyler."

"Speak for yourself." Skyler gestured to the vast space he now stood in. "The vaunted private army of Mr. Prumble."

Prumble chuckled, the sound echoing through the cavernous garage. "Must keep up appearances, you know. Come, come. I want to hear all about the mission."

Skyler followed the man, who'd been his fence and friend since the scavenger crews were first given run of the old airport. Prumble required the aid of a cane and he moved at a languid pace through the former parking garage, which served as a warehouse. Random items crowded every available space, many of them procured by Skyler and his crew. They passed organized sections of electronics, weapons, preserved foodstuffs, furniture, containers, clothing . . . at least fifty sections, organized in a way only Prumble could understand.

"What have you brought me?" Prumble asked.

Skyler rubbed his hands together, then breathed on them. "I always forget to wear gloves when I come here."

"You're stalling."

"I'm cold! Cold . . . and stalling."

"Bloody hell," Prumble said. "Not again."

"We had it. The exact model you requested. Pristine condition, too."

"And what? It fell out?"

"Nightcliff ordered us to land," Skyler said. "When we saw the Elevator vacant—"

"So ignore them, dammit. They wouldn't shoot you down."

"Sam said the same thing."

"You've a keen eye for people," he repeated. "Listen to them once in a while."

Crestfallen, Skyler spread his hands. "They were spooked. So were we, really. Rioters at the gate, the climbers just sitting there, dark, on the cord. I had to land."

The big man grumbled a response. He led Skyler to a specially constructed room, retrofitted into the far corner of the underground garage. Skyler recognized the enormous steel door like an old friend. He and Skadz had pulled it off a meat locker in Perth, a decade ago, at Prumble's request—their first mission for the man.

A keypad on the door served as the lock. "Avert your eyes," Prumble said as he tapped the numbers. The latch released with a dull thud.

An old oak desk, well worn by time and use, dominated the room. An enormous map of Earth covered one wall, marked with hundreds of colorful thumbtacks.

Every flat surface in the office hid under piles of books and papers. Skyler noted technical manuals and medical texts chief among the stacks. Such items were favorites of Prumble. Small and highly valuable. He would spend hours cataloging them. Skyler took the chair by the door, moving aside some books about home childbirth and midwifing.

Prumble went to the map on the wall. From a box on the shelf below it, he removed a blue thumbtack. Skyler watched in silence as the big man placed the marker just north of Kuala Lumpur. Blue represented a scouted site.

"Any subhumans?" Prumble asked.

"No."

He took a green tack and placed it next to the blue. "Anything of value still there?"

"Plenty," Skyler said. "A few trips' worth."

A white tack went up.

Satisfied, Prumble lowered himself into a huge suede executive chair behind the wooden desk and dabbed his forehead again. The handkerchief vanished into his coat, replaced by a yellow pencil.

Skyler pulled his own jacket tighter and wrung his hands together to chase the cold away.

"Down to business, then," Prumble said. His pencil hovered over a thick, leather-bound ledger. "My coveted arc welder is in Blackfield's hands?"

"Sorry about that," Skyler said. Part of him wanted the big man to fly into a rage at the news of another failure. Skyler tried to think of something—anything—he could say to redeem himself. Nothing came to mind.

No admonishment came. Instead, Prumble calmly jotted a note in his ledger. "At least when we scavenge for the Orbitals we can factor Nightcliff's greedy hands into the price. They control the Elevator, and fair's fair."

"He doesn't seem content with that anymore."

Prumble grunted. "If he's going to start rummaging through our bread and butter . . ."

"So he implied," Skyler said.

The pencil hovered as Prumble digested the statement. "I suppose you did the right thing. Landing, I mean. The way Blackfield is behaving, he may well have shot you down just to send a message to the other crews. The man has become unpredictable."

"And the climbers?" Skyler asked. "Think that's a message, too?"

"Yes," Prumble said, "but not to you." His face grew sour.

"This is all posturing. A power loss, even for just a fraction of a second, is disturbing, sure. But to shut all traffic down for a day? Days? No, he's thumbing his nose at the Orbitals."

"Why?"

"Boredom, probably." Prumble's pencil moved over the ledger again. "Traffic will resume. They need our air and water; we need their food. There's no other choice. Right, then. What else did you find?"

From memory, Skyler rattled off the list.

"I can fence the rations and first-aid kits," Prumble said. "Did you bring them?"

"It's all in the truck."

"What else did the bastards take, aside from the welder?"

Skyler recounted the story. In hindsight, it could have been worse. They could have taken everything, even the *Melville*. He shuddered at the thought. Nightcliff's odd exclusion from the Orbital Council had left Blackfield beholden only to his own whims. And by all accounts he had whims in abundance.

"For what it's worth, we found the old man," Skyler said. "The one the roofers wanted closure on. He was full sub, but tell them he was already dead. Brought back a sample, a finger actually." He gently set the sleeve on the edge of the desk.

Prumble eyed it. "That's something. While you were gone I found a hoodwink who can test the DNA. The poor guy doesn't get much work these days. If the sample matches you might at least break even."

"Oh," Skyler said, remembering the stranger. "I also have a letter for you."

"Now you're the postman, too?"

Skyler took the memory card from his jacket and tossed it onto Prumble's desk. "Some bloke in Nightcliff asked me to deliver that. Weird guy. Can't remember his name, but he knew mine."

The big man plucked the card with two thick fingers, eyebrows arched. "Kip Osmak," Prumble said.

"That's him."

Prumble stood and crossed to an old safe, the size of a

refrigerator, and dialed in the combination. The thick door swung open and he began to rummage through the contents.

Skyler couldn't help but peek over Prumble's shoulder. Within the safe he saw an array of high-value items—primarily ammunition. A case of hand grenades. The top shelf was filled with bottles full of seeds, each meticulously labeled.

The big man finally settled on what he was looking for: a yellow envelope. He kicked the safe closed and gave the tumbler a spin before returning to his chair.

Skyler cleared his throat. "Who is this bloke?"

From the envelope, Prumble removed a second memory card and a rigid sheet of white plastic. He set the sheet on his desk and placed both cards in the upper corners. Black text began to fill the programmable "paper."

"Kip Osmak is a weasel of a man," Prumble said without looking up. "A well-connected weasel, as it happens."

"Speak for yourself," Skyler said.

Prumble ignored the jibe, his gaze dancing across the letter before him. His face lit up as he read.

"What is it?" Skyler asked.

"I may have some work for you."

Skyler grunted. "I certainly need it. The crew will mutiny if I offer another spec mission."

Prumble frowned. "Skadz used to run them all the time."

"His were successful."

The fat man's frown grew deeper. "Don't offer missions, Skyler. Lead them."

Skyler had no retort for that. He studied his boots instead.

"When was the last time you pillaged in Japan?"

Skyler winced at the choice of words. "Two years, give or take. This better not be a bloody Tokyo mission. Nothing but bad news up there."

"You have an irrational fear of urban places, my friend."

"I disagree. It's quite rational."

A strange look came across the man's face. Wistful and childlike. "How I wish I could venture out with you. Get away from this tomb. Darwin, I mean."

Then he fell silent, his gaze on the wall map. Skyler

waited. He could think of nothing to say. Prumble did not have the immunity and so would need a special environment suit to leave the city. Skyler knew of no suit large enough to fit the enormous man.

"Can that ship of yours reach the island without a drop from the Elevator?" Prumble finally asked.

Mentally Skyler calculated the electricity burn. The ship's ultracapacitors could handle it, but it would take a few days to spool them unless he paid Woon for a feed. The subtext concerned him more: a long-range mission without using the Elevator meant working off Nightcliff's radar. Given the inspection yesterday, Skyler wondered how easy that would be. "Depends," he said at last.

"Good answer. Read this."

Skyler took the plastic sheet and scanned it. "Toenail clippers? It's amazing how these pricks live."

Prumble removed a bottle from his desk drawer, along with two glasses. "The interesting bit is on the last page. Care for a drink?"

Skyler nodded. He scanned the entire list:

Titanium-oxide powder—4,200/gram
Seeds (citrus), any type/quantity—100 per seed
Gauze and bandages—negotiable
Zigg ultracapacitors, all sizes—6,000 per
Cartridge filter pack for Aqua-Solve M7 membrane
    array—17,500

The list went on, for two pages, covering all manner of desired goods. Vitamins, electronic components, chemicals, and so on. A typical list, in Skyler's judgment. Then he came to the last page:

Prumble,
    An anonymous client wishes the following item to be recovered:
    —NEO Telemetry Logs (cubeSTOR preferred), Torafuku Observatory, Toyama, Japan. Full set marked 93093xxxxx or 97259xxxxx.—200,000 per set (pending verification)

The amount is not a mistake. Knowledge of this request will be denied by myself and my client should it be confiscated.

If this item is not delivered to me at Clarke's on 18 January, I will contact other suppliers.

Skyler whistled, took the offered glass, and threw the drink back in one gulp.

"That last was encrypted."

Skyler felt the alcohol warm his throat and let the sensation fade before talking. "Not fooling around."

"And time critical," said Prumble. "Three days, or he shops it elsewhere."

"Elsewhere meaning Grillo." Skyler uttered the name of Prumble's chief competitor like a curse. Grillo ran a crime syndicate that all but ruled Darwin's eastern slums. He also owned a handful of unscrupulous scavenger crews, using the old football stadium as an air base.

"Grillo, naturally." He handed Skyler a pencil and a sheet of yellow paper torn from his ledger. "Write it all down."

While Skyler copied the list, Prumble sipped his own drink.

"It's risky," Skyler said. "There might be nothing out there. But the payment . . ."

Prumble nodded. "Risk and reward."

"What are these numbers?"

"No idea," Prumble said. "You know these scientists. They speak their own language."

"No kidding. And 'NEO'?"

Prumble shrugged. "The verification bit concerns me. You may retrieve the item, only to have it declined."

"Still, two hundred thousand in stamped council notes. If this pays off, it more than makes up for the last two outings."

"Four outings."

"Well don't rub it in, damn you."

Prumble went back to the map on the wall. "And if it doesn't pay out, certainly your costs will be covered by some of the other items. If you can find them," Prumble said. "Japan is still fairly ripe. Not many subs, either."

"Except Tokyo. I'm not going anywhere near that dump again."

"Fair enough," said Prumble. He traced a finger over the city of Toyama. "This is hundreds of kilometers from there. Rural. Are we in business?"

"Can you front me the spooling cost? I can't charge the *Mel*'s caps fast enough, not without Woon's reactor coupling."

Prumble sucked a breath through clenched teeth. "Skadz never asked for that."

"He had a mind for these things."

"Had. Past tense," said Prumble. An uncomfortable silence followed. "Sorry, I shouldn't have brought him up. Sure, I'll float you. An advance against the goods in your truck."

"Then we're in business. First thing tomorrow if Nightcliff will clear us."

Prumble removed a stack of bills from his desk and passed them over. "This cover it?"

After a rough mental estimate, Skyler nodded. He stood and stuffed the money inside his jacket.

"You can let yourself out," the fat man said. "Be sure to tell your driver about my well-armed guards."

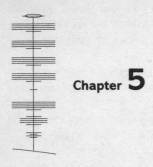

Chapter 5

A FEW DOZEN swagmen loitered near the old airport gate.

They waved with desperation at the sight of Skyler's vehicle and shouted for attention, bare feet splashing in the muddy road. A handful of mercenaries kept them at bay, pushing the ragged bunch back with ease.

Skyler did his best to ignore the sorry lot. They would wait there, day and night, ready to petition any crew heading out of the city. Most often they wanted medicine, offering in exchange their food, or labor. A sister or daughter, in those rarest acts of desperation. Sometimes they would write their requests on scraps of paper and push them through the chain-link fence. A thousand such scraps littered the ground just beyond the barricade; a mulch of ignored hopes. A waste of paper.

He felt sorry for them. They had no other options. Scavengers represented the only way to acquire something from beyond the Aura. Yet he knew their requests were low paying, and often impossible to retrieve. Items rendered useless by time or the elements. Preservall could only do so much. Skyler used to try to explain this, or tried to direct them to Prumble, but he'd given up long ago. Let the short-range crews handle it, assuming any needed work that badly.

Beggars harried the group of petitioners in turn, hands out with palms turned upward, dressed in soiled rags and makeshift sandals.

Part of the crowd, away from the gate, stood in a circle

facing inward. A body lay in the mud at their feet. Skyler squinted, catching glimpses between muddy legs. A child, a girl, he guessed, lay dead. Her eyes were still open.

He sucked in his breath when he saw the telltale rash of a subhuman on her neck.

A commotion erupted near the corpse. The crowd pushed an older man back and forth, shouting at him. He screamed back, naked terror on his face.

"Slow up," Skyler said.

Angus eased off the accelerator as they reached the mercenaries guarding the entrance.

Skyler rolled his window down and waved to one of the men. "What happened?"

The man turned his head and spat. "Crazy sheila was fullblown subby. Ran out from the shanties and started clawing at one of the swags. They beat her till she dropped, Sky. Can't blame 'em."

Skyler nodded. Desperate beggars were known to push children out beyond the Aura, long enough to develop symptoms. They would let it develop until the rash became visible, enough to mark them, and thus make them useful as a sympathy tool. They would pull the poor kids back in, and the Aura would keep the disease in stasis, indefinitely. No worse, no better, for the rest of their pitiful lives. Scrubs, they were called. "A scrub, huh? Looks like she was left out a bit too long."

"Her pa there swears she's never been outside," the mercenary replied. "A lie like that is going to get him killed, too."

Skyler could only shake his head. Such a ridiculous claim meant the father was either incredibly stupid . . .

Or he actually believes what he says, Skyler thought. Insane, more than likely. "Drive on, Angus."

The rain had stopped, giving way to a clear sky and oppressive sun. Heat shimmered off the cracked asphalt at the far end of the airport. Lightning rippled through dark clouds far to the east.

Angus steered the vehicle through the gate and then along a dirt path that paralleled the old runway. The kilometer-long tarmac, once needed for aircraft to take off and land, now served as a foundation for an array of hastily constructed hangars, barracks, and warehouses.

Through the windshield, Skyler watched a fifty-year-old crate hauler descending. Thrusters wailed as the aircraft angled for a landing.

Angus saw it, too. "Whose is that?"

Skyler studied the markings on the side. "One of Kantro's old birds."

"What do you think they're hauling?" the young man asked.

"Soil. That old girl doesn't have much range, so Kantro does the Bathurst run most of the time." The island, some twenty kilometers off Australia's northern shore, was a safe bet for work beyond Aura's Edge. Isolated and cleared of subhumans long ago. The land had been stripped clean as a result. "Miserable work," Skyler added.

The truck jostled over the uneven ground, mud sloshing from beneath the tires. Skyler noted a patrol walking along the high fence that lined the airfield. Volunteers from the crews that made home on the old runway. The sight reminded him to check the duty roster, written on a chalkboard hanging in Woon's tavern, and find out when he should next make the circuit.

Angus pulled the truck off the dirt road and onto the flat asphalt runway, a welcome end to the bumpy portion of the ride. He drove down a narrow alley, created by a gap between a pair of concrete buildings, before emerging into sunlight.

The center of the old runway buzzed with activity. Crews swarmed over their aircraft, unloading cargo or preparing for takeoff. Many more sat idle, waiting for repairs, spare parts, or simply a mission worth flying.

Angus weaved between a dump truck and an ancient sky crane. The enormous aircraft could pick up and move an entire shipping container, and lift a massive amount of weight. *Too bad her range is so limited,* Skyler thought.

They rolled to a stop in front of a weather-beaten old hangar. Angus laid on the horn, four times.

Huge doors creaked and rolled back. The *Melville* loomed in the center of the room. Her name was written on the side in small, simple white letters, just like the first time Skyler had seen her, when she was sitting forgotten on a landing pad in the Netherlands. An old, scarred aircraft painted in olive green. Four massive engines dangled from wings that sagged under the weight, a design that allowed for ample access to the craft's belly. Originally built to carry a small attack force to the far corners of the planet, with gear and one vehicle, the cargo bay provided Skyler and his crew modest room for scavenged goods. What she lacked in space she more than made up for in range.

Ceramic tiles covered the underside, a feature that allowed atmosphere reentry. The squares were charred from frequent use. No one alive knew how to repair the heat shield, as far as he knew, and as soon as even one block showed a crack Skyler would have to retire the bird.

Angus parked to the left of the aircraft and powered off the truck's engine. The electric motors whined to a halt.

"Don't get comfortable," said Skyler, "I need you to round up Jake and Takai."

Angus frowned. "Where are they?"

Skyler jumped down from the passenger seat. "Jake's probably drinking down at Woon's. Takai, well, look for repair work on the strip, and he's probably helping."

"Got it." Angus wiggled out of the driver's seat and dropped to the concrete floor of the hangar.

"Oh, Angus. Ask Takai if he'll jump with us. We need a translator."

"You want *me* to ask him that?"

Skyler shrugged. "Soften him up at least. Make things easier for me. Takeoff is oh-three-hundred."

"So much for sleep."

"I can start flight prep. That'll help a bit."

"Sure thing, Captain." Angus snatched his jacket from a hook on the hangar wall and started off down the runway toward the communal kitchen and improvised tavern at Woon's hangar.

Skyler stifled a yawn as he watched him go. He pondered

getting some sleep, weighed against all the preparation to do. Check the parachutes, load the weapons, prep the *Melville* . . . and, of course, brief the crew.

He decided the parachutes could be done during the flight, and shuffled across the hangar floor to a ladder. He climbed up to a catwalk that ran the entire circumference of the cavernous building. A rough mission plan began to form in his mind as he headed toward the far wall.

Samantha waited for him outside her room, at the midpoint of the catwalk. "Where's Angus going?"

"Nice to see you, too, Sam. He went to get the others. We've got work."

She folded her arms over her chest and leaned against the metal railing, blocking his path. "You and Prumble cook up another treasure hunt?"

"Believe it or not, that walking raincoat last night had a genuine lead."

"And he gave this lead to Prumble? And Prumble gave it to you?"

"That's right."

She narrowed her eyes. "It's pointless, anyway. The climbers are stuck."

"They'll get fixed."

"You hope. What if they don't, Skyler? People are saying the Elevator just gave up the ghost. Quit working."

He understood then the source of her anxiety. The situation had everyone contemplating the worst. Thinking the one thought no one wanted to say aloud.

So Skyler said it. "If that's true then it's over. End of the world." Her nostrils flared and Skyler raised a hand to calm her. "Which is why they'll get it fixed. It will get resolved because it must."

Her eyes danced left and right as she pulled meaning from the words.

Skyler managed a thin smile and pulled from his pocket the wad of cash Prumble had fronted him. "This one has potential," he said, "so relax, back off, and go see if Woon will let us spool the ultracaps from his primary line."

She kept her eyes on his. For a second he thought she might not obey, but then she snapped the money away.

Skyler pushed past her and continued along the catwalk. She followed. "What about food? The storeroom—"

"Empty. I know."

"I don't jump hungry."

Skyler ran a hand through his hair. "Anything growing on the roof yet?"

"Nothing ripe. But I heard some of Kantro's crew saying that Woon is making ramen." Her lips curled in a suppressed smile.

He threw his hands up in sarcastic fashion. "Oh, the delightful irony." Skyler had traded an entire crate of the freeze-dried noodle packets to Woon for some reactor time, a few months back. Spooling wasted on an ill-advised, fruitless mission.

They reached the door to Skyler's room. He sighed and removed a few more bills from his pocket. "Get enough for everyone."

She took it, turned, and headed for the ladder.

"Briefing in three hours," he said after her, then closed his door.

Finally alone, he sat on the edge of his bed and removed his muddy boots. He studied the holes in them, pushing an index finger through one. If this job didn't pay off, he doubted he'd be able to keep the crew going. Tossing the shoes unceremoniously in the corner, he fell back on his bunk and shut his eyes.

Sleep came quickly. He dreamt of falling through a massive engine room, bigger than Darwin itself. He crashed through the floor and continued to fall. Far below, he saw a jungle canopy. Evil lurked there, dark and pulsating, waiting for him in the black space beneath the treetops. Soon branches were slapping at his face. . . .

He emerged from the dream to find Takai standing over him, slapping him gently on the cheek. "All right, all right," Skyler said. "Knock it off."

"Noodles," Takai said, his Japanese accent thick.

Skyler rubbed his eyes. "Yeah, okay. Down in a sec."

Takai nodded, satisfied, and marched to the door.

"Wait," Skyler said. His engineer stopped. "Angus tell you about the jump?"

Takai nodded. His face remained impassive.

"Will you come?"

He hesitated. Skyler knew well the man's aversion to violence, and to the perils of parachuting. Even so, he needed him.

"I get full share?" Takai asked.

"Of course."

The engineer's face twisted in concentration. A full share might mean nothing at all, as recent history proved. Skyler tried to think of some ancillary reward, but before the thought fully formed, Takai nodded once and walked out.

As the dream faded from Skyler's mind, he stood and stretched. A check of his watch showed that more than four hours had passed. He cursed and pulled his boots back on. At the door he paused to look at himself in the mirror hanging there. A worried man looked back. An attempt to pat down his disheveled brown hair failed. He grimaced at the gray coming in. *Thirty-two going on fifty,* he thought, and flipped the mirror around so he wouldn't have to see himself next time.

Stepping out on the catwalk, he saw his team sitting around the rear cargo door of the aircraft. Each cradled a bowl of steaming food.

"Are we spooled?" he called out.

Samantha answered through a mouthful of food. "Three-quarters, all the time he could spare."

"Is it enough?"

She shrugged. "Depends on where the hell we're going."

"Japan." Skyler heard a few groans from the group.

Angus spoke up. "I'd feel better if we could get a lift."

"No lift. Climbers aren't running, in case you hadn't noticed." He regretted the tinge of anger that crept into his voice and took a deep breath.

"Well," Angus said, "Japan is cutting it close."

Skyler clanged along the metal catwalk until he was right above them. "We'll stick to lighter goods, then."

Angus wiped his mouth on his sleeve, set his bowl down, and retreated into the craft toward the cockpit.

Shimmying down the ladder, Skyler joined the rest of the group, taking a bowl of noodles offered by Takai.

The broth nearly burned his tongue, but tasted wonderful.

Samantha broke the silence. "If you say Tokyo . . ."

Skyler chewed a mouthful of noodles, savoring it. "It's out in the mountains, some kind of telescope. Bring up the map, Takai."

The engineer wheeled over a large screen and turned it on. Skyler prized the device, found in the conference room of a mineral prospecting company in Sydney. It contained detailed satellite photos of Earth, accurate to just a few meters, updated only months before the disease rolled across the planet. He could have updated them, the Orbitals had newer pictures, but the ability to see how things stood before the post-disease chaos provided useful insight into the salvage potential at a given location.

Skyler shoveled another wad of noodles into his mouth and crossed to the map. He magnified the region of Japan where they would land.

The telescope complex was nestled into a small valley near the top of a mountain. The circular white dome sat atop a large, rectangular building. A parking lot surrounded the place, along with a few outlying structures. Trees blanketed the land beyond, in all directions.

As the crew looked it over, he wolfed down the rest of his soup and set the bowl aside. Warm food in his stomach helped ease his nerves.

Angus returned from the cockpit, flashing the thumbs-up. "Adjusted the flight plan, Captain. If we keep the throttle low, we should be all right."

"Excellent."

Jake rubbed his shoulder as he studied the image on the screen. "Plenty of hills to make use of," he said. "Are we expecting subs?"

Skyler regarded the man. "It's well outside the city."

Samantha cut in. "What about *immunes*?"

Before Skyler could respond, Jake answered. "The ground looks steep, bad for farming. I doubt any immunes are living out there after all this time."

"Let's follow the usual precautions," Skyler said.

"Why not wait for a lift?" Samantha asked. "The climbers will *surely* be fixed soon. So why not? Can't afford it?"

"Even if I could, we need to keep this one quiet."

Her eyebrows shot up. Excitement filled her face like a child at Christmas. "A smuggling op, then! Kick-ass. What are we looking for?"

Skyler pulled the request list from his pocket. "Some kind of research data."

She frowned. "Boring."

"Maybe, but the price is right. It's a memory cube or something."

Takai reached for the list and Skyler gave it to him.

"Or something?" Samantha asked. "Can you recognize it?"

"Takai can handle it."

She folded her arms again and fixed a withering glare on Skyler. "So he's jumping with us?"

"Sure. He's done it before." Skyler thought he did a decent job of keeping the apprehension from his voice.

"Yeah, once. I'm not babysitting."

"Not asking you to," Skyler said. "I'll partner with him."

Jake and Samantha responded in unison. "You're jumping, too?"

"Angus handled the Nightcliff landing well, he's ready to pilot—"

"Fucking Christ, Skyler," Samantha said. "Takai's second jump. Your first in . . . what, a year? And Angus taking lead on the stick? I missed the 'Amateur Night' sign when I came in."

Skyler felt his fists clenching, and slowly released them. "That's enough, Sam. Let's discuss it in my room."

She got up and came to stand in front of him, her height ever intimidating. "Let's discuss it right here."

Skyler stood his ground and tried to channel the voice Skadz had always used. "The truth is we're on the ropes. It's time we faced it. Time *I* faced it." He clasped his hands and looked at each of them in turn. "This is a hell of a talented team, no question about it. Even so, we haven't hit a winner in some time."

Samantha snickered.

"As I see it," he continued, ignoring her, "we have three assets. The *Melville,* a damn fine ship that can range half the Earth. Then there is Prumble's faith in us. He continues to give us work. I'm not quite sure why."

He glanced around, meeting each of their eyes. "And, of course, our strongest asset: you people. This crew. You're all immune, and you're all the best at what you do. Not a single other crew on this strip can claim either trait. Even Blackfield can't match that. So if there's a flaw in this operation, it's me."

Part of him hoped they would shout encouragements now, but everyone remained quiet. That hurt.

He swallowed hard. "I know things haven't run so well since Skadz left. I know I'm not the leader he was, but I am the senior member, so I'm asking for one more chance." He settled his gaze on the young pilot. "Angus, you're ready to take the stick. I'm trusting you to take good care of our girl."

He nodded once.

The kid could do it, Skyler knew. "If I'm going to lead this mission, I can't do it circling three klicks above you. That's why I'm jumping with the rest of you."

"Huzzah," Samantha said, without enthusiasm.

"The primary goal is finding the data logs in this observatory. Yes, it's a problem that the climbers aren't running. A huge, nasty problem. But it'll pass, and Prumble will fence the goods like he always does."

He stopped there, gauging their reactions. He realized he needed to offer more. "If we find what we need fast enough, and juice permitting, we'll hit the nearest town as well. I've got a list of desirables, plus the usual sundries. Questions?"

Jake asked, "What happens if this mission doesn't hit, Sky?"

Skyler tried to look his sniper in the eyes, and found he

couldn't. He blurted an answer that surprised himself as much as anyone. "I'll step aside."

A bleak silence filled the hangar.

"Who will take your place?" Samantha eventually asked.

"That'll be for you all to decide."

Everyone started talking at once.

"Hey, hey," Skyler said over them, "at least let me fail first."

Angus raised his hand, waited for Skyler to acknowledge him. "And if no one else wants to lead?"

Skyler shrugged. "We disband, I guess."

The sobering thought quieted them.

Let them mull that over, Skyler told himself. As bad as things were, the alternatives might hold less appeal. The misery of daily life in Darwin. Throwing in with one of the other crews, only to be slowed down by their reliance on environment suits and compressed air. Or following Skadz's example, and simply walking out into the world and leaving everything behind.

"I'm asking for a last chance. Let's get the big girl ready to fly, and head into the Clear."

It took the others a few seconds to realize the speech had ended. One by one they stood and started the routine of preparing for a mission.

Skyler sulked back to his room, wondering why he said what he said. *A final chance?* he thought, cursing at himself. He had let the moment take control, and said too much. Right now they were probably all thinking of ways to botch the mission and force him out.

From a locker bolted to the wall of his room he removed his winter fatigues. Russian issue, hardly used. A soft knock at the door distracted him. "Come in."

Samantha pushed the door open. "Nice speech. I liked the bit at the end."

"My offer to step down?"

She shook her head. "You laying down the fucking law around here. Telling people what's what."

He set the thick winter jacket on his desk and turned to her. No words came.

"Pretty good speech," she said. "Too much pussyfooting about, but not bad."

"Let's just hope the mission pays off."

"It better. For your sake."

Before he could reply, she closed the door.

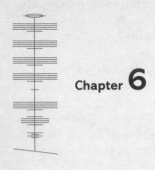

Chapter 6

NEIL PLATZ LEFT the card game a poorer man.

He'd let the skeleton crew win, but they'd all been too drunk to notice his deliberate poor play.

A lonely bunch, stuck here under secret orders, travel restricted to the short distance between Platz Station and Hab-8. A construction crew, so the story went. Neil had cultivated that lie over many months. In truth their job entailed the menial task of sorting and storing supplies.

Neil's arrival, booze in one hand, a set of magnetic-backed playing cards in the other, had been met with smiles and gratitude. A break in the monotony and isolation. The crew set aside their work without a second thought, and poker ensued.

Hab-8, the perpetually-under-construction, long-promised new space station. Quarters for a thousand. Four recreation rooms. The chance for more Darwinians to be lifted from their squalor.

When SUBS broke out, work on the station all but stopped. Materials dried up as Darwin's warehouses ran dry or fell to looters. Workers went idle, their minds on friends and loved ones below. But Neil pushed and pushed over the five years since, counting every rivet made or component installed as a victory, and ultimately finished the job. Hab-8 was done, and should have been handed over to the council months ago, but Neil had a different purpose in mind.

He let the door click shut. The eight-man crew and their

boisterous game would go on fine without him. The gift of scotch, two precious bottles, consumed through special spigot caps, would ensure that. Drunken men in zero-g, always a party.

Neil flipped on the lamp attached to his hat. The corridor filled with blue-white light, and he could see his breath on the chill air. To warm the station, or begin its rotation to generate artificial gravity, would signify readiness and draw unwanted attention. Those comforts would have to wait. He zipped his coat closed, all the way to his chin, and began to drift toward the central hub.

Shadows danced as the beam from his light swept across the cluttered hall. Crates and boxes of every shape, size, and color lined the walls, lashed in place with mesh netting and elastic cord. He let his fingers brush across the containers as he floated along, pleased with the progress in stocking the facility.

Enough supplies for five hundred people to survive six months, his goal. Plus the gear needed to operate a private security force.

All because of Tania and her theory. A theory he'd spent years cultivating in her. Subtle hints and suggestions, dropped casually. The idea *had* to be hers, and she'd finally come to it.

The whole business was a gamble. An epic gamble. Neil knew this. He'd accepted it and moved on, driven not by her innocent speculation, but by the possibilities of what came next. His imagination fueled the rest.

He stopped once, at the door of a crewman who'd begged out of the card game due to an upset stomach. The poor bastard had floated from the common room with both hands clutched around his waist. Neil found the door to be locked. "Okay in there?"

No response came, only the muffled sound of retching.

Poor sod. Satisfied the man would remain in his room, Neil continued his drift along the main corridor.

On reaching the airlock, he opened the circular door and coughed three times, loudly. He swept his gaze, and his lamp, along the direction he'd come, and saw nothing. The sounds of inebriated men at cards had faded to silence. Neil heard nothing but the ever-present hum of air processors.

Kelly Adelaide emerged from the airlock door like a specter.

"I was worried you forgot about me," she said with mirth.

Neil offered his arm to halt her momentum. The tiny woman, dressed in a skintight black outfit, declined his help. She floated to the far wall of the corridor, flipping in air to land feetfirst. Her fluid movements spoke of years spent in orbit.

With one hand she steadied herself. "Dark, no spin. I give up. Where are we?" she asked.

"This is Hab-Eight," Neil said. He handed her a small flashlight.

The woman turned it on, glanced around. "I didn't realize you'd pressurized it."

"If anyone asks," Neil replied, "I haven't."

"Who else knows?"

"A skeleton crew. My brother, Zane, though he doesn't know why I'm stalling. And I told one of my scientists, Tania Sharma, that it is 'close' to completion."

She cracked a wicked grin. He knew she would. The woman, now in her early fifties, had led a checkered life. A daughter of missionaries, her childhood a checklist of every third-world hellhole on the map. She'd learned to be resourceful, to survive. At eighteen she joined the Army Engineering Corps before shifting to Special Forces. After that, a brief stint as a contract assassin, which brought her to Neil. She'd been paid to kill him.

She would have succeeded, he knew that, but SUBS broke out and the world changed. All contracts null and void. Instead of completing her mission, she asked Neil for a job—a life in orbit. His bodyguard, or spy. Whatever he required.

His gut said to take her on, and so he had. He'd learned early in life to trust such instincts.

For the last year she'd spent most of her time sneaking around Gateway, providing Neil with regular reports on everything that went on there. She knew the maintenance tunnels better than the workers who used them, and even played little pranks on them out of sheer boredom. Turning the odd dial, disconnecting random pipes. The people on Gateway spoke of a ghost, and Kelly swelled with pride when she first heard the nickname.

Once a week Neil arranged to have her come up to Platz Station, where she trained select members of his staff in self-defense and basic tactics. For recreational reasons, as the story went. "I should have brought you here much sooner," he said.

Kelly studied the boxes lining the wall behind her. "You've been busy."

"I have at that."

"Show me."

He led her to the second level, and let the station speak for itself. Room after room filled not with furniture but supplies.

Steel canisters of compressed air, stacked in neat rows, filled one section.

"Level three is all food," he said. "Four is water, though we're behind on that front."

Kelly kept silent as they drifted along. Finally she said, "It's like a bomb shelter."

"Astute observation," he said.

"How long have you been hoarding this stuff?"

Neil almost told his rehearsed lie, the one he'd told Tania. Such deception, however innocent, would not work with Kelly. "Almost two years."

"Clearly you know something I don't. What's going on?"

I'll know soon enough, he thought. "Call it a hunch. Change is in the air."

The woman laughed softly. "Why show me now?"

"Because of room seventeen," he said. When she raised an eyebrow, he laughed, too. "This way."

A special lock adorned the door to room seventeen. "Eight seven four four," he said aloud as he tapped the code. "Don't forget."

With a thud the lock disengaged. Neil pushed the door open and waved Kelly inside.

She gasped at the sight within. The large room, intended for recreation according to the station plan, instead served as an armory. Stacks of hard-shell cases in army green or police black, lethal contents packed within. Many months of secret purchases and smuggled shipments led to the cache.

Kelly moved inside with some trepidation. She drifted to the nearest box and threw back the catches. "Sonton 90. Holo sight, mil-spec. Excellent handgun," she said.

"So I'm told."

She ran her hand over the row of identical black pistols. "I get it now."

Neil waited.

"You don't know what half this stuff is, do you?"

"I'm not even sure any of it works," he said. "I'm going to be asking more from you, Kelly, in the months ahead. For starters, I need to know who in your self-defense classes is showing the most promise. I'm also going to give you a list of my staff who have had military experience."

She stifled a response when Neil held up his hand.

"Prep them," he went on. "And send the most promising ones here, to train and plan."

"Plan for what?"

Neil grimaced. "I don't know, yet. I'd tell you if I did."

"Horseshit," she said. "I know you, Neil. You wouldn't do all this without a goal in mind."

Every possible future Neil could imagine, at least those with a happy ending, required people like Kelly to be at his side. And he trusted her, more than anyone perhaps. He'd waited long enough to let someone in.

"Here it is, then," he said. "The Builders are coming back. The next phase in their plan."

"When?" she asked without hesitation.

"I can't tell you that, yet—"

"Wait," she said. "What do you mean, *plan*?"

He spread his hands. "A figure of speech," he said. *Slip of the tongue, more like.* "All I know is they seem to be on some kind of accelerating cycle, and it's about to come around again. Tania Sharma is working on the details."

Kelly glanced around at the crates of weapons. "And you

plan to fight them? With a handful of crusty, out-of-shape infantry?"

"I don't mean to fight anyone," Neil said. "My plan is for this station to serve as a lifeboat, in case we need to clear out for a while. Don't look at me like that. We don't know what they intend to do this time, and I won't let the people I love perish up here if the bastards mean to finish us off. Call it hiding, call it cowardice, I don't care."

She searched his eyes, her face as stiff as a cold breeze.

"I want people who can fight," Neil added, "in case we have to battle our way here. In case we have to fend off a rush of desperate stowaways."

"Okay, okay," she said. "I get the idea. Turn my students into fighters. Is that it?"

"No," Neil said. "First I need you to help me figure out what we have here. And what we're missing."

The beam of her flashlight swept the room. Boxes, containers, and canvas bags were lashed together in rough aisles. They stretched from floor to ceiling.

"I'd better have a look around, then," she said.

"Thank you, Kelly. By all means."

She pushed off toward the ceiling and tumbled around to land with her feet. With deft, precise movement she propelled herself toward the far corner of the room, then quickly vanished behind the tightly packed goods, out of Neil's view.

He settled in by the door, and wondered if he'd gone overboard in this endeavor. He could hear Tania, and her oft-repeated caveat: *It's just a theory.* She would uncover the truth on her own soon enough, and then Neil could feign his surprise and act on the news openly. Besides, Tania could figure out the specifics, the piece of the puzzle Neil so desperately needed. The devil, as always, hid in the details.

"Thought I'd find you here, fuhkerrrrrr!"

Neil jumped at the slurred, raspy voice.

One of the crew floated in the doorway. The sick one, the one who'd left the game with a stomach problem. His face had an odd red pall. "Mysterious room . . . seventeen—"

"—is off-limits," Neil said. "You should be in your quarters."

The crewman ignored the order. Instead he doubled over and gripped his head in front of the ears, as if trying to tear away some invisible pair of goggles. For a second he drifted free, utterly consumed by pain, his face contorted in anguish.

"Bloody hell, man," Neil said. "What's the matter with you?"

The tortured look vanished as quickly as it had arisen. He pushed his way into the room with a queer violence, shouldering Neil out of the way. "Been wondering what secrets you're hiding in here," he slurred. "What the point of this bloody station is."

Before Neil could object, the man collided with the crate of Sonton handguns. The lid came loose and floated open.

"Stay away from that," Neil said. The words sounded ridiculous, weak.

"The hell?" the man said. He picked up a pistol and studied it, alcohol-fueled confusion plain on his face. "Guns? What . . . what the fuck, Platz?"

Be calm, Neil urged himself. *Think.* He shot a glance in the direction Kelly had gone, and found no sign of her.

The man turned. The gun waved casually in one hand. His other hand had gone back to his temple. His fingers probed for relief before drifting lower, scratching along the neck.

Neil noticed the rash.

He froze, unable to believe what he saw right in front of him. It was, frankly, impossible.

The man had SUBS. Of this Neil had no doubt, and it made no sense whatsoever. The crewmen had been stationed here for weeks, no way to have traveled beyond the Aura.

The gun nearly slipped from the man's hand. He caught it and tightened his grip, all the while waving it about like a toy.

Neil had no idea if the weapon was loaded. "Put it back, friend. You're ill, you need help."

"Friend?" The man scratched his cheek and neck with the butt of the weapon, so hard that Neil thought he might draw blood. "You're my bloody boss, not my friend. What's all this for, Platz?"

"None of your concern."

"Bollocks!" the man shouted, enraged now. The disease would amplify his emotions. It would grow worse by the minute until it consumed him.

Something had to be done, and soon.

"Bollocks," the crewman repeated, a darker tone now. He blinked, stuttered. "Something's going on here. I should tell someone. The council . . . yeah."

Neil steadied himself. "We need to take you to quarantine. You're talking nonsense."

The crewman shook his head, an attempt to focus. His breathing became a husky growl, an animal sound. "I slept . . . all my time. Clear now, and watered."

A shadow, along the ceiling, caught Neil's eye. *No, a ghost. Kelly.* She'd turned off her light.

"What did you say?" Neil asked. "You make no sense."

With a heaving cough, the crewman leveled the weapon toward Neil. A shaky aim, but dangerous enough. His mouth twisted into a raw snarl. "Hell with you. *Help me, fucker.* Up on your beanstalk . . ."

Kelly descended from the ceiling in perfect silence, a spider on an invisible web. She landed right behind the babbling man and looked to Neil for his approval to take action.

In the span of a few minutes the disease had almost taken over the man's mind. He'd likely be dead soon, anyway.

Neil nodded to her.

In a single motion she knocked the gun from the crewman's hand and brought her arm around his neck. At the same time she pushed off from the wall.

The pair sprawled into the air, a tumbling mass of limbs. With no purchase, the man—the subhuman—could not gain an advantage. Kelly held her arm tight across the creature's neck.

Neil could only watch, numb with disbelief at the scene before him. A full minute passed before she let go.

The crewman slumped, dead. The limp body drifted into a corner and settled there.

A subhuman, Neil thought. *In orbit.* A litany of other thoughts blared in his head, but that alone drowned them. A man had contracted the disease in orbit, breathing air sterilized by the Aura—hell, inside the Aura. Something Neil never dreamt would happen, or even could happen. It was, by all rights, impossible.

It occurred to him then that this might be the next Builder event. He had assumed another vessel would arrive, like the last three times.

Two times, he corrected himself. Even a mental mix-up of the count was something he punished himself for. The Elevator and the disease, that's what history will say. That line must be toed at all costs. What came before that was his business and his alone.

His focus swerved back toward the present, and the future. He'd been so fixated on the idea that another ship would arrive, it never occurred to him that the next event could simply be a change in the existing circumstances.

The last event, the arrival of a vessel carrying the seed of the SUBS disease, had forced those who could do so to huddle within the Aura. Neil swallowed bitterly as his mind churned through possibilities. *What if,* he thought, *the last five years have just been a grace period? What if they had meant for us to vacate?*

A chill washed over his entire body. Goose bumps sprouted along his back and arms.

He couldn't bring himself to look away from the corpse, bobbing in the corner, legs cocked in inhuman fashion. "Kelly," Neil said. "My God, Kelly. How the hell did it get up here?"

Hands grasped his shoulders and shook him. Kelly's hands—she'd come to him at some point.

"There's nowhere safe now," he muttered. "We misunderstood. We're doomed. . . ."

She slapped him across the face. "Snap out of it," she hissed.

The sting of pain dispelled the fog in his mind. He managed to focus on her. If anyone else hit him like that, he would have sent them back to Darwin's slums in a heart-beat.

"Misunderstood what? Were you keeping that thing here?" she asked. "Some kind of damn experiment?"

"No," he said, incredulous. "Of course not. I have no idea how this happened."

"It got here somehow," she said.

"Listen to me," Neil said. "He's been here, Kelly. For *weeks*. I assigned the man. This . . . this can't happen."

She faced the floating body, as if seeing it for the first time. The anger on her face turned to dread.

I might have seen this coming, Neil thought. *If only Tania's father hadn't blinded me. Foolish, foolish.* He pushed the memory aside. Nothing but pain lay down that road.

"We should alert the other stations," Kelly said. "Initiate a lockdown."

"No," Neil said. "God, no! There'd be chaos. You were in Darwin when the survivors started pouring in. You saw how people acted."

"But—"

"What if he's the only one," Neil said. His words silenced both of them. "A freak of nature," he went on. "There's people immune to the disease, right? Maybe there's some immune to the Aura."

"You're clutching at straws."

A laugh slipped from his lips. "Let's bloody hope so, anyway, or we are well and truly damned."

She took her time to nod. "Then we've got to put him out the airlock, before anyone finds out."

"What?"

"Unless you want chaos, we can't have the body of a sub-human found up here."

"And then?" he asked. "The others will know something's happened. They'll search for him—"

She gripped his chin, forced him to see her. "Then we leave. If anyone asks, he left with us. You had other work for him."

Her words rang true. No matter how vile the business, no other option would work.

He took the lead, moving fast, guiding Kelly and the corpse toward an airlock one level over. The lack of gravity made the task trivial. A strange thing to think about, Neil realized. Murder in zero-g. It sounded like the title of a detective story.

At the inner airlock door, he helped Kelly steady the body, and then entered the access override code. She pushed the body and let it float into the small compartment.

"Did you know him?" she asked.

"Not well," Neil said. He swung the thick door closed and activated the lock again. "Trevor, I think."

Override code still in place, Kelly handled the sequence of commands to open the outer airlock door. Neil couldn't help but watch through the tiny window. In total silence, the black of space came into view. A flash of humidity as air met vacuum. The body jerked and spun, sucked along with the air into the void, slack limbs flopping in grotesque manner. The corpse gained distance with surprising speed.

"I'm too old for this," he said.

"You and me both."

Neil forced himself to look away from the porthole. He turned to Kelly and searched for something else to say to her. Nothing came to mind.

Kelly gripped his shoulder. "What's done is done. Let's get out of here."

He grinned, despite the circumstances. Only he knew his past sins. In this he had a co-conspirator, someone to share the burden with. He could draw strength from that.

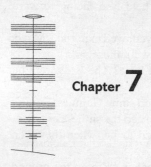

Chapter 7

THREE THOUSAND METERS over the target, the rear cargo door of the aircraft opened and Jake jumped out.

The sun, just cresting the eastern horizon, cast the cloud tops below in a deep red.

Skyler watched until the sniper vanished into the nebulous puffs. Satisfied, he picked up a handheld microphone that hung on the wall and pressed it to his mouth. "He's out, Angus. Slow circles, engines off."

"Copy," the pilot replied through a speaker on the wall. The engine noise faded a second later, until only the rush of wind could be heard. Skyler punched the large red button that controlled the ramp. Hydraulics wheezed as the thick metal door closed.

"Sixty seconds," he said, and set to work strapping on his parachute.

Samantha leaned against the cabin wall, chewing at a fingernail. She'd put her gear on more than an hour ago. A camouflage outfit of gray and white, insulated for winter climates, black combat boots, and her favorite sawed-off shotgun strapped across her chest.

Skyler caught her attention and motioned toward Takai. *Help him out,* he mouthed. She rolled her eyes and began to inspect the engineer's equipment.

"That parachute has seen better days," Skyler said to her, noting the frayed stitching along an edge.

"The whole world has seen better days, Sky."

Takai tried to look, but Sam held him facing forward. "Not funny," he said.

Skyler took a closer look at the yellowed material. "Maybe we should drop on a nylon factory, fix these up."

"Or," Sam said, "a paratrooper base? The Brits were big into that."

"Even better. Hell, we might find some Guinness."

She grinned at him and he returned the smile. For a fleeting instant it felt like things used to be, when they were equals.

Jake's voice came over the speaker. "I'm on the ground. No activity here; it's safe to drop."

However safe it might be, he's whispering, Skyler noted. "Angus," he said into the mic, "are we back over the target?"

"Thirty seconds," he responded.

Skyler made sure his primary weapon, a small machine gun, was securely fastened to his chest. He double-checked his pistol as well, holstered on his thigh. Satisfied, he punched the red button on the inner wall and the cargo door opened once again.

Wind screamed outside. A few kilometers to the southeast, Skyler could see a pair of snowy peaks jutting up through the cloud layer.

He looked at Sam. Her blue eyes were luminous in the dark cabin. Her serious expression said she was ready.

Takai's face said the opposite. Sweat beaded on his forehead, and he fumbled with the pistol Jake had loaned him. Skyler carefully crossed to him, helped him stow the weapon properly, and grabbed him by the shoulders. "You okay?"

Takai managed a smile. "I prefer home, fixing things."

"You'll be fine," Skyler said. "Stick with Sam."

"Stick with Skyler," Sam shouted over the wind. "That was the deal."

Skyler had hoped she'd forget that detail. "That's what I meant. Stick with me."

With a running start, Samantha jumped out the back of the *Melville.* In an instant she vanished into the clouds.

Takai stood frozen in place, staring at the puffy red-gray wall. Skyler began to worry that he would have to push the little man, but Takai closed his eyes and followed Sam's example.

Satisfied, Skyler took the two steps to the end of the ramp and kept going, into the howling wind.

It whipped his hair and clothing with a fury. He tumbled over, facing up, and saw the *Melville* receding above him. Angus had already started to bank, beginning his circular holding pattern.

Skyler rolled over just in time to punch through the clouds.

Far below, Japan rushed toward him.

He steered toward Sam's and Takai's parachutes, both black blotches on the ground below. They had both landed well by the look of it, in a flat clearing that probably used to serve as parking for the observatory complex. Maple and pine trees covered a landscape dotted white by snow.

As he hit the ground, Skyler's foot slipped on a patch of ice and he went down. Waist-high weeds scratched at his face as he fell to one side, the black mass of his chute collapsing around him.

"I see you," Jake said over the helmet comm. "Nice landing, Sky."

"Yeah, yeah," he replied. The chilled air of the descent had numbed his fingers, his nose. On the ground the air hung still, cold and silent.

"No movement at all," Jake said. "I think this place is dead."

Skyler worked frantically to untangle himself. "Roger. Keep us posted."

Clouds kept the rising sun largely hidden, casting the surroundings in muted shades of gray and brown, broken occasionally by patches of snow.

Finished with his gear, Skyler moved through the weeds to where Sam and Takai waited. He crouched with them behind a small earthen berm dusted with fresh snow, and studied the target.

From the vantage point, the observatory looked long abandoned. The semispherical telescope dome had collapsed on one side. A fire had gutted part of the complex at some point, years ago. The blaze had charred one side of the main building and reduced one of the outlying structures to nothing more than a pile of blackened wood.

Sam pointed toward the back of the main building, which faced them. "Door's open," she said, rubbing her hands together for warmth.

She was right: The door hung by one hinge, half-buried in a knee-high snowdrift that had collected along the back of the building. Even from fifty meters away Skyler could make out vicious scratch marks along it, and a large chunk of the frame was missing where a lock should have been. He noted the scratches were on the *inside* of the door.

A feeble chain-link fence stood between the team and the structure, but it had numerous holes in it and wouldn't need scaling. Skyler pressed a finger to his earpiece. "We're moving up, Jake."

"Copy. Still clean," he replied in Skyler's ear.

Samantha didn't need further orders and moved in a low run toward the fence. Skyler hefted his machine gun and clicked the safety off. He motioned Takai to follow and headed for the fence in a half crouch.

When she reached the door, Samantha pressed herself against the outer wall and took one quick glance inside. Skyler moved up next to her. They kept still for a moment, letting a silence settle.

A cold wind picked up, pushing past them and generating a deep, eerie moan from within the building. Skyler shivered. Samantha flipped on the flashlight affixed to her shotgun and looked to him for the sign to proceed.

He turned his light on as well, and waited as Takai removed a smaller handheld flashlight from his belt pouch. He had to smack it against his open palm a few times before it came to life. Skyler, satisfied, nodded to Samantha.

She vaulted over the pile of dirty snow and disappeared into shadow.

Skyler moved in right behind her.

The hallway stretched from one side of the building to the other. A few meters inside he saw the remnants of a small animal. Bones and fur in a tiny pile, the faded carpet below smeared with blood. The carcass had been there for many months. Ahead, Samantha pointed to more signs of habitation. Dried feces, and the gray remnants of what might have been an apple.

"This looks old," she said.

Skyler nodded. His stomach turned at the sight, yet part of him marveled at the animalistic instincts that survived in the subhuman brain, despite the disease. Scientists predicted the diseased would die out within months, but nearly five years later their numbers had grown, if anything. Skyler had seen the children; he'd killed them and the adults alike.

The same instincts must be latent in all humans, he realized, glad he would never have to worry about becoming such a creature.

He shook off the thought and tapped his earpiece again. "We're inside. Hallway is clear."

Jake acknowledged him over the radio. Takai finally crept over the snowdrift to join them.

Satisfied, Skyler tapped Sam gently on the shoulder and gestured toward the nearest doorway along the hall. She led them toward it, keeping close to the wall, her weapon aimed slightly toward the floor.

Reaching the door, she tried the handle and found it to be locked. Skyler motioned for her to keep moving. She hesitated and pointed at faded kanji on the wall.

Takai read it aloud, keeping his voice low. "I think 'Janitor.'"

Sam, incredulous, glared at him. "You *think*?"

"We'll force it later, keep moving," Skyler said to her.

They continued down the hallway and came to an alcove. On one side they found an elevator, useless without power, but beside it an open door gave way to a dark stairwell.

Takai approached another sign next to the Elevator, covered by filthy glass. He wiped a gloved hand across it to reveal a basic map of the building. "Record keeping is basement three," he said. "This is floor one."

Skyler nodded. "There, see? Glad you're here, Takai."

"Yes, delighted," Samantha said.

"Down we go?" Skyler asked.

The woman objected. "We should clear this floor first."

"It's fine, there's nothing here."

"Clear this floor," she said, "*then* down."

Skyler stifled the urge to pull rank. He nodded, instead.

The next door proved unlocked, giving way to a conference room. Water dripped from the ceiling onto a long oval table. Mold grew everywhere. Skyler covered his nose at the stench. Chairs in various states of decay littered the floor.

"That screen looks intact," Samantha said.

Skyler followed her gaze to a large monitor hanging from the wall. Coated in dust, it appeared otherwise undamaged. "Probably dead."

"Components are very useful," Takai said.

"And very heavy. We'll grab it on the way out. First priority is the goods on the list."

They moved back into the hallway. Behind the last door they found a lobby and small gift shop stocked with space-related products geared toward children. Most were electronic. Skyler remembered the list Prumble had supplied him. "Hold up," he said, then removed a large canvas bag he kept folded in his pack. Takai helped him shovel ultracapacitors of all sizes from a circular rack, avoiding those ruined by exposure and time. Skyler then found pairs of two-way radios meant for children, which he knew to have excellent range, and bagged them. In another aisle Takai discovered a locked glass case protecting high-end game tablets. He explained that the screens and memory might be salvageable. Skyler agreed, kicked in the glass, and grabbed the boxes.

He glanced across the rest of the lobby, looking for anything else of value. A receptionist's desk appeared to be the only furniture not ruined from exposure. The surface of it looked barren, save for a postal container covered in dust, packages still inside. "Good enough, let's move on."

They headed back for the stairs. Takai left the bag of toys

in the hallway. Skyler felt himself relaxing, his confidence bolstered by the quiet as much as by Sam's tactical attitude.

The stairway led both up and down, pitch-black in both directions. On the landing one level up, Skyler's flashlight came across the carcass of a cat, long dead. Only fur and bone remained.

"Down we go," Samantha said. She kept the lead as they descended, boots thudding loudly on the metal steps, echoing throughout the stairwell. The sound caused Samantha to move faster, stealth no longer on their side.

Jake's voice suddenly came into Skyler's ear, barely a whisper. "Movement on the tree line."

Skyler grabbed Samantha's shoulder, stopping her halfway down the flight. He tapped his earpiece. "Subs?"

A tense moment of silence followed. "Negative. If you can believe it, there's a deer approaching the building."

Skyler let out his breath.

"I can drop it if you want. Scrawny little bugger, but there might be some meat on it," Jake said.

Skyler felt his stomach twitch at the idea. "Only if it's moving away. For now let's keep things quiet out there."

"Copy that," said Jake.

"What's going on?" Samantha asked.

"Local wildlife. Keep going."

She complied. After two flights of stairs they came across another locked door. On Skyler's silent order, Samantha ignored it and continued down.

Basement level three proved to be the bottommost floor. Sam approached the door and tried the handle.

It didn't budge, so Skyler signaled for her to force it.

One kick from her leg and the door flew open, stopping hard against the wall with a loud thud. The sound of it reverberated through the entire complex.

Somewhere above, Skyler heard movement.

Samantha dropped to a crouch and froze in place. She turned her flashlight on the stairs above. Skyler followed suit.

He saw nothing, yet the sound, like small feet scuttling

across sheet metal, continued. Another cat, Skyler guessed. Perhaps a large rodent.

"I think it's in the crawl space between floors," Samantha whispered.

"Keep still," Skyler said, listening. He crouched there, straining his ears until the sound receded.

"This place is creepy as hell," Samantha said.

"I agree," he said. "Let's get this over with."

She glanced into the space beyond the door and swung her shotgun and flashlight across it. Skyler watched from over her shoulder.

It appeared to be a vast library, about twenty meters square. A strong odor of rot and mildew greeted them. Water dripped from numerous cracks in the ceiling.

Skyler feared the shelves of material would all be water-damaged beyond usefulness, until he noticed the cracks did not have the typical brown splotches that indicated long exposure. Recent, then.

Sam pushed inside, and Skyler followed.

The rows of shelves extended all the way to the far wall, where they could see a single door, closed. Skyler whispered to Samantha, "Sweep this first, then clear that back room, before we turn Takai loose."

"No shit."

He let the comment go, instead looking back at Takai.

The engineer's eyes were wide, his face sheet-white. He managed a nod. "I'll follow."

Samantha set a faster pace, checking each aisle of shelving. Most were stocked with a mix of black binders and beige data cube holders. All appeared to be labeled and organized, a good sign assuming Takai could be able to decipher the scheme used. For now, he set his concerns aside and continued toward the back of the room, where Samantha waited by a door.

He took up a position on the wall to the right of the entrance, a mirror of Sam's stance on the left. He nodded. She turned the handle and pushed it open.

Skyler could hear Takai suck in his breath at what greeted them inside.

A skeletal corpse sprawled in a desk chair, head tilted to one side.

Bits of leathery skin stretched over the bones. Skyler guessed it was a man, judging by the style of the clothing that remained. He appeared to have shot himself through the mouth. A revolver remained clutched in the body's hand, and a spray of dried blood decorated the wall behind.

"Suicide. Dead a long time," Skyler said. Obvious to all, but he hoped to calm Takai down. The short man was breathing hard.

"Better than letting the subs get you," Sam said.

Skyler grunted. "No argument here." He mentally cataloged the rest of room, looking for anything that might be of value. A desk of cheap fake marble jutted from the wall. A computer console, though caked with dust, seemed intact. "Takai, start looking for the cubes." He handed his engineer the paper that Prumble had provided.

Takai practically ran from the morbid scene.

"I'll cover the stairway door. Didn't like that sound earlier," Sam said.

Skyler flashed her a thumbs-up and went to work searching the office for valuables. First came the gruesome task of prying the revolver from the dead man's hand. The weapon had rusted a bit, but Skyler felt it could be cleaned up. Worth a sack of vegetables back in Darwin, if it fired. He unloaded five bullets from it, a nice bonus. Smiling, he unfolded another duffel bag from his pack and dropped the weapon inside.

Everything on top of the desk went into the bag: console, sleek monitor, and an old-fashioned keyboard. Despite being caked with dust they could still fetch a good sum. Then he got down on his hands and knees to inspect the area below the desk. All of the various power and computer cables went into his bag.

On a bookshelf behind the dead scientist, Skyler found a framed photograph. He wiped the dust from it. The image showed four men in casual clothing, smiling in front of the observatory. Two were Japanese, the third a handsome Indian fellow.

The fourth Skyler recognized.

"I'll be damned," he said to himself.

The last man was Neil Platz, the business tycoon who had owned most of Darwin, and nearly all of orbit, before the disease came.

Skyler flipped the frame around and coaxed the picture out. A date on the back indicated 2260, a ribbon-cutting ceremony. *The bastard had his hands in everything back then,* Skyler thought.

On a whim he folded the picture and slipped it into his jacket pocket. Then he realized a glass bottle had been hidden behind the frame, filled with an amber liquid.

"Well, well," he said. The faded label said Lagavulin Whisky, dated more than five decades past. And, more important, unopened. Just the type of thing he could give to a Nightcliff inspector to turn a blind eye.

Jake's voice interrupted him. "How's it going in there?"

"Decent," said Skyler. "We're in the records room now. One rotting corpse is about it so far."

"How much longer?" Jake asked.

"Why, something wrong?"

"Something's boring."

Takai stepped into the doorway, frowning, holding a small, beige data cube container.

"Just a moment," Skyler said, excitement surging within. He raised his eyebrows at Takai. "Excellent! Found them already?"

"Numbers match, but cubes are missing." He turned the empty container for Skyler to see.

In that instant Skyler's excitement crashed. His knees buckled, forcing him to lean on the desk. "You're sure? Searched the whole room?"

Takai nodded, his face a mask.

Skyler took a long, deep breath. "Were any other cubes missing?"

"No," Takai said.

Sitting on the edge of the dead man's desk, Skyler hung his head. He doubted another crew had beaten them here. Rich Orbitals sometimes hired multiple crews to increase their chances, but the place seemed otherwise untouched. No, more likely the intel was bad. Old, outdated, or just plain wishful thinking on some Orbital's part. The end result was the same.

Another failed mission, and worse—one based on the recovery of a single, valuable item. A mission on which he'd staked his very job.

Salvage what you can, he told himself. At least he could leave the others without a debt.

"Looks like we're shit out of luck," Skyler said into his communicator. "Smash and grab, everyone. Anything of value."

He heard Samantha curse in the hallway outside. She kicked something.

Jake's voice was faint over static. "I'll arrange pickup with Angus."

Skyler shook the failed mission from his mind. To dwell on it now would be pointless, and dangerous. "Copy. Takai, bag some data cubes anyway. The Orbitals ask for blank ones all the time."

"Okay."

Skyler rifled through the desk drawers. None were locked, to his relief. He bagged a variety of items: a stapler, scissors, a box of pencils, and what appeared to be a wristwatch, though it had a strange layout.

Next he examined the shelves on the sidewall. On one he found a portable music device, and inside it some zinc-air batteries. He put the whole thing in his bag, which had become rather heavy. He set it back down and slung his rifle over his shoulder to free up both hands.

"I carry," Takai said from the doorway, putting his own pistol away with awkward movements.

Skyler nodded and stepped back. "All yours. Let's get the hell out of here, eh?"

He led the man back to the stairwell. Samantha was gone.

"She went up," Takai said.

Skyler took the stairs quickly and had to wait at the first landing for his engineer to catch up. The next two flights he maintained a normal pace. From the main hallway, he could hear Samantha cursing from frustration.

They found her in the conference room, hands on her hips, staring up at the wall-mounted monitor. "Damn thing is bolted down. I trust one of you brought some cutters?"

Skyler shrugged and turned to Takai. The little man grimaced and said, "In the plane."

"Amateur hour." She pushed past the two of them and stalked back down the hall toward the door they had entered from.

"Wait a second," Skyler said.

Samantha turned around. Her narrow glare brimmed with annoyance.

"Something about this feels wrong," Skyler said.

"No shit," Samantha said. "You goosed it. *Again*."

"Not that. The dead guy."

She folded her arms. "Billions of them around."

Something still nagged him. "No other cubes were missing."

"So?"

"Odd, isn't it?"

Jake's voice crackled in Skyler's ear. "Angus is three minutes out."

"Understood," Skyler said to him. He focused back on Samantha. "Someone offered a small fortune for this. We get here, and it's the one set missing from the entire room? If a bunch were missing, I'd chalk it up to the chaos of five years ago. But the exact set we came to find, gone?"

Samantha gave a grudging nod. "Okay, Sherlock. So where is it? Not in the room, not on the dead guy . . . You did search the body, right?"

He hesitated, felt a knot grow in his gut. "No. Didn't seem right."

She stormed off toward the stairs. "He's not going to mind, Sky."

As her footsteps faded, Skyler realized what he'd missed. He jogged back to the lobby area, bypassing the gift shop in favor of the reception desk. Takai waited at the door, throwing constant nervous glances back toward the stairway.

On the desk in the lobby, Skyler brushed a thick coat of dust off a neatly wrapped package sitting in one of the two mail bins. The parcel's dimensions were identical to the data cube cases Takai had pulled from the shelves in the records room. He tore at the brown paper wrapping, an easy task—the brittle material all but disintegrated in his hands, leaving only a faded shipping label behind. Skyler's hunch proved accurate.

"Takai, have a look."

"We should stay with Sam," he said from the door.

"She can take care of herself," Skyler said. "Come over here."

Takai crossed the room with timid steps. He jumped when a sudden beam of light came in through the tattered drapes that covered the lobby windows. Within a few seconds, the room filled with pale orange shafts.

Dawn.

Skyler tapped his ear. "Status, Jake? Angus?" While waiting for a response, he unlatched the plastic container. Inside, four ceramic cubes were packed in a bed of Styrofoam shells.

"Thirty seconds," Angus said.

Takai appeared at Skyler's elbow, holding the list Prumble had provided them. "Numbers match the second set."

Though he felt a rush of hope, Skyler fought the urge to celebrate. He rummaged through the box and found a folded piece of paper beneath the cubes. Something had been written on it in Japanese.

" 'You must finish what I could not,' " Takai said.

"Hmmm?"

"That's what the paper says. *You must finish what I could not.*"

A chill ran up Skyler's spine. The message, the entire situation, implied that these cubes held something worth every council note offered for their retrieval. He closed the box and slipped it inside his jacket. "Let's get out of here," he said.

He turned back toward the door. Takai ran ahead, no longer content to be led.

In the hallway Skyler found Samantha emerging from the stairwell.

"Found an old phone, and a wallet," she said. "Why are you smiling?"

"Tell you outside," Skyler said. He made a conscious effort to wipe the grin from his face as he ran for the door at the end of the hallway.

Sunlight on snow patches blinded. He stopped their progress just outside the door, allowing his eyes to adjust. In the distance, he saw Jake emerge from the tree line, carrying a small deer over his shoulders. A broad smile graced his haggard face.

"Not as scrawny as I thought." Jake eased the dead animal off his back and rubbed at his shooting shoulder. "Venison stew tonight, I think."

As Sam and Takai admired the carcass, Skyler tapped his headset again. "Angus, ETA?"

The kid replied quickly, voice clear without interference from the building. "How flat is that field?"

Skyler imagined himself trying to land here. "Should work. Favor the east side."

"Any resistance?"

"None," Skyler said, "but let's have a nice quick dust-off, okay?"

"Sure."

"Ultracap level?"

"We'll make it. Just."

A moment later Skyler heard the *Melville*'s ducted-fan engines. The noise grew louder until the four of them were forced to cover their ears.

Angus set the craft down in the southeast corner of the field, a textbook landing. He'd even positioned the rear cargo door to face them, open and inviting. The engines remained on for a quick departure. Skyler admired the kid's work and envied his natural skill.

Samantha once again took the lead, passing back through the chain-link fence and across the weed field. Takai and Jake were last, under the burden of their respective prizes.

Once inside the *Melville,* Skyler punched the red button

that controlled the cargo door and instructed Angus to lift off as soon as the rest of the team was strapped in.

"What about that monitor," Sam asked, "in the conference room?" She held a tool belt.

"Forget it. The caps are running low."

"The parts will fetch a good price."

Skyler patted his jacket and smiled. "Nothing compared to—"

She punched the button to reverse the cargo door and ran off toward the observatory.

"Sam! Dammit." He hit the communicator. "Angus, hold tight, Sam went back inside."

His voice came right back over the speaker. "Kill the engines?"

Skyler weighed the options. The noise would only draw attention, but to spin them down meant spinning them up again, a lengthy process. He glanced at Jake and Takai, who both just stared back. "Keep them hot," Skyler said to Angus.

"Yes, Captain."

"Jake, can you cover me from the ramp?"

In answer, Jake picked up his long sniper rifle and removed the lens cap from the scope. Skyler wasted no time racing back across the clearing. Only when he passed through the fence did he realize he had left his machine gun in the *Melville*.

Before he could unholster the backup pistol kept on his thigh, Samantha emerged again from the building, arms wrapped around the large black monitor. Her face strained from the weight of it.

"Piece of cake," she said.

"Except a lot heavier."

She giggled. "Shut up and help me with this."

With a quick laugh, Skyler grabbed the leading edge. He turned and started back toward the waiting aircraft.

Jake knelt on the cargo ramp. For some reason his rifle pointed well off to the side.

A plume of fire and smoke erupted from the muzzle of the long gun. A split second later the booming sound of the weapon reached Skyler, loud even above the *Melville*'s idling engines. He felt his clothing pulse with the concussion wave. Birds erupted from the surrounding trees. Skyler glanced right in time to see a human form drop into the weeds and out of sight.

"Subs! Run!" Samantha shouted.

Skyler pumped his legs as fast as the weeds would allow. Patches of snow thwarted any hope for an all-out sprint.

He glanced right and saw two more subhumans loping toward them. The closest one ran hunched over, using one hand for balance. In the other hand it held a length of plywood. A club, of sorts. The one farther away had stopped. It coiled itself, preparing to throw something.

Another shot boomed from the plane. The rock thrower jerked and dropped to its knees, toppling over and out of sight.

The runner closed in on Skyler and Sam with terrific speed.

Skyler felt his grip on the heavy monitor failing. His gut told him to ditch the bulky device, then Jake's rifle boomed again. Skyler glanced at the runner just in time to see it tumble into the weeds.

They reached the cargo door, Takai closing it the moment their feet touched the ramp. The engineer gestured toward a blanket he had laid out on the floor. "Place it here," he said.

Skyler and Samantha carefully lowered the screen onto the padded blanket and laid it flat.

"Secure it," Skyler said to no one in particular, and tapped the microphone. "Angus, dust off, but keep it slow until we've got everything stowed."

"Copy that," he replied.

Skyler turned to Jake, finding him already in the process of breaking down his rifle. "Hey."

Jake stopped and turned to face Skyler, rubbing his shoulder more vigorously now, the shoulder where he rested the butt of his weapon.

"Nice shooting," Skyler said.

Jake shrugged. "They made it easy, running straight at you like that."

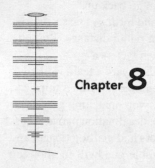

Chapter 8

THE DIGNITARY WORE a perfect business suit and a false smile.

He slipped on the wet steps as he came down from the climber car, his grin faltering in concert with his balance. One hand shot out and found the railing just in time to save him from a slapstick tumble down the rest of the stairs. He righted himself and put his smile back on. "Mr. Blackfield," he said, extending a smooth white hand. "So nice to meet you."

Russell thought that if he opened his mouth he might never stop laughing, so he returned the handshake instead.

"Michael Carney," the man said. "Immigration director, Orbital Council."

He spoke with a strong British accent, punctuated by dangling jowls that shook with each word. He wore glasses, a rare thing in this day and age, perched on the end of his nose so that he had to tilt his head back in order to look through them.

"Immigration," Russell said. "Why'd they send you?"

"I volunteered," Michael replied. He sucked in a breath through his enormous, hairy nostrils. "Haven't been down here in a decade, I wanted to smell the rain."

"Well gosh. We're honored to let you have a sniff."

"Cheers, cheers." If he noticed the sarcasm, he did a good job of hiding it. "Thanks for allowing the climber to come down."

"Thank me when I decide it can go back up."

The man's eyes flickered back and forth. A few secretaries waited patiently behind him, at a polite distance. Russell's own security detail loitered a dozen meters away.

On the opposite side of the loading yard a team worked to detach a food container from the climber. From a third car, a repair crew disembarked. They wore matching gray overalls and were bound for one of the desalination plants across the bay. One of the giant processors had malfunctioned, and Russell felt he'd shown considerable goodwill in allowing the repair team to piggyback on the lone climber.

"Enough with the pleasantries," Russell said. "You're here to negotiate, so negotiate."

Michael glanced around. "Somewhere more private, perhaps?"

"Here is fine."

"Ah . . . right then." The man took a breath and gestured to the container of food. "A peace offering."

"Don't need it," Russell said. "Do better."

The man's eyebrows ticked up, if only for a half second. "My visit proves the climbers are working fine. The power fluctuation last week, while certainly *odd,* should not continue to hamper our trade agreements."

"Odd?" Russell asked. "That's all you can say about it? Odd?"

"We've tripled-checked everything on our end, Russell, and found nothing wrong."

"Try harder, then. Until I get an explanation, the climbers stay put."

"There's nothing left to check, Russell. Perhaps if we could assist in your analysis down here?"

Many years ago, Russell received a piece of sage advice from a wrinkled old con man. "If someone you just met repeatedly uses your first name in conversation, they're either lying to you or hiding something." He'd never forgotten the tip, and it had proved useful many times.

"You think we're doing this on purpose," Russell said. "That we, what, faked the blackout?"

"All I can tell you is we're not ruling anything out," he said with a smug grin.

A politician, through and through. Russell wanted nothing more than to ram his fist into the man's uneven teeth.

Rain began to patter the ground around them. Thick, warm drops. The sprinkle grew to a downpour in the space of seconds.

"Perhaps," Michael Carney said, "we could move indoors?"

Russell turned and stalked away, leaving the councilman scurrying to keep up. He thought of doing the polite thing and guiding the visitor to his opulent office, but a better idea came.

Increasing his pace further, Russell turned toward Nightcliff's massive southern gates. Two huge doors, both patchwork quilts of rusting metal and hasty welds. He angled toward a scaffold stairwell beside the huge entrance and clanged up the steps two at a time.

At the top he paused to let Michael Carney catch up.

The Brit was breathing hard by the time he hit the last step. His once flawless business suit had soaked up the rain like a dry sponge. Drops of beaded water covered his glasses. He removed them, tried to find a place to wipe them off, and quickly gave up and stuffed them inside his blazer.

Russell stepped aside to make room. The narrow walkway ran the entire circumference of the fortress wall, but he knew he wouldn't need to take his guest any farther than this spot.

A murmur started below. Michael took in the view beyond the wall in stunned silence.

The gathered crowd stirred at the sight of a man wearing garb other than Nightcliff black. They sensed it meant something. Something important. The murmur grew, first to anxious talk and then to angry shouts, spreading through the crowd like a shock wave.

Yesterday, after nearly a week of pointless protests, their mood had shifted from riotous to bored. They'd camped in Ryland Square despite the unpredictable weather. They sang songs and played football in the mud. A few rather comical fistfights broke out. Occasionally they threw rocks toward the fortress.

Russell had watched them for a long time and noted how often their eyes turned to the Elevator, hoping to see the climbers moving again. Hoping that a meal would come down the cord.

No meal, Russell thought. *But I've brought a sacrificial lamb.*

"My word," Michael said, his wits finally gathered. He wiped the water from his face and strained to focus on the sea of people. "What are they all doing here?"

Russell clapped the man on his back. "They're dying to hear what you've come to offer them."

Michael recoiled from the edge of the wall. "You can't be serious," he squeaked.

In answer, Russell held out the small microphone he'd been using to address the crowd over the last few days. He'd had it rigged up to a speaker system originally installed to provide alarms if an attack on the Elevator was imminent.

Michael Carney stared at the device as if it were a coiled cobra.

"Go on," Russell said. "Tell them."

The man stammered. He gathered enough of his wits to wave off the microphone. "Point taken, Mr. Blackfield. The people are restless, I get that—"

Russell didn't budge. "You think I'm joking?"

The councilman's eyes grew wide. The rain began to hammer even harder. It poured down the man's face in rivulets.

"Here," Russell said, "I'll do it." He turned to the sea of ragged people and held up an arm. He pressed the microphone to his lips. "We have a visitor from above!"

The crowd surged forward, shouting insults. They were beyond desperate by now. Those who knew how to find a meal in Darwin had long since left the square. Even the Jacobites had given up.

Those that remained were truly pitiful.

Russell went on. "He's come with a peace offering." His

voice boomed across the wide expanse, echoing off the crumbling skyscrapers that lined the far side. The mood of the rabble shifted slightly at the words, and Russell seized the opening. He pointed, swept his arm in a half circle across their hungry faces. "Five containers of fresh food, all for you lot. What do you say?"

They roared in unison. Russell found the sound of it intoxicating.

Michael leaned in. "I only brought the one," he hissed through clenched teeth. "And that was for you and your staff."

"Relax," Russell said. "I'll pull a few from the emergency reserve. You can owe me."

"Owe?! I . . . I can't authorize that."

Russell grinned at the crowd. He threw his arm around Michael Carney's shoulder and turned him to face the cheering mass. "Exactly the problem, *Michael*. You're a powerless twat. So I'll give you a choice. I can push you over this wall right now, or you can go back to your betters and tell them that I've staved off anarchy for a few more days, despite their indecision and incompetence. But in return, they owe me. And more than food."

"What then?"

"Simple. I'll restart the climbers when I'm added to your council."

The man went rigid. He started to speak, then snapped his mouth shut.

Russell continued to wave at the crowd. He nudged the councilman closer to the edge of the parapet.

"A vote will be required," Michael said. "It may take some time."

"You just have to deliver the message, *Michael*. Surely you can handle it."

"What about the climbers? Please! This crowd proves you need food shipments just as much as we need air and water."

Russell sighed. "I suppose I can fire them up temporarily as a gesture of goodwill. In exchange, however, I want to ride one myself. Pay a little visit."

Michael started to object.

"Shut up and listen," Russell said. "I want to meet with Alex Warthen, in orbit, and I want to negotiate through him from now on."

"The task was given to me," Michael said.

"I don't give a rat's anus. Alex I can work with. You? You're a fop and I don't like you."

Color rushed from the man's face. He swallowed, all composure banished.

Russell spun the man so they were face-to-face. He tugged his wet lapels and smoothed out the sopping wet tie. "A business suit?" he asked. "You've forgotten the world we live in, Carney. You're too far removed, all of you."

"I . . . I'm at a loss. I don't know what to say."

"Thank God for that. Just smile and wave, one last time, to the shit-wallowers. Then you can climb back to Platz and the rest of them and deliver my warm regards."

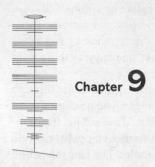

Chapter 9

NEIL PLATZ SCRATCHED at his beard, still unused to the rough hair. When he pulled his hand away, black greasepaint stained his fingertips.

"I can't believe this worked!" he shouted. The rush of wind coming into the water hauler's cabin drowned the words. Neil had asked for the door to remain open so he could enjoy the salty air.

His assistant sat in the middle seat of the bench, flanked by more members of the supposed repair crew. Bodyguards, to a man. His assistant, rigid and green-faced, shook his head in response and pointed to his ear. The poor bloke had vomited shortly after takeoff from Nightcliff and looked close to doing so again.

Neil raised his stained fingers and wiggled them, grinning. The disguise, a black beard and the gray coveralls of an engineer, had worked to perfection. His heart still pounded from the sheer thrill of passing through Nightcliff, under the bastard Blackfield's nose, undetected. No one recognized him, and after spending the last thirty-some years as the most famous man alive, Neil found the sensation of anonymity intoxicating.

Doubly so, since they'd come down on the only climber to descend in six days, carrying a council member to negotiate with Russell Blackfield. "Neil sends his regards," he imagined Michael Carney telling the onerous man. "He regrets he could not make the trip in person."

Neil laughed aloud. He felt alive, like he was half his age. The regrettable business aboard Hab-8 was already a distant memory. Men of power must make choices and move on. No point in dwelling on the past, and anyway there were worse skeletons in that closet. Far worse.

He looked forward to the return trip, to walk through Nightcliff again as a common man. Maybe he should have been a spy, or a con artist. Perhaps he'd missed his true calling, though he suspected many a former competitor would argue he was an accomplished swindler. The idea made him grin even wider.

The gigantic hauler cruised over the bay southwest of Nightcliff, en route to a spit of land called East Point. Neil strained against his harness, leaning out of the aircraft to look straight down. They were far enough from shore now that he could see the rippling ocean below, instead of the derelict boats that crowded the coastline. Whitecaps rolled toward the city. He inhaled deeply, and despite the slight hint of sewage, the air carried with it a flood of treasured memories.

When the engine noise began to drop, Neil looked ahead and saw the shore of East Point approaching.

Six massive desalination plants lined the coast. Square, sky-blue buildings, each surrounded by a nest of pipes in every imaginable size. Intake pipes snaked far out into the ocean, disappearing in the depths. Giant towers spewed white plumes of nuclear-fired steam high into the sky. He swelled with pride at the sight of them, still churning through tons of seawater every day—decades of continuous operation. They were the first piece of the Platz empire that he took over from his father. By the time the Elevator arrived, the plants provided drinking water to nearly all of the Northern Territory, at a time when wars were fought over the commodity.

His father was the real genius behind the construction of the plants. He'd laid the groundwork for the water processors a decade before the need became critical. Bought the land, hired the right engineers, and greased the wheels of bureaucracy. When the alien-built space elevator touched down in Darwin, these plants were what allowed the city to grow so rapidly into a megalopolis.

An amazing stroke of luck for the Platz family, or so everyone said. The truth was a burden Neil intended to take to his grave.

In the post-disease world, these machines were a key reason humanity survived at all. In Darwin, and in orbit. Rainwater drenched the rooftop gardens, sure, but by the time it trickled down to the streets it was a polluted soup. And while the Elevator might protect from the SUBS disease, it didn't sustain anyone. Neil considered that his job, thankless though it may be.

Fifteen other such facilities lay outside Aura's Edge, dotting the northern coastline, lost to the world. They served as spare parts now, occasionally visited by scavenger crews. Only these, on the shore of East Point, could be staffed.

The aircraft angled toward the farthest plant in the line. As the pilot set the bird down on a landing pad behind the facility, Neil felt like a deposed president returning from exile. He reminded himself of his disguise; for the moment he was simply part of a repair crew.

He let his crew exit the passenger compartment first. Neil stepped out last and kept his head low. The engines howled as they wound down, deafening. He walked in a crouch, focused on his balance in the violent exhaust.

Already a team rushed toward the aircraft to begin detaching the empty water container slung beneath. Such productivity made Neil happy.

Inside the facility, he followed his team across the cavernous ground floor. The constant hum of the water processors, each as big as a family home, filled the place. Steam vented from a dozen relief valves. Banks of triacetate membrane arrays filled a quarter of the space, looking like rockets pointed downward.

He saw the intake pipes, tall as himself and dripping with condensation. Neil imagined the seawater rushing through, straight into a series of chambers where it would be flash-heated to separate the salt. He'd run this plant for years and knew each component by heart.

"I'm not happy about this, Neil."

The familiar voice tore his attention from the machinery. Neil turned and confronted the plant manager, Arkin. "Keep it down, would you?"

The man fretted as he fell in beside Neil. "Nice beard," he said.

"Grown just for this visit. I had to pretend my supply of razors ran out. How'd you recognize me?"

Arkin shrugged. "I've known you all my life. You walk like a tyrant."

Neil barked a laugh.

"I'm not happy about this," Arkin repeated.

"Let's get off the floor, and we'll talk."

Arkin led the crew away from the water processing area and into an adjoining warehouse.

He walked at a hurried pace, giving Neil little time to study the contents of the storage area. Rows of wooden shelves held the spare parts that kept the facility running. Some sections looked sparse, but Neil decided now might not be a good time to point it out.

Water containers filled the bulk of the warehouse. The bulky cylinders were stacked from floor to ceiling, held in place by metal scaffolds. Neil glanced at each one, looking for signs of deterioration.

"Would you like to discuss your special containers first," Arkin said, "or your, um, guests?"

"They've arrived, then?"

Arkin said nothing. Instead he led Neil and his team around the last row of water containers.

At the end of the building, near a series of loading docks and garage doors, an armored van waited.

Three guards stood nearby the vehicle, chatting. They came to attention at the sight of their boss.

Arkin stopped short of the van and pulled Neil aside.

"I'm not happy—"

"So you keep telling me," Neil said. "How long have they been here?"

Arkin stifled his concerns. "Ten minutes, I guess."

"Blindfolded?"

"As requested."

Neil looked about the building, then focused on the van. "Let me take it from here. We'll talk about the containers later. I want a full report. We may need to ramp up soon."

"What of the climbers?"

"Don't worry about that. A deal is being struck as we speak."

Arkin hesitated.

"You're not happy, I know," Neil said. "Go about your business. I'll have them out of here soon enough."

Neil motioned for one of his bodyguards to open the van door. The vehicle had thick armor plating, and Neil thought it must have been used for bank deliveries in the pre-disease era.

Inside, on benches that ran the length of the compartment, two men sat facing each other. Both wore black hoods over their heads, but the similarity ended there. The one on the left was rail thin, the one on the right remarkably over-weight.

A third man sat with them, near the door. One of Arkin's security force. Neil leaned in to speak with the fellow. "How'd it go?"

"We found them at a café in the Maze. A place called Clarke's. Tracked the scrawny bloke to it, where the other was waiting."

"And they came willingly?"

"More or less," the guard said.

Neil nodded. "Take the fellow from Nightcliff out. I'd like a word with the other."

With professional calm, the guard took the skinny man by his upper arm and guided him out of the van. Satisfied, Neil stepped inside, took the vacated bench, and slid the door closed.

"You," Neil said, "must be Mr. Prumble."

The fat man's head tilted under the black hood. "At your service, Mr. Platz."

Bloody hell. Neil snatched the black hood away and set it aside. "How did you know?"

"I know your voice," Prumble said. "Heard your speeches."

Neil regarded the smuggler. Sweat glistened on the man's nearly bald head. He breathed with short, stunted exhalations, a side effect of his weight, Neil guessed. In a city full of starving souls, Neil had never seen someone with a weight problem. He found it mildly disgusting.

"Call me Neil. First name?"

"None worth remembering."

"I see. Darwin was a fresh start for you, I take it?"

Prumble inclined his head. "We all made sacrifices to reach the city."

Many used Darwin to hide from their past as much as a disease. *And who could blame them?* Neil thought. "Fair enough. Prumble it is."

The huge man shifted in his seat. His long coat, a brown leather duster, squeaked as it rubbed on the vinyl bench. He made a show of reaching for an interior pocket, from which he produced a metal hip flask. He unscrewed the cap and offered it to Neil.

"No, thanks."

Prumble shrugged and took a healthy swig of the drink. "Forgive my behavior, Mr. Platz. It's not every day I meet an Orbital. Especially someone of your . . . stature."

"Call me Neil," he repeated.

Prumble tipped the flask back again. "Of course. I forgot."

"Let's get to business," Neil said. "You were tasked with finding something for me in Japan."

"Ah," Prumble said. "You're the buyer. I should have guessed from the extravagant reward."

"I wanted to ensure my place atop the priority list."

"Quite. Well, I believe I've succeeded." Prumble returned the flask to his coat and fished around in a deeper pocket.

Neil reminded himself to relax. The stale air inside the vehicle smelled of sweat.

The big man finally pulled out the item from his pocket and presented it to Neil.

A child's toy. A furry green monster with big eyes, white fangs, and one hand raised in menacing fashion.

"Not exactly what I was hoping for," Neil said.

Prumble snickered. He pushed his fingers inside a small hole in the back and rooted around before removing the hidden contents: a small ceramic cube.

"My team found four of these," Prumble said, placing the tiny storage device in Neil's open palm. "Recovered from the facility in Japan, as requested."

Neil took a close look at the object. The cube, a few centimeters on each side, had a white ceramic outer shell. A grid of dark graphene leads lined one edge. Inside, Neil knew an array of crystalline sheets held data in holographic form. A single cube could hold a vast amount of information. "I need to validate this."

Prumble cleared his throat. "The others are safe in my office."

"Naturally," replied Neil. He turned and rapped his knuckles on the van's door. When it opened, he summoned his assistant over. "My briefcase, please."

The silver case in hand, Neil slid the door closed again. He placed his thumbs on each catch, his fingerprints triggering the locks. Inside, a portable terminal screen lit up.

"What will happen to my associate?" asked Prumble.

Neil looked up from the device. "Mr. Osmak has served his purpose. You will work directly with me now."

Prumble grimaced. "That's a bit unfair."

"He'll be paid handsomely," Neil said. "I prefer to minimize the people involved in my affairs. Loose lips sink ships, as they say."

The fat man laughed at that. A sly chortle, full of irony. "That puts me on shaky ground, then."

The manifest from the data cube recovered without error and appeared on the screen. "Perhaps," he said. "Who does your recovery work?"

"What, can't picture me gallivanting about Japan?"

Neil grinned. "Stranger things have happened."

On the screen, he saw a handful of markers—dates, the

observatory logo, Japanese names—that confirmed the data matched Tania's request.

We've got it, Neil thought. He forced himself to quell a rush of excitement. He could almost hear Tania reminding him that "it" might be nothing at all.

Prumble let out a sigh. "I contract with a variety of—"

"Names, Mr. Prumble. Security is a priority for me."

Prumble licked his lips. "Maybe I should keep that to myself. For my own security."

"I could ask Kip," Neil said. "Wag the promise of a life in orbit before him, and I suspect he'll do just about anything."

The big man stared at Neil, his face a picture of concentration. "Are you wagging that prize in front of me?"

"Names."

Another bead of sweat trickled down the man's forehead. He mopped at it with his filthy handkerchief. "Fine. A pilot called Skyler Luiken, and his crew."

"Trustworthy?"

"Extremely," Prumble said, "though I can't vouch for his entire team."

"You'd better. I want them working for me, exclusively."

"Skyler's a good man. Terrible leader, too nice, but a good man. His crew is . . . unique."

"How so?"

"They're immunes. Every last one of them."

Neil couldn't mask his surprise. He knew that some people were immune to SUBS, a few dozen out of the million people still alive. He'd hired a few, in the early years of the disease, to be studied by his medical staff. Nothing conclusive came from the research, and the project was abandoned.

A group of them banded together as scavengers was a smart play. A good business move. The possibilities raced through his mind. They could stay outside for days instead of hours, and would never have to worry about an environment suit tearing. "They could be very useful," he said. "And their aircraft, good ship?"

The fat man shrugged. "It gets the job done, as long as Nightcliff leaves them alone."

There's the rub, Neil thought. Of course such a crew

would suffer additional scrutiny. Still, there were ways around that.

"Well," he said, "we have the genuine article, it seems." He removed the data cube and held it before Prumble. "I'll have my men drive you back so they can collect the remaining three."

"There's still," Prumble said, "the matter of payment."

"When we have the data, you will be paid in full. Plus a retainer, for future requests."

Prumble pursed his lips, as if holding words back. Neil knew the man would be deciding, now, if he could trust such an arrangement. Life in the slums of Darwin was one constant look over the shoulder, and such a state of mind was not easily changed.

Neil extended his hand. A gentle push toward agreement.

The big man reached and shook. A firm, if sweaty, clasp.

"We're in business," Neil said. "Put the hood on, please."

Prumble complied.

Satisfied, Neil put the cube back in his case and pulled the van door open. Outside the cramped vehicle he stretched and called his assistant over.

"Sir?"

"Any news from Nightcliff?"

The man nodded. "The climbers have resumed, for now."

"Fantastic," Neil said. "What did we have to give Blackfield for his cooperation?"

"Carney offered to let him meet with Alex Warthen, aboard Gateway. Blackfield agreed."

"What an idiot," Neil said. He suspected Russell was simply content that they'd offered anything at all. "Perhaps I should have Alex arrest him there and throw him in the brig."

"They say a crowd is celebrating in front of Nightcliff."

"No doubt singing Blackfield's name." The true reason behind the blockade, Neil guessed.

His assistant shifted, nervous.

"Is there something else?" Neil asked.

"Something happened aboard one of the farm platforms," the man said, "an hour ago."

"Well? Out with it, lad."

"Security had to kill a woman. She went crazy, apparently." The assistant swallowed, hard. "They say she had the rash."

"Impossible," Neil said, an easy lie even as his mind raced. The creature he and Kelly dispatched had been no freak of nature. Another subhuman found within the Aura? It signaled a potentially cataclysmic change. One with impeccable timing. A flaw in the Aura's effectiveness now, so close to the next phase of the Builders' plan, could be no coincidence. "I'll look into it," Neil muttered. "A mistaken diagnosis, no doubt."

The comment did little to dispel his assistant's worried look. The man turned his attention to the van. "What are your orders?"

"Take the fat one back to his place. He owes me three data cubes. When you have them, pay him, and leave him with a sat-comm and dish."

The man nodded, then waved to the other guards to get back into the van.

"What about the other one?" he asked.

Neil looked toward the garage entrance, where Kip stood facing the wall, hooded head down. An armed guard waited next to him.

"We won't be needing his services anymore," Neil said. "Double his fee and drop him off at the dump where they found him."

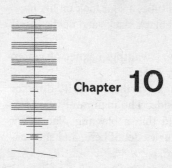

Chapter 10

AT THE MAIN airlock on Red, Tania tried in vain to press the wrinkles out of her lab coat—a task made all the more difficult without gravity. At least she'd remembered to tie her hair back.

A series of mechanical thumps emanated from the large round door. The sound that followed then would normally terrify her, or any Orbital: precious air escaping. The hiss lasted a few seconds as pressure equalized.

"The suspense is killing me," Natalie said. She drifted at Tania's left, wearing a simple white jumpsuit instead of her own lab coat.

"A few more seconds," Tania replied. She'd pulled her assistant away from research to meet some "special guests." The young woman had never met Neil Platz, or his affable brother, Zane, and Tania felt the time was right. Natalie could assist on the special project, something Neil had forbidden. If they'd met, became friends, perhaps he would change his mind. "I'm glad you could take the time to join me."

"You let me out of the lab! I'm the one who's happy."

"I still expect you to finish the debris plots."

Natalie grinned. "Slave driver."

"Shush now."

The airlock door pushed inward and rolled out of the way. Tania wondered if she should have prepared a more formal reception. Too late now.

Neil hovered in the junction tube, a sour look on his face. He wore a gray turtleneck and black slacks and held a briefcase in one hand.

Behind him, two others were waiting, neither of whom was the younger Platz brother, Zane.

Tania recognized one as Alex Warthen, security director and constant thorn in Neil's side. The man rarely came to Anchor, and Tania considered that a blessing. She never understood the need for a security detail here, and she suspected most of her staff agreed.

"Welcome," Tania said, "to Anchor Station."

Neil cracked a broad smile. "Tania, always a pleasure." He floated forward and shook her hand, as if they hardly knew each other.

She gestured toward her companion. "This is my lab assistant, Natalie Ammon."

Neil bowed slightly toward her, his movements fluid and comfortable in null gravity. "Delighted," he said.

"She's a genius at data analysis," Tania added. "Couldn't do it without her."

"Don't underestimate yourself," Neil said. "Have you met Alex Warthen, and Sofia Windon?"

"Alex, hello," Tania said. The man only nodded. He'd visited the station a few times before but never mingled beyond his own security staff. Tania turned to the other guest. "Miss Windon, I've not had the pleasure."

Sofia smiled, polite and nothing more, as she shook Tania's hand.

The woman sat on the Orbital Council, but Tania struggled to remember details about her. Recently elected to her first term, if Tania recalled. A former member of the Australian senate. She was short and plump, and wore a brown business suit with a few visible patches. The black shoulder strap of a messenger bag ran diagonally across her chest. In the absence of gravity, she kept the bag pinned to her side with one elbow.

Few council members bothered to visit Anchor. The bulk of their constituents lived aboard stations at the Earth end of the cord. To travel the forty thousand kilometers out to Anchor just to visit a bunch of anachronistic scientists was an errand they seemed content to avoid. Only Neil, and occasionally his brother, Zane, made the effort.

"Sofia handles resource management," Neil said. "You can thank her for the timely shipments of food, air, and water."

"Nice to meet you," Tania said. "I didn't realize you'd be bringing guests, Neil."

"Neither did I."

Alex Warthen drifted forward, grasping a handhold to steady himself with expert ease. "A last-minute thing. We wanted a face-to-face with the team solving the power problem. The situation has taken a nasty turn."

"More fluctuations?" Tania asked.

"Much worse than that," Alex said. "A subhuman was found aboard Space-Ag Three."

"What?" Natalie asked. "How?"

"Impossible," Tania said over her.

"Not impossible, Miss Sharma. I've got two dead civilians who'd tell you that if they could."

"Oh my God," Natalie said, one hand covering her mouth.

Tania felt paralyzed. She'd heard talk of the outbreak in the halls, but no official word. Few among the station staff even believed the rumor. The Aura had never been anything but infallible; no one ever thought it could be otherwise.

"I want to brief my staff before news spreads," Alex Warthen said. "This should be everyone's top priority now."

Unable to help herself, Tania looked at Neil. Her gaze settled on the briefcase in his hand, and the data cubes she hoped were within. She wondered if Neil would ask her to set the special project aside, given these events.

The timing of the news watered a strange seed of hope, deep within her. The Elevator faltering, a SUBS infection inside the Aura . . . all right when she and Neil decided to start looking for signs of another Builder ship. The coincidence was too great.

Neil ended the uncomfortable silence. "I'll make the priority calls here, Alex—"

Sofia Windon interrupted him. "We'll discuss this in due

time. I must admit, Tania, despite everything the real reason I came is to see the Shell. May we do that, if it's on the way?"

"Of course," Tania said, "no problem. Follow me?"

Taking their silence as agreement, she turned and pushed herself into the curved corridor. Rungs attached to all four sides of the hall aided speed and trajectory.

She frowned at the station's austere décor, a trait she'd never paid any thought to before. Visible pipes and ducts laced the walls, unpainted. Flat areas were used to store things in custom bins bolted to the surface. Little thought had been spent on the aesthetics. Compared to what she'd seen of Platz Station, it all seemed rather mundane.

Natalie nudged her.

"This is Storage," Tania said to the group. "Or Red Level, as we call it. The central hall on each level has a different colored floor, since they tend to look alike. As you've seen, this one contains our primary airlock and docking bay, along with numerous supply rooms."

"There's also a cargo bay on Green, for backup purposes," Natalie added. "Black Level, at the other end of the station, has one, too. But since the Elevator cord doesn't extend there, it's never used."

Sofia asked, "This ring doesn't rotate. Why?"

"It's much easier to pack things in zero-g," Tania said. "Easier to move supplies and maximize our space."

"Yet the hall is curved?"

Neil cut in. "Reuse of manufacturing plans. It's cheaper that way."

The curt answer silenced her. Tania continued along the wide hall, curving ever upward. Large segmented doors spaced at regular intervals lined all four walls. Each door had a code stenciled on it.

"I'll need to survey all this later," Sofia said.

"Of course," Tania replied. "It's all in order, I'm sure."

"The climber problem has everyone spooked," Neil said. "Sofia has a mandate from the council to ensure all stations have ample reserves."

"And," Alex added, "that they are appropriately staffed."

Tania caught a hint of venom in Alex's tone.

"Don't mind Alex," Neil said. "He's fretting over what to wear for his date with Russell Blackfield."

"Someone has to talk to him," Alex said.

"Children, please," Sofia said. She frowned at Tania. "They were at it the whole way up here, like a couple of grade school brats."

After a long series of storage rooms, they came to an open lift.

Tania waited at the entrance and ushered the guests inside. "Orient yourselves so the red floor is down."

She entered last and pressed the control to take them to Green Level, via the central spine.

"Hold on to something, please," she said.

The lift plodded along in relative silence, broken by the occasional lurch as it transferred from Red Level to the central spine, and then into the rotating portion of the station.

Gravity, or the illusion of it, increased the farther the lift moved away from the spine. Soon Tania stood on the floor, and she thought her guests looked much more comfortable.

She led them through the green-carpeted level quickly, passing only one group of researchers who were in a quiet conversation with a maintenance crew. When the workers realized that Neil Platz walked at her side, their responses varied from shy nods to awkward salutes.

Halfway around the long, sterile hall, they came to a series of thick glass doors. Three security guards manned a desk in front. They stood at attention at the sight of Alex Warthen.

Before Tania could speak, Alex approached the men. He greeted each of them by their first names. The guards were tense in their commander's presence, a far cry from their usual relaxed demeanor.

"At ease," Alex said. "I want the squad assembled for inspection in exactly fifteen minutes."

The guards exchanged surprised looks.

"In the meantime," he said, "we are taking Councilwoman Windon to see the Shell. I will personally escort them."

"Yes, *sir*," said the ranking member. He punched a series of codes into his console and the first set of transparent doors silently slid apart.

Tania led the group inside, where they waited as the first doors closed again. After a short pause, the second set opened. Beyond, a long, straight hallway led into the distance, illuminated at regular intervals by pools of dim white light.

They walked in silence until the halfway point, where they passed through an open bulkhead. "Halfway to White Level," Tania said.

Sofia asked, "Why are these two levels so far apart?"

"Fear," Neil Platz said, before Tania could open her mouth. "When we began construction here, to study the damn thing, everyone was worried it might explode. Or some such nonsense. So as we expanded we left a two-hundred-meter buffer on either side of White Level."

At the end of the connecting hall they entered a utilitarian tunnel, replete with unpainted metal walls and exposed ductwork. "I expected white floors," Sofia said.

"This was built first, more than twenty years ago," Tania replied. "The coloring scheme came later."

Sofia looked confused again. "Then why call it white?"

Tania shrugged. "Good question."

Neil cleared his throat. "It was supposed to be eggshell, as in the shell ship, but everyone kept saying white."

The level was cramped, haphazard compared to the others. The hallway jutted at right angles, around exposed ventilation shafts and bare metal pipes. Electrical panels graced the walls like paintings. The group's footsteps clanged on a floor of steel grid tiles. Air flowed in through circular vents that hung from the ceiling.

Neil explained as they walked. "Platz Industries built Anchor Station to study the Elevator, and of course the remnant of the construction ship. A rush job at the beginning. We added on only later, when we realized all the other research that could be conducted with so much scientific activity centered here. The hub of it all, until the plague came."

"What did you hope to learn here?" Sofia asked.

Neil paused in his tracks and turned to face her. He studied the woman's face for a few seconds before answering. "How to build another space elevator. To replicate this incredible gift."

Tania grinned at his enthusiasm.

"For your own profit," Alex said.

Neil shrugged. "Of course. I was a businessman. Even now, it's still a worthwhile pursuit."

"We can barely keep this one running," Alex said. "What the bloody hell would we do with another?"

Neil glared at the security director. "Double our rate of trade? Allow for some raw materials to flow once again? It's essential that we continue our studies here."

"We're all looking forward to some actual results," Alex said. "Maybe you'll be done before this one fails completely."

Tania saw Neil's fists clench. In the uneasy quiet, she struggled to think of something to say. It had never occurred to her that Anchor Station's purpose might be considered a waste of time, especially by a member of the Orbital Council. She wondered if others shared the view. A glance at Sofia Windon gave no hint of her opinion.

Natalie broke the silence. "The Shell is this way," she said, then took a few steps toward the destination.

The natural cheer in her voice diffused the lingering tension and the moment passed. Tania walked toward her assistant and mouthed a silent thank-you to her. Natalie winked in response.

One by one, the others began to follow them.

At last they came upon a large room that resembled an auditorium. Numerous scientists sat at desks facing a bank of enormous screens on the far wall. Nestled in the center of the monitors were two large windows.

Outside, the remains of the Builders' ship dominated the view.

The Shell, now hollow, had served as the hull of the machine that built the Elevator. To Tania the shiny, obsidian-colored object resembled the elongated tail of a wasp, on a massive scale.

Sofia, in naked awe, said nothing.

Tania couldn't blame her. She recalled the first time she'd seen it. She'd been only ten years old at the time, and held Neil Platz's hand as they stood at these windows. Neil had told her all about the ship, but Tania had heard none of it. She'd simply stared, overwhelmed.

"Why did they leave it behind?" the councilwoman asked after a long silence.

"As an anchor," Tania said. "Hence Anchor Station. Literally, a counterweight for the Elevator cord."

"I don't follow you."

"Sorry," Tania said. "Imagine you're holding a long piece of yarn, and you spin in place. What happens to the yarn? It trails and curves, and eventually wraps around you. But tie a small weight to the end and the yarn will pull straight as the weight tries to fly away from you."

Sofia curled her lip and nodded.

A research team outfitted with thick space suits floated next to the Shell. They worked to position a large piece of equipment against the surface. Gold foil and white insulation against the pure black vessel. The ship dwarfed their man-made device.

"One hundred and nineteen meters, tip to tip," Natalie said.

"What are those people doing?" Sofia asked, pointing to the space walkers.

"I'm not exactly sure," Tania replied. "My work is mostly in the observatory."

A scientist at the window turned to them. "Electron aberration imaging. We're compiling a more detailed surface map, at the atomic level."

"What for?" Sofia asked.

"To understand the materials. This object survived a journey through interstellar space, unscathed and still functioning—"

"Could this activity," Alex asked, "be what's causing the power blips?"

The scientist hesitated. He looked to Tania. "I . . . it's a passive scan. I don't—"

"It's unlikely," Tania said. "The climbers get their power from the Elevator cord, which generates it from friction with the atmosphere."

Alex jerked his head toward the Shell. "You're so sure of what's inside? Maybe it doesn't like being probed."

"The vessel is inert," the scientist said, his voice jumping an octave. "We've been doing this for years."

"Thank you, that'll be all." Neil glared at the man, who quickly returned to his work. "Our efforts may seem a waste to some, Sofia. But understanding how this got here, what it's made of, and how the SUBS disease is put into stasis . . . these are all keys to freeing us from being trapped in its shadow. That's why we study it. It's shortsighted to think otherwise."

Alex kept his hands clasped behind his back and stared out the window. "Care to explain that to those who died on Space-Ag Three this morning? We had a subhuman running loose in orbit, for God's sake. The climbers are losing power on an almost daily basis!"

His voice, raised to a shout, brought the room to silence. Everyone stared at him, their work forgotten.

"That's unfair," Tania said. The words tumbled out before she could think to stop.

The security director glanced at her. "Is it?"

"We have an ample team looking into the power issues. A plan is being formed."

"Oh, wonderful. A plan, you say?" Alex turned his gaze to Sofia Windon. "A full audit of Platz operations would prove how the staff is being allocated."

"This," Neil said, "is no time to debate council business."

Tania decided to change the subject before the argument worsened. "Shall we move on to the observatory?"

"Wonderful idea," Neil said.

"Make it quick," Alex said. "I need to meet with my security staff."

"Talk about a waste of resources," Neil grumbled.

Black Level capped Anchor Station, making it the farthest human habitat from Earth.

Dim amber lights lined the main hall. Tania explained. "Red light has the least impact on night vision. Easier to see details when using the telescopes."

"You have carpet up here," Sofia noted.

Tania glanced down. She never thought about it. The red surface, irreplaceable now, had many worn patches. "It keeps noise to a minimum."

"We should arrange a tour for the children," Sofia said.

Tania smiled. Those on staff who had kids left them in the care of others on lower stations. She couldn't remember the last time she'd heard a child's laughter. "That would be delightful."

"I'll speak to our education director."

Natalie tugged at Tania's elbow. "I think I'll get back to work," she said. "If that's all right?"

Tania caught the unspoken request—Natalie would rather return to her research than continue to tag along, which spoke volumes. Nat never missed an opportunity to get out of the lab. "Of course, dear. I can handle this." She added a wink, which Natalie returned before waving to the others.

At the door to the observation lounge, Tania stopped and poked her head inside. On more than one occasion she'd surprised amorous couples in here, sharing the romantic view. Right now the room was, thankfully, empty. She led her guests inside.

Sofia sucked in a breath.

A twin pair of enormous geodesic windows dominated the walls to their left and right. One looked out into space, an impressive enough sight, and the one Tania preferred.

But the Earth-facing window caught the attention of newcomers. It never failed.

Sofia took a seat and folded her legs beneath her, eyes never leaving the grand view. Tania watched her with a twinge of jealousy. A life in orbit provided little chance to see anything new. She loved to watch the reaction of others when they first saw the Elevator from this angle.

Out the window, the tail end of the Shell dominated the view. And some forty thousand kilometers beyond that,

Earth. The planet sat in full sunlight at this hour, a swirl of deep blue oceans and white clouds.

The other rings of Anchor Station encircled the derelict alien ship. As all the rings rotated in unison, they appeared to be at rest. Only Red Level, the ring that didn't spin for gravity, had the illusion of motion.

A few transport shuttles drifted in the distance, yellow warning lights blinking. Both sped toward the next station down the Elevator, almost a thousand kilometers "below," and used the Elevator cord as a guide wire.

"Thrilling," Alex said. He stayed near the door. "Now may I go, mother hen?"

"Alex," Sofia said, "take five minutes to relax and enjoy this. Honestly, you're both too serious."

"I'd rather get to work," Alex said.

Neil snorted. "For once we agree."

"Fine," Sofia said. "Before you run off, Alex, can we at least come to some agreement on how we will address the climber failures?"

The security director shrugged. "As good a place as any," he said. "Thanks for the tour, Miss Sharma. Could you give us a few minutes?"

"She can stay," Neil said. Before Alex could object, he added, "She practically runs this station, and knows the staff better than anyone. If anyone can coordinate the investigative team, it's her."

A brief silence followed. Sofia broke it. "I'm okay with it if you are, Alex."

Tania kept quiet and looked to Neil for any clues as to how he expected her to act. She wanted nothing more than to focus on their secret project, and she couldn't help but glance at the square-edged bulge in Neil's jacket pocket—a data cube case, she recognized.

Alex Warthen was staring at her, she realized. When she caught his gaze, he looked away and shrugged. "Whatever it takes to solve this."

"Good," Sofia said. "First, I think—"

An alarm cut her off.

The sudden noise wailed so loud that Tania covered her

ears without thinking. Three long beeps, grating and obnoxious. It rolled through Black Level's curved hallway.

A prerecorded voice came over the station address system. *"SECURITY TO GRAY LEVEL. SECURITY TO GRAY LEVEL."*

"The hell?" Neil said.

Tania glanced at him, then Alex Warthen. The security director looked composed, his eyes cast upward as he listened to the address. Tania saw a small weapon in his right hand. A gun, drawn so quick and sure she hadn't even seen him move. The weapon frightened her more than the alarm.

A series of dull clicks cascaded along the curved hall.

"What is that?! What's happening?!" Sofia said.

"The doors are locking," Alex said. "Safety precaution."

"Precaution against *what*?"

Alex ignored her. He took two quick steps to the door nearest him and shot a foot out. His timing couldn't have been better as the door slid closed by remote command. It hit his shoe and retracted, half-open.

The alarm began to repeat. Three shrieking beeps.

When the sound stopped, he crouched and checked his pistol. His foot still held the door open. "Tania, how far is Gray Level?"

She heard the question. The words made sense. No answer came to mind. She realized she was shaking and tried to still her hands.

"Tania!" Neil said. They were all staring at her.

"One," she said, hating the fear she heard in her voice. She swallowed and tried again. "One level over. Not far, but you'll need a code to override the junction door."

"I don't need the code," Alex said.

"Of course, I—"

"You all stay here until the alarm ends."

"No," Sofia said. "I don't want to be trapped in this dark little room. The alarm could last hours."

Neil nodded. "She's right. We're coming with you."

"You're not coming with me," Alex said. "End of discussion."

"Gray Level isn't far," Neil said. "What's—"

"The problem isn't on Gray Level," Alex said. His voice was so calm, so collected.

"What the hell are you talking about?" Neil asked.

Alex finished checking the gun. He held it upright, now, and had a finger on the trigger. He was looking outward, toward the hallway, and didn't glance back. "We don't rally security to the location of the problem, especially on a station-wide alert. We rally to the adjacent section, so we can go in together."

Realization hit Tania like a shadow falling.

"The problem isn't on Gray," Neil said, for all of them. "It's here, on this level."

"Yes," Alex replied, and stood. His voice had dropped to almost a whisper, Tania realized. "Wait here. I'll be back soon."

Tania took a step forward. "We could go to scope control. It's just a few doors down. There's food and water there, and a bathroom. In case . . ."

He looked ready to argue, before pushing the door open. "Fine. We're just wasting time. Follow me, but not too close."

The deserted hallway beyond was lit with bright yellow emergency LEDs, running in strips along the edges of the floor. Every few seconds a bank of red lights on the ceiling would flash.

Alex went ahead, keeping to one side of the upward-curving hall. He drew the fingers of his left hand along the wall as he walked. His gun remained pointed at the ceiling. In the brightness, the weapon seemed small, pitiful even.

At the first door, Alex glanced back to Tania, eyebrows raised. She shook her head and signaled with four fingers the number of doors yet to go.

He nodded and went on. Ten seconds later he stopped dead and crouched. Without thinking, Tania mimicked the pose. She chanced a look back and saw that Neil and Sofia had done the same.

She saw a hint of a smile on Neil's lips. Some part of him was enjoying this.

Alex made a soft noise. Tania turned back to him and

found the security director had come back to her. He was crouched right in front of her, eye to eye.

He placed a finger to his lips and pointed back the way they'd come.

Tania turned, her heart hammering inside her chest. She felt her eyes watering and realized she hadn't blinked in some time. If felt as if someone were holding her eyelids open. She forced herself to blink, and felt tears forming at the edges.

Alex put a firm hand on her shoulder and pushed her into swifter motion. He guided her back to the door they'd just passed. Neil and Sofia kept going until Alex made a subtle click with his tongue. They both looked back in unison, then stopped.

With a quiet professionalism, Alex moved beside Tania, stood, and tapped in a code to override the door lock. The thud as the lock disengaged made her jump.

He crouched again and whispered, "Inside. Stay until the alarm ends. *No* noise."

The words left no room for argument.

Half an hour passed in total silence. Then another.

The room, someone's vacant quarters, was even smaller than the observation room. A simple bunk on the far wall, a desk with a terminal, some shelves of books, and a closet. Standard issue, identical to Tania's own. She'd tried the terminal right away, only to find it locked with someone else's passphrase.

Sofia Windon sat on the floor, legs tucked underneath her. She kept near the door as if to be ready to leave the instant they could.

Neil and Tania sat on the bunk. Twice Neil had tried to speak, but Tania waved him off. She tried to focus on sound. Every little noise spooked her.

Each tiny shift in the hum of the air processors. A repetitious grinding from somewhere inside the walls, probably a bad bearing inside a fan. Neil's fingers tapping absently on the blanket.

Her own measured breathing.

As the minutes rolled by, with no activity from outside, no sound of struggle or combat, she felt her pulse drop to something close to normal. The third time Neil spoke, she didn't try to stop him.

"Alex and I might not get along," he whispered, "but he can handle this. Whatever it is."

She nodded. The man had reacted to the situation with surprising poise, she thought.

If Sofia heard, or cared, she showed no sign of it. Her attention remained firmly on the door.

Neil tapped Tania's arm. He'd set his briefcase on the bed between them, and at some point opened it. Inside was a small box. He lifted the lid and spoke in a low voice. "The genuine articles. I hope you can read Japanese."

Tania shook her head. Annoyance rose within her that Neil would want to discuss their secret project now. But the sensation faded. After sitting for an hour, with no indication at all from Alex, a diversion held some appeal. She chanced a glance at the contents of the box.

Four white cubes were nestled inside, each marked with kanji. The tension of their situation vanished as she shifted focus. "I don't read Japanese," she said, "but I can feed them through the translator down in Compute."

"Is that safe?"

Tania shrugged. "It's probably logged," she said, careful to keep her voice low, "but at least I can move the results to my secure cube."

Neil pressed his lips into a thin line. After a few seconds, a slight nod. He looked gloomy to Tania. A trick of the light, perhaps.

"Do it then," he said, "but erase the logs when you're done."

"I have no idea how to do that. And such things are monitored."

"Hell," Neil spat. He wrung his hands together. "Why is everything so complicated?"

Tania leaned back into the wall as his mood worsened. She attempted to impart calm with her voice. A tough thing when speaking in whispers. "It may take some time. If I could get Natalie to help—"

"We discussed this already," Neil said. "It's too early to trust anyone else. Until we know what we're dealing with—"

"*If* there is something to deal with," Tania corrected.

"If? *If?* Of course there is. Why would the Builders send—" He stopped, glancing at Sofia. The woman hadn't moved. Neil lowered his voice further. "Why send the space elevator here, then the bloody disease, only to stop there? A little prank? No, something will happen. It may already be happening."

"What do you mean?" She knew the answer but asked anyway.

He frowned at her and jerked his eyes toward the door. "The power disruptions on the cord? The subhuman on Ag Three? I have a hunch what's going on outside that door, too. I'm beginning to feel these are the signs of the fourth—sorry, third—event. What if, instead of another ship, the Elevator simply expires?"

His words chilled her to the core. She'd never seen him like this, so full of bottled-up fear. Tania closed her eyes and digested his words. "It's speculation. Accurate, perhaps, but speculation. The data will tell us. There's no reason to worry about it until then."

"There's every reason to worry," he said through clenched teeth. He leaned against the wall, too, massaging his temples.

"Neil . . ."

"Let me think."

"No, Neil . . . the door."

A shadow obscured the tiny line of light at the base of the door. A firm knock came and Sofia jumped to open it.

"Find out if another ship is coming, Tania," Neil said as he stood. "Do it fast, but do it alone."

Alex Warthen stood in the hallway outside. He looked disheveled. Tania's eyes were instantly drawn to a splotch of blood on his shirtsleeve.

"It's over now," he said. "I'm keeping lockdown in effect until we can clean up."

No one spoke.

Alex answered their unspoken question. "Another sub. A woman."

Tania covered her mouth with her hands to mask her gasp. "Oh no. Who?" *Please, not Natalie.*

"One of the janitorial crew, I'm told. She thought everything was trying to kill her, and ran until cornered."

"Was anyone hurt?" Neil asked. He sounded tired.

"Six injured, one seriously. The subhuman we had to . . . put down."

"Oh no," Tania said. A death, a violent death, aboard the station. It sounded more alien than the Builders' Shell. She felt dizzy and put one hand on the wall. Her heart raced. She looked to Neil, wanting the strength she'd found there so many times before.

He was staring back at her with an expression hard as stone.

Tania realized he was looking for strength, too.

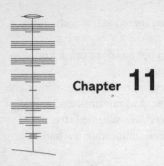

Chapter 11

"PAYMENT," PRUMBLE SAID as he dropped a heavy satchel on the wooden table. Three coffee mugs on the weathered surface rattled.

Skyler stared at the bag.

"In full," the fat man added. He grabbed the only empty seat—a white plastic patio chair, faded and scuffed with age. Grunting with effort, he squeezed himself in.

The tiny coffeehouse had only one table and two chairs. A sign on the wall outside named the place Clarke's, and bragged of "real coffee," a claim Skyler thought far-fetched. He'd left his steaming mug alone despite the pleasant aroma.

Samantha had relinquished her seat when Prumble entered. She now leaned against the wall by the café's grimy window, arms folded, her expression impassive. When Skyler told her the odd location where their fence wanted to meet, she'd insisted on coming along.

For protection, she'd said.

The ground-floor café looked out on a dark, cramped alley, deep within an area called the Maze.

The labyrinthine district butted up against Nightcliff's eastern wall and straddled the territory of a powerful slumlord named Grillo. His thugs patrolled the ad hoc markets that appeared every morning, where people bartered their meager belongings for surplus food. Skyler couldn't fathom why anyone bothered to do business here, between the rampant theft and bribery. The desire to survive, to gain even the smallest improvement in life, must blind people to the risks.

The original skyscrapers hid under a crust of ramshackle bolt-on additions, squeezing the old streets into narrow, unplanned alleyways where sunlight rarely fell. Skyler hated the place. It reeked of human waste.

"Job well done," Prumble said, a satisfied smile drawn across his face. "Just rewards, *et cetera*."

An old woman, with dark wrinkled skin and frayed gray hair, shuffled into the room carrying an antique stainless steel mug. Steam spilled from the open top. "Coffee," she managed in broken English, smiling. With great care she set the beverage in front of Prumble.

"Renuka, my dear, you are an angel," he said.

The old woman beamed at the compliment, a toothless grin stretching across her ancient face.

"Someday I'll buy this place from her," Prumble said as the lady shuffled away. "Just sit here and banter with the locals. Retirement would suit me."

From the sincerity in the man's voice, Skyler knew he meant it.

"Well, say something, man! Count it!" Prumble said.

Skyler lifted the satchel, enjoying the weight of it. A feeling of satisfaction surged within him. Only now did the Japan mission feel like a success. He resisted an overwhelming urge to tell Sam, "I told you so." That little victory he'd save for later.

"It's been a week," Skyler said with as much nonchalance as he could manage. "I assumed the cubes didn't pass muster." With care, he pulled the zipper open.

Outside the dirty window, the citizens of Darwin hurried past, hunched over, ignoring one another. Their festive mood of the last few days, celebrating the resumption of climbers on the Elevator, had already faded. Life returned to normal, and now they probably hoped to get through the day without a shiv in their back.

Most of them would go their whole life without ever seeing paper money that still held value. The satchel in front of Skyler contained stacks of it.

Samantha leaned in close. *For once,* he thought, *she's speechless.*

Unable to resist, he reached in and thumbed through the money. Crisp, flat, Australian dollars. In one corner, the Orbital Council's embossed watermark was plainly visible. In another, the counterstamp of a money broker from Milner Street. The only legitimate tender in Darwin, though few accepted it. For an average citizen it would be hard to spend, but Skyler could. Most of the crews along the runway honored it for supplies, and the odd bit of gambling. He knew a handful of garden owners who'd take it in exchange for fresh vegetables. Even for seeds, sometimes.

The blokes in Nightcliff would take it to turn a blind eye. They knew where the most discerning brothels were.

Most of all, he could use it to purchase a climber lift for the *Melville,* up the Elevator to the edge of space. A drop from there almost doubled the old girl's range. Nightcliff exacted a large sum for the privilege, something few scavenger crews could afford.

Skyler felt a weight lift from his shoulders. For the first time in months, his thoughts turned to pleasure rather than business.

He thought of giving the crew a few weeks off. Perhaps they could fly to a remote island and enjoy some sun. Fiji, or Palau. Catch some fresh fish and cook on the beach. Build a bonfire and dance around it like idiots.

Prumble clasped his hands behind his neck, grinning ear to ear. "The buyer is very happy."

"He should be," Skyler said. "His cut just for passing on the list must have been—"

"No, no, I mean the *buyer.* Kip, that weasel, was removed from the chain."

Skyler set the satchel down as if it were toxic.

Samantha spoke with an uncharacteristically quiet tone. "Murdered?"

Prumble dismissed the idea with a wave. "Nothing so dramatic. The *client* merely prefers to deal with us directly."

"Who is it?" Skyler asked.

Prumble smiled.

"C'mon, who?"

The big man savored the attention. He took a sip from his coffee, swallowed, and set the mug down. "Neil Platz."

"Fuck," Samantha whispered.

"You spoke to him?" Skyler asked.

Prumble did a little jig in his chair. "Even better. I met him in person."

"Not up—"

"Of course not. Me? In orbit? I doubt I'd fit through the airlock," Prumble said, over a rumbling laugh. "No, I was whisked from this very café to a secret location. Neil even wore a disguise."

The ramifications swarmed through Skyler's mind like angry hornets. "This café? Is that why you wanted to meet here?"

"Guilty as charged," Prumble said. "Kip and I meet here often. I'd hoped he might show, so I could make sure there is no ill will."

"And in case there was, Sam and I would be around to help."

"We're a team, are we not?"

"You seem eager to point that out."

Prumble sighed. "Platz and I made a deal. We're to be his exclusive suppliers. Myself, you, and your crew."

"You agreed? On my behalf?"

"Don't worry, I vouched for you."

Skyler looked at the money on the table. "Platz is behind this."

Prumble nodded. "Powerful man."

He wore a disguise. "Powerful enemies."

The smile vanished. "I couldn't refuse him," Prumble said.

"It's just," Skyler said, "we've always kept our hands clean. I deliver to you, you supply your contact, and he deals with *whatever shit goes on from there.*"

Prumble's expression soured. "I thought you'd be grateful."

"It's not that," Skyler said. "Sam, would you give us a minute?"

She shrugged. "What am I supposed to do?"

"Peruse the quaint boutiques along the promenade?" Prumble offered.

She extended her middle finger.

"Or guard the door," Skyler said. "You pick."

She offered a sarcastic salute and stomped out of the room.

When the door closed behind her, Prumble chuckled. "Such a handful."

"She misses Skadz."

Prumble rubbed at his unshaven chin. "Success might ease that. The promise of more."

On reflex Skyler eyed the money.

"I've watched you, Skyler," Prumble said. "You treat them as peers. Make them follow you, not like you. That'll come later."

"Care to wager your cut on that?"

"You know I'm not a betting man," Prumble said.

Skyler snorted a laugh.

The big man lifted his coffee mug. "You haven't touched your drink," he said.

"Talk about a gamble." Skyler eyed the mug with suspicion.

"Nonsense," Prumble said, "you supplied it. The Vietnam mission, a few years back?"

He remembered it. A hospital near Da Lat, where they recovered spare parts for an X-ray machine. In a storage room, Skyler came across a box of preserved coffee. Prumble had paid handsomely for the beans and the special canisters they were packed in. Far more valuable than the instant powdered stuff commonly brought in, he'd explained. "*She* bought them?" Skyler asked, and shot a glance at the old woman behind the counter.

"A gift," Prumble said. "Laying the groundwork for my twilight years."

Skyler took a sip. The strong brew had a spicy flavor, bitterness cut by ample sweetening. "God, that is good."

Prumble raised his glass in salute and sipped.

From the breast pocket of his flight jacket, Skyler produced the photograph. "Have a look," Skyler said. "I found this in a dead man's office inside that observatory."

Prumble glanced at it and shrugged.

"Platz founded the place," Skyler said.

"Yes. So?"

Skyler arched an eyebrow. "It seems odd to me."

The big man shook his head. "Not so odd. He owned many things, back then. He probably felt nostalgic about the research done there and wanted some of it back." He handed the picture back to Skyler.

"None of our business, in other words," Skyler said, returning the print to his pocket. "What happens next?"

"Platz said he'll be in touch. He seems eager to do business, and a lot of it."

A steady stream of work from the most powerful man alive. Skyler couldn't help but smile. It might not be such a bad arrangement, after all.

"A pleasure doing business, Captain," Prumble said, with a mock bow and jovial grin.

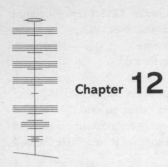

Chapter 12

RUSSELL BLACKFIELD FELT a perverse sense of pleasure watching Darwin shrink below the climber.

The flat monitor, mounted on the climber's cabin wall, displayed a live image of the view outside, aimed straight down the Elevator cord. The city resembled a gray splotch from this height. A stain of ashen vomit on Australia's otherwise glorious coastline. Russell drew a finger along the screen, tracing the circular shape of the city, so distinct from this altitude.

He looked down at his feet, imagining the view below in place of the boring black tile floor. He saw himself, drifting slowly higher like a soul being called to the big party in the sky. The image made him grin. For an instant he could see the appeal of the Jacobite's silly sermons. A ladder to heaven—sure, why not?

The bulky climber inched up the Elevator thread, like a plump spider traversing the first strand of an epic web, eight kilometers into its journey to Gateway Station. The sloth-like pace meant a fourteen-hour trip.

Russell sighed. "The Americans only needed four minutes to get to orbit. And that was three hundred years ago."

The only other person in the cabin, a middle-aged man, lazed in a chair, cradling a thick book with yellowed pages. An Orbital, Russell knew. Overdressed and overfed. And pretending to be overdeaf; that wouldn't do.

"Four minutes," Russell said, louder. "How about that?"

The man looked up from his book. "Well, the Elevator is far more efficient. Resources are terribly scarce—"

"But we didn't build the damn thing, did we?" Russell barked the comment. Too loud, perhaps, as the Orbital flinched. "No, some bloody aliens had to give it to us, and they couldn't even be bothered to stop and say hello."

"Well," the man said, "we built the climbers. The infrastructure."

"Four bloody minutes," Russell said. As far as he was concerned, that settled the matter.

The man swallowed a retort and went back to reading.

Russell eyed him with quiet contempt. He'd studied the cargo manifest for this climber, as he did all of them, and knew the man to be an administrator who worked aboard Gateway Station in resource management. Or, in Russell's view, a man who plotted the looting of Darwin's freshwater supply. He wondered what it might be like to watch the drongo bastard fall from this height. "What's that you're reading?"

The man looked at the cover of his book, where the title was prominently displayed in large block letters. *War and Peace?*

"Never heard of it," Russell said. "Which part are you on?"

"This is book three—"

"The war, or the peace?"

The man stammered. "It's not—"

"Half of it sounds interesting," Russell said. "I don't recall any such book on the manifest, however."

The color ran from the man's face. "I didn't . . . it is a personal effect, surely . . ."

"Have to say, smuggling is not tolerated."

"That's ridiculous! It's a book, for God's sake. I'm no criminal."

Russell sauntered over to the man. He held his hand out, motioning for the thick tome.

The man tried to hold Russell's gaze but relented in a few seconds. With a sigh he gave up the book. "Think I'll sleep the rest of the way, if you don't mind."

"Suit yourself." Russell returned to his seat, enjoying the weight of the novel. He thought the "war" part could be worth a look. He'd tried to read *The Art of War* once. His predecessor had left it on the desk when he vacated Night-cliff. A parting gift, and a boring one at that.

The climber lurched. Motors whirred down to silence and the lights in the cabin flicked off, replaced by dim emergency bulbs.

Russell almost dropped the heavy tome at the change in motion. His companion sat bolt upright, hands gripping the bench on either side of him.

Seconds later the lights came back, and electric motors hummed back to life. Russell could feel the sensation of motion as the vehicle began to climb again. "That gets the blood pumping," he said.

The other man ignored him and looked around at the ceiling and walls, as if trying to see through them. The plain fear in his expression had a comical quality to it.

Eventually he settled back into his seat and closed his eyes again.

Russell laughed softly to himself. The unexplained malfunctions couldn't have come at a better time, almost as if he'd planned it. Almost. "Opportunity knocks," he muttered, and laughed again.

He floated at the airlock while the other seven cargo pods were unloaded. "Why the hell did they put us last?"

The question went unanswered. He looked to his traveling companion for a response and found the man still sleeping.

With a long hiss, the airlock door rotated open, revealing the interior of a flexible white tube connected to the climber. Plastic windows ran the length of the round corridor, revealing an expansive cargo bay beyond, where busy dockworkers floated by with no regard for up or down. The cargo bay's dark gray walls were lit sporadically with small pools of yellow light. The room matched the octagonal layout of the eight-slot climbers, and from Russell's vantage point he could see cargo containers lined all the way to the wall, waiting to hitch a ride up or down.

Russell floated out past a cleaning crew and passengers

waiting for their trip down to Nightcliff. They made room for him to squeeze past, and he recognized each from the manifest he'd studied the day before. None looked happy about their impending journey, as if traveling to Nightcliff was some terrible chore they were being forced to endure.

Fuckers, he thought.

He drifted along the umbilical tube attached to the passenger car, running his hand along the soft material as he went. He checked his fingertips; no dust. They were meticulous up here. To live amid such cleanliness would either be refreshing or boring beyond belief, he couldn't quite decide which.

The title "Director of Nightcliff," a position he'd fought tooth and nail for just a year earlier, had many perks. And now he could add a visit to Gateway to that list. His bluff with the climber traffic had earned the trip, a foot in the door, exactly as he'd predicted.

The council would have to take him seriously.

At the end of the tube, a woman in a white coat and pants waited for him. She had curly red hair and a splash of freckles on her cheeks. Soft skin and a full figure, too—nothing like the bony women in Darwin.

"Are you the welcoming committee?" Russell asked.

"The nurse, I'm afraid. Decontamination is this way."

She pushed off the wall with practiced ease and disappeared around the corner. Russell tried to swim in the air to gain speed, which only left him upside down and disoriented. He grunted as his body impacted the wall.

The woman giggled, a sound she tried to stifle with her hand. Russell heard it, though, and a felt a rage boiling within.

"It takes practice," she said.

Her voice had a kindness to it that he found calming. A lovely smile as well. "Must be hard to shag," Russell said. "Up here. Flailing about like this."

The nurse's smile vanished. "We'll be in gravity soon."

"If that's what you prefer," Russell said with a grin. He winked at her, but the woman turned away.

"Follow me, please," she said. Terse, now.

She led him along a long, white hall, lined with a series of red rungs on one wall. The farther they went, the more Russell felt a sense of vertigo. He mimicked the woman's movement as she started to use the rungs on the wall to guide herself.

Slowly, gravity began to tug at him. He realized then that they were traveling toward the outer edge of the ring-shaped station. The rungs on the wall became a ladder, and soon he found it easier to climb than drift.

At last they reached the bottom, and Russell felt grounded. Up was finally up, down was down.

The nurse guided him through a door and into a stark white room. "There's a shower through there," she said. "Leave your clothing. I'll have them scrubbed."

"Your clothes might be dirty, too," he said. "Care to join me?"

She hurried from the room without a word.

Worth a try, he thought.

Thirty minutes later, showered and dressed, he sat in an uncomfortable metal chair. "Is all this really necessary? I don't have SUBS."

A new nurse, not nearly as cute as the last, sat next to him. She prepped a needle. "The Elevator protects against that," she said. "It's the rest we try to keep out. Colds, flu . . . all the usual suspects."

"I'm sure it was nothing," Russell said as she took a blood sample, "but my companion on board the climber had a bit of a cough."

The nurse's eyes widened.

Russell shrugged. "Just thirsty, maybe? Still, I thought I'd mention it."

"You were sitting with him?"

Oops. "Do I look like an idiot?"

"My apologies," the nurse replied.

Though not as attractive as the previous nurse, by Darwin standards she still looked pretty good. He'd heard all the stories and jokes, among his guards, about Orbital women. *When you could pick and choose your citizens from the herd at large, why bother with the ugly ones?* The thought tickled him. Even at the brink of extinction, people still behaved like people.

"You're clear to enter the station," she said, then departed.

Russell put his coat back on, placed the newly acquired book under his arm, and strode out of the medical bay with a smile on his face.

He gave a curt salute to the security inspector on duty, who allowed him through the checkpoint without a word. It was the first guard Russell had seen, and it occurred to him then how easy it would be to bring a climber full of soldiers up here and overrun the place. If his demands weren't met, it would be an option.

Alex Warthen waited for him on the other side of the checkpoint.

Russell had met the man a few times before, but always in Nightcliff. They were equals, Alex had assured him. Just in charge of different aspects of the Elevator.

The choke points, Russell thought.

And yet Alex held a seat on the Orbital Council, despite presiding over a fraction of the population and an incalculably smaller area. Meanwhile, Russell remained a simple employee, a dog to do their bidding.

I deliver your air and water, he thought. *I can stop just as easily. So a few Darwinites might starve. There's too damn many of them anyway.*

The man looked sharp, as always. Black hair combed to one side, clean shaven, and a face that gave nothing away.

"Taken up the classics?" Alex asked, as they shook hands.

Russell arched an eyebrow. "Classic what?"

Alex pointed at the book.

"Oh," Russell said, "we'll see. How's it going, mate?"

Alex sighed. A long loud hiss of air. "Not good. The climbers are faltering, and now we've had a few subhumans get loose up here. Everyone is on edge."

"The rumors are true, then."

"Afraid so."

Russell knew there was no way such a creature could have made it all the way up to orbit unnoticed. No, someone had contracted the disease inside the Aura. There was no

other way to explain it. He almost grinned at the turn of
events. More wood on the bonfire. "Sounds like you need a
vacation," Russell said.

"No time, nowhere to go. How about a drink instead?"

Russell motioned for his counterpart to lead on. He expected to be taken to an office. Instead, Alex led him to a
tavern, just a short walk from the station entry.

A sign on the wall by the door said TEN BACKWARD. Alex
entered first and pushed through the crowded room.

Russell glanced across the faces within. A mix of men
and women, wearing mostly blue coveralls, filled the dozen
tables, talking and drinking. If anyone recognized him, they
didn't show it. In fact, they hardly reacted to Alex Warthen's
entry, either. Russell wondered how much respect the man
really commanded.

Alex made his way toward the sparse bar. The patrons
huddled there wore mostly black—security personnel. Their
conversation died when they saw Alex, and room was made.

Alex asked, "What's your poison?"

"I'm in a vodka mood."

The bartender bypassed the closest bottle on the shelf
behind him and reached for something with a printed
label, something from *before*. Russell didn't recognize it,
and grunted. Smuggled up, no doubt. A little theater Alex
probably arranged just to irritate him.

As the drinks were poured, Russell took stock of the busy
room. "Don't these people have anything to do?"

"Work, drink, screw, as the saying goes up here," Alex
said. "It's good to mingle with them now and then."

Russell raised his glass.

"Sláinte," Alex said.

They both drank. The chatter in the room had all but died,
Russell realized. He toyed with the idea of making a speech
to the locals. After another drink, he decided.

"Enough dog and pony," Russell said. "Let's go to your
office and chat."

The dreary room felt less welcoming than a Jacobite prayer
hall. Furnishings consisted of a faux granite desk and two

simple metal chairs. No personal touches adorned the desk or the walls; merely the minimum needed to get the job done.

"Nice view," Russell said. The room had no windows. Russell hadn't seen a window since arriving. The realization made the place seem even smaller.

His counterpart offered him a chair, and Russell sat. The seat was hard as rock, uncomfortable in the extreme.

Alex became serious. He rested his elbows on the chair's armrests and folded his fingers together. "I need to ask you something, between us."

"Fire away."

"Are you tampering with the climbers? Causing these power outages?"

The accusation stunned Russell. A flash of anger gave way to pride. Pride in knowing Alex thought him that mischievous. He imagined himself standing at some cartoon lever, throwing it to "off" with a mad cackle before returning it to "on." Russell threw his head back and laughed. "No," he said. "No, but it's not a bad idea. I might ask you the same question."

"We're as baffled as you are," Alex said.

"That's . . . terrifying, frankly."

Alex gave a slow, thoughtful nod. "Well, thanks for starting the climbers again. The council appreciates it."

"Pleasing the council," Russell said. "I live for it."

A pregnant pause followed. Alex deflated slightly in his chair, his eyes dancing from one side of the table to the other.

Russell cleared his throat. "How's our old friend Platz?"

Alex Warthen smiled. "I was hoping you could tell me."

His tone caught Russell off guard. "What the hell does that mean?"

"I heard about his visit last week."

Russell felt his cheeks grow warm. He despised being embarrassed, perhaps more than anything. "What are you on about?"

Alex grinned.

"Are you fucking with me?"

Alex leaned back, clearly enjoying himself. "Either you're getting sloppy or the old man has friends in *low* places."

Russell winced. He didn't like implication. He didn't like the pun, either. "Well, what the hell was he doing there?"

"According to my source," Alex said, "he was buying something from the venerable Mr. Prumble."

"Buying what?"

"I'm working on that," Alex said.

Russell felt lost in the possibilities. "Perhaps I should look into it. Pay Prumble a visit—"

Alex raised a hand in opposition. "Exercise some subtlety, will you? Let things develop."

The revelation boiled Russell's blood. If it proved to be true, the consequences were unsettling. Strict control over what comes and goes through Nightcliff was one of the few pieces of true power Russell held. It meant little if the most famous man alive could slip through unnoticed.

Russell wanted to break something. Someone. Best to change the subject, he decided. "Any progress," he said, "on my request?"

A sour look crossed Alex's face, if only for an instant. "The council voted it down. 'It's the *Orbital* Council. Mr. Blackfield is on the ground.' Their words, not mine."

Perfect, Russell thought. He forced himself to look disappointed. "The ground. It's not just dirt and rock, you know. We have air and water, too."

Alex spread his hands. "Processed at facilities owned by Platz."

"Shipped through facilities run by *me*."

Alex digested the comment like a bad egg. "The council will have none of that."

Russell spread his hands. "They'd probably order you down there with your more-than-capable forces."

"Which," Alex said, "would clearly be a surprise to you."

"Imagine how that would go. Your soldiers stepping out, two at a time, from those cramped little climbers."

"Interesting," said Alex.

A silence followed. Only the sound of air being pushed

into the room by machinery hidden in the walls could be heard. It served as a nice echo to Russell's argument.

He tapped the thick novel on the table. "*War and Peace.* It's the gray area in between where we live, you and I."

Alex kept his face still. "It seems we're at an impasse."

"Then why bring me here? Going to toss me in the brig?"

"The idea was mentioned. . . ."

"Your idea, or the vaunted council?"

"Same thing," the man said. "I'm a member, after all."

"True," Russell said. "The only member in control of armed guards. In fact, between us we command the only remaining military the world has left."

Alex said nothing. His face betrayed nothing.

Russell continued. "We own the choke points, you and I. I don't see why we have to listen to anyone. Especially the old goat, Neil Platz."

Still no reaction.

Russell took that as a good sign, and went on. "A lot of power in our hands, eh?"

"Interesting."

"Food for thought," Russell said. "From my point of view, looking up, Platz just wants to maintain the status quo. To be top dog, like he has been his whole life."

"And what do you want, Russell?"

To be top dog. Not the best thing to voice, he knew. "I want to see a little ambition brought back to the world. As long as we're all trapped, sucking at the Elevator's teat, we should shift focus to making life enjoyable. For *everyone.*"

Alex Warthen, his face a mask, gave the slightest of nods. And that, Russell thought, was good enough.

The seed, planted.

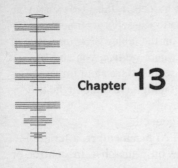

Chapter 13

AT 7 P.M. the interior lights began a programmed drift down to 20 percent brightness and changed hue to a soft silver tone. Moonlight mode. Air circulators adjusted thermal controls to create a subtle chill in the air.

The staff transitioned, too. Research projects and other duties gave way to dinner, then recreation. *Casablanca* played in the cafeteria. Idle processors rendered virtual worlds to be explored in the sensory chamber. The table tennis league held its championship in front of a small, if raucous, crowd.

Three of Anchor's crew remained in the infirmary. A fourth, one of the scientists, fell into a coma and was evacuated to Gateway, which had the best medical equipment.

By midnight, most had retired to their quarters, alone or in pairs. More, in a few cases.

Anchor Station slept.

Tania walked the empty hallways in silence, eschewing shoes for a pair of warm socks. She saw no one as she moved through Black Level. At one point an eruption of muffled laughter broke the quiet—a group enjoying a private game of cards, she imagined. She walked on, one hand resting on her coat, and the data cubes nestled beneath.

Through the connection tube to Gray Level, then White, Tania encountered nobody. Even the observation room that looked out on the Shell was deserted at this hour.

At the bulkhead to Green Level, she used her ID card to

pass through the security doors. A night guard at the desk beyond waved her by with passive interest, a dog-eared paperback open on his lap. Tania thought Anchor Station must be a prized post among the Orbital security ranks.

Support trusses spaced along the walls and ceiling were cast in blue-green hues, reminding her of moonlit trees she'd seen in old films. She followed the slow curve of the hall until reaching a door marked GENERAL COMPUTE LAB. A quick swipe of her ID card unlocked it, and she entered.

The chilled air inside had a bite, her thin coat unable to repel it. She shivered, and moved between the rows of computer terminals. Two researchers were working late, hunched in front of a terminal screen. They talked in hushed voices, so engrossed in their work they hardly registered her entry. Tania reminded herself to act casual. To act as if she belonged here at this hour.

Past rows of terminals, beyond racks of blinking servers, at the very back of the room, she entered a collaborative area with seating for three in front of a grid of massive screens. The Platz Industries logo bounced merrily around in vivid resolution on the display.

She closed the door quietly behind her and sat down in the center seat in front of the console. From her lab coat she removed the four data cubes and a notepad.

After a deep breath, she typed her passphrase into the waiting system. The wall-sized screen cleared, then realigned itself to present Tania's preferred view. Station status, personal messages, and a to-do list filled the left edge. Images from the previous night's telescope activity dominated the remainder.

Tania ignored it all. Instead she inserted the data cubes into waiting slots. Options bloomed on the screen before her. Working quickly, she began the data transfer.

The systems at her disposal proved to be a similar vintage to those used in the observatory, removing her fears about compatibility. The facility must have been outfitted around the same time Anchor was built.

The cubes were dated roughly six years ago. SUBS disease had begun soon after, and across the planet the technical renaissance brought on by the Elevator's arrival all but stopped. Everyone shifted focus to survival, to reaching Darwin before the disease reached them. Tania shivered at the thought. She'd been in orbit at the time, studying, and her parents had insisted she stay in space until "the situation was under control." She never saw either of them again.

Before tears could come, she shook her head and refocused on the task at hand.

The first task for the computers involved cataloging the information in a layout that she could understand. The data set rolled through a linguistics program. She placed markers on the key fields and soon a database began to take shape.

A progress meter traveled across the screen, with anything but haste. Tania began to drift off. She leaned on her elbows, rested her chin on the backs of her hands, and tried to imagine the observatory where the data had been found. Snow-covered peaks, trees from one horizon to the other. A telescope nestled in a valley between the mountains, at the end of a gently winding road.

On the verge of sleep, Tania heard the delicate sound of the door opening. She realized she had concocted no cover story, had no plausible reason to be there. Mind racing, she turned to the door.

Natalie stood there. She looked tired, roused from sleep no doubt.

"What are you doing here?" Tania asked. The words sounded ridiculous even as she said them.

Her assistant waited in the doorway, frozen, taking in the scene. Her impassive face offered no insight into what must be going through her mind. Then she looked once over her shoulder before fully entering the room and easing the door closed. "My computer woke me. We . . . *you* bumped Greg and Marcus off the system. They had an analysis running using a sample from that subhuman, and called me, rather irritated."

Tania realized that the array of screens behind her were full of telemetry data. She stabbed for the key that would blank the imagery, but nothing happened.

Natalie took a tentative step into the room. "What's going on?" She sounded like a child.

"I just," Tania said, then stopped. What could she do? Lying now would be too much of a betrayal. "Nat, I'm sorry."

Natalie came to stand at Tania's side. She focused on the enormous monitor, where a visualization of the database continued to take shape.

"What is this?" Her voice was barely a whisper. "Tania?"

"Listen," Tania said. "I've been given a special project. Something I need to work on alone. I didn't think anyone would notice." She spoke in rapid spurts.

"What kind of project?"

"I can't tell you," Tania said. "You should leave."

Natalie studied the screen, as if she hadn't heard. "That would go a lot faster if you turned off vis and error-checking."

"Nat, please. I must insist . . . wait, it would?"

"Also," she said, "you forgot to flag an index field. It will take forever to search the data later."

Tania glanced at the screen, then back to her assistant.

"Sure you want me to leave?" Natalie asked, a confident smirk on her face.

The warnings from Neil Platz raced through Tania's mind. If what they suspected proved true, everything could change, again. That knowledge carried with it the extraordinary potential to disrupt the already fragile state of humanity. Neil wanted to manage that.

Yet Tania knew she could not do this alone. Natalie had proven her aptitude for information analysis time and again since arriving on Anchor Station a year ago. She'd become Tania's best friend as well. The perfect confidante, Tania decided.

Besides, Nat already stood here, on the brink of uncovering her extracurricular research. *Neil will understand,* Tania told herself. "No," she admitted. "Don't go."

Natalie sat down. "Good, that's settled. A secret project, huh? I love it. I'm in."

Together they realigned the ingestion of data. With Natalie's expertise, the process would take a quarter of the time now.

"You'll have to keep this to yourself," Tania said as they waited.

"*Moi,* gossip?"

Tania shot her a stern look.

"I never pegged you for having a dark side," Natalie said. "I like it. Goes with your eyes."

Tania blushed. Natalie's flirtatious nature was cute, and often riotously funny, but Tania had never been comfortable with such attention.

Tania's mother had been a celebrated beauty in Mumbai; her father, a famous astronaut. Yet both held a deep-seated passion for science, and they met while working for Neil Platz on his first space venture: the purchase of a space station the Europeans wanted to deorbit. Her father had been picked to command the first private space station, a fact that brought him widespread recognition among millions in India.

Tania inherited the better qualities of each, so everyone said, and she often resented her physical beauty. Her mother, rest her soul, had instilled in her the drive to succeed for her mind, not her appearance. A lofty challenge, and one she took seriously.

A chime came from the computer. All the data had been processed.

Natalie edged closer. "What are we looking at?"

"Trajectories of near-Earth objects."

Concern flashed across the young woman's face. "Something going to impact the station?"

"Doubtful," Tania said. "Look at the dates, the origin."

Natalie turned back to the monitor. "All right, fine. Japanese telemetry from 2278. Why?"

"I'm looking for anomalies."

Natalie frowned. "To what end?"

"SUBS started in 2278," Tania said.

"Yeah," Natalie said, brow furrowed. "What does that have to do with . . . oh."

Tania watched as her assistant's eyes lit up.

"They might have spotted it . . . assuming it arrived aboard a Builder ship."

Tania nodded. "Exactly."

A period of silence passed as Natalie thought through the implications. "I don't understand. We know where the disease started. . . . Oh. Holy shit."

"You're quick," Tania said.

"You're trying to find out where it came from."

Tania looked up at the screen full of numbers. "Sort of."

"But," Natalie said, voicing her thoughts as they arrived, "why? I mean, why would that matter? The damn thing probably left the Builders' planet, or whatever, eons ago. Interesting to know, but—"

Tania held up a hand. "Nat, how much time passed between the Elevator's arrival and the outbreak of SUBS?"

The other woman didn't need to think about it. "Twelve years, of course. Well, eleven years, eight months, and ten days, if you want to be super picky."

"Wow. Very good," Tania said. "And, yes, I do want to be super picky."

"Then I'm your gal."

Tania grinned. "Nat, have you ever wondered if they're coming back?"

"Of course," Natalie said. "We all do."

Tania waited.

"Oh," said Natalie. "Oh! If we knew where to look, we could spot it early this time. . . ."

"I knew you'd get it."

Natalie sat motionless for a time, staring at the screen. "I'm amazed it never occurred to me before."

"Can't claim it's an original idea," Tania said. "Neil made a joke about it once, and it got me to thinking."

"So, if SUBS began five . . . sorry, four-point-nine-to-be-picky . . . years ago, we'll get a huge head start this time around. Seven years!"

Tania couldn't help but smile. "You just fell into the same trap I did. Assuming, of course, there's another ship coming, who's to say it would follow the same schedule? It could be seven years, or seven months, or millennia."

As she spoke, Natalie turned slowly to face her. "But you're down here, in the middle of the night, working on it."

"Neil's salivating at the possibility of advance warning. You know how he likes to plan, and how he gets when a project catches his eye."

They worked at it through the night.

Millions of objects were logged, objects as small as a penny, as often as every ten seconds. It proved painstaking at first, cross-referencing each entry with existing catalogs of celestial objects.

At four in the morning, Natalie had the brilliant idea to ask the computer to show them information that did not match the pattern of the rest. Tania had discarded this to eliminate things that might confuse the program. Things like the report title, information on the telescope's settings, and the names of supervising personnel seemed like a waste of time.

In the nonmatching data set, Natalie came across a typed note, immediately below a log entry that blended with all the others. An entry they never would have noticed otherwise.

"Hey, look at his," she said.

The note was in English.

Tania read it aloud. " 'Bizarre! Vector out of band. Validate.' "

They looked at each other. Natalie said, "Let me see if the object shows up anywhere else."

The computer searched the log in seconds and produced one more entry, plus another comment:

> SUGOI! ABNORMAL VECTOR VALIDATED.
> CONFIRM WITH A. R. SHU (KECK).

The room became quiet, save for the constant background hum of the station's air processors. Tania felt her scalp begin to tingle.

"I'd say we have a lead," she said.

"You know who this Shu person is?"

Tania shook her head. "Nope. But a name is a good start."

* * *

Tania returned to her cabin only an hour before the morning cycle would begin. She closed and locked the door, then went straight to her terminal.

After a long series of chimes, Neil answered her call.

"Have you got something?" he asked immediately.

"The logs are genuine. For the most part the information is mundane, trivial. Your basic satellite tracking logs."

"I haven't had my tea yet, dear. Cut to it."

"I found an interesting anomaly." Tania almost said "we." She took a long breath and then exhaled.

"Which is what?" Neil asked.

"It may be nothing," Tania said. "Something marked as an 'unknown entity,' standard classification when something new pops up. In this case, though, there is a handwritten note to go with it: 'Abnormal vector,' and instructions to confirm with an A. R. Shu, at the Keck telescope. It's dated August 2277."

"What does abnormal vector mean?"

"A trajectory that doesn't match the typical objects that cross our path," she said. "Satellites in orbit follow certain paths. Comets and so forth come from fairly predictable angles."

Five seconds passed. "A year before the SUBS began," Neil said, to himself mostly. "Did you get a position? Somewhere to look?"

"It's only listed twice," she said, "and these logs don't contain that kind of detail. Just vector analysis, the positions must have been stored elsewhere. What we need are the finer details."

"A. R. Shu."

"Seems like our best chance," Tania said.

"Anything in the old data vaults about this person?"

"A bit of luck there," she said. "Nothing on this subject specifically. Most of the data we've collected from NASA is rocket schematics and procedure manuals. However, we also have their employment records, and I found an Andrew Ryoko Shu."

"If you tell me we need an expedition to America . . ."

"The mainland, no," Tania said. "Our Mr. Shu was stationed at the University of Hawaii, in Hilo. They had a contract to store all the data for Keck."

She could hear Neil preparing tea in the background, and waited. "Okay," he said at last, "I'll get my team on it. Just tell me which cubes you need, and they'll get it."

"It's not that simple. According to the archives, they were still using antiquated storage techniques, crude even by the standards of their time. The equipment is likely to be massive. Heavy."

Neil grunted. "I see."

They both went quiet for a while.

"I'm hoping you'll say something, here," Neil said.

Tania snorted. "The best option is to try to get their data center online, search for the data we need, and make a copy there."

Now Neil laughed. "Do you have any idea how unlikely it is that any of that equipment still works?"

"It's an underground data vault. According to the archive, a microthorium reactor was installed in 2112 for backup power. It should still be purring away. With a few hours of work, and the right equipment, it should be possible."

"We need to supply them with a portable Ferrine array, too? Jesus."

Tania hesitated. Only a few Ferrine arrays still existed. They'd been designed in orbit, after the disease, for the purpose of interfacing with as many different systems as possible. The complex, fragile devices had been invaluable in syphoning old data before such ventures became too risky.

"Yes." She dropped her voice. "And someone to operate it."

"You're kidding me."

"It's a complex task," Tania said. "These scavengers you hire would not be capable of it."

"Who, then?"

Tania bit down on her lower lip. "We recruit a data tech, someone from Green Level—"

"No way," Neil said, "not going to happen."

"Well, it's me then. Or Natalie."

"I thought we'd talked about her already. Keep her out of it."

"Yes," Tania said, "about that. She caught me red-handed. I had to tell her."

"Oh, Tania . . ."

She sighed. "She was an enormous help. We can trust her. And, for what it's worth, it feels good to have a friend I can confide in up here."

Tania could hear Neil's breathing on the other end of the line. Short and sharp. She waited, letting it return to normal.

"I don't want to send you down there, Tania," Neil said. "It's far too risky."

"I can't ask her to go. I think it has to be me. And besides, these days it's risky just leaving my room."

Neil didn't respond. She waited, and waited more.

"Neil?"

"I'm thinking."

Tania said, "You don't have to decide now."

"No, no. I can't think of any other way to do this, and there's no time to waste," he said. "Get on the next transport down. I'll start making the arrangements."

She balled her fists to stop them from shaking. A trip to Earth. A trip beyond Aura's Edge. *I must be crazy,* Tania thought. Yet no matter how hard she tried to ignore it, the allure of a genuine discovery called. "On my way," she said.

"And Tania," Neil added, "if anyone asks, you're just coming to a meeting on Platz Station. I've briefed Zane; he'll confirm that. You'll need to stop here anyway."

"Why?"

"You're going to need a disguise."

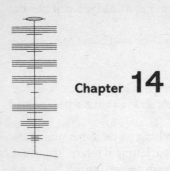

Chapter 14

"NICE AND EASY, Angus." Skyler peered out the dirty cockpit window and watched the twenty-meter-tall barricade of Nightcliff's northern edge pass beneath them. A few guards patrolled the top of the structure, between missile batteries placed at regular intervals.

Angus placed a hand over his headset microphone. "Between you and the control tower, I get the idea."

"Sorry, sorry," Skyler said. "I'm a bit nervous about this mission."

Angus barked a laugh. "You don't say."

"Cleared for staging pad four heading zero niner zero," a voice said over the cockpit radio.

"Copy, tower," Angus said, "landing pad four at zero niner zero."

He slowed the craft even more and turned slightly toward a grid of landing pads just beyond the wall. Vertical thrusters howled under the strain.

"Angus," Skyler said.

"I'm a bit busy."

"Head for landing pad four."

Angus shook his head and chuckled. "Such a wanker."

"This insubordination is intolerable."

"Discipline is in order, I think," said Samantha, listening from the main cabin's intercom.

"Agreed," said Skyler. "Angus, I'm adding five demerits to your record."

"Bullshit," Angus said. "You keep records?"

"Of course. Highly detailed."

Angus began to descend toward the landing pad. "How many demerits am I up to?"

"Let's see," Skyler said. "Five."

"What about me?" asked Samantha.

Skyler checked over each shoulder to make sure nothing was in Angus's blind spots. "Two thousand, four hundred twenty."

The craft gently settled onto the asphalt pad. Hydraulic landing skids creaked as they took on the weight.

"Tower, this is the *Melville*. We're secure on pad four," said Angus.

"Copy, *Melville*," came the voice. "Off engines and prepare for crane attach."

Angus repeated the order and cut power to all four of the ducted-fan engines.

Behind their ship, an old construction crane mounted on huge treads began to approach them. Skyler could just see the mechanical beast over his shoulder.

He removed his helmet as the engines wound down. "Sam?"

"Yes, sir!"

"Be serious now. Prep the hook, and tell Jake to be ready at the rear door."

"Expecting a search *before* the mission?"

"No. We're taking on a passenger."

Angus glanced back, surprised. "What?"

"The hell you say?" Sam asked.

"Not the time, guys," Skyler said. Platz, by way of Prumble, had been very clear that the mission details should be kept secret as long as possible. "Sam, the hook, please?"

"This is a really stupid fucking move, Skyler," she said. "No taxi jobs, that's always been the rule. The risk—"

"Is worth the reward," Skyler barked. "This is not up for discussion."

He took her lack of response as tacit acknowledgment and turned his focus to the water hauler on the adjacent landing pad. Through a misting rain Skyler saw a work crew wearing blue overalls approaching the massive craft. One of them, in the center of the group, moved differently than the rest. *No swagger,* Skyler realized. *That must be her.*

"Jake," Skyler said into his headset.

There was some rustling on the other end. "Go ahead."

"Be ready on the hatch. Open it on my mark."

"Understood," Jake said.

The crew approached pad three, where the massive water hauler rested. The ungainly blue aircraft somewhat resembled a fish skeleton—a huge empty cavity behind the cockpit, surrounded by beams with special couplings that allowed it to pick up and carry a water container the size of a city bus. Two of the workers wrangled a thick hose toward a receptacle on the edge of the pad. They both got on hands and knees to inspect the connection, poring over every last inch of it.

Skyler had seen better acting in school plays.

A third member of the crew pretended to supervise the work, his attention focused not on the crew but the nearby buildings. The fourth Skyler kept a close watch on.

"Here's the crane," Angus said.

Skyler spun in his seat, looking to the other side of his ship. A large construction crane pushed through the mist, red warning lights flashing. It loomed over them, obstructing whatever view the control tower had of their ship.

"Hook is prepped," Samantha said in his ear.

Skyler said, "Good. Help Jake please."

"With what?"

"Get our guest on board," Skyler said, "and the hatch closed, quick as you can." He tried to keep his voice even. Inside his heart hammered.

He could hear Samantha's exhale through the headset. "And if we get inspected again, glorious leader?"

He hadn't considered that. "We'll say . . . we found an immune. Get ready."

"We're ready," said Jake. All business, as usual.

Skyler turned back to the crew working on pad three. The woman moved to the back of the crew's small maintenance cart and removed an oversized briefcase. She turned then and walked swiftly to the *Melville. Too quickly,* Skyler thought, *but it would have to do.*

"Mark," Skyler said.

He could feel the reverberation as Jake and Samantha opened the hatch. Over the intercom, he heard muffled voices.

Another vibration rolled through the ship as the cargo door closed and sealed.

Their guest had arrived.

It took almost ten minutes for the crane to lift the *Melville* off the ground and carry it to the climber loading facility at the center of Nightcliff.

"Angus, can you finish this?" Skyler asked.

"No problem."

Skyler unlatched his harness and climbed from his seat. Crouching, he moved to the back of the cramped cockpit and headed into the cargo area.

Jake and Samantha stood in awkward silence next to the most beautiful woman Skyler had ever seen.

She had jet-black hair, tied back, and smooth dark skin. Indian, or Sri Lankan, he guessed. Her eyes were laced with amber and gleamed with intelligence.

Jake held his flight helmet in his hands, passing it rapidly from one to the other. Samantha had her hands clasped behind her back, her feet crossed. They both stared at the woman openly.

She clutched a silver briefcase like a firstborn child and brightened to see another person enter the cargo bay.

"Are you the captain?" Her voice had a depth to it, not like a man's, but deep enough to imply maturity.

He tipped his cap to her. "I often wonder that myself."

She extended a hand. "Tania Sharma. Research director, Anchor Station."

"Where's that?" Samantha asked.

"About forty klicks above our heads," Jake said.

"Forty *thousand* klicks, actually," Tania said.

Jake just nodded, transfixed.

"Skyler Luiken, at your service. Welcome to the *Melville.*"

He took Tania's hand and shook it. "This is my sniper, Jake, and my ops specialist, Samantha."

Sam stood a head taller than the woman. Despite herself, she smiled slightly. It took her only a fraction of a second to hide it again.

"You're an Orbital," Jake said.

Tania turned to him. "Yes," she said with patience. "Anchor Station is in orbit."

The three of them stared at her. She looked from one to the other, becoming more self-conscious by the second.

"Is something wrong?" Tania asked.

Skyler snapped out of his trance. "It's not often we have a guest, is all."

The lovely woman frowned, but nodded all the same.

"What's in the case?" asked Sam.

Before she could reply, Angus spoke over the intercom. "Everyone prep for lift configuration. One minute."

At the prompt, Samantha and Jake took seats on the starboard side of the cargo bay. Skyler took a seat as well and began to strap himself in, but then realized their guest was still standing in the middle of the compartment. He stood and guided her to the seat he'd been preparing to use, and then folded out another seat facing hers.

Tania stared at the harness, confused.

"Watch me," Skyler said. He used slow motions to attach the first two belts across his waist.

"Twenty seconds," Angus said on the speaker.

Tania started to rush things. The buckles clanged together.

"Relax, plenty of time," Skyler said.

She paused long enough for a deep breath, then latched the first belts together.

"Shoulders," Skyler said, reaching over each shoulder and pulling two additional belts across his chest. He connected them at a special latch above the waist belts.

The woman mimicked his movements. As the belts crossed her, Skyler tried not to stare.

"Five seconds," Angus said.

"Last but not least," Skyler said, and reached above himself to pull a thick metal bar down.

Tania stretched for the bar above her own seat. Her fingertips were short by a few centimeters. She extended farther and the metal briefcase in her lap started to slide away.

The *Melville* began to tilt. Outside, the tow crane had started to lift the nose of the ship. Soon the craft would be pointing nose-up.

"Shit," Skyler said. He pushed his own restraint bar up and unbuckled himself as quickly as possible.

By reflex, he shot a hand out to stop himself from falling. He grabbed Tania's seat just above her shoulder. They were just a few centimeters apart now. She closed her eyes. "What is going on?" she whispered.

Skyler spoke in a low voice as he strained against gravity. "We're being attached to a climber," he said, finally snatching the restraint bar above her seat. He pulled it down and locked it in place.

Tania opened her eyes enough to see the bar and grab hold of it.

"We have to attach vertically or we won't clear the top of the guard tower," Skyler continued. He grunted as he pushed himself back into his own seat. Getting back into his own harness required all his strength, as the ship was at a ninety-degree angle now. In his seat, he looked straight down at her, and she stared straight up at him.

A sickening moment followed, when the crane stopped and the entire ship swayed freely.

Skyler kept a close eye on Tania. "Are you going to be okay?"

She closed her eyes and nodded rapidly. Her knuckles were white on the restraint bar. "Why a cargo climber?" she managed.

"It gets us to a hundred kilometers. The Van Allen Belt. Edge of space."

She let out a nervous laugh. "I'm an astronomer."

"Oh. Of course." Skyler grinned. "Well, it's the only way we can make a round-trip to distant targets. Drop from one hundred klicks, glide above the atmosphere most of the way, save the caps for the way back."

She looked confused. "Why not go higher? Drop from Gateway—"

From across the cabin, Samantha cut in. She played up a thick Australian accent. "Mudders like us aren't allowed up there."

Tania looked at her, then back at Skyler. "Sorry, I wasn't thinking. . . ."

Skyler shook his head slightly, hoping she would let it go.

A loud clang from outside rumbled through the cramped cabin, followed by a low ratcheting sound, as the ship was finally attached to the climber. Angus's cheerful voice came over the intercom. "Cleared the tower. Get cozy everyone; ten hours until drop."

Skyler winced, realizing he sat facing backward. Which now meant downward. The belts of the harness, and the metal restraint, were all that kept him from falling. He already felt the uncomfortable bite of the nylon belts through his jacket.

Ten hours, he thought, and nowhere to look but right at her. He closed his eyes to keep from staring.

The captain's arms extended almost to Tania's neck, his hands outstretched as if reaching to strangle her.

He drifted off during the long tow to the edge of space. The others had, too.

There had been some small talk, at the beginning. The crew seemed anxious to talk about anything but the task at hand. This frustrated Tania no end, but she recognized it as a calming technique. They were risking their lives for her mission, after all.

Well, that and money, she thought. The risk remained.

She'd kept quiet, content to listen, waiting for the right moment to turn their discussion to the task at hand. There would be plenty of time.

But then they'd all fallen asleep. For the last six hours, she'd had nothing to do but stare at their captain.

He almost looked dead, the way his arms floated free, his head lolled side to side. Like he'd drowned.

The situation was worse before, when gravity tugged at him with its full fury. At one point she'd pressed, with all possible strength, into the left side of her chair to avoid a stream of drool that spanned the entire gap between his mouth and her headrest.

She couldn't quite pinpoint the moment when Earth's eternal tug had begun to fade, but she'd watched with fascination as his motions became lighter. The speed at which his face changed from looking tortured, to serene as a baby, was remarkable.

He had a scar on his forehead. An old one, faded now. His brown hair showed early signs of gray, just behind his temples. Thin lips, cracked from exposure. Bags under his eyes implied a poor sleep schedule. Tania realized she had absolutely no idea what life was like for him.

"Or anyone in Darwin," she whispered to herself.

Scraps of faded paper and old photographs filled the wall behind him, taped there in haphazard fashion. Souvenirs from past missions, she assumed. A restaurant menu, a string of bottle caps. Someone's Australian passport. A wedding invitation. Tania found herself smiling at the display. These were the true relics of old Earth, the things no one else thought to collect, or ask for.

One photograph caught her eye. The subject looked familiar, and she squinted to be sure. *It can't be,* she thought.

Working as quietly as she could, Tania released her harness. The others remained asleep as she pushed out of her chair and floated to the wall, to the photograph.

In the picture, four men stood in front of a telescope.

"Papa," she whispered.

Her father stood there, smiling from beneath that horrible mustache he wore, something Tania at eight years old had teased him about. He looked sad, she thought. A ghost trapped in a time long gone.

The odds that this crew would have a picture of her father were astronomical. Of all the people—

And then she saw it. Neil Platz, standing next to him, his

arm thrown around her father's shoulder. Shorter hair, blond, not gray. A younger Neil.

Tania's heart pounded. She held her breath and removed the picture from the wall. With delicate care she turned it over.

A printed note graced the back. *Toyama, Japan, 2264.* The telescope's grand opening, thanks to a grant from Platz Industries. Two years before the Elevator arrived.

"Neil founded the place . . . ," she whispered. He'd said nothing of it when Tania told him where the data she needed was stored. Yet here he was, cutting the ribbon, funding the facility. *With my father.*

She clutched the picture to her chest. Confusion swarmed in her mind. Perhaps Neil had forgotten about it. His company funded many projects, in a time long forgotten by most.

No, a voice inside her said. It felt too convenient. She thought back to how she'd identified the telescope as a source for the information. Neil had listened to her theory with rapt attention, a theory she'd come to after several offhand comments he had made over the years. They'd stayed up late into the night, brainstorming, searching the archives. Had he guided all of it? Could he have led her to her conclusions?

She shut her eyes. It seemed impossible that he would do that. It made no sense, and besides, he wanted the data as much as she did. More, perhaps. She saw no point in speculating about it now. After the mission, she would ask him.

The intercom next to Skyler's head crackled to life. "Captain, you awake?"

Skyler did not stir at the voice, nor did the others.

Tania forced herself back to the moment. She floated back to her seat and buckled in.

"Captain," the pilot said through the intercom, louder.

The captain woke violently. He thrashed once against his restraint, and shouted, "Falling!" before recognizing his surroundings.

Tania realized she still had the photograph in her hands. She slipped it into a pocket.

Skyler's eyes settled on her, his expression shifting to embarrassed. "Did I snore?"

"No," she said, and attempted a smile.

"Good."

"There was some drool."

Skyler cringed and forced his eyes closed. "I'm so sorry."

"That's okay."

He opened one eye. "You must get that a lot."

"Apologies?"

"Drool."

She laughed, despite herself. Then she looked at the others, who were still sleeping. "I have to say, everyone stared when they first saw me."

"They're not used to someone like you," Skyler said.

"An 'Orbital'?"

He shook his head. "More to the point, a beauty."

She blushed.

"Captain?" Angus said, through the speaker.

Skyler tapped the button. "We getting close?"

"Thirty minutes," Angus said.

"Understood." Skyler clicked the microphone off and lowered his voice. "It's a compliment, if you like, but I'm just speaking the truth. Someone with your . . . qualities, is simply not seen in Darwin."

"Why not?"

He broke away from her gaze and began to remove his harness. "It's not a kind place. Enough about that. You're a scientist, so tell me, have you people figured out what's going on with the Aura?"

"We've got a team working on it," she said. "I'm afraid I don't know much else."

"I hope they work fast. Nightcliff thought we caused it. Did you know that?"

"Why?" she asked.

Skyler shrugged. "The first power blip happened at the same moment we were hitting the Aura, coming back in. Bad timing."

Tania studied his face. If what he said was true, she doubted it could have been a coincidence. Perhaps they were just the straw that broke the camel's back, and the Aura really had reached the end of its operational tolerances.

The captain offered her a comforting grin. "Let's get you suited up."

She took the prompt and unbuckled herself from the seat. He showed her how to use a strap on the wall next to her to secure the briefcase temporarily.

Satisfied it wouldn't float away, Tania followed Skyler to the back of the craft. He stopped next to a large metal locker and tugged it open. Inside a bright yellow environment suit waited.

"Your evening gown, miss."

The suit looked ragged, like it had been used for many years. "I hope it fits." *And works.*

"A little baggy, perhaps. As long as the seal is good you'll be all right."

The severity of what she would soon do crystallized in her mind. She pinched the yellow material between her fingers, reassured by the thickness of it. "And if the seal breaks?"

"If it breaks," Skyler said, "we race back to Darwin, hopefully before—"

Tania put a hand on his arm to silence him. She knew the consequences of exposure and doubted they could make it back to the Aura's Edge fast enough to stall the infection. The Aura did not cure the disease, or even kill it. It only put the virus into stasis. Dormant cells would stay that way even after they left the Aura, until they came in contact with a live copy that switched the sleeping cells back on. Because of that, air packaged inside the Aura would be safe to breathe, provided it never mixed with the tainted air outside.

To be exposed for hours would leave most people dead, and the rest devolved into a primal form of human, often with one emotion amplified at the expense of all others. Fear, desire, hatred, rage—one would consume the mind. The thought gave rise to a knot in her stomach.

Skyler removed the outfit from the locker and handed it to her. She took it and, with one arm hooked through a handhold on the wall, pulled it up over her legs. All the while she watched Skyler inspect the seal along the helmet, gloves, and boots she would put on next.

"How did you find out you're immune?" she asked him.

He answered while studying the gear. "I was twenty, a copilot in the Luchtmacht . . . um, Dutch Air Force. When SUBS began spreading up through Africa, we were flying doctors and medical supplies to Alexandria. Then Naples. Madrid. Kept retreating, every day. On the way back from one mission, about a week after it all started, my pilot . . . just lost it. Everything scared the hell out of him. Everything. His own damn shoes were the most terrifying thing he'd ever seen. I had to subdue him. I didn't know what it meant, not then."

Tania let out a long breath, waiting.

"By the time I landed back home, everything was in chaos. It seemed like everyone had been possessed, only no two acted quite the same way. 'Everyone has their own demon,' I remember thinking." He lifted the bulky helmet and placed it over her head, twisting it into place on the ring mount. "I ran, stole a truck. Drove into Amsterdam to try to find my family. It didn't take long to realize the effect had hit everyone but me, near as I could tell. I really thought I was unique. The last sane man."

"Did you find them? Your family?" she asked, while trying to picture herself racing through the streets of Mumbai, only to find her mom dead, or worse. She almost didn't want to hear his answer.

Skyler shook his head, and for a few minutes he said nothing as he finished connecting her suit to an air pack. Then he moved on to the gloves. While slipping the first over her left hand, he said, "Never got close. The whole city had gone insane. An absolute nightmare. I took a gun from a dead policeman and managed to sneak and fight my way back to the open road. That's when I met another immune, a guy named Skadz. He told me the feeds were abuzz with a rumor that Darwin was somehow unaffected, so we stole a transport plane from the base and flew there, more or less."

The man became quiet. Tania sensed he could have included enough detail to scare her away from the journey they were on. Yet something in the calm, methodical way he went about suiting her up instilled confidence in her safety.

After the gloves and boots, Skyler pressurized her suit. A hiss of air was the only evidence that something changed.

"Breathe normally," he said.

"Sorry." She hadn't even noticed her rapid breathing, and willed herself to calm down.

The pilot's voice came over the intercom. "Five minutes, guys."

Jake and Samantha stirred in unison. Instinct kicked in as both of them immediately checked their harnesses.

"Suit checks out," Skyler said. He took her arm and guided her across the cabin. "You've got about eighteen hours of Aura-scrubbed air compressed in that pack, more than enough for the time we'll be in the Clear."

With his help, she drifted back into her seat. The bulk of the hazard suit made movement awkward for her, but at least the gloves were formfitting. She managed to reattach the safety belts on her own.

"Might want to hold on to that bar," Skyler said.

She took his advice, gripping it firmly with both hands. "Thank you."

He winked at her and smiled.

Tania decided she liked him.

It seemed like an eternity passed before Angus's voice came back on the intercom. "Ten seconds. Grab on to something."

Tania could see Skyler mouth the countdown. He pushed hard against his restraint bar, preparing to fight against the force of acceleration she realized was imminent. At "one," his entire face seemed to clench tight.

There was a loud, muffled thump, as the ship was released, followed by a backward somersault of the entire vessel. Tania felt at ease in zero-g conditions, but not sudden acceleration upside down. She closed her eyes.

A rumbling sound started soft, then grew louder. Somewhere behind her, Tania heard something break loose and tumble across the floor. She didn't dare look.

She barely heard the pilot over all the commotion. "Engine's at full."

The sound became deafening.

"You never told us what's in the case," Samantha said, after ten minutes of intense acceleration ended. The ship now glided just above the atmosphere, in serene silence.

"Right, sorry," Tania said, her own voice sounding strange to her inside the helmet of her suit. "Perhaps we should go over the plan?"

"Two hours to kill," said Skyler, "good a time as any." He tapped the intercom. "Angus, come back here, please."

"How much do you know?" she asked.

"Our fence had few details," Skyler said. "Take an Orbital out to some telescope in Hawaii and back, that's about all we know."

"Beats Darwin," Jake said.

Samantha grunted. "Amen."

Tania struggled briefly against her safety harness, to get enough room to remove an envelope from her bag. She handed it to Skyler. "Hawaii is correct, but it's not a telescope. Our goal is inside the University of Hawaii at Hilo."

"A college?" Skyler asked. A pang of worry flittered through his mind. Telescopes were isolated, and at high altitudes. A hostile environment for subhumans. A university could be considerably more dangerous.

"There's a data vault there," Tania said. "Part of a joint venture with NASA, decades ago."

"More data cubes?" Jake asked.

Tania patted the top of the sleek case, made of some kind of brushed metal that Skyler did not recognize. "The facility is much older, before they had such technology. We'll be capturing the data on site, with this."

"What is that?" Samantha asked.

"A Ferrine multi-interface cube array . . ." She noted all their blank stares. "You plug it into old computers and it pulls out the data."

"Is it fragile?" Skyler asked. "From the way you've been cradling it, I'm guessing so."

"Just because we have so few left now."

Samantha said, "How long does this, whatever the fuck, take?"

Tania shrugged. "Depends on how many records are there, and how well organized it is."

"You got photos of the site?" Jake asked.

Skyler pulled two satellite pictures from the envelope and handed them across the aisle.

"I'll check those out when you're done, Jake," said Angus.

Jake flashed a thumbs-up.

Skyler unfolded a larger piece of paper. "Blueprints, even. Excellent."

"Gimme," said Samantha.

He ignored her and studied it.

Tania pointed out the data vault for him. "The data vault is in a basement, here, below these four structures. This building on the right has a landing pad on the roof," she showed him. "I suggest we land there."

The captain sucked in his lower lip as he surveyed the layout. "We could dust off from that, I think. Tania, will this gadget of yours work if there's no power?"

"There's a backup generator," she said, pointing at it on the blueprint. "Thorium, never turns off. We'll switch to it manually if need be."

Samantha cleared her throat. "May I please see the blueprint, oh glorious captain?"

"Study the layout, everyone," Skyler said, and handed it to her. "Ninety minutes until jump. Angus?"

"Yo!"

"Slight course correction, I think."

"On it."

The others pored over the images and blueprints, working out their strategy.

Tania stared at Skyler. "Did you say jump?"

From a storage locker bolted to the floor of the craft, Skyler produced a large backpack with a complicated set of straps.

"This," he said, "is a tandem parachute."

Tania, standing a meter away, made no move to come closer.

"It won't bite."

She looked at Skyler and cocked an eyebrow. A few seconds passed. Skyler imagined her wrestling with an inner voice, telling her to forget this foolishness. But she crossed the cargo bay to stand in front of him. "How does it work?"

He held it between the two of them. "I'll wear it," he said, "and you, well, you'll wear me."

Across the cabin, Samantha snorted back a laugh.

"Or you can jump with Sam," Skyler said, "if that's more comfortable."

"No way," Samantha said. "Sorry, princess, but I jump alone."

Tania kept her attention on the parachute. "It's fine. Just tell me what to do."

He nodded. "Best thing is just to stay relaxed, and when we land, lift your knees as high as you can so that I can get my footing."

"Sounds simple enough."

Skyler removed a second harness from the locker. "I need you to put this on. I'll help, don't worry. Then mine connects to yours, and I'll control the chute."

Tania hesitated. "What happens if you have a heart attack, or pass out, or something?"

"Emergency rip cord," he said, pointing to a red and white pull rope. "I'll show you once we're suited up."

Across the cargo bay, Jake and Sam prepared their weapons. Skyler strapped on his usual complement of submachine gun and high-powered pistol.

"You people don't take any chances," said Tania.

"Sweetie," said Samantha, "this whole business is one big chance."

Skyler tapped his sidearm, looking at Tania. "Ever used a pistol?"

"I've never held a weapon of any kind," she replied in a matter-of-fact tone.

"Okay," he said, "now is not the time to learn. Just keep close to one of us."

"Don't worry."

He looked at the briefcase. "Want one of us to carry that thing down?"

"I'd rather do it myself," she said.

He studied her harness. "Well, let's get it tied to you somehow then."

To Skyler's surprise, the metallic briefcase weighed almost nothing. After a few awkward moments of closeness, and one less-than-gentlemanly brush of his forearm, he rigged it to her chest strap in a way that she could wrap her arms around.

Angus's voice filled the cargo bay. "Two minutes."

Skyler punched the intercom. "Fly over at three thousand meters, then give me slow circles until Jake is in position."

"Copy," Angus said.

They all stood in silence as Jake finished securing his rifle to his harness. End to end, it stood nearly as tall as he did.

"Thirty seconds," said Angus.

Skyler opened the rear cargo door. The sound of rushing wind filled the cabin.

"Broad daylight," Samantha said. "Keep your wits and hide your tits, Jake."

He offered her a mock salute.

"Mark," said Angus.

Jake walked backward off the loading ramp and performed a somersault as he fell away from them, into the white clouds below.

Skyler shook his head and grinned. He glanced at Tania and found her to be frozen in place.

"Don't worry," Skyler said, "I'm no showman."

Her eyes were locked on the sight out the back of the craft, the blanket of white that stretched out in all directions. "Clouds," she said.

"Okay, let's get you hooked up," Skyler said.

She broke her gaze away and moved to stand right in front of him. Skyler connected the tandem harness together and triple-checked the buckles.

"Target in sight," Jake said in Skyler's ear, shouting over

the hiss of rushing wind. "There's a building with a tower. Heading for that."

"How's it look?"

"Good news. There's a light on," Jake said.

Skyler tapped his earpiece. "What, inside? Someone home?"

"No," said Jake, "a beacon of some sort. A radio tower."

"They've got power," Skyler said to Tania. "He's heading for the tall building on the north side. We'll drop on the west building, across from the landing pad."

"Why not on the pad? You could inspect it."

Skyler shook his head. "Don't want to draw any subs to it until we're ready to go."

A quiet, tense thirty seconds passed. Then Jake's voice: "Touchdown."

The transmission stopped, followed by static.

"Are we clear to jump?" Skyler asked. "Jake?"

The static continued, then Jake's muffled voice came through. "Clear" and "collapsed" were the only words Skyler could comprehend.

"Roger," he said in his microphone. "Sounds like he hit a bad spot on the roof, but we're clear. Get ready."

The world below began to tilt and turn as Angus brought the craft around again.

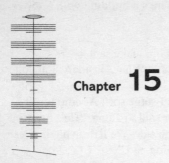

Chapter 15

TANIA'S SCREAM LASTED four seconds.

From terror to bliss, in four seconds flat. She'd never experienced anything like it.

On the word from Angus, Skyler had literally lifted her as he ran down the cargo ramp. She saw Samantha, already impossibly far below them, before they left the aircraft themselves. Tania had closed her eyes and let her fear out.

The wind howled through speakers in her helmet and lashed at her protective suit. Relentless, violent, and ultimately exhilarating.

As soon as they cleared the aircraft, Skyler pulled a cord and deployed the drogue chute. Just before the jump he'd explained that it would slow them to the speed one jumper would normally achieve.

Still above the clouds, Tania took in the horizon. Cottonball clouds covered almost everything, but far to the west the wall of white ended. Beyond lay the dark blue Pacific Ocean, a stark border against the sky. Sunlight danced on the water, and Tania basked in it.

"You okay?!" Skyler shouted.

She barely heard him over the wind and the buffer of her suit. She couldn't help but smile. "Never better!" she yelled back.

"Don't close your eyes, as much as you want to!" he shouted. "This is the best part!"

For a second, she thought he meant their current situation.

Then she looked down just in time to see the thick floor of clouds racing toward them. It took every ounce of courage she had to keep her eyes open. The solid white floor approached faster and faster still.

They hit the puffy whiteness at incredible speed. She felt nothing, as if a sphere of glass were around them, pushing the moisture away. She realized they must be creating a bow shock of air, and laughed aloud.

When they passed through the cloud layer, vertigo set in.

For the first time in her adult life, Tania saw the *real* Earth, beyond Darwin's safe Aura, from a distance not considered outer space.

The big island of Hawaii stretched out below them. She could just make out the telescope complex at the top of Mauna Kea, off to their left. The famous Keck Observatory, which had collected the data she now hoped to recover.

The city of Hilo loomed directly under her. Abandoned skyscrapers lined the coast. Vacation homes stretched from the shore off into the foothills, empty backyard pools just visible in the overgrown vegetation.

"Hold tight!" Skyler shouted. He angled toward the university complex. A sprawling collection of tan buildings choked by wild vines.

Below, she could see Samantha's black parachute unfurl, a small black square against the vast green landscape. Tania placed her arms protectively around the briefcase strapped to her chest and gripped it with all her strength.

Skyler pulled the rip cord.

Before she could think to brace herself the harness around her upper body constricted viciously around her.

Seconds later, the straps loosened and the pain eased.

From the violence of the chute opening, to perhaps the most peaceful moment of her life, in an instant.

The wind became a gentle caress on her environment suit. The campus below drifted closer with each second. Square buildings once white or beige were now covered in the growth of wild vines. The scope and variety of vegetation shocked her, so different from the simple, manicured rows aboard the farm platforms.

"How do you feel?" Skyler asked.

"Overwhelmed," she said, aware how childlike her voice sounded.

She took in the vast Pacific and felt somehow smaller than she ever had looking at Earth from Anchor Station. The blue water stretched to the edge of the world.

"Is Sam headed for the right place?" Skyler asked.

Tania spotted her parachute below them. Her path would take her to the building on the west side of the courtyard. "Yes," she said.

Skyler aimed for the same place. "Remember, legs up, just before we hit ground."

Tania looked north, to the tall building where the sniper had landed. She couldn't see him, but a portion of the roof had clearly collapsed. He might be hurt—a sprained ankle or broken leg. She wondered if any of the crew had medical training. It hadn't occurred to her to ask before.

A few hundred meters below, Samantha landed in the middle of a rooftop dotted by air-conditioning vents and utility boxes. Tania could see her angle just before touching down, moving her legs to hit the ground at a run.

Not a run, a full sprint.

A sharp crack sounded from the tall building, the sniper's direction.

Then another. Gunfire.

Samantha's chute drifted away, released with total disregard for collecting it. Tania saw her raise her shotgun as she sprinted.

The wind gusted. It tugged Skyler's chute off course. Tania could sense him fighting to control their descent.

Below, the roof spun out of view. They would miss it. Tania strained her neck to keep Samantha in view. The woman still ran across the mottled surface, toward a doorway. An open doorway.

A man stood there, wild and filthy. Others loomed behind him.

Samantha's shotgun boomed as the whole roof slid from Tania's view.

Skyler shouted, "Lift!"

Her attention snapped forward. The wind pushed them over the courtyard, away from the target building, across the wide space toward the structure with the landing pad.

She pulled her legs up to her chest, something that took more effort than she expected after the long fall. On instinct she held her breath.

Skyler's feet hit the gravelly surface and skidded out from under him. The loose pebbles offered no traction. He went down hard, on his back. Tania landed squarely on top of him, the impact causing her head to snap backward. Her skull smacked against the inside of the helmet, and she cringed at the sound of it impacting with his chin.

Birds scattered from the roof. More erupted from nearby trees. They filled the sky.

Skyler slid for a few meters before friction won out. He rolled them onto one side and unlatched the belts that had kept her tied to him.

She got on her knees, head pounding. A drip of fluid snaked down her neck. Blood or sweat, she didn't know. The fabric of the parachute occluded the sky. The wind carried it on its course, over them and off the roof.

"What's going on?" she shouted, unable to keep terror from her voice. She knew, yet she had to ask. *Subhumans*.

Skyler ignored her. He worked frantically at the straps holding his gun in place.

More gunfire erupted from the building where Samantha had landed. Then another salvo, from inside the tall structure where Jake was. His shots sounded different, now. Quieter, more rapid. *A different gun,* Tania thought.

The captain freed his weapon, brought the butt of it to his chin, and unleashed a burst toward Samantha's roof, toward the rooftop doorway where the creatures had been. Sparks flew from the metal door and the railing around it.

Tania froze with fear, only able to watch, as Samantha raced to the entrance. Skyler held his fire as the big woman reached the door and kicked it closed.

A sudden, stark quiet fell over the campus.

"Stay behind me," Skyler barked at her.

She pushed herself up from her knees and blinked tears from her eyes. She had no way to wipe at them.

"Are you okay?!" Skyler shouted across to Samantha.

The woman waved, then pointed north. "We have to get to Jake!"

Skyler dusted himself off and turned to Tania. "How's your head?"

"Bleeding, I think," Tania said. "Your chin is, too."

"Listen," Skyler said, "you have to tell me if we should abort. I can't open your suit to bandage it."

Tania's heart hammered within her chest. She willed herself to relax. Her head throbbed, and the blood had spooked her. But the pain felt diminished. "I think I'm okay," she said. The captain had gone still. "What's—"

"Quiet," he whispered.

Tania heard nothing but wind through the speakers in her helmet.

Then, something odd. A sound that chilled her to the core.

From below came the wails, the snarls, of a hundred savage voices. They grew louder by the second. Birds streamed from the trees behind the campus.

"We need to get inside," Skyler said. "Sam! Jake! Meet in the basement!"

"What is that awful noise?" Tania asked. Her knees shook from fear; she felt panic taking over. She knew, had no doubt, what made the sound. She wanted him to say it, so she might draw strength from his confidence.

"Trouble," he said, and grabbed her arm.

Skyler pulled the scientist as fast has her legs would allow. The bulky suit and air tank slowed her as much as her fear, he realized.

Near the middle of the roof, a maintenance entrance jutted from the gravel surface. A three-step stairway led up to the plain white door, paint cracked from years of exposure.

He let go of her arm long enough to turn on the flashlight attached to the bottom of his gun barrel. The poor woman clutched at his jacket, then his backpack. He offered her a reassuring nod, then turned the door handle.

It twisted, unlocked. Skyler took a breath, then yanked the door open and raised his weapon.

A pitch-black stairwell greeted him. He swept his light across and down, and saw nothing.

"Stay with me," he said. Her rapid breaths fogged the inside of her helmet, and he knew he needed to calm her down soon. "It'll be okay."

Tania nodded, but her eyes said otherwise.

After three flights of stairs she stumbled. He just managed to catch her and pull her back to her feet.

"I feel dizzy," she said.

"Rest here a second. Catch your breath." He leaned her against the wall. "There's a water tube, if you turn your head all the way left. Drink a little."

While she settled down, Skyler examined her environment suit. The sensor on the front showed green, no air leaks, but after nearly two decades of use Skyler didn't trust it.

A cursory inspection turned up no rips or holes, so he shifted focus to their situation. Jake might be stuck in the tall building on the north side. Injured by the fall, perhaps, though not so bad that he couldn't fire his gun. Samantha could handle herself, ammo permitting. He wondered how many subs had made the campus their home. From the sound outside, dozens. A hundred, maybe. Too many. They usually formed small packs.

He reached to tap his earpiece, and found nothing there.

"Son of a—" he said, and stopped himself.

"What is it?" Tania asked. Her breathing, though rapid, had calmed.

"Nothing," he replied, no desire to panic her further. The gadget must have fallen off during their rush to get off the roof. Without it he had no way to contact Angus, no way to arrange landing, or warn the poor kid. Jake carried the other radio. "Let's get to the basement, and find the others."

She followed without being pulled now, and Skyler felt grateful for the freedom of movement. He instructed her to keep two paces behind and continued down the steps.

He ignored the doors he came across, marked with decreasing numbers, until they reached one that said B1.

The muffled sound of Samantha's shotgun echoed through the building. It came from everywhere and nowhere.

Two shots, a third. Then nothing.

Skyler fought the urge to race to Samantha's aid. He glanced back at Tania and saw terror there. Less than before, but not gone.

"Go. Help her," Tania whispered, her voice amplified by the speaker on her suit.

"I'm not leaving you here," he said. "Grab my jacket, we'll move faster."

He turned the door handle and slipped into the hall beyond. They were at a corner. Cracks ran the length of the linoleum floor. Parts of it curled where sections joined. Black blotches of mold grew on the walls and ceiling. It stank of age and stagnation, and the hint of human waste. Skyler let a wave of nausea pass.

The idea to abort the mission crossed his mind. He doubted that any of the equipment Tania needed to access here still functioned, judging by the state of decay in the hallway. The place was a wreck.

Her grip of his jacket somehow reassured him.

The blueprint had outlined a square-shaped basement beneath the four buildings above. Skyler guessed that the hall, which went either left or straight ahead, lined the entire perimeter.

"Six of one," he said, and went straight.

Two doors on either side of the corridor ahead were open, blocking his view. A pile of debris spilled from one room—a storage closet, Skyler noted. Cleaning supplies and other basics. On any other mission he would stop to pick through it for useful items. This time he shimmied over the mound and then helped Tania to do the same.

Another corner loomed, fifteen meters ahead.

"Wait," Tania said.

He turned. Her face looked ghostly under the tiny white LED built into her suit's helmet. "Try the lights," she said, and pointed to a bank of switches on the wall beside them.

"Great idea," Skyler said. His flashlight would draw subs like moths to a flame. He crossed the hall and flipped the switches one by one.

Clusters of LEDs along the ceiling came to life, flooding the hall with pale white light. Satisfied, Skyler clicked off the light on his gun.

"Skyler?!"

Samantha's voice, from beyond the corner ahead. "We're here!" he called back.

"It's clear, come to us," she shouted.

Us. She'd found Jake, and he was okay. A wave of relief washed over him. He flashed a smile at Tania and led her to the corner.

Samantha stood halfway down the next corridor, at a wide alcove that fronted a bank of elevators. The entrance to the lower basement, and the data vault, according to the signage on the wall. A set of ugly green chairs and couches occupied the space, along with a series of empty bookshelves.

Jake sat behind her on the floor, back against the wall, legs straight out. White gauze had been wrapped around his head. His arms cradled his stomach. Skyler thought maybe the man had died, until Jake turned his head and nodded at them.

"You scared the shit out of us with those lights," Samantha said.

Skyler ignored her and focused on Jake. A gash on his cheek looked superficial. Blood soaked through the bandage on his head.

Tania stifled a gasp at the sight.

"What happened?" Skyler asked.

Jake winced. "Roof caved in. Water rot, I should've spotted it. I tried to tell you, but when I stood up I just, I don't know, blacked out. When I came around the damn subs were right on top of me. Really aggressive bastards, like those ones in Malaysia. I put down seven or eight before they spooked and ran."

"Worse than Malaysia," Samantha said. "This place is

like a warren, Skyler. I've never seen so many in one place, not since the Purge. They're all over the upper floors."

"And they did that?" Skyler asked, pointing at the wound.

"No," Jake said. "The fall did that."

"I dressed it," Sam said. She took a long draw from her canteen and wiped her mouth on the back of her sleeve. "He'll live."

The sniper coughed and signaled a halfhearted thumbs-up.

"I lost my comm on the roof," Skyler said. "Does yours work?"

Jake shook his head. "Shattered."

The bleak news settled in. They had no way to signal the *Melville*.

"Angus is probably shitting himself up there," Samantha said.

Skyler raced to formulate a plan. He needed to get Tania to the data vault; she'd said it could take her hours to find the data she needed. He checked his wristwatch. "Angus will make a flyby," he said for the woman's benefit, "thirty minutes after loss of contact. We'll need to get his attention, one way or the other, and tell him how long to give us down here."

"Do we know that?" Samantha asked.

"Not until I get started," Tania said, and tapped the briefcase.

While she spoke, Jake pushed himself up to a standing position. He probed at his skull before nodding to Skyler. *I've had worse,* his expression said.

"Okay," said Skyler. "I'll take Tania below and get her started. Make a barricade with these couches and hold here. We'll be back with news before Angus flies over."

Samantha and Jake nodded in unison.

A second passed before Skyler realized Sam had not argued. *Hell must have frozen over,* he thought.

Skyler led Tania down another stairwell, not trusting the elevators despite power being on. The steps descended only one floor and ended at a heavy door. Though unlocked,

Skyler had to give the handle a hard yank before it opened. A waft of cool air hit him as the door swung aside, and they found themselves at the end of a wide hallway.

Something about the place bothered Skyler, and then it hit him: It was clean. The crisp air had a chill bite to it, and carried none of the odors typically found in deserted buildings. He'd been in many places outside the Aura, and Mother Nature had reclaimed it all in some way. Not here.

As his ears adjusted, he recognized the hum of an air conditioner, barely audible but there nonetheless. It knocked and whined, as if it might fail at any moment.

Tania whispered, "Could there be survivors in here?"

Skyler looked at her. The fear in her voice was so obvious that he wanted to hold her. "Doubtful," he said. "Twice in the past we've encountered immunes while in the Clear. One had gone insane over the years and tried to sabotage our ship. The other is my engineer."

The hallway extended for fifteen meters or so before ending at a closed door. A small window, covered in dust, sat at shoulder height.

"Wait here," Skyler said, and jogged to the door. He did his best to keep his boots quiet, rolling his feet with each stride, but they still echoed off the beige linoleum surface.

He wiped dust from the window and peered through. Nothing moved in the room beyond. He tried the door handle, gently, and found it unlocked.

With a wave he signaled Tania to come join him.

When she arrived at his back, Skyler raised his pistol and put a finger to his lips. She nodded. Slowly he opened the door and leaned inside. The room was small. White floors, wall, and ceiling, broken only by a series of gray metal lockers on one wall. A few were open, displaying their contents: white jumpsuits and breathing masks.

Skyler pointed at the clothing. "What's all this for? Is it dangerous inside?"

"I doubt it," Tania said. "Probably just for keeping dust out of the equipment."

"Not something we need to trouble with, then. Still, could be valuable." Skyler opened the satchel strapped to his chest and removed a tightly folded duffel bag. He stuffed it with three jumpsuits and breathing masks.

The other containers were all locked, save one. Skyler opened it to find civilian clothing. He rummaged through the pants pockets.

"What are you looking for?" Tania asked.

Skyler removed a set of keys and jingled them at her. From another pocket he found an access card. "Andrew Ryoko Shu," he read aloud.

"A. R. Shu," Tania said, quietly.

Handing her the card, Skyler said, "Know the bloke?"

"The name was in the Japan data. We're in the right place."

Satisfied, he slung the duffel bag on his back and moved to the door at the other end of the room. Tania kept one step behind him.

This one proved to be locked. Skyler tried the keys he found, one after another. All failed. Then Tania swiped the access card through a slot on the wall, and a firm click emanated from inside. The door unlocked.

Skyler pulled it open. The floor inside sloped upward and then turned ninety degrees. The hum of the air-conditioning was much louder here.

He stepped inside and felt a rush of panic as a tearing sound came from his feet. Looking down, he saw that he stood on some kind of white pad with a sticky surface, covered in faint, dusty footprints.

"To remove the dirt from your shoes, I think," Tania said.

Skyler continued up the ramp. Turning the corner, he came into a large room with a high ceiling lined with bundles of cables. Row after row of equipment filled the vast room. Most appeared to be functional, judging by the myriad of small blinking lights.

"This is it," Tania said.

Skyler looked over the room. "Where do we start?"

She pointed toward one of the equipment racks that still had power. "That one is as good as any," she said.

Skyler checked his watch. "Is ten minutes enough time to get set up?"

She nodded.

"Okay," he said, "a quick sweep of the room and it's all yours. Wait here."

He scanned each row. All were empty except the last, where Skyler found a toolbox on the floor. Someone had abandoned their work many years ago. On instinct, Skyler went through the box and removed a handful of useful tools, placing them in a pouch within his jacket.

Satisfied the room was safe, he returned to Tania. "You're on," he said.

She walked to the computer rack and surveyed its contents. Then she moved around to the other side of the row and opened the access panel on the back side of the same section. Inside, a chaotic mess of colorful cables snaked through metal loops, connecting all the systems together.

Tania removed the briefcase strapped to her chest and set it on the floor. She opened it to reveal a gleaming, streamlined device, clearly far newer than anything else in the room. She opened a small display on the top of it and powered it on.

Skyler watched, fascinated, as she methodically searched through the cables inside the big cabinet, tracing where they started and stopped.

"These gloves make it difficult," she said.

Through some criteria that he couldn't understand, she finally settled on one, and tugged it aside from the others.

Next, she pulled a similar cable out of the briefcase. On the top of the device, she slid open a covered section, revealing a bank of various connection ports. Tania scanned them quickly and plugged the cable into the one that matched.

She took the other end, found her isolated cable inside the old computer rack, and held it between two gloved fingers. From the case she grabbed another wire with two pronged clamps on the end.

"Careful," Skyler said. With all the violence around them, if she ended her mission by poking a hole in her suit . . .

Tania paused, steadied herself. With deliberate care she punctured the cable and locked the clamp.

"I'm amazed any of this stuff still works," Skyler said.

Tania's gloved fingers danced across the screen inside the briefcase. "It's all solid state, no moving parts. With proper power and cooling, it will last a century or more. I just hope the data is stored in a standard format."

Information flooded the interface. She watched it like a hawk, tapping on certain elements and swiping others to the side, creating columns where none existed before. Order from chaos. Skyler didn't understand a bit of it, and used the quiet moment to study her. He never harbored much desire to become an Orbital himself—too boring, too confined—but the idea of spending more time with this woman had definite appeal.

Almost five minutes passed before she reacted to something on the screen. "I've found the data I need," she said. "Good news: I should only need an hour."

Skyler checked his watch. "I should tell the others. You'll be okay here?"

She nodded, absently, keeping her eyes on the screen. "Sure. Take the key card."

He pocketed it, impressed by her bravery but unsure whether to believe her. He decided he had no choice. "Back as soon as I can."

She looked at him through her hazard helmet and smiled bleakly. "Good luck, Skyler."

Her smile thrilled him.

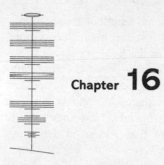

Chapter 16

AT THE ENTRYWAY, Skyler left Samantha to defend the barricade and took Jake to the roof. On the way, he stopped at the mound of cleaning supplies blocking the hall and gathered ten rolls of white plastic trash bags.

"I have an idea," Skyler said as they climbed the stairs. He had to pause twice when Jake stumbled. The man's eyes were cloudy, and his hands shook.

On the roof, Skyler asked Jake to look for the lost communicator while he set to work on his backup plan. From the courtyard below and the surrounding land he could hear the muffled grunts of the subhumans. Occasionally one roared, a pained and eerie sound. Others took up the cry before settling down again.

The reams of white plastic bags rolled out into perfect lines. He worked fast to write his message in giant block letters: "30м."

Skyler had just put the finishing touches on the makeshift display when the *Melville* drifted overhead. Angus turned and dropped lower to make another pass. This time he tilted the wings back and forth to indicate he'd understood.

"Half an hour," Skyler said to Jake. "Let's make it count."

"Take a look at this," the sniper said. He stood at the edge of the roof, leaning over.

Skyler moved to stand next to him and looked down. Subhumans filled the wide outdoor space, four floors below. There were a hundred at least. Most were naked; all were filthy. Some carried found, primitive weapons—thick sections of tree branch, the occasional length of copper pipe.

He'd only seen a group so large once, many years before, during the Purge. Back then, in the fledgling days of Darwin's role as "last city," the subhuman population in Australia was massive. Large groups happened more by accident than anything else. In the years since, the population across the planet had dwindled significantly. Now they usually formed small packs of four or five, and spent their days fighting one another when they weren't eating or sleeping.

"It's like a bunch of swagmen took speed and decided to have an orgy," Jake muttered.

Skyler barked a laugh. Too loud.

One screeched, a wild sound of raw anger.

The creature stared directly at Skyler. Like a chimp in a zoo, it began to jump about, waving its arms in rage and frustration.

More took up the cry. Soon they were all looking up, and feeding off one another's disease-fueled bloodlust. A few retreated to the corners of the yard and cowered, the disease amplifying their flight reaction. Others began to throw rocks, which fell short.

"This is bad," Jake said as the volume of the inhuman cries rose. Out of pure habit he'd already unslung his long rifle and pulled the lens cap from its scope.

A couple of the stronger ones started to climb the side of the building, using the overgrowth of vines, cracks in the concrete walls, and windowsills to pull themselves up.

Skyler hoisted his machine gun and flicked off the safety. "Retreat to the door," he said, and began to backpedal.

Jake followed.

At the door, Skyler yanked it open and moved inside. He allowed enough room for Jake to come in as well. The sniper crouched and leveled his long gun toward the edge.

When the first head emerged over the rooftop, Jake fired. The poor creature's skull snapped backward and then it disappeared, back to where it came.

Before Skyler could compliment the shot, the man reaimed and fired again. Another dropped.

More appeared now. Six or seven. Jake fired in rapid shots but couldn't keep up.

The subhumans ran very fast, their lean bodies corded with muscle. Skyler aimed and squeezed off a burst, taking one in the chest. A female, he realized. She toppled over in a heap.

Still more came. They streamed over the rooftop now.

One stood out. It had a mess of wild gray hair and wore tatters of old clothing. The leader, Skyler realized, as the sub raised its arms and bellowed.

Jake saw it, too. His shot exploded out the back of the leader's head, spraying blood and brains across the faces of those behind it. The being went down in an unceremonious heap.

The others faltered. Some turned back, confused. A few did not, and started to laugh as they ran past the body. Jake's rifle took on a drumlike rhythm, *pat-pat-pat,* as he ended their sorry lives. He worked so fast that Skyler had no time to aim.

Quiet settled. Even the birds had gone silent.

A dozen bodies littered the roof, right on top of the "30M" sign Skyler had drawn. Blood spilled on the white plastic bags in stark contrast. Pools and splatters of deep red.

Skyler wiped the sweat from his brow. His heart pounded from adrenaline, he could feel blood throb in his temples. He took a long, measured breath. "Bloody hell," he said after a moment. "Nice shooting."

Jake kept his focus on the edge of the roof, and said nothing. He expected more to come, and for good reason. If the creatures were anything, they were persistent.

"We should get back downstairs," Skyler said.

"You go," Jake said, reloading his gun. He laid his extra clips in a line on the ground in front of him. "I'll thin the herd."

Skyler stared at the back of the man's head. "Sure?"

"If Angus is going to land here, we need to clear these bastards out," Jake said. "Besides, this is much more fun than cowering down there in the dark."

Skyler clapped his friend on the shoulder. He turned and

ran down the stairwell, taking two at a time, and reached Sam at her barricade within a minute.

"What was all that noise?" she asked.

"The maestro at work," Skyler said. Despite the relative safety, he crouched behind the stack of bookshelves she'd piled up.

Samantha grinned at him. "Think Angus got our message?"

"He got it," Skyler said.

"Will we have enough juice to get home?" she asked, voicing their greatest fear. It'd be one thing to go down fighting, another thing altogether to get stranded out in the Clear.

"Gonna be tight, I think," Skyler said. "You have this under control?"

She nodded, eyes glued to the hall beyond her barricade.

"I'll head back down then. Retreat to the basement if things get interesting."

"What about Jake?"

"Remind me to keep him on our side." With that, Skyler turned and ran to the subbasement.

He followed the same path they took earlier and found Tania right where he'd left her.

"Did you reach Angus?"

"He'll give us thirty minutes, all the energy we can spare."

Tania studied the screen. The readout indicated thirty-eight minutes left. "I need more time," she said.

"No choice, sorry. We stay any longer, we won't get home."

Tania searched his eyes. "I hope it's enough, then."

Skyler pulled a folded duffel bag from a pants pocket. "Going to scavenge a bit, won't be far."

Despite concern in her beautiful face, she managed a single, stiff nod.

Skyler moved through the computer room. From some of the cabinets near the back, which lacked power, he disconnected every cable he could find and tossed them in the bag. Spare parts always found a buyer.

From the front of the racks, he yanked out any removable

component. Charred power leads marred some, but he bagged them all regardless of condition. Takai could sort them out.

Next he went to the power junctions along the sidewall. He kept his distance from the ones that still seemed to be functional, not wanting to disrupt Tania's work. From the others he removed circuit breakers and three large wiring harnesses.

Satisfied, he slung the heavy bag over his left shoulder and slipped the strap over his head, letting the strap run diagonally across his chest. He returned to Tania.

"You don't fool around," she said.

He turned so she could see just how full the duffel was. "Pays my crew."

Tania frowned. "It does a lot more than that."

"What do you mean?"

"The work you do, people like you, it's the only reason anyone can survive in orbit."

In almost five years of scavenging, Skyler rarely went a week without someone offering thanks, praise, or a compliment. Even something simple, like a new bicycle chain, could make all the difference for someone trapped in the Aura. Every person who claimed the world would end without scavengers just added to the pressure.

Tania's words cracked that barricade. She meant it with total sincerity, and Skyler knew in that moment that all of his work had been for her, and those like her. People striving to do more in the world than just survive. People who kept hope alive for a better future.

He found it impossible to articulate any of this, so he looked away and mumbled his usual response. "No offense, but we don't do this for the greater good. It pays—well, sometimes— and keeps me and my crew fed and sheltered, which is more than most—"

Gunfire rang out, somewhere above their heads. Not the sniper rifle, with its loud single cracks, but the booms of a shotgun.

"Sam's in trouble," Skyler said. He checked his watch. "Ten minutes still. Son of a bitch."

"Go help her," Tania said. Her fearful tone contradicted her words. She was shaking.

He grabbed her by her upper arms. "Eight minutes, no more. Got it?"

She nodded.

"Can you find your way back to the stairs?"

Again she nodded.

"Deep breath, Tania. They won't get past us, I promise."

She drew a long breath and let it out slowly.

He gave her wrist a squeeze, using the opportunity to glance at the gauges mounted on her suit. The air level read just above half. Satisfied, Skyler ran for the stairs.

At the door he almost ran into her.

She backed up, and they stood side by side in the doorway at the bottom of the steps. Six bodies had already piled up on the stairs, with a fresh one just tumbling to a stop halfway up.

"Better position behind us," Skyler said. "This is too close."

"Lead on," Samantha said.

He closed the door to the stairwell—a nearly useless gesture since it didn't have a lock—and retreated to the data vault entry door with the shoulder-high window. Skyler slammed the door behind them, and with the butt of his rifle he smashed the glass.

Flipping the gun around, he pointed it through the space the glass had occupied, and waited.

Sam reloaded her weapon at the same time. "These fuckers are really far gone, Skyler. Never seen them so aggressive."

"And in such a large group. I don't get it."

The door to the stairwell burst open and Skyler answered with a spray of bullets. With the awkward angle, aim was out of the question, so he fired for effect.

Another of the creatures dropped, skidding to a sickening halt, blood spilling from wounds on its chest and legs.

"I'm low on ammo," Samantha said.

Skyler fired again, a short burst. "We're going to be trapped in here."

"Where's the map?"

Skyler looked down at his jacket. "Inside pocket!" he shouted, over the crackling sound of his gun. Samantha reached and took it.

"Go get Tania," Skyler said. "I'll hold them off."

"We can both go. Look, below the computer room. There's a subbasement marked SHIPPING AND RECEIVING. A ramp leads out of it, back up to the surface."

She set the map against the door. Skyler studied it and let off another burst from the rifle without even looking. Sure enough, a sloped road led from the subterranean loading dock to a parking lot some fifty meters distant. "We'd be far from Jake, and outdoors," he said.

"Yeah, but all the subs will be in here. We can come back through the trees, to the rear of the building."

He fired again through the window. A wild yelp of pain came from the diseased human sprinting toward the door. It fell in a heap.

"You're assuming there's a way through the floor."

"I'll make one if I have to. Beats the hell out of this."

Skyler led the way, moving as fast as his legs would carry him. Behind, they heard the snarls and growls of subhumans trying to open the windowed door.

They found Tania in the data center, already packing up her equipment.

"You get it all?" Skyler asked.

She shook her head. "Eighty percent. It will have to do."

Samantha turned the map in her hands, getting oriented. "Over here, I think." They followed her to the back wall of the room. Samantha opened a door, which displayed an assortment of warning signs related to electricity.

"We're fucked," she said. The room inside the door was barely a meter deep and contained some sort of electrical junction, which filled the entire space.

"Down there," Tania said, pointing at the floor. Conduits from the equipment disappeared through large panels, set into the floor like tiles. Skyler crouched and, with Samantha's help, tried to dislodge one of them, but there was no gap to insert their fingers.

Tania turned and ran back toward the front of the room.

Skyler shouted after her, "Where the hell—"

"Help us, you bitch!" Samantha shouted.

Tania removed something from the wall near the front of the room and ran back to them. A metal handle, oversized, with two large suction cups on either end.

She slammed the thing down onto the floor tile, and then lifted. The square panel came away with ease. Tania tossed it aside and faced the two of them.

"Ah," Samantha said, "Sorry about the 'bitch' thing."

"Can we go?" Skyler asked.

Beneath the floor they stood on was a crawl space, packed with bundles of cables and a variety of cooling and power conduits. Below that, more tiles.

Samantha sat down on the edge of the opening, and kicked. The weaker tile below cracked in half and fell away. Through the hole, darkness. Skyler turned his flashlight back on.

"Four-meter drop," Samantha said.

Skyler laughed. "You're almost that tall, you go first."

"Flip a coin?" Sam said.

In the hallway outside the computer room, they heard a crashing sound, followed by hideous screams.

"No time to argue. Down you go."

Samantha lowered herself down into the floor between a gap in the conduits. She grasped the metal girder that framed the space where the tile used to be, and hung from it. Finally she let go, dropping down into the dark room.

"I'm okay," she called up.

Skyler looked at Tania, found her white as a sheet, eyes wide with terror. He followed her eyes to see a subhuman turning the corner at the far end of the computer room.

Naked, covered with dirt, blood, and old scars—more gruesome than most. It had an open wound on the side of its face, rancid with infection, revealing the bone beneath. The creature tried to scream at them, but all that came out was a sick gurgling sound.

Skyler aimed and squeezed off a burst. Bullets tore through the pitiful being's face, snapping its head back in grotesque fashion. It flopped to the ground, heaved once, and went still.

The noise from the gun brought a cry from Tania. She wavered on the verge of panic.

"Get below!" he shouted at her, but she was incapable of movement. Skyler slung his weapon and grabbed her wrists. He forced her over the hole in the floor and lowered her down as far as he could.

Tania stared into his eyes, tears streaming from her own. He dropped her into the darkness below.

Another subhuman entered the computer room, and Skyler sprayed the last of his clip toward the creature. He managed to wing it in the leg, enough to put the creature on the floor.

Sucking in his gut, Skyler stepped as far as he could inside the little power closet. Then he grabbed the door handle and jumped through the hole in the floor. The fall, combined with his grip on the handle, caused the door to slam closed above him.

He hit the floor below and felt jarring pain shoot up through his knees. He toppled to the ground, grabbing his legs in agony.

Samantha was over him in seconds. "Fuck. Anything broken?"

He shook his head, grunting.

"Can you walk?"

"I'll damn well try," he said through clenched teeth. "Reload my gun."

Samantha took the offered weapon and removed a spare clip from Skyler's belt. The last he had.

"Tania, are you with us?" he asked the scientist.

She clutched the briefcase to her chest again. Her lip quivered.

"Brilliant idea, using that . . . whatever the hell it was. You saved our asses," Skyler said.

"Slab sucker," Tania said.

"Huh?"

"The boys on Green Level call it a slab sucker." Her voice came from a faraway place.

Samantha whispered in Skyler's ear. "She's in shock."

"I know," he said back. Then louder, "Let's keep moving, eh?" He let Samantha help him to his feet, ignoring the pain in his legs.

She cocked her shotgun and then led them toward the exit.

A large segmented door, big enough for vehicles, marked the rear of the building. They emerged to unnerving quiet, on a pothole-infested access road that wound up and out of view. Weeds grew waist-high from every crack in the surface.

Samantha led as fast as Skyler's knees would allow. She stayed a solid ten meters ahead, her body in constant motion as she checked every direction for approaching subs.

At the end of the access road, she halted behind a thicket to survey the ground between their position and the cluster of buildings. Skyler judged them to be a hundred and fifty meters from the building where Jake waited on the roof. He couldn't see the rooftop, or any subhumans on the ground around it. A parking lot filled the space between them. Wildflowers choked every gap in the asphalt surface. Scattered about were the remnants of vehicles, left behind to rot as people fled the disease.

Skyler couldn't help but catalog useful parts as he surveyed the vast lot. A hard habit to set aside, no matter the imminent danger. Fabric from the car seats, LED bulbs in the headlamps, dashboard components—the list went on and on.

A deep hum filled the air. The *Melville,* Skyler realized, high overhead. The only thing that sounded better than those engines was Tania's calm, measured breaths. Her gaze might still be vague and distant, but his confidence grew that she would recover soon.

Samantha rose from her crouch. "No time to waste."

She ran. Skyler wanted to scream from the searing pain in his knees, but with each step the sensation abated. Despite his aching legs, he moved faster than Tania. She didn't complain when he grabbed her elbow and pulled her along. Despite the weight of her environment suit, the woman showed no signs of exhaustion. Skyler realized she had not complained about the bulky outfit once.

The hum of the *Melville*'s engines grew like approaching thunder.

At the back entrance, Samantha flashed five-and-five to Skyler before rushing through the back door. She wanted ten seconds to clear their path.

Skyler guided Tania to the outer wall and hunkered down in front of her. He couldn't see the aircraft, and had to gauge her distance by the engine tone. Close now, but still not in vertical landing mode.

"Mother of God," Skyler whispered.

The cacophony generated by the ship's engines drew subhumans like moths to a flame. He stared in horror at the tree line beyond the parking lot.

The creatures streamed from the forest. Some galloped on all fours, like apes. He'd never seen so many in one place, focused on the same goal, as if they'd formed a clan.

Tania gasped. She clutched at Skyler's sleeve.

"Run," he said. "Don't look back. Go!"

She ducked inside to the sound of shotgun blasts from deep within.

We're surrounded, Skyler thought.

All the while the thunder from the approaching aircraft grew, until the noise drowned everything, even the cries of the subhumans.

Skyler saw no point in wasting bullets. There were far too many. The roof was all that mattered. He followed Tania, pausing only to shut the door.

She waited at the stairwell entrance. Samantha stood at her side, her breaths loud and labored. A few pitiful bodies were sprawled in the corridor beyond.

"To the roof, now," Skyler said. He went first, and heard their footsteps on the stairs behind him.

Two flights above he stepped around the body of a subhuman, shot in the throat. *Jake may have come down,* he realized.

At the top he found the door to the roof open. Bodies littered the gravel surface. Beyond them, the *Melville* rested on the building's landing pad, her engines at idle now. Skyler could see Angus's face in the cockpit window, white with fear.

He paused. "Is Jake aboard?!" he called.

Angus read his lips, then shook his head.

Skyler looked across the rooftop. "Jake?" he shouted out. No response came.

"Jake?!"

"He must be inside," Samantha said. "You saw that body on the steps. Give me your weapon."

He handed her the gun. "I'll be right behind you."

Bracing her shotgun on an armpit, and holding the submachine gun in her other hand, Samantha disappeared into the darkness without another word.

Not five seconds elapsed before Skyler heard gunfire below.

He removed his pistol from the holster on his leg. "Let's get you aboard," he said to Tania.

She set the pace, somewhere between a walk and jog, crouching under the swirling winds of the *Melville*'s thrusters. Skyler threw an arm over his face to fight off the maelstrom of dust and rock kicked up by the engines.

"Where are the others?" Angus shouted from the open cargo ramp.

Skyler waved him back. "Be ready to take off!"

Angus hesitated, then returned to the cockpit.

Skyler ushered Tania through the door and tossed the duffel bag in after her. "Close the door, but be ready to let us in."

"Skyler—"

"Do it!"

Tania flinched at the barked order, and pressed the button to close the ramp. The captain disappeared out of her view as the cabin sealed.

She found herself alone, the aircraft dead quiet save for the faint hiss from the engines. There were no windows in the cargo bay. She threw her briefcase into a seat and went to the cockpit door.

Angus glanced back at her and offered a sympathetic nod. She leaned in to see through the cockpit window. An odd angle with her bulky suit helmet.

One of the aircraft's engines blocked much of her view. She could only see Skyler from the torso down.

He ran from the ship to the stairway entrance, his pistol held in both hands, aimed dead on the open door. The wind generated from the *Melville*'s engines whipped his clothing about and filled the air with dust. Bodies of subhumans lay everywhere.

Tania held her breath. The contrast of death and paradise brought tears to her eyes.

Skyler entered the stairwell, and darkness, gone from her view.

The stairs had become a slaughterhouse. He stepped over two more dead subhumans before reaching the bottom, and guessed the carnage wasn't over yet.

A shot rang out from the direction of the barricaded alcove, and Skyler ran.

He found Samantha kneeling over Jake's limp body. She cradled his head in her lap, tears streaming down her cheeks. Skyler stopped and fell to a seated position a few meters from them.

A pistol dangled from Jake's fingers. A stream of blood ran from the corner of his mouth and down his neck, smearing on Samantha's pants. The woman's hands, which held the dead sniper's head, were coated in blood.

"He ate a goddamn bullet," Sam muttered. "Rather than letting them—"

Skyler clenched his teeth and looked away, fighting his own tears. He wanted to punch something, to exact some kind of revenge. "It's my fault. We should've landed together. I'm sorry, I'm so sorry."

Samantha came to him. She gripped his shoulder with one hand and squeezed. Her other hand, coated with Jake's blood, slipped around his neck and she pulled him toward her until their foreheads touched. "We don't always see eye to eye, Skyler, but I don't lay this at your feet. I'd never do that."

He blinked tears away and looked at her. "You have to crouch for us to see eye to eye," he muttered.

A laugh escaped both their lips. Sam head-butted him, a gentle rebuke to his gallows humor. "That's the Skyler I know. Enough of the waterworks, all right?"

"What do we do about Jake?" he asked, staring at his friend's limp form.

"We're scavengers," Sam replied, dragging the back of her hand across her nose. "We take his shit and get the hell out of this godforsaken place. Just like he would have done if it were one of us lying there."

Five long minutes passed with no sign of them. Tania stared at the maw of the open stairwell, ignoring the pilot Angus as he fretted nervously. For now, at least, the subhumans were gone. Elsewhere, she thought, or all slain.

A figure emerged from the door—Samantha, alone, her head down and shoulders slumped.

Tania's breath caught in her throat. Then she saw Skyler, just behind the stocky woman. A few steps into the sunlight, the captain faltered, his knees buckled. Samantha turned and caught him in stride. She carried him toward the plane, out of view.

Tania felt an enormous pit open in her stomach.

She raced back to the rear door of the craft and opened it just in time for Samantha to climb the ramp and dump Skyler on the floor.

Unchecked rage showed on the tall woman's face. She slammed the "close" button and the red intercom button in unison, so hard Tania thought they would break.

"Get us the fuck out of here," Samantha said.

The pilot made no reply. The engines answered for him. They roared back to full strength and the craft tilted as it left the ground.

"Belt in," Samantha said to Tania, without looking at her. Tania moved to help Skyler up, but he stubbornly waved her off and pulled himself into a seat. Feeling lost, she took the seat next to him and buckled herself in.

Samantha pounded the butt of her shotgun against the wall, over and over. Each impact was weaker than the last as her strength, if not her rage, drained. In the end she stumbled through the cockpit door and closed it behind her.

Tania watched Skyler for a time, as the *Melville* sped away. He slept, or pretended to.

She felt numb, completely exhausted. Eventually she reached out a gloved hand and took his, held it firm. When his fingers tightened around hers, she fought to hold back tears. They'd lost one of their crew for her mission. A man had died, somewhere in the depths of that horrible building. Alone in the dark, those creatures cackling as they tore at his face . . .

Guilt would hang over her for the rest of her life. She knew that with total certainty. Tania retreated, found a place in her mind that she could make sense of. The lab on Black Level, her work, her research. She wanted nothing more in the world than to be back there now, and so she closed her eyes and took herself there.

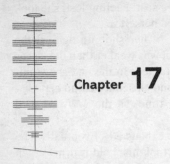

Chapter 17

FROM HIS VANTAGE point, Darwin looked like scattered glowing embers, as if God himself had stood at a fire pit and kicked the smoldering coals in pure frustration.

Russell Blackfield liked to imagine himself in the role of God.

He spent most nights here, relaxing on a tattered old recliner on the roof of his headquarters in Nightcliff, a patio umbrella to keep the rain off his head. He brought three things: a lantern, the shipping manifests for the next day, and whatever bottle of alcohol he could get his hands on.

From midnight to dawn, he memorized the shipments that would come through Nightcliff the next day. It was his secret. Among the administrators and inspectors, his knowledge of all things coming and going had acquired legendary status. In truth he was never more than a day ahead, and the memorization process took him hours.

He allotted himself two swigs from his bottle per climber memorized, until the task was done. Then the floodgates could open. He would drink, and watch the city wake up. A million souls, or so the estimates went. His own sleep would come with the sun.

But tonight his mind drifted. Events beyond his control clawed at his attention, like hungry kittens. Word of a subhuman running loose in orbit had spread like wildfire across the city. It dwarfed the news that a few had appeared inside the city as well—that, at least, could be explained.

Power outages continued to plague the climbers, more occurrences happening by the day, and no one had a good explanation. Not even the council. Or perhaps they just weren't sharing. Scared shitless, more likely.

Russell took a swig of vodka and drew his arm across his mouth. Change didn't scare him. Change meant opportunity for those willing to grasp it.

He heard footsteps behind him and sat up slowly. His staff knew to leave him in peace up here. Footsteps meant something important.

"Sorry to disturb you, sir," came a voice.

Russell turned to see a uniformed guard. Too dark to distinguish whom, not that he cared much. "What is it?"

The man stopped at a respectful distance. "The missing worker from yesterday's climber."

"What of it?"

"There was a scavenger ship that went up just after—"

Russell felt his temper rising. "The *Melville,* yes?"

"It just returned, sir."

Russell set his bottle down. "To the old airport?"

"No, sir," the man stammered. "We ordered it here. It's in the yard. The crew has been quarantined."

Russell held back his surprise. Quarantined, no less! Competence like this deserved a toast, so Russell pressed the bottle to his lips and tilted it back. "And our missing woman?"

"One of them matches her description. We've put her in a separate room."

"You . . . ," Russell started, then paused. "You've done well. I'm shocked." He handed the half-full bottle to the man. "Get yourself rotten. I'll take it from here."

Quarantine situations were handled in the basement of the old asylum, conveniently situated within Nightcliff's walls. Russell strode inside and was greeted by the nurse on duty.

"Status," he said.

The heavyset woman fell in step next to him. "Got three of them together in room D. The fourth I was told to set

aside, so she's in room H. Real looker, she is. You'll like her.
In shock, I think."

"Shock? From being captured?"

The woman shook her flabby head. "Nah, she was like
that when they pulled her from the ship. Seems they got into
a bit of a scrap out there."

Russell picked up the pace. "Out where?"

"Hawaii, they said."

That matched the flight plan put in when the *Melville*'s
captain purchased lift rights.

"Is she exhibiting any symptoms?" he asked.

"She had a hazmat on. The rest say they're immune."

"They are, I know them. Room H first," Russell said.

The obese woman had to jog just to keep up with him.
Waddling on her stubby legs, she led him through a series of
empty hallways and abandoned waiting rooms.

The quarantine rooms consisted of two sides, one for the
patient and one for the observer, separated by a wall-sized
one-way mirror. Russell entered the observation area
ahead of the nurse and looked through the glass at the
woman on the other side.

Tile covered the walls, floor, and ceiling in the holding
cell. Once gleaming white, the grout had now blackened,
and mildew stains bloomed everywhere. The detainee sat
on a metal bench, the only furniture in the room. She hugged
her knees to her chest and rocked gently back and forth. Her
eyes were closed.

"She is lovely, isn't she?" Russell asked.

"Told you so," the nurse said. The hag licked her lips.

"You get a name?"

"No," she said. "She keeps mumbling about someone
named Jake, that they left him behind. Then she said she
wanted to speak to Neil Platz. Can you believe that?"

Russell smiled. He could believe it, in fact. "She looks a
bit dirty," he observed. "We should clean her up. What do
you think?"

"Very prudent, sir."

Russell found a simple chair in the corner of the observation room and pulled it close to the glass. "Right, then. Get someone in there and give her a good scrubbing."

The ugly woman broke into an evil grin. "Right away," she said.

"Tell them," Russell said, "to be thorough." He settled into the chair, leaned back, and crossed his hands behind his head.

On the whole, the resulting show disappointed. The gorgeous woman had an exceptional body, no question. But she never *struggled*.

He sighed. His cock barely twitched the entire time.

"In shock. What an understatement," he said to himself.

They left her sitting naked on the narrow bench, still dripping from the buckets of cold, soapy water thrown on her. She made no effort to cover herself after the medics left the room. Instead she stared straight ahead, straight at Russell, as if she could see him through the mirror.

Maybe when she gathered her wits she'd put up a bit of sport. Then Russell could swoop in, play the helping-hand card. Whisk her to his private quarters, away from such savage behavior.

But not yet. Bored, Russell left the observation room. The head nurse waited for him in the hall. "What should I do with her?"

Russell paused. "Let her stew in there. I'll be back."

"What about her clothing?" the nurse asked.

"Burn it," Russell said. "And I suppose you should examine her closely for any signs of infection. Can't have a goddamn sub get loose in here."

A disgusting smile grew across the old woman's face. "Thank you. Very good."

"Same goes for the others we brought in," he said.

"Yes, certainly," said the nurse. "I'll start with her, I think."

Russell paused. "Hurt her in any way, and I'll cut your fucking hands off."

She recoiled, almost tripping on her own feet. He doubted he would have accomplished the same reaction had he physically slapped the shrew.

* * *

The *Melville* rested on the same landing pad from which it had departed. When Russell arrived, a team of cargo inspectors at his back, the ranking guard on duty greeted him.

"Evening, Mr. Blackfield, sir," the boy said.

Russell read the name off his uniform. "Officer Decklan. What have we got?"

"Craft is Dutch Air Force, built in 2204. Registered as the *Melville,* owner Sky—"

"Skyler Luiken," Russell said for him. "I know all this. The scow's been through here many times before. What's *inside*?"

Decklan stammered. "One full bag, and one metal case, locked."

"That's it?"

The guard swallowed, and nodded.

All the way to Hawaii for so little? "And in the bag?"

"No idea, sir. Orders were not to touch anything."

Russell nodded. "Well done." He motioned to the three inspectors he'd brought along and pointed them toward the open cargo ramp. To Decklan he said, "No one in or out, without my permission."

"Yes, sir!"

Russell followed his inspection team up the ramp.

The ship's cargo hold, packed full on the last inspection, stood nearly empty now. Laid bare, the bird looked her eighty years. The fact that she still flew regular missions spoke volumes of the love her captain had for her. That, or the skill of whoever repaired the thing. Russell made a mental note to find out who the engineer was and try to woo him away.

"Sir, have a look," one of the inspectors said.

Russell knelt over the metal case. Well made, from brushed aluminum, Russell guessed. The locks looked military grade. "Not the type of thing a wag from Darwin would carry about," he said.

The inspector, with a gesture of permission from Russell, picked it up and turned it over, examining all sides. "It's got the Platz logo, here," he said, pointing.

Russell smiled. He couldn't wait to tell Alex about this.

"Want me to open it?" the man said.

"Not yet," Russell replied. "Give it to me for now."

One of the other inspectors had opened the large black duffel bag. He stretched the opening for Russell to scc. A random mess of cables and other spare computer parts filled it.

Russell looked around at the rest of the cabin. He recalled his meeting aboard Gateway. "Exercise some subtlety," he said, echoing Alex's words. It had a nice ring to it. "Take a handful each, no more."

"Sir."

Time to consult with his counterpart above, Russell decided. "I'll be back. Conduct a thorough search, lads. I want a list."

The three men nodded in unison.

He took his time returning to his office, climbing the twenty flights of stairs to the top floor with no great hurry. The stairs always gave him time to think, and got his heart beating nice and fast.

Inside, he first went to his desk and removed an old camera. Setting the briefcase on his desk, Russell photographed it.

Next he powered up his antique terminal, transferred the picture to it, and dialed Alex Warthen.

It took some shouting before Gateway's graveyard shift agreed to wake their boss.

"Three in the bloody morning, this better be good," Alex said.

Russell sent the photo to Alex as he spoke. "I have the most exquisite woman down here. Snuck away to Hawaii with a scavenger crew. She's demanding to speak with Platz."

"Who is she?" Alex asked.

"Not sure yet. I was hoping you could help with that," Russell replied. "Are you near your computer?"

"I can be."

Russell struggled to keep his patience in check. "I've sent

you a picture of a briefcase the woman was carrying when we apprehended her."

"What's she look like?"

Russell closed his eyes, remembering the examination. "Medium height. Fit. Black hair. Of Indian descent, I'd guess. Very pretty. Small mole on her left ass cheek."

"Pardon me?"

Russell laughed. "She'd been outside Darwin. A full examination was required."

A brief pause from the other end. Russell could hear Alex activating his computer.

"Well," Alex said, "my guess is the woman is Tania Sharma, a scientist from Anchor Station."

"Long way from home," Russell said.

"The briefcase . . . looks like a standard secure model."

"There's a Platz logo on the bottom."

Alex took a moment to reply. "Tania and the old man are acquainted."

"Why would she be down here? Cavorting with smugglers outside the Aura—"

"That," Alex said, "is a damn good question. Maybe something to do with these power failures, and the subhuman outbreaks. If they're researching it on the sly, they must know something."

Russell ran his hand over the sleek object. "Maybe I can sell it back to the old prick. The girl, too."

Alex let out a long breath into the receiver.

How bloody annoying, Russell thought.

"I have a better idea," Alex said. "I'm going to send you down a small tracking device. I'll—"

"What good does that do me?" Russell asked.

"Hear me out," Alex said. "Platz is up to something. If we figure out what, we'll have the upper hand."

"We have the upper hand now. The case, and the woman."

"The woman is nothing," Alex said. "What's in the case, what she risked a trip to Hawaii for, that we must determine."

It made sense, Russell had to admit. "So we attach this device. Then what?"

"Let her go. I've got agents on every station. Sleepers. We'll see where she takes it and find out the details without tipping our hand."

Russell drummed his fingers on the case. He didn't like the idea of putting his playing cards in Alex's hand, but fostering a sense of teamwork might have advantages later. And sleeper agents? Alex had alluded to such a plant inside Nightcliff when they met before, and now he admitted to more. Russell wondered just how wide the net had been cast.

"Look," Alex said, "if Platz thinks we're on to him, the trail stops."

"Fine," Russell said. "Once the case is tagged, I'll let her go."

"Unmolested."

Russell laughed at that. "Unharmed. I have a reputation to keep."

Tania lost all track of time. She sat on the cold bench, shivering and naked, unable to focus her mind in any meaningful way.

Some time ago, hours it seemed, a nurse had come in. The old woman was very sweet, sickeningly so, and her hands were cold as ice. The lengthy, probing examination she performed would have been humiliating, repulsive, had Tania been able to bring herself to care.

In her mind she kept seeing the look on Samantha's face when she had emerged from that cursed building. The way Skyler's knees had buckled. They had lost one of their own, for a cause they knew nothing about.

Then she recalled the way Skyler had shouted and struggled in vain when they separated Tania from the others upon entering the infirmary. He'd punched a guard before they tackled him. Even after the loss she'd caused him, he still fought for her.

When the door finally opened again, Tania hardly noticed. Two men entered, one carrying a folded gray jumpsuit. She did not move. Instead she kept her eyes locked on her own reflection in the mirror. She pretended to be that woman, the one watching with numb disinterest. They lifted her to her feet and dressed her, guiding her legs into the stiff, scratchy cloth, using their hands more than necessary as they pulled the garment above her waist and chest.

A voice in her head screamed at her to fight them, to struggle, but she couldn't. There was no point.

She'd come to Earth, set her feet in the soil for the first time in a decade. She had seen trees and wildflowers, growing in unplanned natural beauty.

And she'd seen a strangely human face torn in two by a bullet.

She had seen death.

Growing up, she'd been taught the dangers of living in orbit. She had felt pride in knowing how brave they all were for existing so close to the void.

Ridiculous.

She knew real danger, now, and had been truly frightened for the first time in her life. The indignities she now suffered were nothing compared to what Jake must have gone through in the bowels of that building.

All to serve my theory, which I can't even tell them about.

The men finished dressing her. "Let's go, sweetheart. You're due at the climber port," one of them said. His voice sounded far away. "Back to Utopia, har har."

They led her through the stained halls of the miserable hospital and across the main yard of Nightcliff.

Out in the open, she sucked in the salty air and looked up at the sky. The soaring thread of the Elevator. The way home. The only way.

She heard a distant voice: her own, but far away, telling her to find Skyler. To tell him what his friend had died for, that she would make it mean something.

The voice faded.

If she had a chance to ask to speak with him, she missed it. Her captors loaded her into a passenger carrier and began the preparations to send it to space.

"The case you kept asking for," one of them said to her. He pushed the metallic briefcase into her hands.

Tania stared blankly at it.

"Crazy sheila," he added, under his breath.

Perhaps that's true, she thought. *Perhaps I've gone insane.* She pondered the idea while they attached the compartment to a climber.

She sat alone in the austere cylinder as it lurched onto the thread.

When Russell Blackfield entered the cell, goon squad on his heels, Skyler balled his fists. A fight was suicide, he knew. They were outnumbered and outgunned.

They were naked, too. That didn't help.

Skyler had been in tough situations with his crew plenty of times, but he couldn't remember being more uncomfortable. Eight hours they'd spent, the three of them, stuck in the small room without clothing.

"Quarantine," their jailers had said. "Clothes had to be burned, so sorry."

Screw it, odds be damned, Skyler thought. He was prepared for the consequences, except for one thing: He wanted to know where Tania was.

"Skyler Luiken, we meet again," Russell said.

Skyler bit his tongue and tried to hold the man's gaze. Russell's eyes, however, had gravitated to Samantha's bare chest.

"I would think," Russell said casually, "after eight hours in here, you'd have thought of something to say." His attention shifted slowly back to Skyler as he spoke.

Through clenched teeth, Skyler said, "Where's my other crew member?"

"She's part of your crew? You honestly expect me to fall for that?"

Skyler held his tongue.

"Or did you mean poor Jake, left behind in Hawaii—"

Samantha's punch flew so fast it caught everyone off guard. She connected squarely with Russell's jaw, knocking him clean off his feet.

He fell hard against the wall and grunted when his body hit the floor.

One of the guards jabbed Samantha in the stomach with the stock of his rifle. The wind left her lungs and she collapsed to one knee.

Skyler and Angus both surged forward.

"Enough!" Russell struggled to his feet, wiping blood from the corner of his mouth. "That was my fault. Sore topic. Loud and clear."

Samantha fought to control her breaths.

Russell shook his head, dazed. "Christ, woman. A hell of a hook you've got. If you need a new job, my door is open."

She spat in his face.

The man did not flinch. Wiping the spittle off, he said, "I'd like to know you better before we exchange bodily fluids."

Samantha drew herself up to her full, impressive height. The defiance in her eyes blazed, wild and raw.

"Seems I'd need a stool, too," Russell said, looking up at her. Some of the guards laughed. "Perhaps another time." He snapped his fingers at two nurses near the back of the group, and they came forward with fresh clothing.

Russell seemed to be waiting for them to dress, but Skyler made no effort to reach for the garments. Sam and Angus followed his example.

"Suit yourselves," Russell said. "Ah, no pun intended. You're free to go, cleared from pad four."

Skyler squinted at him. "What about—"

"The woman will remain here. House arrest, pending questioning."

"I want to see her."

"Denied."

Skyler opened his mouth to argue.

"I suggest," Russell said, "you stop there. Assuming you ever want to fly in my airspace again, or hitch a ride upstairs."

Skyler could feel the cold stare from Samantha without turning to her. He swallowed his words.

"Give them ten minutes to get dressed and leave, or throw them out," Russell said to his guards as he turned and left the room. In the doorway, he stopped and leveled a lewd gaze on

Samantha. "You have an open invitation for a rematch, any time," he said. "Clothing is optional, of course."

He left the room before Samantha could respond.

Nine and a half minutes later, the *Melville* lifted off.

The short flight to the old airport, two kilometers away, felt longer than the trip back from Hawaii.

Samantha had not spoken a word to him since the guards had escorted them from that dismal room. She stormed out the cargo door almost before the *Melville* settled on the tarmac, stomping toward the makeshift kitchen and bar down at Woon's hangar.

A stiff drink didn't sound like such a bad idea, but Skyler decided to unload the ship first. It would give Samantha time to settle down, if nothing else.

Truth be told, he needed time himself.

"Take the night off, Angus," he said to his pilot. "I'll do the postflight." He gave the craft a gentle pat.

Angus shrugged and made his own way toward Woon's tavern, head down and hands in his pockets.

It took hours for Skyler to run through the postmission checklist. Far longer than normal. He checked each engine even as they burped excess heat and spooled down. He checked the flaps and hovering thrusters, and visually inspected each ceramic tile on the underbelly for signs of cracks or wear.

He did a thorough job. The work stood between him and a collapse into self-pity.

Satisfied with the health of the ship, he turned his attention to the cargo bay. Tania's briefcase proved missing, of course. He had expected as much when they were taken into quarantine. Russell Blackfield would probably demand a healthy price for it, if he had any sense.

Surprisingly, the duffel bag full of other spoils remained on board. Lighter than he remembered, but there might still be enough inside to cover their spooling costs and drop rights.

Before leaving the ship, he noticed something else: a blank space, where the photograph he'd found in Japan had been. The image of a young Neil Platz, standing in front of the telescope. He wondered if it now graced Russell Blackfield's office wall.

Platz paid for the mission to the telescope, a place he helped build. Skyler couldn't wrap his mind around that. If a reason existed, it eluded him. *None of my business,* he thought, then dismissed the idea. The less he knew, the better. Part of him hoped that Platz would pull the contract with Prumble after this debacle. Life could return to a semblance of normal, minus one friend and sniper.

"Evening, Skyler," someone said.

Skyler turned to see a fellow scavenger captain ambling past. "Kantro, my friend."

"Heard about Jake," the man said. "He'll be missed."

Skyler nodded. He didn't want to talk about it. "I hope your day went better. Good scavenging out there?"

Kantro shrugged. "Aborted before we even stepped out. A whole mess of subs swarmed us. Newsubs, my crew is calling them. Never seen 'em so . . . organized."

"Same thing happened to us," Skyler muttered. The thought sent goose bumps along his arms. "Newsubs, eh?"

The other captain waved it off. "Maybe the bastards finally unionized," he said with a good-natured laugh. "See ya 'round, mate."

Skyler wandered inside, wrestling with the idea that the subhumans might be changing. That the behavior they'd witnessed in Hawaii might be widespread, the new norm. The idea chilled him to the core.

He wound up in his room, exhausted, lying on his bunk. When he closed his eyes the mission kept replaying in his mind. Memories of Jake. Tania, in her cell in Nightcliff. His imagination ran wild. Opening his eyes proved the only recourse.

Sleep would have to wait.

He pulled the blanket from his bed and wrapped it around his shoulders, picked up the first bottle he could find, and made his way to the roof.

The meager rooftop garden smelled of citrus and soil and rain. Skyler wandered through it and took stock of the plants sprouting there. They'd have plenty of tomatoes, papaya, and bananas from the look of it. Rambutan, too, which he shunned for its strange texture. The others could eat it. He dug out a small weed from beneath the lone starfruit tree and tossed it into the compost bin before continuing to his destination: a small patch of roof at the back of the hangar.

He spread the blanket out and sat. The noise of activity along the main runway barely reached this spot. He lay down, one arm behind his head, and watched the climbers inch their way toward the planets and stars that filled the clear sky above. A crescent moon shimmered in the heat near the horizon.

He drank for Jake, first.

The quiet one, devoted to his role as sniper. Everything he did seemed to be with the goal of improving his ability. Target practice, exercise, meditation. Once, on the return leg of a mission, he'd parachuted from the *Melville* over Darwin's eastern slum, the Maze, for no reason other than to see if he could find his way out. "If I'm not back by midnight, drinks are on me," he'd said. He made it with an hour to spare, let Skadz pour him a drink, and never once bragged about the accomplishment.

Next, Skyler drank for Tania.

He tried, hard, to imagine her being treated fairly by Blackfield. He tried harder not to imagine her alone, in her own decon room, subjected to the bastard's questions. Or worse.

The thought made him shiver, despite the balmy night. He drew another swallow from the bottle and let the warmth of the alcohol fill him from within.

For a time he toyed with the idea of going back, attempting to rescue her. But to what end? He'd never fly in Nightcliff's airspace again, and he couldn't exactly get Tania approved for a lift home, either. He couldn't imagine her living in the squalor of Darwin, cut off from her gleaming space station, forever.

At some point he drifted off. When he awoke, Samantha was sitting next to him. She held his bottle, dangling it from two fingers.

"Angus," she said with a slur, "passed out in Woon's kitchen." She erupted into a booming laugh, full of snorts and wheezing breaths. "Facedown! Middle of the sodding floor!"

Skyler propped up on his elbows and shook the fog from his head. "What time is it?"

"Fuck knows," Sam said. She tilted the bottle back and took a full gulp.

"Should we go get him?"

Samantha shook her head. "Woon threw a coat over him. Probably more comfortable than his cot."

They sat for a while without speaking. Skyler turned his attention to the night sky again. Far above, he could just make out the winking beacon of a climber. Looking lower, he scanned the checkerboard of lights, marking the few pockets in Darwin where electricity still flowed.

Lower still, he tracked along the fence line of the old airport. Shacks and tents had been erected right to the edge, a stark contrast to the weed-infested expanse within.

In the middle of the field of weeds, Skyler spotted an enormous rat, devouring some stolen morsel. He made the shape of a gun with his hand and pretended to fire at the rodent.

Samantha watched with grim fascination. "Jake coulda made that shot," she said.

"One time," Skyler said, "back during the Purge, Jake and I were sighting down on this crap little village near Weddell. A whole bunch of subs had overrun the place. But they were all spread out, not like that clan in Hilo. Just the two of us were out there, long recon, you see?"

He reached for the bottle and Sam handed it to him. She stretched her arms across her knees and laid her head down, looking sideways at Skyler.

"We were about a klick away, gone to ground on a hillside. Doesn't matter. Jake, he's studying the hell out of the place through his scope. I'm just trying not to piss my pants."

Sam chuckled. "Scared shitless, eh?"

Skyler waved her off. "No, my bladder really was about to rupture. We'd been hiding out there for, hell, six hours.

Then, all of a sudden, Jake tells me to prep the LAW rocket. He stretches his fingers like he's about to take a shot."

Watching him with droopy eyes, Samantha nodded.

"We're a klick out, remember. No backup. You weren't in the Purge, but you can guess how we immunes were used. Sent far and wide to scout things out, report their numbers and pack locations.

"Anyway, I'm about to piss myself. But I get the rocket tube up on my shoulder anyway." Skyler gulped again from the bottle, nearly empty now. "Without warning he fires. *Boom!* Sounds like lightning. Or thunder, whatever the hell. I'm looking at each sub in the village, waiting for one to drop. But none do."

"Fuck . . . he missed?"

"No. No, no. This is Jake we're talking about. Suddenly all the subs turn toward the center of the town. And then I hear it."

"What? Hear what?!" Sam asked.

"Church bells."

"The fuck?"

Skyler smiled at the memory. "Jake hit a bell in the church tower, size of a teakettle, from a klick out. The sound drew 'em like a swarm of cockroaches." He shivered, visibly. "I can still hear their screams. Not like yesterday. These were desperate, angry. The confused early herd in dire need of thinning. Anyway, the damn things poured into the old church at the center of town, through the doors and windows. And then I understood."

"Tell me!"

Skyler grinned wide. "I could see them, climbing the church tower, through a couple of small windows along its height. Tripping and falling over each other to find a fresh kill up at the bells."

"Oh, shit," Sam said, reaching the conclusion before he told it.

Skyler nodded. "I put a rocket into the base of the tower. The blast was terrific, but, Sam, when that tower collapsed . . ."

"Jesus," she whispered.

"Had to be at least fifty of them in there. The way he told the story, it was my heroics. But that's bullshit. He shot a bell from a kilometer away and sent those things to peace. One bullet."

"Efficient," Sam said.

"Maybe three crawled away, all broken and twisted," Skyler added. "Jake didn't even waste bullets on them. 'No need,' he said."

"The man was smooth, I'll give him that."

With a grunt, Skyler nodded. "Best part? We'd finally found something a church was useful for."

Samantha laughed from the depths of her belly. Guilt, driven by sorrow, eventually restrained her mirth.

Skyler lifted the bottle to the sky and drank half the remnants. He passed the remainder to Sam.

She poured it on the roof and hurled the empty bottle at the rat in the darkness.

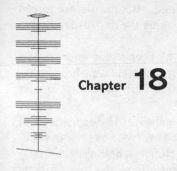

Chapter 18

THE KLAXON WAILED so loud Neil found it hard to think straight.

In every corner, in every room and hallway of the vast station, his staff suffered the same obnoxious noise.

"EVACUATE, EVACUATE!"

The synthetic voice boomed in between the long, droning alarm. The whole thing sounded like a parody, Neil thought. Something out of a bad science fiction movie from the golden age. Whoever designed the emergency systems had a sense of humor, that much was obvious.

He flipped the switch from "test" back to "normal."

"Let's hope we never have to listen to that again," he said into the handheld microphone. A few among the gathered staff laughed politely. Most shook their heads or worked their jaws to clear strained ears.

"Right," Neil said. "On that horrific note, I'll turn things over to my brother, Zane, for the evacuation rehearsal." He glanced right.

Zane stood close, an amiable grin on his jolly face, hands clasped in front of him. The dark blue business suit he wore matched his eyes. Though he was only two years younger than Neil, his hair still retained a lot of its original sandy blond color. The staff loved him, probably because he was perpetually in a good mood. He'd never shown the business acumen that Neil possessed and had long ago been relegated to simpler tasks—running charities, keeping the family home in order, and, after the disease forced them to relocate to orbit, managing the day-to-day operations aboard Platz Station.

Zane took the microphone. "It's been a year since our last drill," he said, "and in light of recent events, my brother has asked me to hold these more often. Perhaps he'll reconsider after that wonderful serenade."

Nervous chuckles from the audience. The appearance of multiple subhumans in orbit had everyone on pins and needles. Continued outages of the climbers, however brief, only fueled the growing unease. Neil offered the best smile he could muster. "I leave them in your capable hands," he said under his breath, and stepped back.

His brother launched into the details of the evacuation plan. Leads for each level were named, exit points reviewed. Neil listened to all this as he walked. He took his time, offering casual nods to everyone he passed. He saw excitement in their faces, despite the general anxiety. The evacuation rehearsal made a convenient diversion.

"This drill will simulate a hull rupture on the Earth-side levels," Zane's voice said over the address system. "As such, we will evacuate via the topside climber port."

Exactly as Neil suggested. A masked order, in fact. He cared little about station safety procedures. What he wanted from all this was a crew fresh with the knowledge of how to move *up* the Elevator on a moment's notice, to Hab-8, in case trouble came from below. From Nightcliff, from Earth.

"Going down with the ship, Mr. Platz?" a woman asked, walking with a group toward the nearby junction hall. They all smiled at the joke.

"Oh, was there an alarm? I didn't hear it," he said. They laughed and he offered a sly grin as he waved them off. "Carry on. This is serious business."

Before long he had the office to himself. The crew would be in the topside climber bay now, reviewing the process for activating the lifeboats and attaching them to the Elevator cord. Neil figured he had two hours of blissful quiet. More than enough time for what he intended to do.

Inside his office, he closed and locked the door. He went

to his safe and used a combination of thumbprint and numeric code to unlock it. When the heavy steel door swung open, Neil knelt down in front of a second safe tucked inside. An antique, purely mechanical, as small as a shoe box. No complicated electronics to fail, no need for some computer expert to have maintenance access.

He spun the dial from one side to the other, inputting the series of numbers. The combination hadn't been used in more than twelve years, yet it came easily to him.

A *click* as the lock disengaged. Neil closed his eyes and drew a lungful of air, then slowly released it. Indecision crept into his thoughts the instant he wrapped his fingers around the handle. After all, the contents had been secure all this time. No one but Neil knew the secret contained inside. Surely he could keep it, if only to honor the memory. Perhaps to study it, maybe even let the scientists have a look—

No. He hardened his resolve. It must be destroyed, and today. He should just take the entire safe and push it out an airlock. Let the truth drift for eternity in the vast, freezing void.

And yet his hand tilted, pulling the handle on the safe's door. It opened.

With a sigh, Neil reached inside and removed the only item within. A data cube, unmarked. Nothing outwardly special about it. He closed his fingers around the cool ceramic object.

One last look, he thought. *Then it's the heart of the sun for you.*

He held the cube in both hands as he walked to the sensory theater. It felt like a dream, he thought, to walk through the empty station. The place felt cold—creepy, even— without its inhabitants bustling about. He half-expected to see a schoolboy ride by on a tricycle. Or twin girls in matching blue dresses, hands entwined around the hilt of a bloody knife.

He chuckled. The laugh echoed in the empty hall and carried with it an immediate sense of guilt. The business at hand was nothing to joke about.

Neil put his focus back on the cube. If there were any ghosts in this place, he held them in his hands.

He stepped into the sensory theater and flipped the systems on. A semicircular red couch graced the center of the round room, surrounded by floor-to-ceiling screens, each capable of more resolution than the human eye could discern.

The crew treasured this room, and the vast library of entertainments stored on the station's array. New and old, from fully interactive sensory experiences in which the viewer could participate to the simple, passive, popcorn fare of centuries ago.

Neil perched himself on the edge of the cushioned red seat and placed the data cube into a port atop a sleek black pedestal.

The cube held only three recordings. Before Neil could entertain any more self-doubt, the system accessed the file and began automatic playback.

Dread and wonder began to build in him. He kept one hand on the cube, ready to rip it from the machine, and watched the events unfold for the last time.

An odd thing to see the world through a dead man's eyes.

The footage, from the tiny camera mounted on Sandeep Sharma's helmet, presented the scene from his perspective. It infuriated Neil, watching, that he could see everything except the man's face. No way to read the emotions there. No way to truly say goodbye, to say sorry. To see that hint of Tania in her father's eyes.

"If only you'd trusted me," Neil whispered.

The image showed the interior of a shuttle cockpit, crowded with gauges and colorful terminal screens. Sandeep sat at the controls, only his arms and the tops of his knees visible in the frame. He looked to his right, at a young Neil Platz in the navigator's seat, suited up in similar astronaut gear.

How I've aged, Neil thought. Forty-four years since that damned mission, and he felt every day of it. *The weight of the world has all but killed me.*

A bob of the camera as Sandeep nodded. The younger Neil flashed an eager grin and a thumbs-up.

The view returned to the cockpit and the forward-looking window. Still too far from the object for the camera to discern it, but Neil knew it was there. The idea of sitting through the event again, of watching Sandeep and his younger self see the object for the first time, the unchecked excitement in their faces and voices, disturbed him. He fast-forwarded the footage until they were right on top of the damned thing.

Foreshadow, they would dub it later, when they understood its significance. A ridiculous name, and yet so perfectly apt. It was the first of the Builders' ships, parked in orbit almost twenty-eight years before the Darwin Elevator arrived. Undetected by a population turned inward, a population apathetic to the overdue promises of science and bogged down by resurgent religions.

The rest of the planet thought the Darwin Elevator to be a surprise arrival, the "first-contact" event for the history books. Some noted the absurd luck of the Platz family, owners of the land in Nightcliff and so many industries that would be key to the exploitation of the Elevator. Consumed with awe of the alien device, the populace largely ignored such questions, and in time those voices retreated to the lunatic fringe.

Neil knew the truth. Sandeep did, too, until his demise. The only other person Neil ever told was his own father, the true business tycoon. The old man convinced the two young astronauts to keep the discovery secret, and together they began to shift Platz Industries toward taking full advantage of the finding.

All because of that bloody room, Neil thought.

He fast-forwarded again. Through the portion of the recording where Sandeep flew them past Foreshadow Station for the first time. A smooth black sphere tucked at the end of a mottled conical hull. Exotic materials, never understood. Neil sped through the hours of footage as they circled the object, until he reached the portion where their robotic probe touched the device. An accident, Sandeep's excitement pushing the small vehicle too fast. And yet it started it all.

Neil slowed the footage to normal speed. He heard his own excited voice as the door opened. Sandeep urged caution, but young Neil demanded they push forward.

The probe drifted inside. Neil fast-forwarded again, to the part where he and Sandeep entered the station themselves, in space suits, to see it with their own eyes.

Foreshadow. The cursed room at the heart of it.

Six-sided, each "wall" nearly fifteen meters tall. Four were blank, then. Two had strange murals, vividly displayed as if painted with light, but not like a terminal screen. These had a physical nature to them. Neil felt he could reach right in and feel the things shown there.

The first mural they recognized immediately. It depicted the station itself. *Foreshadow*.

The next mural depicted something astonishing. Neil paused the video to study it again, for the last time.

A simple image. Alien in style, yet unmistakable. Earth, at the bottom—a portion of it, at least: Northern Australia. Darwin.

And jutting from that spit of land was a simple line, stretching all the way to the top of the mural, ending in a black oval.

He listened with mild amusement as his younger self and Tania's father debated what it meant. They would think, for the next twenty-seven years, that the message was for them to build the device. That the mural was some kind of blueprint. A space elevator, long the dream of space enthusiasts and science fiction writers, long the butt of jokes by engineers and physicists.

They realized even then that such technology would take many, many decades to develop and deploy, and yet they would pursue the goal, the resources of Platz Industries at their disposal. The mural told them it could be done, and that was motivation enough.

They were still frustratingly far from even starting construction when the alien Elevator arrived. Only then did they realize what the mural meant: a foreshadowing. A message to whoever discovered the six-sided chamber, announcing what was to come.

Knowledge of the future, a bloody powerful thing to have. Enough to drive men insane.

Neil and his father had sought to guard the knowledge with extreme prejudice. Sandeep would be pulled along with the plan, but never fully on board. He harbored the desire to tell the world. A desire that festered until it became something twisted.

Stupid, stupid . . .

Fast-forward. The exploration of the station sped by, until the recording ended.

Another followed, taken thirty years later. Their return, a tough mission to arrange. It had been Sandeep's idea. There were six panels, he'd pointed out, and only two with images. Perhaps with the Elevator's arrival . . .

He was right. Neil skimmed the footage until the part where he and Sandeep entered the mural chamber again.

The third panel was lit. Neil still remembered the rush of excitement that coursed through his entire body upon seeing it. They held in their hands perhaps the most powerful thing any human ever had: foresight.

Neil found he couldn't pause the video here. He couldn't stare at that cursed image any longer than necessary.

Such a simple pictograph. So obvious now what it meant, so damned confusing back then. Neil sighed. If only they'd figured it out. So many lives could have been saved. Not all, no, but many. Millions.

But they didn't understand. The third mural, almost identical to the second, showed Earth at the bottom. Darwin, and the Elevator, but with a critical difference.

A vague, ghostly column stretched the length of the cord. Iconic depictions of strange buildings crowded the ground within the column. Disks were spaced evenly along the cord itself, all the way to the top. All within the column.

Nothing existed outside that ethereal shape. Only blackness.

They'd thought it to be another guidance. Build a grand city around the Elevator. Build space stations. The rest of the planet didn't matter now, so it had been left out of the picture.

The version of Neil in this video, now past sixty, quipped how they were well along this path. Darwin had blossomed since the Elevator arrived, and it showed no signs of slowing. Platz Industries had already begun construction of a number of space stations, just like the mural showed.

They would understand, shortly after SUBS began to sweep the planet. When they realized Darwin was safe, in an eight-kilometer circle that stretched to the top of the Elevator. A cylinder, with blackness outside. So goddamn obvious, after the fact.

The mural had been a warning. *Contain yourselves here, puny humans. A purge cometh.*

A tear rolled down Neil's cheek and he wiped it away with an angry swipe. The end of the footage loomed like a sentencing. He knew he should stop here. Why suffer such torture again? Nothing good had ever come of it.

One last look. So I never forget.

The third video segment began, twelve years after the last. Just weeks after the SUBS outbreak. The footage began like the others, except this time the passenger seat was empty. Sandeep had taken the shuttle, alone. The beginning of his swan song.

"Billions are dead because of your greed," he'd raged earlier that day, over the radio. Neil, safe in Darwin, had listened in silence. "And *still* you want to go on! To keep the future for yourself! Can't you see it is a curse? I will not go along, not anymore. The world, whatever's left of it, will know the truth. Tania will know the truth!"

Neil wondered, for the thousandth time, if he should have gone along on the mission. Maybe if he'd been there with him, in person, he could have talked sense into the man. But he'd asked Sandeep to make the trip to Foreshadow alone that time. There was too much chaos on the ground, too much to do.

Faced with Sandeep's threats, Neil did the only thing he could think to do. He'd sent the remote commands needed to shut down the tiny outpost station. The air processors stopped. The data feeds to ground died. Soon Sandeep would, too. Neil could claim a malfunction and that would be that.

The footage rolled on, like a bullet train heading toward a ravine. Neil couldn't bring himself to fast-forward now. He sank deep into the couch and watched.

Sandeep took the only action he could: He went to the shuttle and powered it up. It would buy him air, and thus time. He sat there for a while before launching. He could have made a desperate run for the Elevator, to dock with one of the stations there.

Alas, no. Sandeep had only one thing on his mind, and it wasn't survival. Reason had long left him. He took the shuttle straight to Foreshadow, suited up, and began construction of his bomb.

A simple device. Crude, yet ultimately effective. Compressed fuel canisters, a clever detonator made from parts yanked out of the shuttle's cockpit. For the next hour Sandeep went back and forth, from the shuttle to the mural chamber, bringing the components and connecting them.

And with maddening, deliberate care, he kept his gaze away from the fourth mural. Above all else, he didn't want Neil to know what image displayed there.

Neil had watched this part of the video a dozen times, frame by frame, trying to catch a glimpse. But only a tiny portion ever came into view, enough to know the fourth panel had indeed lit up, but nothing more.

Finally ready, Sandeep rested. He sat for a while and stared at his makeshift explosive. Then, at the end, he removed a grease pen from his utility pack and wrote a note on the side of one fuel canister. He drew out the block letters with calm deliberation and then stared at it, making sure the video caught his words.

I DO THIS TO END YOUR MADNESS, NOT MINE
YOU HAVE THE BLOOD OF THE EARTH ON YOUR HANDS

Static, then.

The deed was done. Foreshadow Station, the first of the

Builders' vessels, became nothing more than a cloud of debris expanding into the emptiness of space, or into the atmosphere to burn up.

No record existed of the fourth panel. No possible way to ever see the fifth or sixth. Neil carried only the knowledge of *when* the events would occur. The schedule, mapped out with simple markings between the murals. Earth's orbit around the sun as a constant, shown in multiples and then fractions. Sandeep worked out the pattern: each event a 0.42 reduction in time from the last. Neil had spent the last year trying to coax Tania into figuring out the pattern on her own, lest he be forced to admit his insight into the plan.

Neil glanced at the data cube, and the printed label on the side. Numbers, random to anyone else, but to him they laid out the time between each of the six events.

$$27.86, 11.70, 4.91, 2.06, 0.87$$

Twenty-seven plus years between Foreshadow and the Elevator. Almost twelve before SUBS arrived. The five-year gap since then arriving imminently.

Neil had yet to wrap his head around the meager two years they would get before the fifth event, and not even a single trip around the sun before the finale.

He alone carried the Builders' timeline, like a one-ton boulder shackled to his ankle. That and the knowledge that he'd killed Sandeep. He'd murdered Tania's father. And now, in a twist of fate that chewed away at his gut, she was helping to fill in the blanks left behind by her father's actions. He'd even sent her out to Hawaii, among the subhumans. He'd asked her to risk her life to discover what he already knew, simply to let someone else figure out the schedule. To earn valid pretense to act more deliberately, to get a head start.

Sandeep had failed, in that sense. Neil's madness, if the term applied, never abated. He felt more thirst than ever to know what the Builders would do next.

The future, *his* future, depended on it.

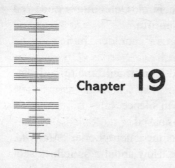

Chapter 19

WHEN THE COUNTDOWN ended, nothing happened. The ship should have fallen out and away—a backward swan dive from one hundred kilometers.

"Where's my release?" Skyler asked.

They were well above the atmosphere, yet the *Melville* remained firmly attached to the climber.

Angus reached above his head and toggled the release-readiness switch. Twice, and then a third time. Despite showing green, nothing happened. "Canceling the push-away," he said. "Malfunction?"

"Jesus. Ours?"

"Has to be theirs. We're green on this side."

Skyler leaned forward, trying to scan the cockpit displays for errors that Angus had missed. Ultimately Gateway had final control over release. A safety mechanism, to prevent the ship from separating too early, or too late. The indicator from their side showed green as well. "Maybe that power blip earlier caused it?"

Angus shrugged. Hours ago, at the start of the ascent, the climber car had stalled for a few seconds. Nightcliff control had said, in a pointedly worried tone, not to worry.

The intercom crackled. "What the fuck, guys?" Samantha said through the speaker.

Skyler elbowed it, forcing it to the off position.

In the pilot's seat, Angus held up a hand. They could both hear the voice through their headsets.

"*Melville,* this is Gateway control. Detecting a code red failure in the primary latch. Confirm."

Skyler put a hand on Angus's shoulder, indicating he would handle it.

"Control, this is *Melville.* Confirmed, we're still attached."

They waited thirty seconds in silence.

"Did they hear you?" Angus asked.

"Control," Skyler said into the microphone, "*Melville.* Confirm primary latch failure. How about a switch to secondary?"

"*Melville,* there is only the primary," came the voice.

"Why the hell is it called 'primary' then?" Skyler muttered.

An uncomfortable minute passed.

"*Melville,*" came the voice, "we have to bring you on up to Gateway to troubleshoot."

Angus turned in his seat to look directly at Skyler. His eyebrows arched so high, they almost disappeared under his helmet.

"Control, repeat please. You're bringing us up there?"

"Affirmative, *Melville.*"

Skyler grinned. "Copy. How about a grand tour while we're there, eh?"

"Negative," the voice said. "You will remain on board at all times."

"How long is this repair going to take?" he asked.

Another long delay. "Unknown," they came back with, after a few moments.

The possibility that the mission might end before it started tugged at Skyler. More than a week had passed since the return from Hawaii with no news, and no new requests, from their benefactor.

Skyler had tried, twice, to get information on Tania's status. The guards at the Nightcliff gate turned him away, though he suspected they didn't know anything. A crane operator, whom Skyler found in a hookah bar not far from the fortress, was friendly enough and, after a small bribe, willing to ask around. He didn't come back the next day as promised.

Then Prumble had received a specific order from Platz for a set of spare filtration units that were, hopefully, sitting in a long-abandoned warehouse in Abu Dhabi. The mission came as a welcome break in the monotony, and Skyler figured Prumble could ask about Tania when the goods were ultimately delivered.

Samantha opened the cockpit door and floated halfway inside. "What the hell's going on?"

"We're stuck," said Angus.

"No shit. Takai looks like he's going to piss himself back here."

"Not now, Sam," Skyler said.

It took another hour for the climber to reach Gateway. A pair of robotic arms extended from the inner ring and began to unload the cargo containers attached.

Skyler and Angus watched as two workers, in full space-walk gear, drifted out from an airlock just above the main cargo bay. They floated past the *Melville*'s canopy and disappeared from view.

After twenty minutes of silence, the radio crackled to life. "*Melville,* Gateway. Clamp's frozen in the locked position. Going to take about eighteen hours to fix."

Skyler shook his head. "No can do, Gateway. We're not outfitted for an extended stay. Not enough air."

"We will extend a transfer tube."

"No airlock for it. We're only designed to drop from the Van Allen."

Another long pause on the other end. "All right, *Melville.* We're going to disconnect the whole climber section and bring it and your ship inside. We can do the work in here."

"We're supposed to stay in here for eighteen hours?" Skyler said.

A different voice came over the air. "Without proper decontamination, you must remain—"

"Decon us then," he said. "Nothing we haven't been through before."

"God," Angus said, "not that again."

Another long period without a reply. Then, "You and your

crew will be under escort, and must remain in Section B. You will leave all weapons and contraband on board."

"Section B," Skyler said. "Sounds thrilling."

Before long, the *Melville,* with a large portion of the climber attachment, was tucked safely inside one of the giant cargo loading docks. After thirty minutes of waiting for the huge room to pressurize, the crew received permission to exit the ship.

A man in a yellow hazard suit and protective mask greeted them. He led them through a tunnel to the outer edge of the station. Gravity slowly returned to normal as they traveled toward the rim.

At the entrance to Decontamination, the man directed Samantha to a separate medical area. She made a rude gesture behind her back as she walked away.

"This way, please," the man said to Skyler, Angus, and Takai.

Skyler thought the contrast between here and Nightcliff couldn't be sharper. Clean white walls, air that didn't churn the stomach, and a professional staff.

"Please disrobe," the man said, "and enter through there. I'll have your clothing disinfected."

Skyler followed the instructions silently. Angus and Takai followed his example. The door led to a narrow industrial shower. Takai made his way into the room last, and the moment the door closed all three were inundated with hot water from nozzles on the ceiling. The liquid smelled like it contained additional chemicals.

Under the warm water, Skyler began to relax. He tried to remember the last hot shower he'd taken, but came up with nothing. "I could get used to this," he said.

Angus grunted agreement.

Decontamination went by much faster compared to the medieval methods in Nightcliff. Drying himself, Skyler wondered if Tania was still down there, and how she fared. There had been no word of her fate since Skyler and crew were released eight days earlier.

An idea came to him, as part of a daydream. He could

deliberately incur another inspection and thus another trip through the fortress. He saw himself staging a breakout, rescuing the gorgeous doctor, fleeing into the danger and chaos of the Maze. The brigand hero and his dark princess, escaping the madman's castle—

"You lover boys enjoy the shower?" Sam asked as they exited the medical center.

The daydream faded. "Sam! Hardly recognized you all cleaned up."

She grabbed her crotch and squeezed like a rugby captain. "They've got a tavern here. How cool is that?"

Skyler turned to their escort. A true guard now, wearing a black security uniform, armed with some kind of stun gun. "Is that in Section B?"

"Yes," said the man.

"Well, lead on then."

They passed through the wide reception room. Skyler continued to marvel at the cleanliness of the place. Compared to the run-down state of Darwin, Gateway looked like it had been built yesterday. Skyler had risked his life many times to find spare parts for places like this. Seeing it in person gave him an odd sense of pride.

Angus kept the guard's ear busy as they walked. Skyler fell back a few paces to be alongside Samantha. "Keep your ears open," he muttered. "Might as well try to drum up some business while we're stuck here."

She stifled a laugh, shaking her head. "Never a boring mission with you in charge."

"What, this is my fault?"

She looked down her nose at him. "Skyler, I'm in orbit. First time, probably last. I'm going to have a drink, in orbit. Relax, in orbit. You handle the business, in orbit. Sound good?"

Picking up her pace, she moved ahead to walk with Angus.

When they reached the bar, things did relax. Angus and Samantha eventually wore down their guard and convinced him to have a drink.

Skyler took a table on the far side of the crowded room. Takai joined him.

"I think," Skyler said over a truly delicious cider, "you should head back to the ship. Offer to help with the repair, or say you're uncomfortable in here. Something. I'm not happy with them crawling all over it."

"Agreed," Takai said.

"Trick will be getting word back to us, if something is—"

"Skyler Luiken?"

A middle-aged man approached their table, flanked by two others too grim to be there for leisure.

"That's me," Skyler said.

He leaned in close and dropped his voice. "I represent Neil Platz. He'd like to have a word with you."

Skyler searched for deception in the man's face, and found none. He looked to the bar. Sam and Angus were laughing with their supposed escort. "Here? We've got a chaperone."

"I wouldn't worry about that," the man said. "Platz is in his office. It's a short walk."

"My crew?"

"They should remain here," he said, leaving no room for debate.

Skyler and Takai exchanged a glance. "You'll be okay?"

Takai shook his head. He kept his eyes on Skyler's.

Skyler frowned and turned to the man. "Thing is, there's a problem with our ship, and we need to be ready—"

He leaned in close. "The business with the latch?"

Skyler said, "Yes, that."

"The latch is fine," he said under his breath. "We needed an excuse to get you up here. Let's not waste any more time, eh?"

Skyler hesitated.

"Your ship will be fine."

"What does Platz want with me?"

The man looked Skyler up and down. "Wondering that myself," he said. "Shall we?"

The three men led Skyler from the crowded bar to a junction hallway that he assumed linked Section B to the "upper" sections. They stayed behind and directed Skyler to walk ahead.

A woman greeted him at the other end.

From the gray in her short hair, Skyler put her age at fifty. Still, her tight jumpsuit showed a muscular, lithe figure.

"Kelly," she said, extending a hand. "Kelly Adelaide. Though some call me the Ghost."

Skyler shook it. "Interesting title. What's your role in this organization?"

"Whatever delicate tasks Neil needs done."

Skyler grinned. "How's that going for you?"

The hint of a smile crept into the corners of her mouth. "I'm a busy woman. Where's the guard they assigned to you?"

"Drinking," Skyler said, "with the rest of my crew."

She nodded and led him through a series of corridors. When the silence went from polite to awkward, Skyler asked, "Does Platz own this station?"

"Not anymore. Though he does 'own' Section H, keeps it as a satellite office. The rest is under the jurisdiction of the council."

"Doesn't he lead the council?"

She cast him a sidelong glance. "He tries."

Skyler considered that. "Why'd he give up control in the first place?"

"Ask him yourself," she said. "We're here."

A large pair of double doors opened to reveal the famous face of Neil Platz.

An image, ten years old, burst into Skyler's mind. Posters and billboards, plastered all over Darwin, kindly reminding the citizens that Neil toiled away, up above their heads, growing crops and manufacturing the things they needed to survive.

It wasn't long before his iconic face became vilified. Food shortages, faulty product, and numerous other miscues made him public enemy number one on the ground.

"Mr. Luiken, a pleasure." He extended a hand.

"Mr. Platz, uh . . . sir."

" 'Your excellence' is preferred."

Skyler faltered in his handshake. "Your ex—"

"A joke, young man. Everyone calls me Neil."

His legendary charisma exceeded Skyler's expectations. "Neil, then. Call me Skyler."

"Dutch?"

"Yes. From Utrecht."

Neil smiled broadly. "The Flying Dutchman, eh?"

"That never gets old."

The elder man laughed. "Join me for a drink," he said. He turned and began to walk, expecting Skyler to follow.

"It's your show," Skyler said.

They left the entryway and entered the main portion of the orbiting office complex. The ceiling soared much higher here compared to other portions of the station. *A shocking waste of precious living space,* Skyler thought. Golden light bathed it, casting a strange yellow pall. Much different than the blue LEDs everywhere else.

Platz followed Skyler's gaze to the display above them. "Natural sunlight, reflected in. One of my favorite things. Come," he said.

They passed through another door into a lounge area. Two steps led down to the sunken center of the room, where a pair of couches faced each other.

Skyler felt his stomach lurch at the sight of the far wall, or lack thereof. Earth dominated the view, slowly spiraling below them due to the rotation of the space station.

"If the view gives you vertigo, I can close the blinds," Neil said.

Skyler shook his head. "I was surprised to see guards carrying firearms. How thick is the glass?"

Neil puffed with pride. "It's no ordinary glass. A borosilicate variant. Manufactured here in orbit, in my zero-g factories. It would take a tank shell to rupture it."

"And the walls?"

"Multilayer Kevlar and ceramic fabric, woven with our proprietary technique."

"Proprietary?" Skyler said. "You have no competition."

"Not at the moment, no."

Skyler bit back the desire to argue with the man. It had never occurred to him that Platz would still be thinking like a businessman, given the state of humanity. "Amazing," he managed to say.

"A luxury, of course. It's a hell of a thing keeping the temperature in check." He pointed to special vents along the edge of the ceiling.

Skyler raised a hand and felt warm air blowing. It had the sterile smell of a hospital room.

"Have a seat," Neil said. He placed himself on one of the two couches. Skyler took the other.

"Sorry for the business with your ship."

Skyler spread his hands. "You could've just invited me."

"Not really, I'm afraid," Neil said. "Things are . . . complex, right now."

"No kidding," Skyler said. "Look, before we go any further, have you arranged for Ms. Sharma's release?"

"Tania? Release from what?"

Skyler leaned far back into the plush fabric of the couch. "She's okay then."

Neil perched himself on the edge of his seat, confusion filling his face. "I'm afraid I don't understand."

"We were detained," Skyler said, "at Nightcliff. After the mission. You didn't know?"

Platz shook his head.

"They said . . ." Skyler had to start over. "Blackfield, that son of a bitch, said that they were going to keep her for questioning. I thought she was still there."

Platz took a deep breath. He stood and went to the window. Silhouetted against the spinning planet, he said, "Tania has told me nothing of this." His tone was grave. "I hope she . . ." His voice trailed off.

Skyler kept quiet, watching the famous man as he stood and stared at the blue orb of Earth. For his own part, he felt as if an enormous weight had been removed from his shoulders. Tania had returned, unharmed.

"All she told me was that the mission was successful," Platz said. "She was unusually terse, in hindsight."

"I thought maybe you brought me here to try to plan a rescue," Skyler said.

Platz turned from the window and moved to a cupboard

on the wall opposite Skyler. He opened a panel and began to prepare two drinks. "No," he said, "thank God that won't be necessary." He returned to his seat on the couch and set the glasses on the low wooden table between them. "I owe you a great deal of thanks for bringing her back safely. She's the key to . . . well, she's critical to my operation."

Skyler took a sip of his drink and let the liquid warm his mouth. He took his time swallowing. "I take it this new mission to find your fancy water filters is a ruse?"

Neil placed his fingertips on the table. "Something more urgent has come up. I needed to discuss it with you in person."

"I work through Prumble."

"There's no time."

Skyler decided the moral stand could wait. He'd cut Prumble in no matter what Platz said. "Go on."

Neil's face turned grave. "You're aware of the sporadic power failures on the cord?"

Skyler nodded. "One happened on our way up. Good thing the climbers are designed to grip when power is cut; otherwise it's a short trip back to the bottom."

"Indeed," Neil said. He stood with a sigh and crossed to stand at the window. For a moment he said nothing, as if caught up in the view of Earth. "You may have also heard rumors of SUBS appearing within the Aura."

A pit opened in Skyler's gut. He remembered the girl, lying dead on the ground outside the airport, her father claiming a new infection. "I'd hoped they were nothing more than rumors."

Neil half-turned, considering the response, before returning to the view. Whatever the man wanted, Skyler realized he couldn't make eye contact.

"We noticed something," Skyler offered, "in Hawaii. The subs were acting different. Grouped in a big clan, working together. Other crews have reported the same thing. Newsubs, the scavengers are calling them."

"That's . . . interesting," Neil said. "Related, maybe. Bottom line is that something is wrong with the Aura."

The pit in Skyler's gut grew deeper. His mouth went dry.

Neil continued. "We had a subhuman get loose aboard one of the farm platforms."

"In orbit?" Skyler asked. "That isn't possible."

"So we all thought. The Aura is . . . malfunctioning, it seems. Or being tampered with."

Skyler stared at the back of the legendary man. The blue and white marble of Earth spun gently, far below. Always so peaceful in appearance, no matter what ailed it.

"You're going to fix it, Skyler."

Skyler coughed. "What the hell can I do about it?"

"More than you think," Neil said. He finally returned to his seat, then took a peanut from a bowl on the table and popped it into his mouth. "Contrary to public knowledge, the Elevator itself does not generate the Aura. It's more like a broadcast antenna."

Skyler went still. He sensed that very few people knew what he was now being told.

"The Aura is actually created by a . . . machine . . . deep below the surface, below the end of the cord itself."

"I had no idea."

"It's a guarded secret," Neil said with a wave of his hand. "We explored down there, back when the Elevator arrived. A shaft was dug to ease access. Poked around for a while but eventually decided the object was another anchor, like the shell ship. Deadweight."

"What changed your mind?"

"SUBS broke out," Neil said. "Didn't take long to realize the Elevator offered safe haven. We sent a team back to the bottom, to see if the Aura extended the entire way, and they found the object was no longer inert. In fact it was generating quite a lot of heat."

"Switched on," Skyler said to himself. "Maybe it's switching off, now."

"Quite right."

Skyler ran a hand through his hair, buying time to think. "Why aren't you still studying it? Send a team back there."

"That's where you come in."

"Me?"

Neil held a hand out, motioning Skyler to be patient. "A

decision was made, five years ago, to seal the place off. As control of Nightcliff, and thus our access to the place, shifted to authorities on the ground, it became clear to me that it would be better if nobody was going down there and doing any tinkering with it."

"They might break it," Skyler said, nodding. "Cause a malfunction."

Neil's eyebrows slowly rose. He looked at Skyler as if he'd never seen him before. As if the comment marked a revelation. The expression faded. "Which brings us to our present situation."

"Doesn't answer my question, though. Why us?"

"If this is being caused by some malcontents trying to break the thing, I don't need scientists down there, I need people who can stop them."

"I see where this is going," Skyler said.

Neil shook his head. "There's more. It could truly be a malfunction. The Aura generator is, itself, outside the Aura, which makes it complicated for most of us to visit. Your crew, on the other hand . . ."

"What do you expect us to do, exactly?"

"For now, go down there and have a look around. It's information we need. Look for . . . anything. Signs of decay or failure. Malfeasance."

"We're not scientists," Skyler said.

"What you are is immune. And you understand the business end of a gun. You can go in quietly and stay awhile. You can take care of saboteurs, if needed. You can look around, if not. Any team I send will be detained by Blackfield."

Skyler glanced out the window at the planet below. "Is all this related to the data cubes we went out to retrieve?"

"No," Neil said.

Skyler figured he had little to lose by challenging the man. Worst case, he'd get thrown out and sent back to Earth, where he could return to a regular routine. Business as usual. He decided to push. "You're lying."

Neil Platz stared at Skyler for a long moment.

I'm lying, too, Skyler thought. Business could never go back to "usual" now.

The man eased back into the cushions of his couch and folded one leg up over the other. He spread his arms out along the back of the seat. "The truth is, we're not sure yet."

"What was on those data cubes?"

He looked down at the fabric of the couch, running his hand over it. "I'm not at liberty to discuss—"

"Look, if you want my help, I need to know what the hell is going on. I already lost one of my crew over this, and whatever payment you plan to offer now won't cover *that*."

Neil slowly closed, then opened, his eyes. "I'm very sorry. I had no idea."

"He knew the risks, but his sacrifice still holds."

Platz stood again and walked to the window, his steps heavy this time, and slow. "What would you say to living up here?"

The words hung in the air. Most people in Darwin dreamt of being lifted from the squalor to a life in orbit, yet few ever were. The first problem was simply one of living space; there was no room, unless someone else got kicked out, or died. Even then, the children of existing Orbitals took precedence.

The second reason had to do with the quality of the person. Most of Darwin's population could dream of ascending all they wanted, but it wouldn't change the fact that they had nothing to offer. No applicable education, no skill set to bring along. With so little space, the last thing needed in orbit was deadweight.

"I'm hardly the right stock," Skyler said.

Platz spread his hands wide. "On the contrary. I need people like you. Leaders. Fighters."

"I'm not much of a leader. But fighters, what for?"

Neil ran a hand over his mouth, as if trying to take the words back. "What fighters do."

Skyler shook his head. "Isn't that Alex Warthen's job?"

"*Loyal* fighters, Mr. Luiken."

Skyler turned to the giant window made from exotic materials. "You're really going to wage a war? In this place?"

"War . . ." Neil paused. "I just need to protect my interests. Present and future."

"What about my crew?"

"Of course, they could come, too." He downed the contents of his glass. "But first . . ."

"First the Aura."

"The Aura, yes. By the time you've reported back, Tania will have completed her analysis of the Japan and Hawaii data. I promise you, once I have more information, I'll explain everything."

Skyler picked up his drink and took another sip. It had a spicy but pleasant kick to it. "Assuming I can get my crew to go along, how do we get into this shaft below Nightcliff?"

"The primary entrance is in the basement of the climber port, but it's been sealed permanently."

"Primary . . ."

"Which implies a second, yes."

Skyler stifled a laugh. *Not always.*

The old man turned and leaned against the glass. "You're aware of my old family home within Nightcliff's walls? Good. Wasted on long-term storage now, I'm told. There's an access tunnel from the basement that leads into the silo. It's well hidden, but I'll give you access. Go in, snoop around, then report back to me. Your friend Prumble has a paired comm."

"How do I get into Nightcliff itself?"

"You're the resourceful one. Figure something out."

A loud knock came from the door, and the woman named Kelly entered.

"I asked for no interruptions," Neil said.

Her face looked flushed. "Something's wrong down at the bar."

Skyler stood up.

"Warthen's men stormed the place," Kelly said between breaths. "There was a fight, shooting," she said, the words tumbling out.

"My crew," Skyler said. He went for the exit.

"Wait!" Neil shouted. "Dammit. Kelly, go with him."

"What should I do?" she asked.

"Keep him out of their hands. We're not done—"

Skyler raced out the door, and Neil's voice faded.

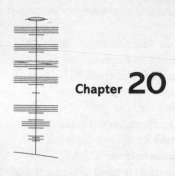

Chapter 20

ALARMS WAILED AS Skyler rushed toward the commotion at Ten Backward.

He had no plan, no weapon.

The station's usual dim blue lighting had been augmented with spinning red beacons at nearly every corner.

Sucking in breaths, his heart pounding from exertion, he reached the main hallway that spanned the entire torus of Section B and paused to gather his senses.

Beyond, just before the point where the hall curved out of view, was the tavern.

He could see a platoon of security guards splayed out in front, crouched behind whatever cover they could find. At least one body lay at the center of the floor inside the room. Skyler only saw the legs, but the clothing was unmistakable: the flight suit he and his crew wore.

One of the security guards glanced Skyler's way. "The other one! Behind us!"

The frightened guard raised a weapon, a gun unlike any Skyler had seen before.

Someone grabbed Skyler from behind and pulled him through a doorway on his left.

Inside was a narrow passage lined with hundreds of pipes and utility panels. Kelly pressed him against the wall.

"Let me go," Skyler said. "My crew is in there!"

"Your crew is captured," she replied, "or worse." Her fingers danced across a keypad on the wall. The door locked.

Outside, Skyler could hear the muffled sound of boots on the hard floor.

"Seal off this level," someone said from the other side of the door, followed by a symphony of footfalls.

"Dammit," Kelly said. "We need to get back to Section H. Platz has a shuttle—"

"I'm not going fucking anywhere. *Let go!*"

Her eyes darted back and forth, calculating the options. "What about your ship? Can you fly it?"

"Sod the damn ship. I've got to help them—"

Kelly gripped him by the chin. Her hand was rough and strong as a vise. "Forget your crew! They killed one of Warthen's men. There's nothing you can do—"

They both jumped as something slammed hard into the door from the other side. The guards, trying to break it down.

Kelly shifted her grip to his forearm. "Your choice. Stay here and end up dead or in jail, just like your crew. Your ship will be forfeit. Or flee with your craft and regroup. Fight another day. This is just the beginning, Skyler."

Another smash, even louder. Skyler heard straining metal and knew the door wouldn't last.

The logic in her plan increased with each passing second.

"Fine. Let's go," he said.

She wasted no time, sprinting along the utility tunnel that snaked through the station in a bizarre assortment of twists and turns. Skyler fought to keep his despair in the back of his mind, and did everything he could to keep up.

At a junction, she stopped and checked all directions. Behind them, somewhere, they heard shouting, and boots on the hard floor.

Kelly removed a small, sleek device from her belt. On top it had a single button and two metal prongs protruding from it. "Take this," she said, handing it to Skyler. "Good for one use only, I'm afraid."

He didn't complain, and accepted the offered weapon. "What about you?"

She ignored him and kept moving. They took a right turn, continuing at her blistering pace.

Skyler almost ran into her when she stopped in the middle of the hall. She opened a bright yellow box mounted to the wall, revealing an assortment of emergency tools. She removed two pipe wrenches and a small utility blade.

One wrench she handed to Skyler. It was nearly half as long as his arm, and satisfyingly heavy.

"Beggars can't be choosers," she said.

"Agreed." He slipped the small stun gun into his belt.

Extending the utility razor, Kelly went to work cutting a bundle of wire along the wall.

"How do you know all this?" Skyler asked.

She kept working on the wires. "I used to lurk here. Four years, off and on, back when things were a little less organized. Keeping an eye on things for Neil."

Skyler grunted his approval. "He's got quite a diverse operation."

"Grab my belt," she said as the bundle started to give.

"What?"

"My belt. Quick!"

Skyler took hold of the leather belt just as the cable snapped.

The tunnel plunged into absolute darkness.

"Don't let go," she said, already moving again.

She slowed her pace, for which Skyler felt grateful.

"Do you know why Neil brought us up here?" Skyler asked.

"Vaguely. He took a big risk, that's for sure."

Skyler bumped his head against a low pipe on the ceiling. He winced at the pain and crouched lower. He couldn't see anything in the absolute darkness.

"Neil may have inherited his empire, Skyler," she said as they ran through the darkness, "but he can judge people. Usually instantly, and always accurately."

Skyler thought back to the meeting. Platz may have withheld the larger details, but he had said a lot. It hadn't occurred to Skyler the level of trust that must have taken.

"Quiet now, we're here," Kelly said.

A thin vertical line of light appeared in front of them, and it grew wider as she opened a doorway. Beyond was another area of the station, seemingly deserted. She led him across the wide hallway and into an alcove.

Skyler realized there was no ceiling when Kelly began to climb a ladder bolted right into the wall.

"We can't use the lift. It'll trigger an alert," she said.

Skyler shoved the large wrench through his own belt and began to follow her toward the inner hub. He grew less comfortable as gravity began to diminish the higher they went.

At the top, they moved as if on the moon. Kelly opened the door in front of them and peered through.

"It's clear," she said. "Quickly now."

In the low gravity she moved much faster, with a grace and confidence that came from years of experience. Skyler struggled to keep up. The inner ring consisted of a wide hallway, arching steeply up and away.

Kelly stopped at another door, which Skyler recognized; they'd come through it when they were brought off the *Melville*.

"Ready?"

Skyler nodded.

"Stay behind me, and act casual." She removed her wrench and turned it over in one hand, familiarizing herself with the balance of it.

Skyler did the same. "I'll try."

She opened the door and entered with a remarkable air of confidence.

Drifting in behind her, Skyler focused on keeping his motions slow and loose. Over her shoulder, he saw his ship. It waited exactly where they had left it. He felt his pulse quicken at the sight of a group of guards crowded around it.

The guards were focused on two handcuffed engineers.

Kelly wasted no time. She launched herself forward and crashed into the nearest guard, sending him tumbling. Before the others could react, she swung her wrench. It hit the next guard square in the face with a sickening crunch, blood exploding wildly in the reduced gravity.

Skyler tried to mimic the way she had jutted forward, but he pushed his legs too hard and at the wrong angle. He ended up in a high, arcing jump. Sailing over the heads of the guards, he latched his feet around the neck of one and pinched his legs together for purchase. The surprised man flailed his arms, trying desperately to remove Skyler's feet.

Skyler swung the wrench downward with all the strength he could muster. The thick metal end impacted the poor man on the top of his forehead. Skyler heard the crack of bone, and the man went limp beneath him, tumbling with the force of the blow.

An unfortunate result, as Skyler was perched on the man's head. The dead guard's motion whipped him toward the floor. He released his feet from the now-limp neck with only an instant to put his hands in front of his face. He met the floor with a painful thud. The impact sent his wrench bouncing away, out of reach.

Skyler rolled over as another guard leapt on top of him. The guard had a small weapon in one hand, a stun gun by the look of it. Skyler managed to slap it away with the back of his hand. The guard took the loss in stride and began to throw punches. One arm raised for defense, Skyler used his other hand in a frantic search for the small stun gun Kelly had given him.

Pain exploded into Skyler's mind as the guard on top of him landed a vicious blow, just above his right eye. Everything blurred, then turned to double images.

Nearby, he could hear Kelly scuffling with the other guards. The handcuffed workers were both shouting, even screaming. Skyler could hear someone else, across the room, shouting for help.

His hand finally brushed across the small device. He grasped it, pulled it from his belt, and punched the two prongs into the stomach of the guard on top of him. A rapid clicking sound came from the weapon.

The guard's entire body heaved, an involuntary jump almost a meter high in the microgravity. The man's mouth and eyes stretched open, wider than Skyler knew possible. His arms and legs jerked violently.

It lasted only a few seconds. Released from the coursing electricity, the man drifted back down and slumped over Skyler, emitting a horrible deep groan.

Skyler kicked as hard as he could, sending the limp guard spiraling across the room. He rolled onto his stomach and pushed himself up from the floor in time to see Kelly land a fatal blow on another guard. Her wrench, hands, and forearms were splattered with blood.

"Get the engines started! I'll figure out the airlock!"

Her tone left no room for argument. Skyler bounced toward the *Melville*'s open door. He was finally starting to move with some agility, but his head throbbed with every step.

The cockpit door had not been tampered with, and for that he was grateful. He climbed over the navigator's seat, making a clumsy landing in the pilot's chair.

Running through the bare minimum of a preflight check, Skyler spun up the engines. To his right he saw Kelly enter a control room and seal the door behind her. He watched her through a window as she began to examine the control panel.

Then she ducked. A series of holes appeared across the glass, a web of cracks spidering out from each. The cavalry must have arrived. They were behind him, out of his field of view. Likely swarming toward the ship or the control room. Or both.

He made a snap decision and gunned the ship's engines. It was a level normally not enough to achieve liftoff in Earth's gravity, but here the ship lurched up off its landing skids and began to hover.

Skyler hoped the sudden rush of air from the engines would knock any nearby guards off their feet. He couldn't see them, but the sound of bullets bouncing off the *Melville*'s hull said he at least had their attention.

He took a glance at Kelly. She seemed dismayed, frantically scanning the array of controls in the small room.

Pulling back on the flight stick, Skyler moved the big craft rapidly to the left, then the right. He turned in place, a full circle, to survey the room. Most of the guards had taken cover behind an equipment cart. A few lay on the ground, clutching at smoldering clothes. Skyler grinned with satisfaction.

Red beacon lights on the walls began to blink and rotate. A loud horn could be heard, even through the cockpit window.

The guards bolted for the door.

Blinding light flooded the cavernous room from above. The ceiling, which served as the airlock door, began to recess to one side. The pressure differential between the room and the vacuum of space caused anything not bolted down to flush outside, limp bodies chief among the flotsam.

Skyler felt the *Melville* drifting upward as well. He took one last look at Kelly. She stood at the window, pointing above the ship, urgently.

"I'm going," Skyler said aloud, mouthing the words clearly for her to read from his lips. "Thank you."

He punched the engines: once, twice, and then again. Each burst increased the ship's speed, and in seconds it cleared the station.

The *Melville* wasn't built for extended use in orbit. He could generate minimal thrust with the small maneuvering rockets. They carried only enough chemical fuel for a few trajectory corrections, and the gauge already read 50 percent.

Drifting in the serenity of open space, the magnitude of what just happened became clear.

His crew, captured or worse. He'd killed a few guards himself during the mad escape.

The bizarre, harebrained scheme Platz had asked him to partake in. Save the Aura, and a life in orbit awaits. Not the most tantalizing reward for an immune, but the payment didn't really matter. If the Aura failed, that would be the end of everything.

Despite a burning desire to turn around and try to rescue his crew, he knew that the task Platz gave him took precedence.

There really was no decision to make, he realized. He must return to Darwin. Regroup, somehow.

Skyler waited until he was well clear of Gateway Station and the thread of the Elevator. Then he fired the thrusters and began to descend toward Earth.

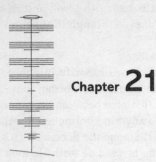

Chapter 21

THE MOMENT HE hit the atmosphere, Skyler realized he was going to die.

Something prevented the *Melville* from staying at the proper angle to deflect the heat of reentry.

He remembered the urgency on Kelly's face as she pointed frantically above the craft. She wasn't telling him to hurry and leave: She was telling him the climber latch was still stuck to the top of the ship.

The damn thing had the aerodynamic profile of an elephant, complete with tusks. The two large arms extending from either side of the latch mechanism must be sticking out beyond the *Melville*'s profile, causing friction with the air.

The ship shuddered as its computer made thousands of small corrections to keep from flipping over backward. If that happened, disintegration would be instantaneous.

Skyler closed his eyes, and came the closest he ever had to praying.

Something tugged at his memory. Something Neil had said.

The stuck latch had been a ruse.

The simplest solution possible was what Skyler needed. He reached up and toggled the release switch that had failed them earlier.

The effect was immediate.

"Yes! Occam's razor!" Skyler shouted as the latch released.

He heard the metal structure detach. An instant later, he heard it shear through the rear fin of the craft.

"Occam, you prick . . ."

Warnings lit up all over the cockpit. Skyler gripped the stick with both hands and put all his strength into holding it center.

Onboard computers sensed the loss of control from the rear fin and shifted to using the maneuvering rockets to keep the vehicle stable. But the hasty exit from Gateway had left them almost spent, and at an altitude of twenty kilometers, the rockets ran dry and the craft began to spin and tumble. Regaining control would be impossible now.

The *Melville* had no ejection seats.

Body pressed painfully into one side of his seat, Skyler decided to turn off the autopilot and level the craft out. Keeping on course for Darwin, at this point, was less important than surviving the trip down.

Falling at a terrifying pace, spinning out of control, Skyler shifted his focus to bailing out.

He clawed his way over the pilot's chair, then over the navigator's chair, and through the door into the cargo bay. The craft lurched from the turbulence. It took all the strength he had left to keep from getting bounced into the ceiling.

The scream of rushing wind outside grew ever louder. Skyler guessed he had about thirty seconds to get a parachute on and exit the doomed vehicle. He pulled himself up the wall and opened the locker where the chutes were kept. Quickly he threw on the pack, buckling only the main clasp. The rest he would have to deal with outside.

On a whim, he opened the next locker over, where the weapons were stowed. Grief swept over him when he saw Jake's sniper rifle, Samantha's shotgun beside it.

He shook his head clear and yanked out his machine gun, along with two clips of ammunition.

Fighting his way to the back of the cargo bay, he grasped a safety line with his free hand, wrapped it twice around his forearm, and then punched the red button.

A deafening howl of wind greeted him. The vortex pulled his legs out from under him, and Skyler just managed to hold on. If he let go before the door opened fully, he'd hit it on the way out.

He closed his eyes in pain as the line constricted around his arm, pinching off circulation.

Just below the rushing wind, Skyler could hear the hydraulic motor of the rear cargo door shut off.

The door was open.

He let go.

Wind buffeted him from all sides as he left the ship. As fast as his fingers would allow, Skyler finished strapping on his chute and securing the gun. He yanked the rip cord.

The chute deployed, whipping him around and upright, belts and straps constricting with brutal force. Then, peace. As if floating on a pillow of warm air, he drifted downward.

The urgency and altitude he'd misjudged. From the size of the buildings below him, he guessed he was a good thousand meters up. He could do nothing but watch as the *Melville,* his livelihood for the past fifteen years, spiraled toward a small city below.

The ship smashed into the side of a building at the center of town. Rock and fire spewed from the tremendous explosion.

He'd truly failed, now. Loss of crew and ship, a captain's worst nightmare. He didn't even have the nerve to go down with his vessel.

Anguish threatened to consume him, but somehow survival instinct won out. He had a window of opportunity to guide his fall. Shelter, water, and food were about to become the only concerns in his life. They always were, he supposed, but never in such a tangible way.

Using altitude to his advantage, he turned in a slow circle, scanning the horizon. The memory of doing the same for Tania rushed in. It may as well have happened years ago.

The sun filled the sky with an orange-colored haze to the west, above a landscape of mud flats and a sliver of ocean beyond.

Below, the deserted city loomed. He realized he didn't have the height to steer himself outside it, so he looked for a good place to land. As far north as possible, he decided.

Every inch closer to Darwin was one less he would have to walk.

A strong, warm, southwesterly wind pushed him over low, dilapidated buildings. Weeds choked every available opening. Abandoned vehicles crowded the streets. Desperately he tried to make a mental map of the town, looking for areas of commerce, areas where food might be stored.

Flames now engulfed the building struck by the *Melville,* a few hundred meters northwest of him. A column of black smoke roiled up into the darkening evening sky.

He drifted lower, guiding his chute to keep himself aloft as long as possible. Looking down at the rooftops, through holes worn by time and weather, Skyler tried to spot the telltale signs of subhuman life. Abandoned buildings were like caves to them.

He didn't see the rusty antenna until it caught him in the legs. A spike of pain ran through him as the old brittle metal sliced into his calf. Skyler gritted his teeth, felt warm blood run down his leg. The aerial collapsed from the impact, over the edge of the roof.

It crumbled into a noisy heap in the dusty street below.

With the sound came a wild cry from somewhere below him. It echoed off the buildings. Others answered, from farther away.

The ghost town came to life.

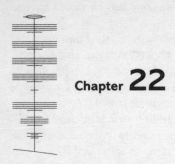

Chapter 22

AFTER AN HOUR of lockdown, security finally came for Neil Platz.

He'd spent the time in his private office, running scenarios through his mind. What if the pilot Skyler hadn't made it off the station? What if he failed to report back? A backup plan would be needed for inspecting the Aura's generator deep below Nightcliff.

Neil toyed with the idea of explaining it to the council. Hell, even to Russell Blackfield. In the end he'd discarded that line of thought. If others knew of the generator's existence, word would spread. Blackfield would be tempted to go poke around, perhaps making things worse. He might even do it on purpose.

All it took was one nutcase to go down there and set off a crude bomb, just as Sandeep had done to Foreshadow.

Neil was still struggling with his options when he heard a commotion in the lobby beyond. Shouts, and tension thick as fog, came through the closed doors.

He stood and pressed the wrinkles from his slacks. After one last long look at Earth, he strode to the double doors and threw them open.

"What the devil is this about?" he roared.

His secretary stood behind his chair, pressed against the wall in the face of a squad of armed security guards.

"Search the entire place," Alex Warthen said at the head of the group.

"Do no such thing," Neil said.

The guards ignored the conflicting order and streamed by.

"This is an outrage," Neil added.

Alex Warthen, pale-faced, mouth drawn in a tight line, stepped forward until he was just a few centimeters from Neil. He spoke in a quiet, deliberate tone. "What's outrageous is the size of your damn testicles. You brought smugglers aboard my station under false circumstances."

"I have no idea—"

"Enough, Neil. You've gone too far this time. You leave me no choice. I have four dead guards lying in the infirmary, along with two of your scavenger friends. One's in the brig, and once she's ready to talk, she'll confirm what we already know."

"This is all news to me," Neil said. Two of the scavengers, dead. One captured. All he could think was whether Skyler had escaped. Warthen's trigger-happy idiot brigade might have doomed everyone, and they'd never know it.

"We know one of them was here," Alex said. "We have security cameras on the station, as you may be aware."

"I can't control every jackass who comes to this door. Present company included."

Alex shook his head. He turned and waved to a guard behind him. The man came forward and handed Alex a portable terminal screen. Pad in hand, Alex tapped away for a moment before turning it to allow Neil to see.

"Watch," Alex said.

"What is this?" Neil asked.

Alex produced a sad smile. "The earpieces my guards wear have cameras. This was recorded by the poor fellow assigned to escort the smugglers."

"Roddy, what kinda piece they let you carry?" a young man asked. Neil had asked Prumble for a description of the entire *Melville* crew, and he guessed this was Angus.

The guard, Roddy, looked down at his drink. He picked up the glass and swirled it. "Just a little stunner."

"Not the size that matters, eh?" a woman said with drunken

mirth. Samantha, Neil surmised. The only woman in the crew, according to Prumble.

Roddy glanced up. The woman sat next to him, the young man just beyond her. "Only enforcers are allowed to carry coilguns. Too dangerous up here for the rest of us lugs."

Samantha took a swig of her drink. She was uncommonly tall, with thick blond hair. "Can that little thing even put someone down?"

Roddy removed the device from his belt holster. He held it up in front of him. "Sure. The prongs go in, toxin releases, and whammo. Like they had a seizure."

"Wonder if it could slow a sub down," Angus said.

Roddy focused on him. "If one gets in here, I'll find out—"

Samantha, studying the weapon, said, "Doubt it would work."

Roddy looked from her, to the gun, and back. The motion of the video made Neil a bit nauseous. "You've faced one?"

"One? Hell, we've faced dozens."

"Really?! What . . . I mean, how do you . . ."

Angus nudged Samantha with his elbow. "Company," he whispered, just loud enough for the camera to pick it up.

Samantha whipped around to face the door, and Roddy followed her gaze.

The recording showed a squad of uniformed guards at the entrance to the bar. They fanned out to either side, while four entered and walked directly over to Sam and Angus.

They carried exotic weapons, Neil saw. He knew about coilguns: built for use in places where flames were something to avoid at all costs. Magnetized coils inside the body propelled special bullets that wouldn't spark. No combustion and little recoil. Lethal at close range, but safe inside a space station. A few crates of the weapons were safely tucked away inside Hab-8, though Kelly said the risk of fire from a regular gun was actually quite low, and they need not bother. But Warthen's people had regulations to conform to. Without such concerns, Kelly preferred overwhelming firepower, and trust in the fire suppression systems.

Roddy stood abruptly. "Evening, Commander Weck. Is something wrong?"

Commander Weck was a short man. Bald and soft, with a scowl saying he wanted to prove otherwise. "Who owns that boat in bay four?"

Roddy looked past the man, to a table in the far corner. Neil saw the last smuggler sitting there, the engineer named Takai. The poor fellow looked white as a ghost. The other chair at his table was empty. Skyler must have occupied it.

Roddy answered, "He's right over . . . Well, he was over there. I . . ."

"Yes," Commander Weck said, eyes darting toward the bar, the drinks. "Amazing that he escaped under your vigilant watch."

Samantha came into frame, on her feet now. She dwarfed the watch commander. "Is there a problem, Bonaparte?"

"Who the hell are you?" Weck asked.

"Sam. I crew on that 'boat,' and my captain probably just stepped out to take a shit in your precious station. He might even do it in a toilet."

The camera tracked Roddy's frantic gaze from her to the young pilot. Angus winced at the woman's slurred words.

"Ah," Weck said, "you're familiar with such a device?"

Samantha smiled. "Your face reminded me."

On reflex, he put a hand on his slung weapon.

"Know how to use that thing, Hightower?" Samantha asked.

"Take it easy, Sam," Angus said.

Roddy moved between them. "Commander, relax. They're just waiting until the repairs are done."

"Bollocks," Weck said. "There's nothing wrong with their ship. Someone sabotaged it. And now their captain is missing. Coincidence?"

Angus spoke up. "Impossible. I'm the pilot, and that latch—"

"Someone ask you a question?" Weck said.

Angus snapped his mouth shut.

Watching, Neil felt his mouth go dry, and he swallowed.

"Enforcer Nichols," Weck said over his shoulder.

Another guard behind him stepped forward. "Sir."

"Take them to the brig, have their ship searched, and find—"

Samantha kicked the commander square in the chest. He tumbled into a nearby table.

"Bloody hell," Neil whispered to himself.

She wasted no time, picking up the weapon Roddy foolishly left on the counter. She fired the toxic prongs into the guard called Nichols. Within seconds, he was convulsing violently.

"Sam, what the hell?!" Angus shouted.

She dove forward, landing on the third guard as he fumbled with his rifle. Her fist flew into his jaw with a deep thud.

Roddy watched all this without moving. He saw Takai, the engineer, crouched low, moving along the wall toward the door. He probably intended to leave and find Skyler, or run for their ship.

The melee raged in the center of the tavern. Guards dove on top of Samantha. Workers scrambled out of their seats, pressing themselves against the walls.

Roddy turned to look at Angus, perhaps thinking he should finally perform his duty as a guard. But Angus had moved already. He crouched down over Weck, who lay limp on the floor, and wrestled the man's rifle away.

"He's armed!" Roddy shouted.

Guards leaned in from either side of the entrance, raising their weapons.

Angus tried the trigger, but the weapon didn't cooperate. He frantically fumbled for the safety.

"Drop it, now!" yelled a guard from the door.

Angus found the button and pressed it. He raised the gun and pulled the trigger. But Commander Weck, who'd come around, kicked wildly at the pilot's ankles. Angus lost balance just as the gun chattered, spraying bullets wildly along the ceiling.

Panic erupted.

Most of the workers still in the bar dove under their tables.

A few ran for the door, escaping an instant before the guards there began to return fire.

Roddy crouched behind his bar stool. He watched as Angus jumped behind the only solid cover in the place, the bar itself. The guards sprayed bullets in short bursts toward him. In a panic Roddy threw his arms over his face. Neil heard the sound of bullets hammering into the walls, the crash of the mirror behind the bar as it shattered.

As his comrades scuffled on the floor with Samantha, Roddy began to crawl for the end of the bar. He took frustratingly few glances at the conflict unfolding all around him.

The sound, however, told Neil enough. This was no simple fistfight, and no simple denial would satisfy Alex. Investigations and endless council meetings would result, and Neil couldn't afford that kind of nonsense right now.

Roddy stopped at the end of the bar. Only a few seconds had passed since the combat erupted. The last immune, the engineer Takai, could be seen at the door now. The little engineer threw a punch at the guard closest to him, a weak blow that glanced off. Neil watched, helpless, as the guard jabbed the butt of his gun into Takai's face, sending him sprawling.

Angus must have sensed the opening. Neil could hear gunfire, much closer. Roddy jerked in reaction to the loud noise, his gaze still on the action at the door. Bullets tore through the guard who had hit Takai. Red splotches appeared under the torn fabric across his chest.

Angus released another burst toward the other side of the opening, but the guard there had already ducked away, the special bullets shattering as they hit the wall.

"Sam, get back here!" the pilot shouted.

Roddy glanced at her. In the footage, Neil could see the tall woman on all fours, her face contorted in pain, blood on her shirt. A combat knife lay on the ground in front of her.

Beyond her, Neil saw Takai try to stand, one hand covering his bloodied face. Angus shouted a warning.

A burst of gunfire from the hall outside ripped through Takai's shoulder and chest. He fell, life gone from his body.

From behind the bar, Angus shouted with primal rage. He

let loose a hail of bullets toward the door. The guards there disappeared behind the wall again.

The guard Roddy finally overcame his cowardice, or shock—both, Neil guessed—and started to round the bar. He came out of his crouch and tried to wrestle the gun from Angus. The pilot, in the grip of bloodlust, kicked Roddy back and turned his weapon on the guard.

Neil almost looked away as the salvo flew. Roddy staggered back, the camera swinging up to the ceiling and then over to the side as the poor guard fell. He landed on the floor, one limp arm covering half the camera's view. The picture, now tilted ninety degrees, showed the center of the tavern.

Samantha picked up the knife in front of her. Screaming through clenched teeth, she buried the blade in the already dead body of the guard under her.

Angus came into view. He grabbed her by the shoulder and tried to pull her toward the bar. She brushed him off, picking up a gun from the floor.

"Get back here, dammit!"

She ignored him and limped toward the door, her rifle coughing bullets.

The barrel of a gun appeared around the wall of the entrance: a guard, firing blind.

"Get down!" Angus yelled. Then he stopped, almost frozen in place. He looked around, confused, then down at himself. He had his back to the camera, but Neil knew.

Angus dropped to his knees, then toppled to one side.

Samantha hadn't even noticed; her sights were on the door. She tried to fire again, but the rifle only clicked. Visibly defeated, she tossed it aside as guards stormed in from the door and tackled her.

The image on the screen vanished, replaced by an exclamation point and the words "stream not found."

"The fuck is this?" Alex said.

Neil hoped his brief smile went unnoticed. He knew immediately what had happened.

Alex Warthen fiddled with the device, frustration growing

by the second. The guard who provided the gadget tried to help, but Alex waved him off. "Go find another one," he barked.

"I still don't see what this has to do with me," Neil said. He struggled to hide the shock in his voice.

"We've reason to believe a murderer is being harbored here," Alex said. He gave the device a smack with the flat of his hand. "Dammit," he said through clenched teeth.

"Nonsense," Neil said. "Who?"

"Kelly Adelaide."

"Haven't seen her in months, since I fired her."

"Lie all you want," Alex said. "We'll see what the footage has to say, once we've gathered it all."

"Sir," the guard said, "this one has the same problem."

"Try another feed," Alex said.

"I can't access any of them," the man replied.

Neil watched as comprehension washed over Alex's face. "Son of a bitch. She's erasing the archive."

"Sounds like a tight operation you're running here," Neil said.

Alex ignored the jibe. He turned away and began to blurt orders into his handheld. Something about wanting a team at the data center right away. Neil smirked, despite himself. Kelly would be long gone by the time they arrived. She knew the maze of maintenance tunnels and ventilation ducts aboard Gateway better than anyone.

The security chief whirled on him. "This is a serious offense, Platz. If I find out you gave the order—"

Neil dismissed the tirade with a casual wave of his hand. "Looks like an unfortunate barroom brawl to me, combined with inept data management. You can leave now."

Alex Warthen seethed. A response came to his lips, only to be interrupted by the return of the men he'd sent inside to search the office.

"No one here by her description, sir," said one of the enforcers.

Alex held Neil's intense stare. "Keep the station on full lockdown," he said to the guard, "until we've sorted this out. Perhaps the scavenger in my infirmary will shed some light, if she lives."

"Yes, sir."

"Make yourself comfortable, Platz. I still have witnesses to interview, and backup data to restore."

Neil stood firm, and offered Alex nothing else to go on. He knew he'd won.

Neil sat with his staff in the office lobby, eating a simple meal of hummus spread between slices of a stiff potato bread, when one of Alex Warthen's underlings came by to tell them the lockdown had been removed.

"They caught her?" Neil asked, too quickly.

"Can't find her."

"What of the pilot? The scavenger pilot."

"He escaped on his ship," the guard replied. "I'd better not say anything else."

Neil nodded, dismissing the man. He'd heard nothing from Kelly since she ran from the office to follow Skyler. And while he doubted now that she'd escaped aboard the scavenger's ship, he felt he could not stay around to wait for her. Gateway Station had become unfriendly territory. Best, he thought, to vacate in favor of Platz Station, farther up the cord. He didn't want to be around when Alex Warthen finally produced evidence linking the scavengers, or Kelly, back to him. Evidence he should have, by all rights. The endeavor had come off in sloppy fashion. Loss of life, and the scavenger captain forced to flee without his crew of immunes.

No, let Alex try to yank me from my own home. I can dig in with the best of them.

"Let's get the hell out of here," he said to his employees. During the lockdown, Neil had instructed them to pack anything important and be prepared to leave, and so they had.

To the receptionist he said, "Shut everything off; lock the doors behind us."

"When should I reopen?"

"I'll let you know. In the meantime, you have a new job: wanderer. I expect you to spend a lot of time roaming around the station. Send me daily reports on what you hear, and who you hear it from."

"Of course."

"Things will get *tense* around here. Anything out of the ordinary, you lct me know immediately," Neil added.

The man nodded, a serious expression on his face.

"The rest of you, with me."

Neil carried a stuffed briefcase in one hand and a portable comm in the other. He led the group at a brisk pace through the hallways. The corridors were empty save for Warthen's guards, who made themselves far more visible than normal. Two weie stationed at almost every junction.

To Neil's surprise and relief, the guards simply watched them go. He couldn't blame the anger on their faces. Some of their own had died today. Murdered, Alex said. By Kelly. Violence, even bloodshed, in orbit was almost unheard of. Anyone guilty of such a crime would be pushed out the nearest airlock, or sent back to Darwin. There was no room for extended jailing in orbit, and no tolerance for people who couldn't contribute.

He came to the docking bay on the "top side" of the station. Inside, he ushered everyone into his personal climber, instructing them to pack tightly. He had no desire to make two trips. Within minutes, the vehicle jutted out from Gateway Station, using the thread of the Elevator as a guide wire.

As the modest craft drifted away from Gateway, Neil considered the situation. He knew he needed to stay a move ahead of Alex if his plans were to succeed. Action must be taken or he'd be at the mercy of Warthen's guards.

He excused himself from the main cabin and entered a small room, alone. He activated the comm and dialed Platz Station.

"Put Karl Stromm on," Neil said to the woman who answered.

It took five minutes to find him.

"This is Karl."

"Neil Platz here. Kelly tells me you're someone I can trust, someone who can get things done."

"I do my best," he said.

"No time for modesty."

"Kelly's a smart woman," he offered.

"Good enough," Neil said. "Consider yourself promoted. Self-defense training time is over."

"All right," he said. "What happened?"

Neil quickly recounted the events aboard Gateway. "Keep quiet about this. Kelly is incommunicado, so I'm calling you directly. First, contact every station where we have representatives. Tell them to be vigilant. Take care who they talk to, or where they talk. Warthen all but admitted he has spies all over. Not to mention his damned guards."

"No problem. I'll get the word out."

"Everywhere but Anchor," Neil said. "I want you to handle that personally."

"How so?"

"Pick a few of your best pupils and prepare to travel there. You'll need a cover . . . a replacement janitorial crew, maybe. Talk to Mr. Brill in personnel; he can be trusted to an extent. I'll send him a note authorizing it."

"What do we do when we get there?"

"I'm still working on that," Neil said. "Just be ready to act. If you don't hear from me directly, you're to do whatever Tania Sharma asks. Until then, no matter what happens, lie low. Clean floors, listen, and keep me informed. Most of all, keep tabs on Warthen's men. Their shifts, patrol routes, whatever."

"I think I get the picture," Karl said.

"Good man. Safe travels."

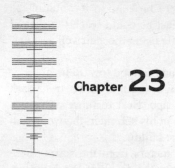

Chapter 23

SKYLER AIMED FOR a dried-up pond, centerpiece to a public park on the southern end of the town. Once it might have been a nice space, with families strolling along the paved walkway under the shade of irrigated trees. The pond, now bone dry, dominated the piece of land. From above it looked like a bomb crater, lined with skeletal trees for victims.

When he hit ground a sharp pain lanced up his leg. The gash from the rooftop antenna seared, and warm blood trickled down his leg into his boot.

He stumbled and rolled in the dusty bowl of the former pond. With no further need of his parachute, and no time to collect it, he let it drift away in the hot wind.

From all around, the disturbing howl of subhumans grew to a fever pitch.

Skyler put sunset at an hour away. He needed shelter, some place he could defend while bandaging his wound.

Grunting with effort, he limped to the rim of the pond, unstrapped the rifle from his chest, and scanned the town. Most of the structures were small shops in various states of decay. Farther north, toward the center, he could see the tops of small stores and a church steeple. Some distance west an office building, perhaps ten stories high, stood against the red sky.

Nearest to his position, he spotted a two-story building with some sort of shop on the bottom. A stairwell outside led up to a covered walkway that ringed the second floor.

All the exterior windows were broken, so it wouldn't be much use as shelter. But at least he could reach the second floor and get his bearings while using the stairwell as a natural choke point.

Good enough, he decided, and limped toward it.

He didn't bother to keep low, now out in the open—a dark figure against a sandy landscape. Best to move as fast as possible. He ignored the pain in his shoulder, the wound on his calf, and jogged toward the building.

When he was still twenty meters from the stairs, three subhumans came around from the front of the building. They moved as one, protecting one another as they hunted. A typical pack, and Skyler felt glad for it. Not the collected mass like in Hawaii. He took a knee and opened fire, dropping them easily. They hadn't even seen him yet.

Throughout the town the howls grew louder, and he knew there were far more subhumans here than he had bullets for.

At the sound of more scuffling footsteps coming from the street, Skyler sprinted the rest of the way to the stairs, grunting back the searing pain in his calf.

Reaching the stairwell, he tossed the gun's strap over his shoulder and climbed, two steps at a time.

Halfway up, the rusted stairs collapsed under his weight. Skyler heard the bolts splitting an instant before the structure fell, and he used his last step to jump toward the walkway at the top. His arms just made it over the lip of the landing, but they immediately began to slip on the dusty concrete.

Below him the stairs crashed into the dirt, creating a calamitous sound surely heard for blocks.

He had to ignore it. Reaching to his left, he grabbed a rusted iron bar—part of the railing on the second-floor walkway. To his amazement it held. Pain bloomed anew in his shoulder as he struggled to lift himself onto the platform. Legs dangling, kicking for momentum, he groaned through clenched teeth. It took all the strength he could muster to pull his upper body onto the walkway.

Below, more subhumans arrived, hissing and growling like primates. A child led the way, perhaps ten years old, with filthy wild hair and a mangled arm. It jumped with astonishing power toward Skyler's dangling legs, sheer savagery in its bloodshot eyes.

He felt the small hand grasp his boot, and then Skyler felt its added weight in his tenuous hold on the rusty iron bar. Without thinking, he reached down with his right hand and swatted the subhuman's filthy fingers from his boot.

The child fell.

Only then did he realize his mistake.

The gun, slung over his right shoulder seconds before, slid down his arm. Skyler fumbled for it, but the strap slipped past his fingers, and he watched helplessly as the weapon dropped to the ground below. It landed in the wreckage of the flimsy stairwell.

Skyler flung himself over the railing and onto the walkway proper. He lay back on the platform, clutching his wounded leg with both hands, and forced his breathing into a regular rhythm.

He stayed still for a long time, staring at the sky. Around him, the cries of the formerly human receded with the setting sun. He could hear a group of them sniffing about below, grunting at one another like dingoes.

He fought against heavy eyelids, not wanting to sleep. Sleeping felt like giving up.

Give up, he thought to himself, darkly amused. Then, *Give up what?*

He thought of everything he'd lost. The *Melville,* Samantha and the rest of the crew—his entire world. The weight of it all brought tears to his eyes.

I haven't got a damn thing left to give up.

Skyler put the thought out of mind. *Focus on the immediate,* he told himself. *Survive.*

As the last light of the sun faded, Skyler set to work bandaging his leg, using fabric torn from his shirt. He knew he could not stay here long. The creatures below might eventually lose interest, but clearly the town was infested with them. There would be no easy way out.

Satisfied with the wound dressing, Skyler rolled over and pushed himself to the edge of the walkway. In the darkness below, he could make out the shapes of a few subhumans. Some milled about, most crouched in the dirt, still as death. He focused on the wreckage of the stairs, and thought he could see a glint of light coming off his dropped weapon.

As he considered his options, one of the subhumans—the small one again—noticed him and began to snarl. The sound, so inhuman, paralyzed Skyler. The other creatures took up the call. As if spurred on, the small one began to leap for the platform where Skyler lay, but it fell short by half a meter. Then it started to use the wall beside it as leverage, and sent Skyler's heart racing with a swipe that missed his face by mere centimeters.

Skyler knew the next attempt might succeed; yet he lay still, frozen in place. *I'm going to die here,* he thought. The subhuman child leapt again, savage hunger plain on its face.

The tip of one dirty fingernail scraped Skyler's nose. No more than a tickle. The child-creature's mouth curled in frustration as it fell back to the ground. It landed on the stairwell debris and stumbled, its ankle folding in an unnatural way. A howl of pain erupted from the poor animal as it rolled in the dirt.

The tingle on the end of his nose coaxed Skyler from his fog. He crawled back from the edge of the walkway and sat up against the wall, intent to be silent and invisible. Let the monsters below get bored and move on.

Several hundred meters away, against the crimson sky, he saw the silhouette of the one tall office building.

High ground. The first step in figuring out where he was, and what his path back to Darwin would be.

The clouds above were thinning. From where he sat, Skyler could only see the southern sky. He decided to crawl around the walkway to the north face of the building and scan the horizon for telltale lights of climber cars on the Elevator cord. If he was close enough to Darwin, and the sky clear enough, it would give him his bearings.

His leg throbbed. The ache in his shoulder, from the melee aboard Gateway, flared whenever he lifted his right arm. He rubbed at it, coaxing out the tenderness.

The idea of crawling around the walkway suddenly seemed

like an impossible journey. As far away as Gateway Station itself. He felt the energy drain from him as the surge of adrenaline wore off. His focus shifted to simply breathing in long, regular measures. His vision blurred from sheer exhaustion.

With nowhere to go, and no energy to move anyway, Skyler lay down and closed his eyes. One hand rubbing at his shoulder, the other clutching the bandaged wound on his calf.

Sleep never came.

His mind instead replayed the chaotic escape from Gateway. Guilt consumed his thoughts. No matter how he tried to justify it, he'd left his crew behind. He'd fled. Whatever sense that decision might have made at the time, he struggled to recall it now.

He tried to picture the crew, languishing in some high-tech brig aboard the space station. He could hear their conversation, wondering where he was. If he was okay. Would they assume he was being held separately? Or maybe that he'd died, in heroic fashion, trying to save them?

He lay still on the cold concrete until well after dark, imagining a heroic death. A preferable outcome to dying here, cold and alone, in God-knows-where.

The mere thought of hiking his way back to Darwin, however far it might be, exhausted him. Part of his mind kept offering the same question: *Why bother?*

Platz and his dubious plan to save the Aura, if it even needed saving, could go to hell, Skyler thought. What did an immune need with the Aura? If it failed and the rest of the ungrateful world perished, he could finally have some peace and quiet. No more scavenging, no more damn request lists and desperate pleas.

"Stop it," he whispered to himself. He shut his eyes and willed the pessimism back into the corners of his mind.

His thoughts turned to Prumble. If nothing else, he should find Prumble. Tell him what happened. The big man could help, or give him a corner of his vast garage to convalesce in.

And then Skyler remembered that Prumble had a sat-comm.

A direct link to Platz. At the very least, Skyler could find out what had happened to the crew. That, he thought, would dictate what he would do next.

It was a first step, a tangible goal.

Hours passed. A crescent moon offered poor light, augmented every few minutes by lightning that rippled in clouds to the east like a distant war. A poor way to navigate unfamiliar territory, but the subs should at least be dormant now. Sleeping, conserving heat and calories like any wild animal.

Skyler sat up with a grunt. He checked the bandage on his leg and found that only a little blood had soaked through. The wound looked minor despite the pain. He could only hope that infection would not occur.

Time to get moving.

With care not to make noise, he crawled to the edge of the walkway where the stairway had collapsed, and studied the ground below.

The subhumans had indeed wandered away. Either that or they were well hidden in the pitch-black shadows below. He held his breath and listened for a time. No sounds of their ragged breathing.

Skyler gently lowered himself over the edge, hanging on by his fingertips. The ache in his shoulder returned as he began to swing his legs. When the pain became unbearable he let go, swinging his fall to land away from the pile of metal and concrete.

He took the impact on his good leg, rolling as he landed, vaguely proud of the nimble move. Standing, he pushed himself back against the wall of the building and waited. No cries arose from the surrounding buildings. Satisfied, he knelt before the remains of the stairway and retrieved his weapon.

The weight of a gun in his hands bolstered his confidence. He crouched and did a half-walk, half-run along the wall, gun pointed at the ground a few meters ahead. He peered around the corner into the wider road beyond. Dusty and trash strewn, and blessedly empty. The building he stood next to had once been an art supply store, so the faded sign told him. The windows were empty, and he didn't need to see inside to know the place was a ruin. He tried to think of anything useful to scavenge from an art store but came up blank. Not worth the time to look.

More shops lined the rest of the street, all in similar states of disrepair. None was more than three stories tall. Skyler suspected that nothing in this poor town remained unscathed by the ravages of rioting, abandonment, and plague. He'd seen a hundred just like it. In his mind he pictured his beloved Amsterdam, languishing in a similar state.

All the great cities of man, left to rot. All except Darwin— and Darwin would be along soon enough.

He looked for the office building to get his bearings. At least four hundred meters west, and perhaps a hundred south. He knew from experience that subhumans were drawn to sound and movement. Most had lost their ability for higher thought, but their primal senses remained. Indeed, the curse of SUBS was that one primal emotion would intensify to the point it drowned out all other thoughts, a phenomenon made all the more unpredictable by the fact that one never knew which emotion would take over. Anger, fear, lust . . . even humor. He'd seen a few in the early days who laughed hysterically at everything around them. They tended not to survive for long.

Gun held low, safety off, Skyler set out. Many of these buildings likely served as shelter for the subhumans, and they all looked straight out onto the road. He needed a path that kept him out of view.

He crossed the street to the building directly opposite, formerly a bookstore, and stopped to listen. He heard only the barest whisper of wind, and pressed on past the broken shop windows to an alley just beyond. The narrow space, barely the width of a car, was pitch-black.

This he followed one careful step at a time until it met the next junction. The street beyond appeared to be simply a wider alley, something the shop owners could use for deliveries. To the west Skyler could see the brick and glass office tower, looming black against the starry western sky.

Another three hundred meters, and now straight ahead.

He stepped up his pace and moved to the end of the back-street. A wide avenue crossed his path, dotted by the husks of abandoned cars and a commuter bus that had burned. Charred passengers still sat in some of the seats, dry and black. A sculptor's demons set against a nightmare background.

The alley's end marked the edge of the business district. Adjacent was a residential section of town, with evenly spaced homes nestled in weed-infested yards. One section had succumbed to fire, years earlier. He ran along the road between businesses and burned-out homes.

A soda bottle ruined his silent passage. In the near blackness, he kicked the old thing, sending it rolling and hopping along the cracked asphalt. The clicky-clack sound went on and on, calamitous in its volume after so much silence.

Like clockwork, the cries of newly agitated subhumans returned, emanating from the empty buildings that lined the street.

Skyler ran.

Pumping his legs as hard as his injury would allow, he beat a direct path to the office tower. He could hear rapid footfalls behind him.

A quick glance over his shoulder—at least ten of them were in pursuit, and gaining. He forced his attention ahead and in doing so caught movement to his right. Another sub emerged from an old house and raced toward him. Skyler squeezed off a burst of bullets from his hip. The poor creature pitched forward to a sliding stop, utterly limp.

The deafening crackle of the machine gun brought a chorus of mindless howls from every direction.

Skyler pushed himself harder, lungs burning as he sprinted the last few meters to the building.

Thick planks of wood and pieces of sheet metal covered the entrance, with rows of razor wire nailed across it in haphazard fashion. With despair he ran past the barricade, circled around to find the side door in the same state, and kept running toward the rear of the building.

In back there was a small parking area secure behind a tall wrought-iron fence. An electric gate provided the only way in, but it had been chained closed and padlocked. Next to it was a small white ticket booth.

With panting, snarling sounds just meters behind him, Skyler angled toward the tiny structure. The booth's windows were intact. Skyler fired a single round into the one facing him and watched it transform from a clear pane to thousands of tempered shards. He leapt at the last second with his gun held before him, shattering the glass in a shower of sharp bits.

There was no time to waste. Skyler stood up. Broken glass fell from his clothing and crunched under his feet. He ignored a few small cuts and aimed. A subhuman jumped through the open window even as he fired. Bullets tore through the creature's chest but momentum carried the body straight into Skyler's torso, driving him back into the far wall of the tiny shack.

Air rushed from his lungs. Something cracked, and pain lanced up his side. His head snapped backward and knocked into the wall with a deep thump. Stars swam before his eyes. Gasping, unsteady, he pushed the limp body off him and fired again at the next one. This sub had some sense of self-preservation and ducked away. Those that followed it slowed, too, and looked at one another as if deciding what to do.

Skyler grasped the opportunity and stumbled out the thin door of the booth. Inside the gated parking area now, he hobbled toward the building's rear entrance, fighting to keep his balance the whole way. His torso burned, the pain growing with each movement.

Desperate now, he fired blindly behind him while studying the back of the building. He limped toward the double door in the center of the wall, ignoring the fierce agony coming from his ribs.

The doors were locked.

Skyler spun around and saw four subhumans scaling the gate. He hoisted his gun with a grunt. The weapon felt like it had a sack of stones tied to it. Searing pain flared along his torso with the effort but he could do nothing about it. Skyler aimed at one sub as it reached the top of the barrier. He pulled the trigger.

Click.

He fumbled for his last clip of ammunition, which he'd stuffed into his jacket as the *Melville* plunged toward Earth. The black metal case slipped through his fingers and fell to the ground.

For a split second Skyler welcomed his fate. He slumped and waited for the devolved human beings to come and tear him to pieces, as the disease had programmed them to do.

Something caught his eye to the left. He glanced and saw a stairwell tucked up against the side of the building, leading down into darkness.

He went for it, pausing only to grab the ammo. Each limping step toward the stairs produced a spike of pain in his ribs that felt like knives. He shouted through it as he slapped the clip of bullets into the center of his gun.

The stairs he took three at a time, more of a controlled fall than a descent. A door loomed at the bottom, and it was all Skyler could do to raise one arm as he reached it. He expected a hard impact, but his weight and momentum flung the door wide.

Skyler fell, hard. His cheek slapped against a carpeted floor that smelled of mold and something else. Something feral, like an animal's cage. His vision began to blur at the edges and then grow dark.

He spun onto his back and aimed back up the stairwell even as the first subhuman crested the edge. Skyler squeezed the trigger and kept firing until the bullets ran out.

As consciousness began to fade, he was vaguely aware of crawling toward the door, reaching for it.

The rest was blackness.

Chapter 24

WELL AFTER MIDNIGHT in the Gardens, a poorly named slum in southern Darwin, a caravan of armored trucks surrounded a crumbling old parking garage.

Half the vehicles skidded to a stop in the street outside. Black-clad police leapt out and moved into defensive positions. To anyone watching from the shadows their maroon helmets announced them as Nightcliff security, not that any doubt existed.

The other half of the caravan did not slow down. They followed one especially large truck adorned with a thick corrugated steal wedge bolted to the front grill. The truck's electric motors surged as it smashed into the metal gate at the garage's entrance. The old bars broke away from their brittle joints, clattering away into the darkness.

The vehicles flowed into the open hole like roaches. They barreled down the concrete spiral, spewing sparks whenever their rough-plated edges scraped the cracked sidewall.

Hardly dented from the first impact, the lead truck accelerated through the final corner and made short work of the feeble chain-link fence at the end. The barricade collapsed and parted easily, leaving nothing but a large door between the intruders and the interior of the building.

This door didn't hold, either. When the ram hit it, the old wood splintered, sending a shower of debris into the warehouse and headquarters of Mr. Prumble, noted smuggler and a chief supplier of Darwin's black markets.

As the mighty vehicle backed out of the way, police flowed into the hole.

Russell Blackfield enjoyed watching his elite do their work.

He entered behind them, carrying only a pistol. From inside he heard shouts of "clear" as his men fanned out through the building. Above, he knew they would be working through the upper floors, though reconnaissance said those were long abandoned. Worth a look anyway, he had decided during the planning session.

According to the intelligence Russell had paid for, Prumble kept a payroll of forty toughs, protecting the goods stored in this rank tomb of a hideout.

"So much for resistance."

The massive room held no one at all, save for Nightcliff men. *Someone tipped him off,* Russell thought. He should have arrested the informants who sold Prumble out. Recoup the bribes, exact some revenge if it didn't pan out.

His soldiers maintained a professional aggressiveness despite the lack of an enemy. Russell strode past aisle after aisle of organized merchandise, meticulously stacked. The urge to scatter it all required more self-control than he usually exercised.

At the very end of the last aisle in the room, he came across the only obvious hiding place—another room, retrofitted into the far corner of the underground space.

Five of his guards waited there, guns trained onto the solid metal door. It looked just like the giant refrigerator entrance in Nightcliff's cafeteria.

"Open it," he said to one of his men. The others fanned out on either side.

The officer grabbed the handle and his entire body jerked. Every limb shot straight out, except the arm connected to the door. He let out a sickening, guttural sound, and his hair began to smolder. Another officer had the presence of mind to hit his electrocuted companion in the chest with his rifle, knocking him away from the door.

The room plunged into darkness. Somewhere below, the hum of a generator faded.

Some of the soldiers had lamps on their helmets or attached

to the underside of their guns. Within seconds they all came on. Russell removed a small, handheld flashlight and trained it on the victim.

Dead, or near enough. The scent of burning hair and skin filled the stagnant air. "For fuck's sake, someone get him out of here," Russell said, holding his nose.

Someone grabbed the cooked man by his collar and dragged him away.

"The power is out. Try it again," Russell said. One of the men approached the door and tapped the handle with one finger. Nothing happened, so he gave the handle a full tug. It didn't budge. He tried again, this time straining with effort. No movement.

"Enough," Russell said. "Use the onc-rope."

Another officer came forward with a coiled yellow cord. He unwound a length of it and stuck it to the door in an oval pattern.

Russell cupped his hands around his mouth to amplify his voice. "If you're in there, Prumble, better hide under the desk. Assuming you can fit."

A few of the men chuckled. Russell turned and led everyone back to the main entrance. The explosives expert arrived last, unspooling a thin blue wire as he moved. He crouched down next to Russell.

"Fire in the hole!" he shouted. After a pause, again, "Fire in the hole!"

Russell covered his ears.

The guard pushed the wires into a small object in his hand and pressed a button on the side of it.

The building shook. Brown dust shook loose from everywhere and filled the stale air.

Russell felt the explosion in his bones. His own clothing buffeted in the rapid shift of air pressure. *Hell of a thing, that rope.* He'd appropriated it from that immune scavenger's ship. The bloke had said he fenced through Prumble, a delicious irony.

It took a good minute for the smoke and dust to clear, at least enough to see a few meters. Russell wanted no more time wasted and used a hand signal to indicate his men should proceed inside.

Two by two they entered, their lights making the thick smoke somehow worse.

"Clear!" Russell heard from the far end of the room.

Goddammit! Not what he wanted to hear. Two well-paid informants, plucked off the street outside yesterday, had sworn Prumble was inside. Russell's own watchers said no one had left.

Now Russell looked every bit the idiot. He made a mental note to find those two-faced tossers and dump them outside Aura's Edge.

He walked into the small office. The portion of the door removed by the onc-rope had torn through the room, shearing off part of a large oak desk and badly denting an old file cabinet. Debris and papers littered the floor.

"Check that desk," Russell said, "and be careful. I've smelled enough barbie for one day."

He loved giving orders to no specific person and noting who took initiative. It served as a key method for choosing whom to promote.

"Those of you not in here," Russell said loudly, "pack everything into the trucks. Nothing gets left behind."

A chorus of unenthusiastic "Yes, sirs" resulted. They'd come for some action and were disappointed to find an empty building instead. "Whatever you can fit in your pockets, you can keep," Russell added. The grumbling abated a bit after that.

"Some kind of ledger here, sir," said one trooper, looking into the file cabinet. He handed Russell a leather-bound notebook, filled with page after page of handwritten information.

"Paperwork, exactly what I dreamt of finding." He flipped through the pages anyway. The scrawled notes were cryptic at best. Initials, abbreviations, numbers. The type of thing only the author could understand, and Russell guessed that was the point. He flipped to the end and found something peculiar.

The last entries all began with the same initials: "N. P."

"Sat telem," Russell read, sitting down in the worn leather chair. The cushion was rock hard—compressed by Prumble's gigantic ass, no doubt. "What are you looking for, Platz, you old goat?"

The soldiers ignored him, stuffing their pockets with anything that fit.

Two of the Platz entries were marked as "Sat telem." Satellite telemetry, Russell realized.

Why? What would I do with that?

Satellites. Military satellites. Orbiting weapons from an era long gone. Something Platz could use against the ground, against Nightcliff. Something that would give him the upper hand again. Russell felt a chill run through his entire body. Had he underestimated the goat? Could Neil really be that clever?

Even if wrong, this provided ample pretense to crack some skulls.

He closed the book, then smiled. It was time to call Alex Warthen.

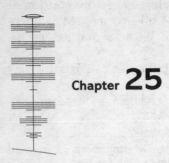

Chapter 25

TANIA PUSHED IMITATION eggs around her plate, creating artful yellow swirls on the purple plastic dish. The improved aesthetics did little to help the bland flavor.

Across the table, Natalie worked on a bowl of fresh fruit. "Any news from Platz?"

Scientists bustled into the cafeteria from all over the station, in for their morning meal. Tania had chosen a two-person table in the far corner, one that said "go away" to anyone looking for a breakfast chat, or so she hoped.

She shook her head. "He's mired in some political fallout from a 'security incident' on Gateway. Wouldn't tell me more than that."

Guilt chewed away at her. She didn't know why, but when Neil asked about the mission to Hawaii she'd left out all the horrible details. *I've got the data, and I'll start looking at it right away.* The rest she'd kept for herself, a fire in her gut that she kindled whenever it started to fade, despite every instinct telling her to put the molestation behind her. Telling Neil would just make him fuss over her, and he would make justice a project. He had enough projects already, and this one she felt was hers to resolve.

"I heard some Darwinians managed to sneak in," Natalie said. "Turned into a big tangle with Warthen's guards. Jacobites, I'd guess. They're always going on about 'purging the heathens from Jacob's Ladder,' you know?"

Tania glanced up from her plate. She doubted the world could get any crazier.

"Good thing we're so far away," Natalie said.

"Cheers to that," Tania replied. They toasted with apple juice in hard plastic cups.

Natalie grinned at her friend. "Feeling any better?"

"The healing power of having work to do," Tania said. "Just need to keep busy."

"Speaking of," Natalie said, checking her watch, "we should have our pictures in soon."

"Not long now," Tania said. She'd set her timer as well.

"Any trouble last night?"

"None," Tania said with a half smile. "Greg and Marcus will be annoyed I bumped them, but I'll say it was a typo. An honest mistake. Canceling their task was easy enough."

Natalie looked around them and dropped her voice even lower. "What do you think we'll find?"

Tania shrugged off the question. "You know I don't like to speculate."

"Oh c'mon, hon, humor me."

Tania set her fork down and folded her arms on the table in front of her. She took a long look at her friend. "I suppose you must have a theory, Nat?"

"Sure. I can't stop thinking about it."

"You first, then."

Natalie wiped her mouth with a cloth napkin. "I think they're sending a giant passenger ship, full of their people."

"What?"

"Like the *Mayflower* or something."

Tania stifled a laugh. Natalie's energy never failed to lift her spirits.

"I mean it," Natalie said. "Think about it. First they sent the Elevator, gave us a way to get up here. Then they sent SUBS, *forcing* us to get up here. Survival of the fittest, right?"

"Go on," Tania said.

"They give us a chance to vacate, plus one city to survive in as a token offer. Maybe they can't breathe in an atmosphere that doesn't have SUBS floating around."

"Why not give us more time? Or a whole continent?"

Natalie shrugged. "Maybe they can't make an aura that big."

"I see one big flaw in this idea," Tania said.

"Do tell."

"Why give us a chance to leave? Why kill ninety-nine percent of us but stop there?"

Natalie's grin faded. Her eyes raced back and forth. "Okay, enough of my idea, what's yours?"

"I don't like to speculate."

"C'mon!"

"I'll tell you what Neil thinks," Tania said. "He thinks they're coming to finish the job."

At that Natalie grew somber. When she realized Tania would say nothing more, she went back to eating.

A few minutes later, their watches beeped in unison.

"There's our pictures," Tania said.

Natalie hesitated.

"What's wrong?" Tania asked.

"It's just . . . I'm not sure if I want to know any more."

Tania took her hand. "Nonsense. We're scientists. True discovery is a once-in-a-lifetime chance."

The hallways had lost their nighttime forest feel with the arrival of dawn on the planet's surface below. The overhead lights now simulated full sunlight. Tania preferred the way it looked at night. Now it was just a white hallway with green carpet.

Natalie swiped her badge to open the door, and Tania breathed a sigh of relief at the sight of an empty room.

They walked straight to the giant multiscreen setup in the back room at the far end of the lab. Natalie went for the center console seat.

"I'll drive," Tania said, guiding her aside. "The data is keyed to my account."

Her assistant took the direction in stride and moved behind the chair to let Tania sit.

"Let's see what we've got," Tania said. She entered her passphrase and waited. Natalie placed a nervous hand on her shoulder.

The aging computer took several seconds to respond, and then another minute to access and display the raw images from last night's sky survey. On the screen before them, a panoramic map of the cosmos appeared.

"I used the Japan and Hawaii data," Tania said, "to calculate the likely vector the first Builder ship would have taken. Adjusted of course for changes in Earth's, and our solar system's, position." She highlighted a section of the star chart, and hundreds of small boxes appeared along it. Each one gradually filled in with a small image. "The yellow squares are the pictures we took last night. The rest are old."

"There's a lot of yellow," Natalie said.

"It gets worse," Tania said. "For each yellow square I took a sequence of six images, so that we could detect movement."

"This will take ages," Natalie said. "What if we wrote a program to automatically scour these for anomalies? Greg could knock that out in his sleep."

Tania shook her head. "We've got one already, rather sophisticated. But it sucks up all the compute resources, which would really set off some alarms."

"Damn."

"I know. Let's save that for a last resort."

Tania selected the first yellow box and an ocean of stars filled the three screens. Other than subtle variation in color, they all looked the same.

She closed the image and opened another.

Natalie frowned in concentration. "Can I drive for a second?"

Rolling her chair aside, Tania watched as Natalie stepped forward and leaned over the keyboard. She worked quickly, her fingers a blur. With each tap the view shifted into a new configuration.

A minute later Natalie stepped back. "Try it now."

Tania rolled her chair back to the machine and selected the next yellow box. When it highlighted, a cluster of five adjacent boxes lit up as well. They all expanded at once, evenly spread across the giant displays.

"Tap there," Natalie said, pointing.

Tania did, and the next images in each sequence came in. She tapped again to see the third. "Brilliant," she said.

"Not as much detail, but we can look for movement more easily."

"And in six places at once," Tania said. "Great idea."

Natalie rested both hands on Tania's shoulders. "Thirty minutes until breakfast is over and people start poking their heads in here."

Tania nodded. She began to work quickly, bolstered by the clever scheme Natalie had set up.

After twenty minutes, Tania could feel her eyes begin to glaze over. The images started to blur together into a random assortment of stars. She shifted in her chair and rubbed at a knot in her shoulder. Natalie brushed her hand aside and took over the task, kneading with just the right amount of pressure. It felt good, if mildly distracting. Tania did her best to ignore it and redoubled her focus on the pictures.

A dozen more sequences went by without any signs of motion.

"Wait. Go back," Natalie said.

Tania stopped the sequence and rolled back through the images slowly.

"Stop. Focus on the second one from the left."

Tania stared at a perfectly average picture of stars against the blank void of space. "What is it, Nat?"

"In the corner," Natalie said, pointing.

In the bottom left, nearly off the edge of the frame, she saw a dark gray object, nearly invisible against the black background. Definitely out of place. Tania selected the image to expand it across all three screens. She adjusted the positioning to move the gray speck into the center, and rolled through the sequence.

The blurry object moved over time, unlike the background stars.

"I'll be damned!" Natalie said.

Tania frowned. "It could be an asteroid or something."

"Argh! You're such a pessimist. It's the Builders!"

Tania did think the gray blob vaguely resembled the shape

of the shell ship. "We need to be sure before contacting Neil. Let's task the telescope for a high-res shot on the next pass."

Natalie bounced on her toes. "This is amazing! They're back, and on some kind of schedule!"

"We'll see," Tania said. It took all her self-control to stave off Natalie's infectious enthusiasm. In truth her gut had already reached the same conclusion Natalie voiced. Possibilities, and their ramifications, swarmed her mind. All paths led to the same place, though: Their world would change, again.

"We'll see," she repeated, for herself.

Chapter 26

NEIL PLATZ STRODE through the double doors of the council chambers. He paused long enough to order his entourage to remain outside.

A large conference room served as the council's meeting place, dominated by a long rectangular table and twenty high-backed leather chairs. A Platz Industries signature window dominated the far wall.

The rest of the council already sat at the table, engaged in quiet conversation, waiting.

The chairs at either end of the table were left empty, a custom. In the old days, Neil and his brother, Zane, would sit at either end. Now they had to sit as equals to the others. A silly change, yet one the upstart council had vehemently demanded.

In recent years, the council had taken to meeting only once every other month. The issues were always the same: How much food could we send down, how much water and air would they send up?

"Am I the last to arrive?" he asked of no one in particular.

Michael Carney, head of immigration, frowned. "Some of us have been waiting half an hour."

"Good Lord, how did you survive? I see you didn't resort to eating your assistants." The other members turned at his raised voice. They had each brought one or two secretaries.

Two stone-faced guards, in plain clothes, framed Alex Warthen. "I've got a killer on the loose," the security director said. "How about we dispense with the chitchat and get started, eh?"

"Agreed. Now that we're all here, let's begin," Sofia Windon said in her even, cool voice.

Neil liked Sofia, to an extent. She performed the thankless job of resource management with precision and fairness. Unfortunately, her voting record on the council often proved the tiebreaker, and she showed no allegiance to any specific faction.

Sofia leaned in. "First—"

"First order of business," Neil said, "I move that this meeting be council members only."

Sofia glared at him. She took her task of running these meetings seriously. "Why?"

"Call it rumor control," Neil said. "We have delicate issues to discuss, and I'd rather be candid for once."

"That's never been a problem for you," Alex said.

Before Neil could reply, Sofia held up a hand. "Fine, vote. Those in favor?"

Only Alex, and manufacturing director Charlie Williams, kept their hands below the table.

"Motion passes," she said. She looked around the room at the litany of support personnel. "If you would all please leave us . . ."

Some were slow in reacting to the order, looking to their bosses for confirmation. Alex glanced sidelong over his shoulder and jerked his head toward the door. His two bodyguards left without a word.

The matter settled, Sofia continued. "The purpose of this meeting is to discuss two issues. First, the security incident that occurred here on Gateway on February fourth. Second, the continued disruptions in power along the Elevator, which may be allowing the subhuman disease to take hold inside the Aura. It's also disrupting air and water shipments from Nightcliff."

Amanda McKnight, who ran a fledgling education department, leaned forward. "Can we also discuss the lack of terminals for the children—"

"Sure," Neil said. "They can all tap away on them as they suffocate."

"That's uncalled for."

"Air and water, Miss McKnight. A trifle higher on the priority list."

Alex Warthen leaned back in his chair. "I'll add a third item to the itinerary. The continued smuggling of contraband to Anchor Station, and the secret research going on there." He paused for effect. "Dare I say, related to the 'security incident,' the skittish Elevator, and the erratic shipments."

Neil felt his skin prickle. Alex stared at him with smug confidence. *He knows something.*

"Let's go over the security situation first," Sofia said. "Alex?"

He nodded. "I have obtained a useful body of information from the prisoner, one Samantha Rinn, a hired gun on the Darwin scavenger ship."

"What of the vessel itself?"

Alex shrugged. "It deorbited but never landed in Darwin. The stuck harness was still attached. We're assuming it crashed, no survivors. The authorities in Nightcliff have been alerted as a precaution."

"Authorities. That's rich," Neil said. He kept his face and tone steady even as his mind raced through the implications. If Skyler was dead, he had only two choices regarding the Aura: let everyone in on the Aura generator's existence, including Blackfield, or keep his mouth shut and hope his larger plan could be initiated before the Aura failed completely.

Neil decided to keep his mouth shut.

Alex went on. "The prisoner claims their ship was not released from the climber due to an equipment malfunction on our part. Our investigation shows the control switch was deliberately sabotaged."

"By whom?" Sofia asked.

"The investigation is ongoing," Alex said. "We're questioning the operators who were on duty, but my gut tells me Kelly Adelaide is responsible."

"Yes," Sofia said, "your report mentions her numerous times."

"She killed three of my guards."

"Allegedly," said Neil.

"The footage may have been wiped, but I do have witnesses."

"But no perpetrator."

"All in good time," Alex said. "Which brings me to my first request. I would like the council's permission to search Platz Station. We think she's fled there."

Neil shot forward in his chair. "Ridiculous."

"Miss Adelaide is your employee, is she not?"

"Was," Neil said through clenched teeth. "That's in the past."

"Is it? I wonder."

"I won't sit here and listen to baseless accusations."

"They don't seem so baseless," said another council member.

Neil glanced left at Dr. Bettina Moore, who ran all the medical clinics and associated staff. She'd shared a bed with Alex, years ago, and they were still on good terms. She tended to take his side.

Sofia turned to her. "Dr. Moore?"

"Neil formerly employed the woman. No one disputes this," she said in a clinical voice. "The report says Gateway has been searched end to end, twice. It's certainly plausible she has fled to familiar ground. Whether Neil or his staff are aware of it is immaterial."

"Warthen provides security for my station just like everywhere else," Neil said. "I doubt she could slip past such a vigilant staff."

"My *staff* are denied access to anywhere but the loading dock, by your orders."

"Which is where she would have entered from, if I'm not mistaken."

"Gentlemen, please," Sofia said. "Neil, the Orbital Stations Security Act, which you signed, allows for unfettered access to any station by the head of security or his representatives."

"With the approval of this council," Neil corrected. "Don't lecture me on the rules of this so-called government, Sofia. I set the damn thing up after all."

Alex took the opening. "Let's put it to a vote then."

They did. Five to four, in favor of giving Warthen access.

An uncomfortable silence followed. Neil drummed his fingers on the table.

Oliver Devanneaux cleared his throat. "If we could please move on to more pressing matters," he said, quietly. His area of responsibility: consumables.

"Air and water," Sofia said. "Certainly, proceed."

"Nightcliff has threatened to stop shipments yet again, claiming worry over these power fluctuations, which are happening almost hourly now." Oliver looked around at the rest of them. "They have refused our offers to assist and now have built up a backlog of nearly twenty climbers."

"Blackfield will cave when the food runs out," someone said.

"Alex," Sofia said, "you met with him on Gateway. What's your view?"

The security director shrugged. "He wants a seat on the council. You all know that."

"Oh good," Neil said. "*That* will fix the climbers."

"Perhaps we should address the root cause," Alex Warthen said. He stared directly at Neil.

A deep silence settled over the table.

Sofia finally spoke. "Which is?"

"I've been to Anchor Station," the man said. "Recently. They've been probing the shell ship with some intensity—"

Neil snorted back a laugh. "We've been doing that for years," he said.

"I'm not finished," Alex said. He swept his gaze across the table. "These scans are the deepest they've ever done; one of the scientists there said so. Not only that, but I've been informed that Neil recently took a trip to Darwin, to purchase something from a group of smugglers."

No one said a word. Neil felt their looks but kept his focus on Alex.

"The same smugglers," Alex added, "who killed four

guards on this very station, three days ago. If you ask me, it's all interrelated."

"This is rich," Neil said. "Are the Freemasons involved, too? Go on, please."

Alex ignored him now. He spoke to everyone else. "First Neil visits Darwin, without any council approval. In disguise, I might add. Then we find out about these 'deep scans' of the shell ship, which coincidently start around the same time as the odd power fluctuations. Let's not forget the appearance of two cases of SUBS in orbit. And finally, one of Neil's prize scientists, Tania Sharma, personally undertakes a dangerous trip outside the Aura aboard a scavenger ship. The same ship that was then brought to Gateway under dubious circumstances."

He looked around at all of them. "I'm telling you it's all related. Their probes of the shell ship are causing the power fluctuations, the SUBS outbreaks. Neil's scientists are working with reckless abandon. This investigation should be centered on two places: Platz Station, and Anchor Station."

Neil swallowed. He scarcely remembered the offhand remark made by the researcher at Anchor about doing a detailed scan of the shell ship. The damned thing was derelict and everyone knew it. The mapping effort was completely innocuous and unrelated, but that didn't matter. Alex had seized the bit of information and now used it in bloody clever fashion.

To his credit, Alex pressed the attack. "Russell Blackfield, in my opinion, has every right to worry. The power blips are an annoyance right now, but they are getting worse. A climber falling back to Earth would drop on Nightcliff like a bomb."

"They can't fall, you *idiot,*" Neil said. "Their state of rest is to grip. My engineers aren't fools."

"We have only your word," the man replied. "An independent review—"

"Now you're just being an asshole," Neil said. He glanced at the rest of the council. "He and Russell are pigs in a blanket. He's just jockeying to get Blackfield to this table."

"Is it not obvious," Alex said, "to everyone here, that

Nightcliff is critical to this equation? Take a deep breath if you don't believe me. Feel the air in your lungs. Go on, sip your water."

No one said anything.

Alex stood and put his hands on the table. "This council, the nine of us, is only fifty percent of the picture. Russell Blackfield, right now, controls the other half. It's too much power to put in one man's hands. You've heard of the riots down there? Let me tell you, it's us they curse, not him. We will take the blame for all this unless we get him here."

Sofia spoke with abundant patience. "Neil, your thoughts? Does Russell have the people of Darwin behind him?"

"Of course," said Neil, focusing on her. "All they know of orbit comes through him. Other than Alex and Michael, who here has visited Earth in the last six months? Gone *outside* the fortress in the last year?"

Silence in the room.

Neil went on. "I was there two weeks ago, that is true. Arranging—"

"Arranging a purchase from smugglers," Alex said.

"Critical information for my researchers," Neil shot back.

"Right. We're all looking forward to the fruits of your discoveries up at Anchor Station, Neil. I'm sure our grandchildren will be anxiously awaiting it, too."

"Gentlemen, please!" Sofia said, smacking the table with the palm of her hand. "Alex, you had something to say earlier."

He placed his hands on the table in front of him. "This would be easier to resolve if Blackfield had a seat at this table. It would make him one-tenth the equation, not one-half. It's worth it."

Neil grunted. "We're not going to vote on this *again,* are we?"

"The situation has changed. Blackfield isn't just a gatekeeper anymore. He runs the whole place and has solidified his power." Alex looked at each of them in turn, except Neil. "Like it or not, he and the fortress are critical to our wellbeing. Better to bring him into our circle—"

"Not a chance," Neil said, voice deep and loud. "Remove

him from power immediately and install someone we can control."

Everyone began talking at once.

Alex shouted over them. "I will not send my security forces to subjugate Nightcliff—"

"Perhaps we have another personnel change to make, then," Neil said.

"Get used to losing council votes today, Neil."

Neil said nothing. The conversation at the table finally dwindled.

"His hold on Nightcliff is too strong," Alex said. "It would cost a lot of lives and precious resources to try to oust him. Especially when the alternative is to simply let him sit here at this table."

Neil turned to the other council members. "Where he can extend his power to orbit as well."

"Where we can control him. The price for his entry would be that this council's authority expands to include Nightcliff and Darwin. Bend him to our agenda," Alex said.

Neil shook his head. "He'd never agree to that, and you know it."

There came a knock at the door.

"Come," said Sofia.

Neil's secretary peered in and, on the beckoning of Sofia, entered the room and went straight to Neil. He whispered in his ear for a few seconds, and then stood straight.

"I request a recess," Neil said. "I've some important business to attend to."

Sofia glanced at each of the members in turn. Alex seemed on the verge of arguing. Then he sat.

Sofia bowed her head to Neil. "It's three P.M. now. We will reconvene after dinner, at eight."

Chapter 27

TANIA WAITED ANXIOUSLY at the desk in her room.

Her terminal displayed a detailed image of the object now approaching Earth. The high-resolution picture, taken the previous night by the main telescope, left no doubt as to what it was.

Ten minutes after she had first contacted Neil's secretary, he finally picked up the communicator on the other end.

"Sorry," he said between gasps, "didn't want to take it on the station. Too many of Warthen's goons around. I jogged all the way to my climber."

"That's okay," Tania said. "Are you alone then?"

"As much as I can be. Let's have it. There's nothing coming, is there? All of this has been for naught?"

She hesitated, tripped by the uncharacteristic pessimism in his voice.

"I knew it," he said. "The Aura failing, that's the next event. Goddamn—"

"There's another shell ship coming," she said.

Neil missed a beat. "Are you sure?"

"Yes," Tania said. "Exactly like the one we have here at Anchor, as far as I can tell."

A long silence followed. "Is it headed for Darwin?"

"Impossible to know," Tania said. "We need more time."

After a few more seconds, he said, "Well, what *do* we know?"

"It's rather close," she said. "Natalie is trying to re-task the telescope for another shot tonight, which will tell us how fast it is moving, but not its rate of deceleration."

"How long will that take to work out?"

Tania thought about it. "Three or four days, I think."

"Why so long?" Neil asked.

"We're sharing telescope time up here. The others are going to get suspicious if we keep changing the tasking program."

"Who else is using the scope?"

"Greg," she said. "Greg and Marcus."

"I'll send them a note," he said. "Something suitably cryptic, telling them that their project is on hold and to give you full run of the thing."

His ability to take such monumental news and immediately turn to practical issues amazed her. "I thought you'd be more excited," she said.

A weary sigh came through the earpiece. "I'd convinced myself that the failing Aura was our next Builder event. Hell, it might still be."

His tone confused her. Every time they talked it was like he'd already accepted that the Builders would keep returning, in some endless series. She reminded herself whom she was speaking to. Neil had a laser focus on the future, on opportunities and consequences. He wasn't one to let events simply happen, to relish in the act of discovery.

"Things are not going well down here," he went on. "The council is about ready to cave to Russell Blackfield's demands. We're going to have to act swiftly, before he gets a toehold."

Tania felt her heart beat faster at the mention of Blackfield. A vision flashed in her mind, of Anchor Station crossed with the quarantine room at Nightcliff. She clutched the zipper on her jumpsuit and pulled it all the way up.

"Things are going to happen very quickly, Tania. We need to be ready."

"Can I ask you something?"

"Of course, dear."

Tania swallowed, and closed her eyes. "Did you know about the data in Toyama, before I asked for it?"

"Pardon me?" he said. "Of course not. What's this about?"

"But you'd been to the telescope."

"I don't think so—"

"I saw a picture," she said. "You and my father, standing in front of it."

"Perhaps you're mistaken?" he said. "Or, who knows . . . your father and I funded dozens of science facilities in our heyday. It may have slipped my mind."

Tania could hear the lie in his voice. A subtle change in tone, something that took a lifetime of friendship to detect. "Perhaps so," she said, staring at the picture in front of her. The time did not seem right to confront him. He might have simply forgotten.

"If it makes you feel better," he said, "I can check our records."

"No, forget it," she said.

"Stay focused, dear."

"I'd feel better if I knew the plan."

"You will," he said, "when it's safe to tell you. But the critical piece of the puzzle is that ship. The what, when, and where."

"I promise you'll know as soon as I do," she said.

"Good. And Tania?"

"Yes?"

"Watch yourself. Warthen tried to spook the council with talk of 'secret research.' Don't forget he still runs the security staff there."

"We're being careful," Tania replied. It almost sounded true.

Chapter 28

SECLUDED WITHIN HIS personal climber, Neil lay in a plush chair and let his mind drift back to the Elevator's arrival.

Darwin had almost twelve years to grow around the Elevator at Nightcliff before the plague came. There was extraordinary luck in the location of it—an easily defensible piece of land, bordered on two sides by ocean, in a small but prosperous city within a nation at peace with the world. It couldn't have been better, for Earth and for the Platz legacy.

Neil pictured the Darwin Elevator, stretching up from Australia, static electricity roiling along its length due to friction from the atmosphere. On up into space, through Gateway Station, and up, and up, and up, all the way to Anchor. To the shell ship.

And then he envisioned another. Another shell ship, floating into position next to its sibling. What purpose would it serve? Spin a mirror image of the original, all forty thousand kilometers of it? System redundancy—it made a kind of sense.

The first Elevator was faltering. Power seemed to be running out. A replacement, perhaps? A real possibility as far as Neil was concerned.

Whatever the case, he knew what must be done: regain control of Nightcliff.

And the council.

To achieve his goal, he needed more resources in orbit. More workers, more fighters, more weapons. He was getting old, and things were going too slowly. He cursed himself for relinquishing power in the first place.

Time to put all the cards on the table, he decided. Before it's too late.

He could not wait for Tania's analysis to be finished. *Something* approached. Therefore something had to be done.

Neil decided to work under the assumption that another ship would arrive over Darwin. Whether it came to repair the original, or replace it, or for some other purpose was impossible to know. Would remain impossible until it was too late to act.

He had to roll the dice. A replacement Elevator he could wrap his mind around.

He let himself out of the chair and made his way across the private docking bay, back into Gateway Station. Neil climbed down through the empty corridor that connected like a spoke to the outer edge of the ring-shaped structure. He could feel the artificial gravity slowly grab hold of him.

The satellite office had been deserted since he pulled everyone back to Platz Station after the security incident. Neil wandered the halls. The council would not reconvene for hours, and he was in no hurry to return to their company.

He needed a bargaining chip. Something that would keep his enemies from unleashing their superior firepower. Something that would force them to bargain, or even better, to cede power.

A plan began to take shape in his mind.

Before anything else, Neil needed to change the decoupling codes.

Since the company first started building space stations along the spine of the Elevator, Neil had insisted on manufacturing them in a central location and then moving them to their ultimate position. It was too expensive to move the manufacturing infrastructure to each location.

The added benefit was that the stations could be repositioned. It was a complex and difficult procedure, not often used. He knew the various station crews rarely reviewed the process. If not for the recent project to realign the farming platforms, Neil wondered if anyone would know how to do it without lengthy training.

As it stood, his scientists at Anchor would know what to do. Tania would know.

But first, the codes. He couldn't let anyone cancel the procedure, once started. Neil went back to his climber, activated his terminal, and began the process.

The rest he would have to plan as things progressed.

Despite the dizzying array of hurdles before him, Neil couldn't help himself. He felt excited. Alive. For the first time in years, he looked forward to a future of unknowns.

A future to be conquered.

Sofia Windon leaned forward in her chair, fingers folded in a tent on the cold marble table in front of her.

"The ayes have it," she said softly. "Russell Blackfield will join the council."

Alex Warthen locked an expectant stare on Neil, watching for some reaction. Hoping, perhaps, that Neil would fly into some rage.

Neil smiled, instead. "Well then," he said. "It seems this meeting is over."

Sofia said, "We still have a litany of issues—"

"Not me. I resign from this council," Neil said.

His voice resonated in the room, with more authority than he thought himself capable of.

Alex Warthen coughed. "Excuse me?"

"I will not submit to a search by you and your incompetent security force. I will not negotiate for the water produced at my own desalination plants. I will not have the integrity of my research staff questioned," he said, voice gaining volume as he went on, "and I *will not* share this table with Russell Blackfield."

Alex didn't move; he was dumbfounded. Sofia's mouth hung open. The rest of the council sat perfectly still.

"You want the food produced by my farms?!" Neil shouted. "You want the water purified by my plants? I'll consider any reasonable offer, from my headquarters. Good day to you all."

He stormed from the room before anyone could respond. Even his brother, Zane, looked stunned.

Let them chew on that, Neil thought, while preparations are made. If he stayed a step ahead he would win this race.

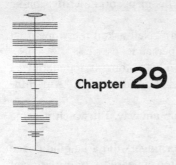

Chapter 29

THE PASSENGER CLIMBER ports on Platz Station featured standard Earth gravity, a unique feature Neil had insisted upon during the station's construction.

Eight S-shaped guide rails carried incoming climber cars away from the Elevator's thread and off to reception ports on the outer rim of the station's upper and lower rings. Individual rails could be retracted to allow some cars to remain fixed to the climber, allowing them to pass through the station entirely, or be unloaded at a more traditional dock in the central hub, where a lack of simulated gravity eased unloading of supplies.

Guests could exit their climber car with the dignity of walking on two feet, while workers and supplies could be brought to the center levels for easy distribution.

The apparatus had one drawback: complexity. A room full of equipment and twenty-four-hour monitoring by an actual person.

Neil stood behind the climber operator, a middle-aged woman with shoulder-length black hair and a strong Venezuelan accent.

They both stared at a schematic displayed on the large monitor on the room's longest wall. All traffic on the Elevator could be tracked from here, but Neil's focus was on a single climber that barreled toward the station from Gateway.

The climber's manifest and layout were listed as "unavailable." He'd never seen that before, not that it surprised him. Alex was coming to do his inspection, permission be damned.

"When can we get a visual?" Neil asked the woman. "I need to know which cars are personnel carriers."

She studied the display for a long moment, then tapped a few commands into the panel at her fingertips. "Any minute now, Mr. Platz."

"Neil," he said. "Bring it up anyway. I'll watch it come into view."

She nodded slowly, then her fingers did a languid dance across the input panel. A frame appeared within the giant wall-sized display above, quickly filled with a high-resolution image of the Elevator cord. Earth loomed far below, mostly in shadow. Despite the excellent contrast of the cord against the dark planet below, the approaching climber was not yet visible.

"Shall I call you when it arrives?" the woman asked.

"Why?" he asked. "I'm here now."

"It's just . . . I'm due for my break."

She'd been pensive since he'd come in the control room, and had hesitated at each request from him. Not the type of person who works well under scrutiny, Neil decided. His presence had that effect sometimes, but now was not the time for such nonsense. "Forget your damn break," he said. "We have an unannounced climber speeding toward us. I need you here."

She slumped in her chair.

"Would you rather be relieved?"

"No," she muttered. "I—"

"There it is," Neil said, pointing at the display. "Enlarge that."

The woman hesitated, again.

"Enlarge it!"

"I need a glass of water," she muttered, standing.

"Bloody hell," Neil said. "Sit down. I'll get your damn water. You get me a clear picture of that climber."

He stomped to the door and threw it open. A few of his staff milled about outside, talking in hushed tones. They jumped when he stormed from the room.

Skittishness and tension. He had found it at every turn since returning from the council meeting. News of his resignation beat him to the station, of course, and no one knew what to make of it. Neil had isolated them, and many had family or friends aboard other stations.

He considered sending one of them for the drink, but stopped short. A brief walk might do some good. It wouldn't do to be all frayed and overanxious when the climber arrived.

The common room was a quarter ring away, and Neil made a conscious effort to slow himself. He clasped his hands behind his back and strolled down the center of the burgundy carpet that spanned the entire ring.

Warthen was coming, of that Neil had no doubt. The man had to make good on his threat to search the station, or else lose whatever momentum he was trying to build with the council.

Neil ran through the scenarios in his mind, for the hundredth time. He'd already had the resident Gateway security contingent locked in the central cargo bay, ready to be sent away. He'd ordered all the reception rooms on the landward deck sealed, the door codes changed. When Alex's climber arrived, Neil would have each personnel car separated and sent to different reception rooms. Split them up, confuse them. They would be expecting to arrive in the central cargo bay.

Once they were divided, Neil would address them. *Take your comrades and go home, you're no longer welcome here.* Something to that effect. His privately trained fighters, stationed outside each reception room, were ready in case Alex Warthen decided not to listen. Neil hoped they could remain behind the curtain, but he would use them if he had to.

A solid plan, he thought, *as such things go.* By the time he returned to the control room with the silly cup of water, he felt relaxed.

Happy, even.

* * *

"Here's your drink," Neil said. He handed the red plastic cup to the woman, his eyes on the big monitor behind her.

The enlarged feed showed the approaching climber from a top-down view. A cylindrical center that housed the climbing mechanism, and eight spiderlike booms stretching out from it where cars could be attached.

Only four cars hung from the climber's arms, all personnel-style. *Perfect,* Neil thought.

"When will it reach the splitter?" he asked.

The woman glanced across the various status readouts. She took a slow sip of the water as she studied them. "Three minutes," she finally said.

"Route each car to the lower reception areas. I need to know which rooms they will arrive at."

She turned in her seat, facing Neil but looking at the floor. "I'll need a few minutes," she said.

"We don't have it. Are you feeling ill or something?"

"No."

"Then what the bloody hell is your problem? This is urgent."

Instead of responding, the woman turned back to the screens.

With one swift motion, she dashed the contents of her cup across the console.

Sparks flew, screens flickered and went dark. Pale blue smoke shot out from gaps, yanked upward by hungry air panels in the ceiling.

The woman ran.

She flew out the door and into the hall before Neil could comprehend what had happened. He simply stared at the screen where the image of the climber had been.

"Stop her!" he yelled. "Someone stop her!"

Neil went through the door, knocking over a bystander. He looked left and right, along the curved corridor, and saw nothing. The woman had disappeared, just like that.

"Which way did she go?" he demanded of the man he'd toppled. The staffer pointed to Neil's left.

He started after her, ignoring the complaints from his old muscles. But after just a few steps, he stopped.

The shock of the betrayal had consumed his mind. Neil recognized this feeling and allowed the event to become just another facet in the larger scheme of things.

He considered the rapidly approaching climber. And then his teams of handpicked fighters stationed at the reception bays where no cars would arrive, thanks to the sabotage.

His men were in the wrong place, and precious seconds were passing.

Neil considered allowing Alex to board. Accommodate him, and even facilitate his search. After all, the man was unlikely to find anything that would help him. Kelly Adelaide was not aboard the station. Indeed, she remained on Gateway, right under their snouts.

Neil kept no records of his meetings with her or of his other various secret projects. Hab-8 had a perfect cover story. Tania's research was all off the record. Since he'd destroyed the Foreshadow files, there was nothing outwardly serious for Alex to find.

No, he thought. A stand must be made. If Neil allowed the search, Alex would take the opening and never leave. Security officers would be here for days, longer perhaps, and that would make things very difficult indeed.

The traitor would have to wait.

Turning, Neil raced to a nearby emergency alarm, flipped the protective lid up and away, and pulled the red handle down.

Instantly Klaxons began to wail. He did his best to ignore the earsplitting sound and rushed into a nearby room. He slammed the door shut and fished a handheld radio from his pocket.

"Zane, come in."

"I'm here, brother," the response came. "Any idea what the alarm—"

"Listen carefully," Neil hissed. "Find our night operator for the climbers and get them on duty, now. The main terminal has been sabotaged. I can only hope there's a backup."

"Sabotage?" he mumbled. "What—"

"Make it happen, and now. I want the climber incoming

from Gateway to be turned around before it even docks. We've got minutes. Less than that."

"What of the alarm?"

"Get on the PA and tell everyone to remain in their quarters. I'll explain later."

"Okay," Zane said.

Reversing the climber was a long shot, but it would put a quick end to the intrusion if done in time. Neil knew he still needed to be ready for the alternative. He tapped the screen on the radio, switching to a private preset.

"Climber controls have been compromised," he said. "Get to central docking, on the double."

His four commando leaders, newly trained, each responded "affirmative," in sequence. Kelly had done her job well.

The cream-colored hallways of Platz Station blurred into a morass of doorways, bulkheads, and warm light as Neil jogged toward the central docking bay.

He'd started at a sprint, only to find his old legs unable to keep up the pace.

A betrayal of a different sort, he mused.

The thought of arriving at a confrontation with Alex out of breath and haggard gave Neil all the excuse he needed to ease up.

Zane's voice came over the handheld. "Neil, the backup climber controls are at L-Four J-Two."

A primary spoke junction on the very level Neil ran toward. It made sense, having the secondary controls near the cargo bay.

"Thanks," Neil said. "What about the night shift operator?"

"He wasn't in his room," Zane said. "We're still looking."

With sudden certainty Neil knew they wouldn't find the man, at least in any condition to operate the climbers. The saboteur had probably run straight to the poor bastard's room after fleeing from Neil.

Smart.

"Keep at it," Neil said. He decided to keep his deeper

fears from Zane. Dealing with stressful situations wasn't his brother's strong suit.

Neil switched to the private frequency again. "Rally at L-Four J-Two," he said.

"We're here already," one leader replied. He was shouting over a loud hiss.

"What's that noise?" Neil asked.

"Steam!" the man replied. "They're cutting through the damn airlock!"

Neil forced his legs to move faster. The very fact they they'd brought a water torch meant Alex had anticipated being locked out. There would be no simple stalemate.

"Dig in there," Neil said. "I'm almost to you."

He could only hope Alex hadn't anticipated an armed resistance.

Team three joined up with Neil just before he reached level four. He let them take the lead and grunted back the fire in his thigh muscles as he ran to keep up.

He heard sporadic gunfire before the junction came into view.

Steam roiled in the air, pouring down from "above," where the junction corridor led up to the central docking bay. Neil could only see a few meters into the cloud. The constant hiss from a cutting torch, high above them in the spoke, drowned out even the warning Klaxon.

"Report," he said to the first commando they reached.

The woman was pressed against the wall, using a support truss for modest cover. "They're through the airlock door. Surprised to see us, I'll tell you that."

"How many?"

"Twenty," she said. "Thirty. Hard to say. We got off a few shots before they pinned us here. Brought some serious weaponry."

Thirty men. Neil's four teams had four members each. Almost two-to-one odds. "If they're through the door, why are they still cutting?"

Someone lost in the steam ahead answered. "They're working on a side door, halfway down the spoke."

Another team arrived, their presence feeding Neil's confidence. "Warthen's going after the climber controls," Neil said to all of them. "They mean to destroy our ability to leave the station, and we can't let that happen."

He saw nodding faces in the roiling steam.

"They're sitting ducks in that tunnel," someone said. "Smooth walls, weak gravity."

The station's rotation provided Earth-normal pull here at the outer rim, which decreased the farther one traveled up the spoke to the central bay. Neil hadn't considered that this might make the enemy's movements slow and awkward. A small advantage, but he'd take it.

"Concentrate fire," Neil said. "Everyone together."

"We can't see anything in this steam," the woman said.

"Fire blind," Neil shot back. "It's a narrow tunnel—you're bound to hit *something*. One burst from each of you ought to show them we're serious."

"Each team take a corner," one of the leaders said.

They fanned out and began to fade into the swirling vapor. Neil felt naked without some kind of weapon in hand, despite the fact that he'd only held a gun a few times in his life. Swallowing, he took a few tentative steps into the cloud, moving just fast enough to keep the back of the last commando in view.

"On three," he heard someone say. "One . . . two . . ."

The shooting began. Muzzle flashes lit ghostly figures within the steam cloud, as all sixteen fighters leaned in and fired upward into the access shaft, like revolutionaries celebrating a coup.

Cries of surprise and pain came from above.

A body drifted down the vertical corridor, falling faster as the mock gravity took hold. It hit the ground with a thud, and two more followed seconds later.

One of them lost his gun in the fall. It skittered over the tiles and tumbled to a stop near Neil.

The tone of the cutting torch changed, then stopped.

"Get back!" Neil shouted just as the mists cleared.

Alex Warthen's troops answered the attack with a relentless barrage. Bullets hammered against the floor of the hall for what felt like a minute. The special munitions gave off no sparks but left hundreds of small pockmarks in the floor.

Neil heard bullets ricochet in every direction, clattering across the tiles as they lost momentum.

He saw one of his men take a round in the calf. A splatter of blood like spilled paint on the floor. Two of his squad mates pulled him out of the line of fire, ignoring his anguished cries.

The dropped weapon lay near Neil. He reached for it, his fingers just brushing the black metal when more shots rang out from above. Warthen's men had an opening and they were seizing it.

Neil yanked the weapon toward himself as he skulked away from the danger zone.

Somewhere above, mixed with the constant bark of firing weapons, he heard the sound of metal striking metal. Repeated, powerful blows, as if someone were taking a crowbar to a computer.

He realized that might not be far from the truth. They were in the climber room, smashing it to pieces.

Bullets fell from the vertical shaft like rain. And then, as suddenly as it had started, the gunfire stopped.

Neil's ad hoc commandos were shell-shocked. Two appeared to be wounded. He decided to take the initiative and stepped forward, into the open area below the spoke corridor.

He saw men climbing up, toward the cargo bay airlock at the top. Others waited there, looking down, guns at the ready. They were holding fire to let their comrades retreat from the control room.

Neil raised his gun and pulled the trigger. The snub rifle barked and spat. It slapped into his shoulder with vicious strength and almost vibrated out if his grip. His shots sprayed wildly up the side of the shaft, toward the top and across the men climbing. The arc crossed the men waiting at the top, forcing them to push away for cover. A slow and clumsy movement in zero-g, where they were.

The gun fell silent, out of ammo. Neil thought he might

have hit one of them in the back before they were pulled out of the shaft.

But the damage was done. He could see hazy smoke spilling out of the backup climber control room, halfway up the shaft.

Warthen's men, peering down from the cargo bay, recovered from Neil's barrage and lifted their weapons. Neil stepped back, feeling suddenly calm. He let them shoot. Waited it out.

When the bullets stopped, he knew they'd retreated.

Minutes passed in silence. Neil's men eventually organized again and risked the climb up to the cargo bay, but he waited in the hall. He knew they would find it empty.

By now Alex and his men would be zipping along the Elevator cord toward Gateway Station, just fifty kilometers below.

All things considered, Neil counted the skirmish a draw. Alex failed to get into the station proper and did not achieve his desired "inspection." Plus he had no presence on Platz Station at all now, which meant Neil could move forward without those watchful eyes.

But the climber controls were gone. They would have to rely on other stations to guide their traffic in and out. Stations controlled by Warthen's guards. A huge problem, by any estimation, but even as Neil helped drag bodies from the bullet-ridden hallway, backup plans formed in his mind.

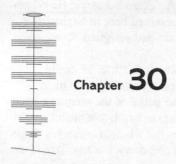

Chapter 30

ON THE HORIZON west of Darwin, lightning danced through deep purple clouds, creating pockets of bright violet over a calm sea.

Russell Blackfield counted the seconds until rolling thunder washed over the city. He stood naked in the warm wet-season breeze, on a balcony high above Nightcliff's western wall. A hotel, once, for the thousands of people who came from all over the world to gawk at the alien device.

A whore lay on the bed in the room behind him, sleeping already. He'd worn her out, given her more than she bargained for. He took a deep breath and stretched. Russell never felt like sleeping after sex. In fact, what he needed was a good run.

He returned to the room and collected his clothing, careful not to disturb the sleeping woman.

"Whore" was unkind, he decided. She'd been genuinely willing, and asked for nothing in return. Not overtly, anyway. They all wanted the same thing—status, and ultimately a trip up the ladder to a better life.

Russell paused after pulling on his pants, and sat on the bed next to her. She lay on her side, back to him.

The thought came out of nowhere, a thought that had never crossed his mind before. *Perhaps I should take a wife.*

Word had come yesterday, from Sofia Windon herself. He had been elected to the Orbital Council, a post that would allow him free access to any station. He would even be assigned quarters in Gateway, for extended stays. He was an Orbital now, even if his job remained here in Nightcliff.

On top of all that, Neil Platz had resigned. Convenient, that.

Yes, a wife. For the first time in his life, he could legitimately offer life in orbit as a perk for being with him.

He traced a finger along the curve of the woman's back. She had a well-toned body. Thin as a rail, like most Darwinians, but good proportions on the whole. He ran his finger over the arch of her buttocks and down her hip. Would she make a good wife?

Russell tried to imagine himself wed to this woman. Sleeping with her every night.

What was her damn name?

True, she had pleased him this evening, and a few times previously. How long could that last?

She'd been so willing. So utterly boring.

He wanted someone who would be shocked at his bedroom demands. Someone with rounder, softer curves. Someone he could corrupt.

Someone with a name worth remembering.

His thoughts drifted to Tania Sharma.

All in good time. Russell stood and finished dressing.

In the main yard, he splashed through puddles left by the storm that now faded into the eastern sky. He picked a barracks at random and burst through the door without knocking.

A soldier, who had been sitting in a creaky wooden chair by the door, leapt to his feet. His surprise turned into a salute when he realized who had entered.

Russell felt pleased the guard had not been asleep, but hid this.

"Get everyone up," he said. "We're going for a run."

"Yessa!" the guard said. No more than a boy.

"I'll be out front. You have thirty seconds." He enjoyed the youngster's reaction, all slack jaw and clumsy stammer. Russell spun on his heel and walked back outside to the sound of shouted orders and frantic men rolling out of their bunks.

Sixty seconds later, the guards were standing in a rough line, two deep, in front of him. While a few had managed to get into uniform, most were still in their undershirts and shorts. He let the tardiness go.

"I feel like a jog," Russell said. "How about you?"

They shouted their agreement in perfect unison.

"Good. Once around the wall, I think," Russell said. He turned left, toward the main gate, and began to run. Behind him he heard the satisfying sound of eighty feet landing in unison with his.

He kept the pace brisk, took a sharp turn just before the huge gate, climbed the stairwell there to the top of the wall. A route he did frequently, often with a random platoon trailing behind. They knew the drill.

The wall made a rough circle around the base of the Elevator, except when following the coastline, with a total circumference of just over five kilometers. It stood more than fifteen meters high, with steeply sloped sides, and only a fraction of it had guardrails to protect one from falling.

For most of it, including the entire stretch along the ocean, there was only flat, weathered concrete, slick with sea spray. One misstep would result in an unfortunate meeting with asphalt to the east or south, or craggy shallow rocks to the north or west.

Few actually fell. Hell, the last one even survived, if Russell remembered right. About as useful now as a horse with two legs, but he survived. A run in and of itself was a mind-numbing activity. Add a little risk, though, and you had something.

The group started to spread out by the time they reached the one-kilometer marker. Only a small portion of the guards could keep up with Russell, and by the end he knew that it would be him and perhaps one or two others.

Russell thought it was a good way to find candidates for his elite guard. And of course, the men knew that he would often reward those who finished next to him with a willing woman.

Good motivator, that.

And good for the woman, too, as far as Russell was concerned—practice makes perfect.

At the midpoint on the north wall, by the old jetty, he heard a voice calling for him. He assumed it was one of the guards behind him, pleading to slow the pace, and ignored it. But on a second call he realized the voice came from below. Russell looked down and left and saw someone waving both arms.

"What the hell do you want? I'm running!" he shouted at the dark figure.

"Gateway is on the comm; they say it's urgent," the man yelled back.

"Did you tell them I'm running?"

The man stammered.

"That was a joke," Russell shouted. "Be right there."

Russell took the call in his office.

"This is Blackfield," he said into the microphone.

From the other end came a jostling sound. He heard muffled voices in the background.

"Russell, hello."

Alex Warthen. He sounded tired.

"What can I do for you? There's been no sign of that scavenger, Skyler what's-his-name, if that's why you're calling."

"There's a situation developing up here, and I need your help."

Russell grinned. *One day, and already I'm indispensable.* "You sound like shit."

"Took a bullet," Alex replied, "in the shoulder. Collarbone is all cracked to hell."

"Shit," Russell said, leaning forward. "You've got my attention. What happened?"

Alex recounted the story of the failed raid on Platz Station. "He was ready for us. With well-armed fighters. Luckily my sleeper agent aboard his station had the sense to act before Platz could divide my men. We would have failed completely without her help."

"What's Neil's angle?"

Alex paused. "What do you mean?"

"Why," Russell said with a sigh, "did he fight you? Couldn't he have just turned your climbers around from the start? Avoided the whole thing in the first place?"

Another pause. He must not have considered that. Then Alex said, "I have to assume he wanted to cause casualties, not avoid them. One thing's for sure: He's got something worth killing for hidden in that station."

Russell tried to work through the ramifications. He felt a headache coming on. "Where do I come in?"

"We need reinforcements, supplies. My men don't have the numbers or the training for something like this."

"You're going to try again?"

"Hell yes," Alex said. "Platz isn't just a former council-man now; he's a cold-blooded murderer. The stupid old sod has given me the excuse I need to shut him down, per-manently."

"Us," Russell said. "Given *us* the excuse."

"Right. Of course."

Russell turned his chair to look out the dirty window at the Darwin skyline. Shadowed against the dawn light the buildings looked like so many tombstones.

Alex interrupted his train of thought. "Well?"

Russell crossed to his door and waved his assistant in. "I'll have an anti-riot battalion on the way within the hour. Real hard-hitting bastards." To his assistant he said, "Squads four and six, full gear, in the yard in thirty minutes. Go."

The man nodded and ran for the stairs.

"With them will be air and water," Russell said to Alex.

"Food, too, if you can. The farms are above Platz Station, so he effectively has a hold on them. I know there's a *short-age* down there and all . . ."

"Har, har. No problem, enough to feed an army."

"All right," Alex said, "see you soon then. Doc is here, ordering me to rest. Which reminds me, I'm pretty useless with my shoulder like this. Captain Larsen, my second in command, will be acting on my behalf."

"Any good?"

"I just met him, actually," Alex admitted. "He's been run-ning security up at Hab-One."

"He runs a major thing like that and you just met him?"

"Never needed to," Alex said, "because he's been doing the job so well."

Russell understood this. His best people were the ones he could assign a task and then forget about. "I look forward to working with him. Blackfield, out."

He switched off the connection and stared out at the horizon. Slums, as far as the eye could see. A million hungry mouths and diarrheic asses.

As soon as Platz was well and truly defeated, Blackfield would announce a new way of doing things down here. He would release the food and fire up the rest of the desalination plants.

The people would cheer his name. He could practically hear it carried on the rolling thunder.

The men aligned in an uneven grid. Russell walked up and down the rows, nudging them into line with swift strikes from his baton to the back of the calf. It didn't take them long to realize he was serious.

Two hundred men in all. Many of them even carried the same gear, appropriated from the Australian army after the collapse. A few had weapons acquired on their own, and as a rule Russell never questioned how they came across such equipment. They just had to prove that it worked reliably, and that they had ammunition in sufficient quantity.

Russell stopped at the front of the assembly, his back to them. A light rain fell, just more than a mist. He looked up at the cord of the Elevator, which faded into the mist just a few hundred meters above.

His eyes turned to the busy dockworkers in front of the array of soldiers. Ten cargo climbers were being prepared for the journey. Per his instructions, each would carry the maximum load of eight containers: two water, two compressed air, two food, and two personnel.

A crane loomed overhead, waiting to lift the massive vehicles and swing them into position, where another crew would clamp them onto the cord itself. Billions of microscopic legs inside the climber's central shaft would then grip the thin thread and begin to crawl upward.

Russell turned to face the men. They snapped to attention, more or less in unison.

He began his address. "I know you all enjoy our weekly jaunts into the square outside to quell the rioters."

This drew some laughs, and more than a few *whoops* of agreement.

"And I know you're all disappointed that you weren't sent out to patrol Aura's Edge and have some target practice against these supposed packs of 'newsubs.'"

A mix of grumbles and assent this time. Everyone wondered about the rumors. Subs working in large packs, coming in from the Clear and rampaging through neighborhoods. Russell didn't believe it, but he'd sent a few squads out to make a show of effort.

"Well, I have a different task for you lot. Something much more interesting."

Silence, now. He had them hanging on every word.

"Playtime," Russell said, raising his voice, "is over." He paused for effect, enjoying the sight of two hundred grins being whisked away. The yard grew silent, save for the rain that dripped from the rooftops—and the busy climber crews.

He continued. "Today will be a turning point. The start of a new era, where we Darwinians no longer live off the table scraps of those who sit above us." Now he had their undivided attention. "Yesterday a routine security inspection, led by my Orbital counterpart and friend Alex Warthen, was ambushed on Platz Station."

A murmur ran through the troops. Russell held up a hand and waited for quiet.

"Neil Platz has fired the first volley in a conflict that I aim to end. Today."

The men shouted in unison, a single whoop. Russell felt a twinge of pride, and fed off it.

"Commander Warthen took thirty of his best men into Platz Station, and they were repelled. The commander himself took a bullet." Russell began to pace through the ranks, hands clasped behind his back. He'd seen the behavior in an old war movie, and liked it. "They retreated to Gateway," he said, pointing upward, "just four hundred klicks that way."

Russell stopped in front of one of the soldiers, a black man with bloodshot eyes. "Any idea what he did when he got there?"

"No, sir," the man said.

Russell looked the soldier up and down and nodded with satisfaction. He turned back to the group at large. "He called me. And *begged* for help!"

They shouted again, louder this time.

"You see, they've got it pretty easy up there," Russell said. "His men are soft. What Warthen needs right now is a bunch of skull-cracking, badass sons of bitches who know how to keep squabblers in line!"

The last part of this was lost in the hollering of the men, now smacking their rifles with the palms of their hands.

"Are we going to hide here, in the safety of these walls?"

"No, sir!"

"Are we going to cower here, waiting for another shipment of rotting fruit?"

"No, sir!"

"No, sir, that's right." Russell returned to his position in front of them. "What we're going to do is ride to the rescue."

"Yes, sir!"

"What we're going to do . . . is kick some Orbital ass."

"Yes, sir!"

"And we're not leaving," Russell said, lowering his voice to draw them in, "until Neil fucking Platz pays for his cowardly ambush."

They cheered again, loud enough to wake the whole of Nightcliff, and much of Darwin, Russell thought.

"And mark my words, Neil fucking Platz will never again dictate the affairs of Nightcliff. Of Darwin."

The men roared.

Russell turned to face the climbers again, mostly to hide his broad smile.

This was going to be fun.

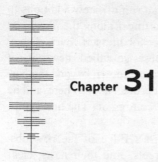

Chapter 31

THREE NIGHTCLIFF SOLDIERS cowered in the dusty ground-floor storefront. The acrid smell of burned gunpowder filled the hazy air, and spent shell casings littered the concrete floor.

One stood at the open doorway, leaning out to view the street beyond. He held his AK-47 in a white-knuckled grip, braced against his armpit. Sweat and blood dotted his face. Smoke still curled up from the tip of the gun's barrel.

Abandoned cars clogged the street outside, many still occupied by the remains of those who had almost made it to Darwin, to the Aura's safety, five years earlier. They'd made it as far as the shifting, rippling Aura only to die in the traffic jam, unwilling to leave the safety of their cars as subhumans swarmed the area. The no-man's-land had been left to rot ever since.

Until tonight.

Ramesh looked down at his own feeble pistol. An antique, with his last four bullets in the clip.

"We're cut off," the third man said, from his crouched position by the large square hole in the wall that a shop window once filled. "We'll never make it back to the barricade."

"Shut up," the man by the door said. His maroon helmet had a nasty dent in it from a newsub who'd swung a tire iron at him. "There's more coming. I hear them."

"We're fucked," said the one by the window.

Ramesh agreed, silently. Four of their squad mates lay in

the street outside. Two others had run off, new additions to the enemies' numbers. He ran a finger along the pistol and decided he'd save the last bullet for himself. Even if they survived another wave of these so-called newsubs, it wouldn't matter. They'd been pinned down beyond the barricade too long. The Aura didn't protect as well here, and he could already feel the headache coming on. The first symptom, everyone knew that.

Blackfield's order: Clear Aura's Edge of the newsubs. Quick sorties into the dark streets, find their nests, clear them, and get back. In reward, volunteers would be placed on the list for Orbital duty.

Not worth it. Not even close. Ramesh could hear their inhuman grunting in the street outside, close now.

"Our reinforcements should get here soon," said the guard at the door. "We hold here. Got it?"

The one by the window rose to his feet with a grunt. "Why wait? Fuck this. Let's get back to the barricade with the others. We'll end up diseased if we stay any longer."

One of the subhumans screamed, a sound so awful Ramesh wanted to clap his hands over his ears. Then the cry ended sharply.

Gunshots rattled off in the street, lighting the sides of the abandoned buildings in brief flashes. Ramesh moved to the window, unable to stop himself. "Reinforcements?" he asked.

No one needed to answer. The gunshots were coming from *outside* Darwin, not toward the barricade. Subhumans loped over the derelict cars toward the sound, their scrawny forms lit with each salvo from some unseen position down the street. One's head snapped backward in midair and it fell, lifeless, just outside the empty window frame. Three more fell in as many seconds.

In those flashes of light, Ramesh saw a man standing atop the shell of a van. He swung his weapon in quick arcs, rattling off shots with unnerving calm. The rifle sounded different than an AK. Quiet, more refined.

"Who the hell is that?" the soldier in the doorway said.

Ramesh didn't care. Could be Jesus H. Christ, or the

Devil himself. Either way the man was killing subs one after another, and that was all that mattered.

A subhuman rushed toward the man from beyond the Aura, from his blind side. Ramesh aimed and squeezed a shot off. He missed, but it slowed the creature, and in the next second its body convulsed as bullets tore through it.

"Help him," Ramesh managed to say as he fired again. Two bullets left.

His squad mates finally took action and began to provide cover fire.

The man saw them then and leapt from the van. He jogged toward their position while still shooting, one arm wrapped around his torso.

Skyler plowed through the doorway and slid to a seated position by the back wall. His ribs felt as if on fire, and he wanted to faint as soon as he reached the wall.

Three men in the storefront room stared at him with wide eyes. "Don't stop shooting on my account," Skyler said.

The one with the maroon helmet by the door turned and started to fire again. A Nightcliff guard, then. The other two looked like street thugs. One, an Indian man, crawled to Skyler's position. "I'm Ramesh. You okay?"

"Just need a second," Skyler replied.

"That was amazing," he whispered. "What you did—"

"Won't matter if they get in here. Keep shooting."

"Out of bullets," Ramesh admitted.

Skyler pulled a Sonton pistol from a shoulder holster. He'd found the gun on his miserable trek home, on the corpse of a dead traffic cop. He flipped the weapon around and stuffed it into Ramesh's waiting hand.

The shooting from the others subsided as the newsubs retreated.

"Who are you?" the man asked, eyes fixed on the fine pistol.

"Skyler—"

"Skyler?" the one by the door said. He swung his AK-47 around and pointed it at Skyler's chest. "Blackfield's got a huge reward out for you."

Before Skyler could say a word, a subhuman flew through the open window. It tackled the thug who crouched there, slashing at his face even as they toppled into a heap in the center of the room.

Skyler broke for a rear door that led farther into the building. He had no idea where it went; he just knew he had to get away.

"Come back!" The shout came from Ramesh, and Skyler ignored it.

To his dismay, the passageway was not an exit but a stairwell, going up. Skyler took them three at a time, flight after flight. The sounds of battle receded behind and below.

At the fourth floor, Skyler stopped and ducked into a side hall. The condition of the space was no different than the first floor—concrete floors and a grid of exposed support columns. He listened at the stairs, hearing only the battle below.

That would change, and soon. Whichever side won, Skyler had to assume the building would be searched.

He jogged to the empty windows along the outer wall. Skyler leaned out and studied the street below, just in time to see a burst of fire from the leader's powerful rifle. The sound of the gun echoed through the deserted buildings along the narrow street, like a succession of thunderclaps.

Gunfire also erupted from behind a pile of debris in the road. Skyler couldn't see well but guessed reinforcements had arrived to rescue the men below.

Subhumans were everywhere. Loping to and fro, dodging weapons they understood at some primal level, dancing toward their attackers.

Skyler looked left, toward the trash barrier that marked the outskirts of Darwin's slums. Then he looked up and saw the tightly packed rooftops against the night sky.

Rooftops.

He raced back to the stairs and continued to climb, ignoring the searing pain in his ribs. He'd wrapped his chest in gauze two days earlier, but the dressing did little to help.

After six more flights he broke through a badly corroded metal door. Skyler skidded to a halt. Numerous holes marred the uneven surface, caused by erosion from pooled rainwater that could not find an open drain. He picked his way carefully across, to the Darwin-facing side of the building. In the sky above Nightcliff, he saw a strange sight. Fifteen climbers by his count, inching up the Elevator into the clouds. In all his life he'd never seen more than seven or eight at once, well spaced out. These were bunched together, less than a kilometer separating the first from the last.

Worry about it later, Skyler thought. He looked at the adjacent building, hoping for a spot narrow enough to jump across, and saw something even better.

A crude bridge, constructed of old stepladders bound together, spanned the short distance between his rooftop and the next. Even without considering the height, the bridge looked terrifying.

However, it was a path, the only path, so Skyler took it.

He stepped over the edge of the rooftop and gingerly tested the ladder with one foot. It bounced under his weight. Skyler gulped and stepped back. The route suddenly seemed like folly.

Behind him the metal door creaked. Decision made. He moved in rapid, even steps out onto the bridge, rolling each footfall to minimize its springing effect. The ladder strained under his weight but held.

"Stop there!"

"Hell no!" Skyler shouted, halfway across. He could taste the other side.

A shot rang out. He heard the bullet whiz over his head. *A calculated miss?* He doubted these guards were that skilled.

Skyler paid no heed and leapt for the roof opposite. He landed feetfirst on a low wall that surrounded the edge. His momentum carried him over and onto the roof itself, just before another bullet buried itself in the low wall behind him. Skyler rolled to a stop, then rolled backward to get cover behind the waist-high lip.

Skyler heard the voice of the squad's leader from the other roof, talking low but not low enough.

"Get him?"

The other sounded confident. "Think so, in the back."

"Go check," said the leader. "I'll cover—"

Skyler popped up into a crouch and aimed his rifle at them, squeezing off a burst. He had precious few bullets remaining, even after finding two fresh clips during his nightmare trek home, but he needed to dissuade them. The leader deftly dodged to his right. Skyler's bullets caught the other man square in the chest, sending him sprawling.

The leader lifted his gun over the lip of the opposite rooftop, firing blind. Skyler had seen this attempted many times, always with the same result: People overcompensated, firing low. No exception this time. He ignored the salvo and instead leaned over the small wall. He grasped the end of the ladder-bridge and shoved. It fell away easily, tumbling down into the darkness below. Skyler ducked back behind his shelter wall and listened to the satisfying crash as the ladder hit the ground.

He took a deep breath and then started crawling to the left, along the roof edge.

"We'll find you!" the leader shouted from the other building.

When he reached the corner, Skyler moved into a crouch and turned toward where the other man had been. He jutted upward just enough to get a view of the other roof and found it to be empty.

Standing, he moved diagonally across the surface, heading for a doorway that led into the building below. He moved like a crab, keeping his weapon trained on the other roof. No sign of the Nightcliff thug. Perhaps he'd given up.

Doubtful, Skyler decided. He put himself in the other man's shoes and guessed he was racing back down the stairwell now, intent on catching Skyler as he tried to exit this building.

Skyler moved to the western edge of the roof. The adjacent building was a full floor lower, but close. He backed up, got a running start, and jumped.

His feet took the initial impact, and he quickly tucked into a roll, putting his good shoulder forward.

Raw pain lanced across his rib cage. Skyler rolled to a stop and lay curled in a ball, drawing shallow breaths until the burning sensation faded. Every corner of his mind told him to stop, to rest.

Not yet.

He used the same technique to traverse one more rooftop, and only then began to descend. The building appeared to have been used for migrant worker housing, back when such people flocked to Darwin for jobs creating the infrastructure that went into orbit. Room after room of bunk bed frames, in various conditions. The mattresses had all been taken, along with the spring coils and anything else not bolted down.

Skyler kept to the main stairwell, moving as quickly as his fatigued legs and burning ribs would carry him. Minutes later he peered out a hole where the front door used to be.

A wide avenue fronted the building. Along the middle of it stood a mound of trash five meters high. Darwin's edge.

On top of the debris barricade, about a hundred meters off to the right, a group of men stood and waited. For what, he couldn't see. They were looking, Skyler guessed, down the street where the fight had occurred minutes earlier.

He left the shelter of the building and jogged away from them, keeping close to the buildings. When they were out of sight, Skyler crossed to the barricade and scaled it.

He peered over the top and saw the very edge of Darwin's densely inhabited slums. A stark contrast to no-man's-land, the streets on this side of the barricade teemed with people. Campfires illuminated them, erected in chaotic intervals along the middle of the street. One fire burned in a flipped-over refrigerator, and another in an old rowboat. Around each were crowds of people, huddled together. Some were cooking things over the flames. Rat, Skyler guessed. What else was there? He decided it was better not to know the answer to that.

So ingrained was their fear of SUBS that they all kept a safe distance from the barricade, and that was all that mattered right now. Skyler pulled himself over the top of it and crawled down the other side.

Home. I'm home.

* * *

The storm came out of nowhere, and in less than ten minutes the city had gone from a balmy evening to a torrential downpour. The streets cleared somewhat, and that suited Skyler just fine.

He kept to himself, head down, gait purposeful but never hurried. Each breath he drew felt like a thorn twisting in his side. He hid his gun beneath his flight jacket, as best he could. No one in this part of Darwin could afford a weapon like his, much less hang on to it. Best not to advertise.

The old airport appeared like an oasis.

At the high chain-link fence that ran the perimeter of the airfield, he stopped and leaned against it. He waited, hoping a patrol would come by. Someone he'd know. All of the airport's residents chipped in to patrol the fence.

Warm rain soaked his clothes. After ten minutes, it became clear that no patrol marched the circuit. Something was wrong.

He studied the row of hangars along the old runway. The flat pavement, no longer needed for rolling takeoff or landing, had long ago been put to use as a foundation for hangars. More than a hundred such structures spanned the length of the airstrip. Even in this storm, there should be activity.

Skyler gave up waiting for a patrol. Instead he set off walking, along the fence line, toward the airport's main gate.

Well before reaching it he saw an armada of Nightcliff armored vehicles parked in sloppy fashion around the entrance. Blocking it. A handful of maroon-helmeted soldiers milled about. Most loitered in front of Woon's tavern, the communal kitchen at the beginning of the runway. Skyler could just make out a few of his neighbors; they were having animated discussions with the soldiers.

Soldiers who held guns at the ready.

The sight crushed all hope of finding refuge here. Worse, his misfortune now affected the other crews.

He risked moving closer to get a view far enough down the runway to see his own hangar. Maybe the guards were here for some other reason. It was a false hope, and he knew it before even setting eyes on the door to his home. Still, the sight of it hit him like a hammer blow.

A steady stream of soldiers moved in and out of the hangar door, carrying whatever they could. He even saw two of them working together to move one of the bunks into the back of a truck.

Skyler turned and walked away from the fence, and headed back into the city. His mind raced. He needed a place to hole up, to think. To plan his infiltration of Nightcliff. And he needed resources.

He needed Prumble.

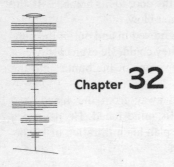

Chapter 32

TANIA RUBBED THE sleep from her eyes and read the message again:

Speak to no one.
    Go immediately to Room 32, Gray Level. Password: Antelope.
    —N.P.

Neil, here? A chill ran down her spine; a million little bumps rose on her arms.

She pulled on a jumpsuit, her mind racing.

A thick air of tension gripped Anchor Station. After word came of the battle on Platz Station, security began to block access to the docking bays.

Orders, they said.

Rumors spread of the turmoil in the council. Some said Neil had resigned; others said Alex had. She'd even heard that Alex had thrown Neil in the brig for "treachery."

And now, her first word from Neil. The cryptic nature did little to help her anxiety.

Stepping out of her room into the dark hallway, she considered waking Natalie. Whatever happened now, they were in this together, and Tania found she craved the comfort of a confidante.

Speak to no one.

She heard the words, in Neil's authoritative voice. Memories came with it, of sitting under an avocado tree, of watching ants devour a lone straggler fallen from the maze of branches. He'd spoken to her in that voice then, urged her to take on the project alone. She'd betrayed him then, but wouldn't now.

Moving at a natural pace, Tania made her way to Gray Level. She rarely visited the section, but the layout mirrored the others. As she walked, she wondered if a guard might stop her. In the past few days, some of her staff had complained of being questioned when moving between levels.

Again, orders.

She considered contacting Alex Warthen directly, demanding an explanation, and the thought made her miss Neil even more. She always took such concerns to him and knew he would champion her causes in front of the council.

She reached room thirty-two unscathed. From the faded sign on the wall, it was a typical station conference room.

Trying the door, she found it locked. A swipe of her access card did nothing. On the manual keypad below the card slot, she tapped the numbers that spelled *Antelope*.

The lock disengaged with a subtle click, and she opened the door to a room full of people. Neil Platz was not among them.

"Come in and close the door," a man at the table said. Tall and thin, gray hair in two tufts over each ear, and wearing square-rimmed glasses. He looked vaguely familiar.

She took one step inside and let the door click closed behind her. An oval-shaped table dominated the room. Chairs had surrounded it, but they had been pushed to the far wall.

Roughly twenty men and women stood at the table, studying maps of the station splayed out across the surface. As Tania entered, they all stopped and stared at her.

She thought she had seen a few of them around the station, but she couldn't name a single one.

"What's going on here?" she asked. "Who are you?"

"Karl Stromm," the balding man answered.

"Do I know you?"

He shot her a friendly smile. "I served you breakfast this morning."

The memory jumped to the front of her mind, clear as day. This man, in an apron, dishing out her imitation eggs. She looked over the rest of them, and the pieces fell into place. Low-level maintenance workers, cooks, cleaning crew.

People who went unnoticed.

"I take it that Neil did not brief you," Karl said.

Tania shook her head.

He nodded, once. "Join us at the table. We need your help."

"Help with what?" she asked, cautiously approaching the map-laden surface.

"Neil wants to stay a step ahead of the enemy."

She felt her pulse quicken. "What do you mean?"

"Mutiny, Miss Sharma. Mutiny."

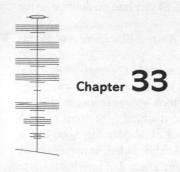

Chapter **33**

IN THE MIDDLE of the road, Skyler dropped to his knees and erupted into a bitter laugh.

The gate to Prumble's garage lay in a broken pile of twisted iron. Debris littered the street in front of the building, a pair of rag-clad pickers filling burlap sacks with the choicer pieces. They scattered at the sound of Skyler's laugh.

My ship destroyed, my friends killed or captured, my hangar looted, and now this?

Skyler glanced over his shoulder at the Elevator. It had never seemed farther away.

Numb, he forced himself onto unsteady feet. One foot in front of the other; repeat. He lumbered to the garage entrance and shuffled down the ramp. The smell of smoke overwhelmed his senses. He pulled his shirt up over his mouth and nose.

At the bottom of the ramp Skyler flipped on the light attached to his gun barrel. The inner door leading to Prumble's warehouse had been smashed away, along with most of the surrounding wall. Beyond lay charred, shattered shelves and overturned plastic bins, their sides partially melted.

Prumble must be dead. Dead, or gone. Nothing of value remained here. It had been ransacked, then scuttled. At the back of the garage, Skyler found Prumble's office. The meat-locker door lay on the ground, crumpled like a discarded lager can. Scorch marks marred the ground around it.

They'd used high explosives. Skyler had no doubt who the culprit was.

New goal, he thought. *Find Russell Blackfield and put his eyes out with a hot poker.*

One more check box on a growing list of impossible tasks.

He left the garage, his feet moving on their own, for he had no will to keep going. He took shelter from the rain in a building across the street and doubled over from pain. A pain born not of his injuries but of despair. His hope of fixing the Aura, and returning to orbit, faded, stomped out by the cards that fate had given him. He had to turn his focus to survival now.

Maybe he could go to Grillo and beg for a job piloting one of his shitty boats. To come this far, only to join up with that bastard? It almost seemed the perfect end to this series of tragedies.

Perhaps he should just walk away, into the Clear, as Skadz had done. Leave this mess to those forced to wallow in it.

He thought back to the day he'd met Prumble at the café. The feeling he'd had seeing that satchel full of pristine bills.

The café. Prumble had joked of retiring there. Half joked, Skyler thought. He certainly knew the owner well enough. And he did say it was where he met his contact from Nightcliff.

Skyler thought that maybe if he waited at the coffeehouse long enough, the man from Nightcliff might come in again, looking for Prumble. He lived in Nightcliff, and that meant a potential way in.

Or perhaps the old woman who owned the place had heard from the big man. Maybe she even knew if he'd survived the attack on his home.

Near exhaustion, devoid of other options, Skyler did the only thing he could do: walk.

He arrived very late. Between the hour and the heavy rain, the streets were mostly empty. Only one other shop was open near Clarke's: a one-room card house. The occupants, four elderly men, huddled around a table playing mah-jongg. They barely registered Skyler's passing.

He breathed a sigh of relief. The café was open. Even better, it was empty.

The old Sri Lankan woman sat behind the counter, knitting. She eyed him with suspicion but flashed a toothless smile nonetheless.

Skyler couldn't recall her name. He asked for coffee, plus a bun filled with some kind of bean mash. He tried not to imagine the origin of its contents, and wolfed it down before he was even seated. Belatedly he wondered how he would pay for it.

When she brought the coffee, Skyler thanked her, and said, "Do you speak English?"

"Little," she said.

"Have you seen Prumble? The fat man?"

Her eyes narrowed. The smile remained. She shook her head slowly.

"Please," he said, "his garage was attacked. I have to find out if he survived."

"I no know him," she said.

Terrible liar, Skyler thought.

He looked at his coffee cup. "He gave you the coffee beans, yes?"

Her eyes shifted, uncertain.

"I retrieved those for him in Vietnam. You know Vietnam?" She just stared. "Prumble sent me to retrieve some parts for an X-ray machine. We dropped on a military hospital, looking for them."

The crone just stared at him. He wasn't sure if she understood any of it.

The details of the mission flashed through Skyler's mind like a daydream. "I remember we found the parts we needed straightaway, and had some time to explore. Skadz and I went to a house on the base; it belonged to some Communist Party official. There was a whole cache of supplies stacked in the basement, including a case of preserved coffee. Coffee, yes? In a special can." He approximated it with his arms. "Had a white stripe across it, diagonal, like this."

Her eyes briefly shot toward the bar. Skyler hoped he was getting through to her.

"Coffee," she finally said.

"Yes. From Vietnam. From Prumble."

She shuffled away, under the flimsy wooden plank that was the bar, and through a curtained doorway.

"Look," Skyler called after her, "Prumble met a man here a few weeks back. A man in a long overcoat. I need to contact that man. If you can help. . ."

No sound from behind the curtain. Skyler gave up and sipped his beverage, enjoying the rich flavor.

He looked out the dirty window and watched the rain pummel the alley beyond. Merciless, tonight. He looked up the side of the building directly across. On every windowsill, containers of all sizes and shapes had been set out, precariously, to catch what water they could.

He wondered if anything would ever change here. The city was gradually dying. Entropy would win.

Sound from behind the bar caught his attention, and he turned back.

Prumble stood there, leaning on his cane, a huge grin across his face.

"I can scarcely believe my eyes," he said.

"Prumble!" Skyler stood and embraced the man.

"I figured you were dead," Prumble said, laughing.

"Likewise. I went to the garage. . . ."

"Ah, yes. Blackfield's work. I was inside at the time."

"And you survived? Well, clearly. What were they after?"

Prumble sighed. The old woman set a cracked mug in front of him, and he thanked her. To Skyler, Prumble said, "Dirt on Platz. Something tipped them off."

"I may know something about that," Skyler said.

"Oh?"

Skyler leaned in closer. "Have you heard anything about Sam, or the others?"

The fat man shook his head. "I've been keeping a low profile. But your question fills me with dread."

"A lot has happened."

Prumble picked up his mug. "Come with me, and tell me all about it. I prefer not to sit next to a window under Nightcliff's shadow. I'm a wanted man, after all."

Skyler followed him through the curtain behind the counter, and up a narrow, steep flight of stairs.

"Renuka was kind enough to offer me a room," Prumble said as he foisted his girth up the steps, "as long as I need it. Her husband and her son have both passed away, it seems."

They entered a small room, with Prumble only just fitting through the door. It stank of old socks, and measured barely three meters on a side.

However, devoid of furniture, it provided enough room to survive. Instead of a bed, layers of threadbare carpet and blankets covered the floor. Moth-chewed pillows filled one corner.

"It's comfortable enough," Prumble said, carefully taking a seat on the floor. Skyler sat opposite him.

Prumble busied himself for a minute, adjusting the stack of pillows behind him to support his bad back. "Tell me," the fat man said.

"In a moment," Skyler said, lying down on the soft floor. It felt warm, and smelled of cinnamon. He closed his eyes.

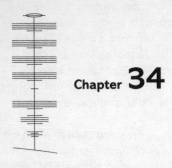

Chapter 34

TANIA KEPT HER gaze on the floor. She pulled down a baseball cap she'd borrowed to hide her face. Surprise would be
lost if anyone recognized her too quickly.

Two guards manned the security desk. They hunched
over a well-worn board game and paid little attention as the
cleaners arrived. Routine behavior, their reaction said. Both
were lightly armed, with handheld toxin-based immobiliz-
ers and standard batons. Both were out of shape.

"Your weapons please," said one of the cleaners. Another
opened a canvas bag and held it out to them. "Slowly."

The two guards looked up from their game, bewildered.
From the back of the group, Tania observed unnoticed. The
guards focused completely on the weapons now pointed at
them. After a brief exchange of glances, they placed their
weapons in the offered bag and slumped back, waiting.

"Show me the duty roster," the leader said.

One of the guards cautiously picked up a clipboard from
the desk and handed it over.

The cleaner did not so much as glance at it. Instead he
passed it over his shoulder to another in the group. His attention never left the two confused sentries. "Access cards."

The men hesitated, if only for an instant, before produc-
ing their key cards. These, and the clipboard, made their
way back to Tania. She glanced at them and flashed a quick
nod at the leader of their mutinous party. She realized she
had forgotten his name.

The guards waited, confused.

"Where are your quarters?" the leader asked.

One of the guards said, "Green fifteen."

"Green seventeen," said the other.

"Lead the way." Four of the supposed janitors followed as the two guards stood and shuffled toward their rooms. The other cleaners took positions around the security desk, pretending to do their jobs.

Time for Tania to play her part. Without a word, she turned and ran along the upward-curving hallway. After a few hundred meters she came upon another large cleaning crew milling about the door to the main computer lab, which had been propped open with a black plastic buckct.

Tania acknowledged them with a flashed thumbs-up and moved through the open door without breaking stride.

Inside the lab, she took a sharp right and angled toward a pair of double doors marked SECURITY PERSONNEL ONLY.

Karl waited there. She showed him the keys, flashing a smile, hoping it conveyed confidence. In truth, she felt nothing but dread at what they were doing.

"Good work," Karl said. "Any problems?"

"They cooperated. I didn't have to talk to them."

A loud *clack* emanated from the lock as she swiped the card through the reader.

"No one enters," Karl said to the crew at the main door. Then he led Tania inside the Anchor Station security control room.

She went immediately to a panel of monitors, swiped the card again, and tapped the screen until they were looking at Red Level. The cargo dock.

Karl stood next to her, and together they watched the second phase of their plan unfold.

On the screen, a maintenance crew mingled with four security guards. Tania replayed their planned story in her mind. The workers would tell the guards on duty that they were being punished for a well-intentioned but poorly executed prank against their boss. Their penalty: perform a full inspection of all climbers in dock, and check all the airlock doors for leakage. The guards laughed and waved them in.

Play on the universal disdain for bureaucrats, Karl had said.

Brilliant, Tania thought.

Fully inside the docking area, the disguised workers floated into positions around the laughing guards. Red Level duty was considered a "short straw" security post, unlike the two slackers Tania's group had encountered. These guards would be younger and prone to fight back. Karl's words, and right again.

A melee erupted on the screen; a clumsy battle in the weightless environment. One guard had the sense to turn and push himself, flying toward an alarm panel ten meters away. No one gave chase.

The guard reached the lever and pulled it. And pulled it again.

"So predictable," Karl said, tapping away on the adjacent monitor.

Tania watched as the man turned back to the fight. The other guards were clearly losing. And now three workers fanned out to take on this last. Tania held her breath. Weapons were drawn, and the idea of more bloodshed on the station terrified her.

Thinking better of his choice, the remaining guard let go of his weapon and raised his hands. The gun drifted away, and Tania breathed a sigh of relief.

Within a minute the guards were bound and gagged. According to the plan they would be locked in one of the offices on Purple Level, pending further instructions.

"It's time, Miss Sharma," Karl said.

Tania hesitated. "Can't you do it?"

Karl gave her a gentle pat on the arm. "I clean toilets," he said, "as far as these people know. A voice of authority is critical now. A familiar voice."

She nodded. He was right, but it did not make this easier. "This is all happening so fast," she said, watching the guards on the monitor get escorted offscreen.

"Neil has a plan," Karl replied. "We've got to trust it."

Tania wondered if Neil had really thought all this through. More than anything, she wanted to speak with him. *No,* she thought. More than anything she wanted to get back to her research and have no further part in activities like this.

Instead she would have to speak to the entire station. With trepidation, she picked up the microphone.

"Attention please. This is Dr. Tania Sharma. Due to an increasingly dire rift that has formed within the Orbital Council, I've been asked by Neil Platz to take control of the security situation on Anchor. Be assured I take no pleasure in this act. However, after a violent and unprovoked attack on Platz Station yesterday, I felt action was necessary to ensure the safety of everyone here. I have Neil's full blessings in this matter.

"Security personnel have been temporarily relieved of duty, due to their association with Alex Warthen, who ordered the attack on Platz Station."

"When the differences within the council are resolved, the situation will return to normal. Until then, Neil has appointed me director of Anchor Station. I ask that you go about your normal duties. The station is supplied with ample food, water, and air.

"It saddens me to inform you that external communications have been temporarily suspended. I know many of you have family elsewhere in orbit. I promise you this will be reversed as soon as this crisis is resolved.

"I've called a meeting at ten this morning with all department heads so I can answer questions and explain the situation in greater detail. Please direct your concerns to them. Thank you for listening."

Tania turned off the microphone and buried her head in her hands.

"You did fine," Karl said.

"It won't matter," Tania said through her hands, "if Neil doesn't resolve this soon."

The important part done, Karl set to doling out specific orders to the rest of his group. "I need to think," Tania said, and wandered to the back of the lab.

Alone, she slipped into the research room and logged in. The high-resolution image from the telescope's nightly scan awaited her. She took one more glance at the door and then filled the bank of screens with the picture.

The Builders' ship sat in the center, a dark mass against the blackness of space. She enlarged that portion and studied the telltale oblong shape. Because of the dark material there still wasn't enough detail to discern any purpose, but she could just make out what looked like a shield covering the nose of the vessel.

Tania walked around the desk to stand directly in front of the screen. She traced a finger along the vessel's length, looking for any other differences, and found none.

She stepped back and took in the whole scene. A few small discolorations caught her eye. On the left monitor, near the top corner, a tiny gray blob could just be seen. Another sat near the center. She studied the monitor on the right and found another.

"Multiple ships?" she whispered.

Concerned, Tania moved back to the console and set up Natalie's program again, flipping the image through the entire sequence captured by the telescope. Only three images had been captured, but when they were shown in sequence Tania could see the tiny blobs moving in loose formation with the new Builder ship, which dwarfed them in size. Even with just three pictures to study, Tania realized the small objects were breaking away from the craft.

She counted five in all, and what purpose they served she couldn't begin to imagine.

Chapter 35

INSIDE THE PRIMARY cargo bay on Gateway's lower ring, the Nightcliff men floated around like balloons set adrift. Only a few managed to keep with Russell as he moved for the exit, where a stocky Gateway security officer waited for him. The man had a face like a bulldog and kept his sand-colored hair closely cropped. Ex-military, through and through.

"Jarred Larsen," the man said, extending a hand to Russell as he drifted in.

"I was expecting a horde of nurses and decontamination showers," Russell said.

"There's no time."

"So we depart for Platz Station soon?" Russell asked, grabbing a handhold. Two of the three soldiers who had followed him across the room found something to grab, and landed reasonably well. The third bounced off the wall and drifted slowly away.

Russell wrinkled his nose.

Jarred either didn't notice, or didn't care. "No need. They came to us. Platz's men hold the upper ring, but so far we've managed to contain them there."

"They took the offensive? How did they even make it off the climbers?"

"Didn't use climbers. They came on lifeboats. Somehow they sealed the section remotely," Jarred replied.

"Bold son of a bitch, isn't he. Where's Warthen?"

"Still in the infirmary, sedated. You got here just in time. We're about to try to retake the section. On any other day I'd have your men trade their weapons for coilguns, station regs, but we'll make an exception today."

Russell turned to his soldiers. Slowly they were managing to orient themselves and float toward the exit. "I need a word with your dockmaster."

Jarred called out to a woman on the far side of the bay; she was directing a team who were unloading supplies from the first climber. She heard her name and launched across the bay with expert precision. One of the Nightcliff soldiers nearly collided with her as she sailed past.

"Listen," Russell said to her, "there are nine more climbers right behind this one. I realize the supplies are badly needed, but if you'd be so kind as to, uh, assist my soldiers in getting to the outer ring?"

"Sure," the woman said. "Anything else?" She directed the question to Jarred.

He shook his head. The woman, Williams, nodded to each of them and returned to her crew. Russell and Jarred watched as she had her team efficiently gather the remaining infantry, who floated around the room like so many dead fish, and deposited them along the wall near the exit. A rail ran the length of it, and luckily the men were smart enough to grab it.

"She could be useful," Russell said, "for training my men to fight up here."

"I agree. Hadn't thought about it until now. I think our men will handle any zero-g business until then."

Russell continued to watch for a few more seconds, mesmerized. His attention eventually returned to the task at hand. "Lead on, Captain Larsen."

The burly man moved quickly along the access tube that led from the inner cargo bay to the outer ring. Russell mulled the skipped decontamination. He'd never heard of that happening before. The situation must be dire indeed.

The access tube gradually changed from something they moved along to something they fell down. Red metal bars spaced along the walls turned from handholds to the rungs of a ladder.

Captain Larsen stopped suddenly in front of a large schematic on the wall. "There's a map at each main junction," he said. "Best to memorize it, though." His tone had more authority than Russell cared for, but he allowed it. He already envisioned this man as a platoon leader; might as well let him get comfortable in the role.

The men studied the map. One asked, "Where's the conflict now?"

Russell pointed at three locations marking junctions between the uppermost deck, in terms of distance from Earth, and the one next to it. "Platz basically owns Section II. He has a suite of offices there. Some storage. He sealed these doors remotely," he said, indicating them, "preventing us from stopping them at the climber bay."

"Platz is with them?"

Jarred shrugged. "I use the name loosely. We don't know."

"Are the doors still closed?" Russell asked.

"Not completely. We were in the process of forcing them open when the shooting started. At this point, we're just managing to keep them contained to Section H."

"How many are we talking about?" someone asked.

"Unknown," Jarred said. All business, no bullshit— Russell really liked this guy. "Four small shuttles docked, but we don't know how many were aboard."

Blackfield studied the map. "Is there any other way into that area?"

"Via the climbers," the captain said, pointing along the Elevator thread. "You'd be a sitting duck coming out of one, though. Surveillance cameras, when they were working, showed they have the cargo bay well guarded."

Russell had an idea. "I need a volunteer," he said to his men. No shortage; every hand went up. He picked one at random. "Listen up. Go back to the dock. Your mission is to lead the rest of the troops, as they arrive, to the three combat zones, until you hear otherwise. Spread 'em evenly, got it?"

"Yes, sir," the man said. He seemed to regret volunteering to miss the battle.

"While you wait," Russell continued, "see if you and the dockmaster can find some empty air canisters. Load a climber full of them, rig it with something that looks like a fuse, and send it up to the climber bay in Section H."

"Sir?"

"Keep them on their toes," Russell said. "They'll waste time and people on it until the jig is up."

The soldier smiled, as did the others. "Good idea."

"Get moving," Russell said. As the men turned and hustled back the way they had come, Russell turned back to Captain Larsen. "Lead on."

Not thirty seconds later, an alarm sounded.

Jarred stopped in his tracks and tapped the small communicator in his ear. All of the Gateway security personnel wore them, Russell realized. The little device added a certain air of importance to the wearer. He made a mental note to ask for one.

The captain listened for a few seconds and then shot a sidelong glance at Russell. "Trouble at the brig."

"What?"

"An escape attempt," Jarred said, still listening to the report. He began to run, and shouted over his shoulder. "This way!"

Russell ordered his men to secure the entrance to the brig. He followed Jarred into the small room that fronted a row of four cells.

A guard waited there, his face pale and flushed. He kept one hand pressed to the back of his head. "I was just sitting here at the desk," he told Jarred. "Then . . . nothing. I woke up a few minutes ago."

"You were alone?"

"No," he muttered. His eyes shot left toward the only open cell door. "Found Barry in there, instead of the prisoner. He's dead."

"Step aside," Jarred said. Instead of going to the cell, as Russell expected, he went to the desk. "Cameras may have captured something."

As he tapped away on the terminal, Russell walked

around to the cell door. It appeared undamaged. Inside, a guard lay on the floor, one arm folded awkwardly underneath him, bruising around his neck. "The prisoner lured him inside, perhaps?" Russell said, to no one in particular.

"No," Jarred said. "Take a look."

The screen in front of him showed the view from a camera mounted in the ceiling.

"Fifteen minutes ago," Jarred said.

In the footage, the guard at the desk waved as another guard approached, carrying a covered bowl. Food, Russell guessed. There was no sound, but Russell could see the two men chat for a few seconds. Then the food carrier moved on to the cell block.

Ten seconds passed. Then the man at the desk stood up abruptly and turned around. He'd heard something.

A person approached him from the entrance, toward his turned back. A woman, Russell saw. Small and lithe, wearing a skintight black outfit. She hit the guard on the back of the head with something—a gun, perhaps—and he dropped like a bag of sand.

What happened next startled him. The woman reached over the desk, without even looking at the terminal. Her hand raced across the keyboard, and the video feed died.

An absolute pro. Russell whistled appreciation. "Who the hell is that?"

"The 'Ghost,'" Jarred said. "Kelly Adelaide. Works for Platz, though he denies it. An enormous pain in the ass."

"And who was in the cell?"

The dazed guard answered. "A scavenger from Darwin. A woman."

"The immune? Samantha?" Russell asked. When the guard nodded he turned to Jarred. "Tough as nails, that one. I've had a run-in with her before."

"Good to know."

"They can't be far," Russell said, clicking off the safety of his pistol.

Jarred shook his head. "She's with the Ghost. They're long gone, trust me. They've been trying to find her for almost a week."

A week. Russell found it hard to believe, in a tin can like this, that anyone could even get thirty seconds of privacy. "Well," he said, looking over the scene, "standing around here is pointless, then. Let's go crack some skulls."

Halfway to Section G, Jarred pressed a finger to his ear and began to run. "They've broken through," he said to Russell. "Pushing our men back." His own soldiers, four in number, ran ahead with him.

When the combatants started to come into view, Russell slowed down. He turned to his twenty men. "Listen up," he said. "They're all using pansy tactics. Pop up, shoot, duck, repeat. I'll have none of that. We're going to barrel in there like a bunch of subs and scare the hell out of 'em."

Everyone nodded. They were smiling. Russell realized he wore a wide grin, too.

Russell turned toward the battle and started to jog. The jog turned to a run as his men caught up to him. Some even passed him. Bloodlust took over, and he loved it.

They rushed forward as if they were playing rugby, shouting as they raced toward the enemy, shooting wildly. A shocking and effective tactic.

Platz's forces, caught off guard, crouched behind whatever cover they could find under the hail of bullets and bloodcurdling cries. Before they could return fire, the Nightcliff guards were right on top of them. Russell ran as hard as he could, and still he fell toward the back of the group. Their boldness filled him with pride.

A slaughter ensued, beyond Russell's expectations. In seconds, five Platz soldiers lay dead or dying. Some already on the ground received a second bullet.

Blackfield's soldiers pushed on, into the junction corridor, leaving the shocked Gateway guards to secure ground already gained. The junction hall was a narrow space—no more than three people wide—with nothing to hide behind along the twenty-meter stretch. They surged forward.

Russell passed Jarred Larsen, who was crouched behind a metal table turned on its side. Jarred shouted something. It sounded like a warning. Russell laughed and ran on.

Jarred shouted again, much louder. "Blackfield! Ambush!"

He heard the cry two steps before entering the corridor. Something in Jarred's tone resonated. At the last step he angled into the wall next to the door.

A storm of gunfire erupted from the Platz-held end of the junction. Men screamed and toppled.

Fish in a goddamn barrel, Russell thought. *Oops!*

Whipping around, he held a hand up, ordering the men still behind him to halt. Most were able to heed the call, angling to take cover along the wall next to their leader. A few could not overcome their momentum and died in the open doorway.

Jarred moved up and took a place on the wall next to Russell.

In the junction, on the other side of the wall, the wounded men screamed. "I guess we got carried away," Russell said. No one laughed.

One soldier managed to crawl out, a bloodstain spreading across his lower back. Russell pulled him through to safety.

"How many up there?" he asked the fallen man.

Through clenched teeth he said, "Couldn't see. They're dug in."

Russell took stock of his men along the wall. Ten of the twenty were still standing. A sobering number. Russell saw no fear in the survivors' faces, but the cockiness had definitely been smothered. He leaned to the next man on the wall. "We hold this position, until the rest of the boys arrive. Spread the word."

As the orders spread down the line, Russell pulled Captain Larsen aside. "Second squad is bringing tear gas. That'll clear them out."

"Can't do that. The circulators will suck it in and spread it all over the station."

From within the junction corridor, Russell heard a deep clang. The sound reverberated through the floor and walls. "The hell?"

Jarred moved up to the doorway and chanced a quick

glance inside. "Son of a . . . they've sealed it. The emergency bulkhead."

Russell leaned in and saw it, too. A massive metal barrier, right at the halfway point of the connecting hall.

Jarred grimaced. "We should check on the other junctions. Maybe they couldn't seal all three."

"I'll join you," Russell replied. "You," he said to the closest soldier, "you're in charge. No one gets through that door, got it?"

"Understood!"

"Lead on, brother," Russell said to Jarred.

He stood before the fourth set of emergency bulkhead doors that blocked Section H. Twenty minutes ago, after he and Jarred had found them all sealed, Russell had demanded some onc-rope be brought up and sent four men to fetch it. Jarred had gone with them, so he could report in to Alex Warthen.

Russell kicked the thick barrier with the bottom of his boot. "Where the *hell* are my explosives?" he shouted.

A number of men milled about, and all suddenly tried to look busy.

Jarred Larsen appeared a minute later, alone and empty-handed.

Russell spread his arms. "Are we supposed to claw it open?"

"Alex said no explosives," he replied. "Can't risk the damage to the station."

"That's great," Russell said. "Let the bastards slip away."

"I sent a team to get a water torch from maintenance," Jarred said. "They didn't show?"

Russell made a show of looking around.

"Dammit," Jarred said. He produced a small handheld communicator. "This is Larsen, where's my torch?"

Nothing but static from the other end.

A voice finally crackled over the small speaker. "Fiske here, sir, I'm near maintenance. Want me to track them down?"

"Yes, please."

An uncomfortable silence followed. Russell paced back and forth in front of the door, struggling to control his rage. He could picture Platz's men, grabbing anything useful and stuffing it into their lifeboats.

Minutes later the radio crackled again. "Fiske here, sir. We've got a problem."

"What's going on?"

"They're dead. Looks like an ambush."

Jarred slapped his own forehead and dragged his hand down his haggard face.

Russell felt the same. The enemy was supposed to be contained within Section H. "How the hell? Oh . . . I get it. The 'Ghost' and the prisoner."

"This is a right bloody mess," Jarred said. He lifted the radio to his mouth. "Everyone listen up: We've got a couple of infiltrators on the loose. Two women. One we know: Kelly Adelaide, short with close-cropped brown hair. The other is Samantha Rinn, abnormally tall and strong. Blond hair."

Russell ground his teeth together. *Samantha*. She'd spat in his face, and clocked him in front of his men. He rubbed absently at his jaw. Even now, weeks later, it still ached from her blindside punch. He'd let her go, shown leniency, and this was his reward.

"Okay, everyone," Jarred said, "stay sharp and hold your positions. No one goes anywhere alone, understood?"

"You're not sending search parties?" Russell asked.

Jarred covered the microphone. "No one knows this place better than Kelly Adelaide. Let her come to us."

Russell thought it over and gave a stiff nod. He turned to his soldiers, who were standing by. "You," he said to the only one he recognized, "take three men from each door and get back to the docking bay. I don't want these bitches anywhere near our supplies."

The man saluted and began to pick his team.

"It's time I spoke to Alex directly," Russell said to Jarred.

* * *

He found Alex to be awake and alert.

The infirmary bustled both with wounded and those treating them, making the place ill-suited for talking strategy.

Luckily, Alex had been afforded some privacy. His bed had been pushed to the far corner and a medical curtain erected around it.

"You made it," Alex said when he saw the leader from Nightcliff push through the fabric wall.

"Brought some friends, too."

"So I've heard." Alex tapped a small handheld communicator on his bedside table. "Been keeping tabs as best I could."

"How's the shoulder?"

"As long as I don't move, it hurts like hell."

Russell looked around for a chair and, not finding one, sat on the edge of the bed. "The old man's tougher than we thought."

Alex frowned. "I don't know where he got all these weapons, and people who know how to use them."

"Sneaky bastard."

Jarred Larsen stuck his head in through the curtain. "Permission to enter?"

Alex nodded, wincing slightly from the pain of the motion. His second in command stepped through the curtain.

"We finally cut through a door up there," Jarred said. "They're gone. Other than a few crude booby traps, no sign of them. They, uh . . . they cleaned the place out."

Alex closed his eyes, his frown growing deeper.

"At least we kept them contained in Section H," Russell said.

Jarred cleared his throat and kept his attention on Alex. "I don't think moving beyond Section H was their objective, sir."

"Explain."

"They didn't bring enough men to take control of the station, and frankly, they did break our line on Section G at one point, but did not press."

"So what the hell were they after?" Russell asked.

Jarred kept his focus on Alex. "ERVs," he said, then

explained for Russell before he could ask: "External repair vehicles."

Alex asked, "How many did they get?"

"Six in all," Jarred said to Alex.

Russell chuckled. "Platz is gonna give the station a paint job?"

"What he's doing," Jarred said, "is staying a step ahead of us. It's a smart move, frankly."

Alex squirmed slightly in his bed, wincing with pain at the move. "He's building a transportation fleet, since we shut down his climbers."

"So," Russell said, "he's got a few runabouts. What's the problem?"

"It's us I'm worried about," Alex said. "We'll be vulnerable to the same situation."

"How?"

"Adelaide," Jarred said. "And the other."

Russell began to understand. "You mean sabotage."

"Yes. Just like we did to him."

"If they manage to blow up the climber controls," Russell said, "are we trapped here?"

"Not quite," Alex said. "There's a whole graveyard of transport ships at the old dock in Section E. Once the climber system was installed, they became obsolete, but they should still work in a pinch."

"Christ," Jarred said. "We need to secure that room. I'll take care of it."

He pushed through the privacy curtain, already barking orders into his headset.

"Hardly ideal," Russell said. "We need to put an end to this, soon."

"I agree," said Alex. "I'll speak with the council—"

"No," Russell said. "Neil isn't playing by the rules, so neither should we. You and I are the only two members with power anyway. It's time we initiated what we discussed."

Alex closed his eyes, his face tightening. He was in serious pain, Russell realized.

The anguish abated after a moment, and Alex said, "I'm in no condition to lead a counterattack."

"No problem. I'll handle it."

Alex sighed. "I was thinking more of Captain Larsen."

Here it is then, Russell thought. Two allies positioning themselves for the aftermath of victory. "Great idea. Besides, I've got a different mission to lead," he said. At Alex's arched eyebrow, he went on. "I suspect if we attack Platz Station, the goat will just abandon it and move up. We need a bargaining chip. Something precious to him."

"Anchor."

"Exactly." Russell smiled. "I'll take a few squads in some of these ERVs. We'll get him sandwiched, cut off in his stupid headquarters. And with his research, not to mention the brainiacs doing it, under our control. He'd have to surrender."

"Indeed," Alex said. "Your plan isn't half-bad."

Gosh, thanks! "You'll miss all the fun," Russell said. "I'll put a squad together. Who can help get these old boats out of storage?"

"Larsen can point you in the right direction. A couple of my older guards are rated to fly them."

"Good. Rest up; we'll deal with this."

"I've got an agent in Anchor Station," Alex said as Russell turned to leave. "She can help you get set up."

"Name?"

"Natalie Ammon. Tania Sharma's assistant."

Russell cracked a sly grin. "I like the way you think, Alex."

Without warning, the power went out, plunging the room into blackness.

In the dark, Alex said, "Get going, then. I've got a vermin problem to deal with."

Beyond the curtain, they heard the medical staff scrambling through the dark before emergency power kicked in, bringing a soft green glow to the room.

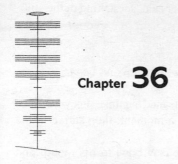

Chapter **36**

Darwin, Australia
10.FEB.2283

SKYLER AWOKE WITH a shudder. He jerked upright, tense and confused.

The motion brought fresh pain to his cracked rib. He padded the area with his fingertips and, though it was still unpleasant, he thought the worst had finally passed. If he moved with care, he could live with it.

Prumble sat next to him. Two bowls of steaming noodle soup waited on the carpet by the door. A stick of incense burned in a small brass holder, filling the room with the rich aroma of cinnamon.

"Good morning," Prumble said.

"How long was I out?"

"Sixteen hours, if you can believe it. The rain has passed."

"Sixteen? Hell."

"You woke once," Prumble said, "for a sip of water. And promptly fell asleep again."

Skyler sat up and grunted. He leaned against the wall and flexed the stiffness from his arms and legs. He rubbed the sleep from his eyes and scratched at the stubble on his face. "Did you salvage anything from your garage?"

Prumble cracked a sardonic grin. "They didn't quite wipe me out. Something you need?"

"How about a new plane and the crew to man it?"

The fat man's grin half faded. "Fresh out, I'm afraid."

"Your sat-comm, the one Neil Platz gave you?"

The grin disappeared entirely. "Blackfield took it."

"I'll settle for a razor," Skyler said, scratching at the stubble on his neck.

"You're in luck."

"That's a start then."

Prumble handed him a bowl of soup and began to slurp from the other.

Skyler set his aside, and leaned against the wall once more. He closed his eyes for a moment, then stared at the ceiling.

Prumble waited, lifting the clay bowl to his mouth and shoveling in hot noodles with a pair of well-worn chopsticks. "For my money, Skyler, the great ramen heist you and Skadz pulled off . . . when was that?"

Skyler held up three fingers.

"Three years ago," Prumble went on, "is never to be topped."

"That's why it's called 'Top Ramen.'"

The fat man groaned at the lame joke, then chuckled between mouthfuls.

"Everything we worked for is gone," Skyler said. To his own ear, his voice sounded distant and hoarse.

"I am well aware."

"What will you do now?"

Prumble sighed. "Retire, I suspect, and enjoy my twilight years. Buy this place if I can. Or barter my way into a rooftop commune. We know one that owes us a debt of gratitude, don't we? That finger you brought back? It matched, by the way. They were very pleased. Yes, I could call upon them. 'Don't worry, I won't eat much!'" He fell into a hearty laugh, hugging his massive belly.

Skyler studied his old friend. "No thirst for revenge?"

The big man grinned. "I said 'enjoy,' did I not? Revenge means stewing over the past, and that doesn't agree with me. You could join me in retirement, you know."

"Someday, maybe. Turns out I still have a job to do."

"Oh? Do tell."

Skyler explained the meeting with Platz and the mission to investigate the Aura generator. He also recounted the tale of his escape from Gateway, and subsequent crash-landing in Gunn. How the subhumans had chased him into the basement of a medical office building, a basement that turned out to be a veterinary clinic, a stroke of incredible luck amid such terrible events. He'd passed out there, awoken hours later, and paused only long enough to bandage his wounds. Lastly, Skyler told of the misery of his hike back to Darwin, the only bright spot being his discovery of a long-abandoned police van, parked in front of a wealthy enclave, in which van he'd found a few precious clips of ammunition that fit his weapon. Prumble listened intently, asking only a few questions.

Skyler's hunger finally won out and he picked up his bowl. The room fell quiet as both men ate.

"I've heard interesting rumors around here," Prumble said. "Blackfield elected to the Orbital Council, Platz resigning in protest."

Skyler paused, mid-bite. Nothing good could come from an expanded power base for Russell Blackfield. The phrasing Neil Platz had chosen, about leaders and fighters, came to mind. "The old man won't go quietly," Skyler said.

"It's said that Nightcliff is sending climbers full of troops up the ladder."

"I saw them, on the way here. Looked like a strand of pearls."

Prumble studied his friend. "What are you planning to do, Skyler?"

"I need a way into Nightcliff. Platz said the entrance to this generator is below the old mansion."

"Seems like a fool's errand," Prumble said. "No offense."

"None taken."

"And after that? You have no way to deliver him your findings."

Skyler leaned forward. He set the empty bowl aside. "I need to get to orbit, then. Back to Gateway, at least. I can send him his bloody information, then find out what happened to the crew. If necessary, offer myself in exchange for their freedom."

Prumble coughed. "Nothing so ambitious as a garden commune, then."

Skyler shrugged. "I've got nothing left here. Can't imagine

rebuilding, and I can't shake the feeling that I left my people behind up there."

"The Aura is everything," Prumble said. "You did what you had to do."

"And with such success," Skyler said. "The idea was to save the ship. Made a fine mess of that. Once again, my leadership shines."

"Better to have stayed? Wound up dead or in jail?"

Skyler shrugged, unsure which outcome would be best.

"Enough with the self-loathing," Prumble said. "You're upsetting my delicate stomach."

Skyler stared at the trail of smoke from the incense stick.

"So," Prumble said, "a way into Nightcliff?"

"I was hoping you might have some ideas," Skyler replied.

"I can do better than that."

Skyler met his smiling eyes.

"Up for a bit of a walk?" Prumble asked.

Skyler walked next to Prumble through the narrow alleys of the Maze. The rain had lifted, true to Prumble's word, and the city bustled in the reprieve. Rain would have been preferred. Rain can't pick pockets, or drive a knife into the small of the back.

Yet the crowds parted. Prumble strode through the morass with total confidence. Chin up and arms turned inward like a body builder, his leather duster trailing in the wake. He held his cane in one clenched fist, as if he might lash out with it on a whim.

The sight of some Jacobites, preaching to a small crowd in a side alley, brought a taste of bile to Skyler's throat. Swallowing, he kept his eyes forward.

Prumble took a bizarre, twisting path, full of sharp turns, sudden stops, and retraced steps. He paused the march frequently, ducking into shops or small alcoves, where he would massage his aching leg.

"We can sit somewhere," Skyler said, "if you need a rest."

"The leg is fine," Prumble said, leaning on his cane while

he rubbed his knee. "But my belly is rather distinct, and I fear Blackfield's agents are still looking for me."

Another dozen turns transpired and Skyler became truly lost. Then Prumble turned down an alley that stopped at a dead end. He kicked away the only tenant of the bleak space: an enormous gray rat. At the back of the alley was a nondescript steel door. Prumble produced a key ring from his jacket, selected one key from the hundreds that hung there, and opened the door. He propelled Skyler through it by the elbow, following right on his heels.

Down a damp stairwell, the pair approached a padlocked door engraved with POWER & WATER CORP and MAINTENANCE ACCESS ONLY. It looked at least a century old. Prumble shook his key ring, thumbed through the silver and brass objects, and selected another.

The small room beyond was just big enough to fit its only feature: a round steel hatch on the floor.

A ladder led down into darkness and the pungent smell of sewage.

"You clever bastard," Skyler said as they reached the bottom and entered the wide sewer tunnel. "This leads into Nightcliff?"

"Yes," he said. "Well . . . sort of. You'll see."

From another jacket pocket, Prumble produced a small handheld LED lantern. The wan blue-white light hinted at a cockroach infestation of epic proportions. The insects scattered from the light source and gave every shadow a swirling, shimmering depth.

The tube-shaped tunnel was perhaps five meters wide. A meager stream of putrid water, maligned with rotting chunks of unidentifiable refuse, meandered along the bottom. Running along one side was a narrow walkway, lined by a rusted old railing. Skyler had to lean to his left to keep from scraping his head.

"Amazing," he said. "I never knew this existed."

"Few do," said Prumble. "I found this place by accident."

Skyler glanced in both directions. "You'd think there'd be more water."

Prumble shook his head. "It's the original system, from

when Darwin was little more than a town. The modern system of microtunnels is just above us; that's where most of the runoff goes."

A familiarity in Prumble's words told Skyler the man had spent a lot of time down here. Prumble probably moved his wares through here, or paid others to do so.

The fat man inhaled deeply. "Not too bad down here after a good rain!"

The stench made Skyler's eyes water. He could hear the chattering echo of rats, somewhere distant. "Who else knows about this?"

"Occasionally I come across other people down here, usually lowlifes moving their drugs. They're easy enough to scare off."

"How far does it go?"

"Covers the extent of the old city," Prumble said. "Though some tunnels have been blocked with grating or even filled with concrete." They walked to the first intersection of tunnels. "How are you for supplies?"

Skyler tapped his weapon. "Enough ammo to stop an army. Provided that army is only two men."

"We'll make a detour then," Prumble said.

Most of the journey passed in silence. After thirty minutes, Skyler felt nauseous from the stench. Finally they left the walkway and climbed another stairwell, which led to a heavy, locked door. Prumble had the key.

Skyler followed the giant man into a room stacked full of metal lockers and various sundries, like a miniature version of Prumble's garage. A table made of thick wood dominated the center of the space.

"What is all this?" Skyler asked.

"My private reserve," Prumble said with a flourish. "We are directly below my garage. As luck would have it, I was down here when Blackfield struck. They didn't find the secret hatch." The giant man moved to the left wall and started opening cabinets.

"Holy Mary Mother of God," Skyler said.

Weapons, of all shapes and sizes, filled the cabinets.

"Some judicious skimming of your deliveries, in truth. Hope you can forgive me."

Skyler walked forward and picked up a high-powered assault rifle.

"I plan to sell most of this," Prumble said. "It is all I have left, after all. But you, my friend, are welcome to take what you need for your suicide mission."

Skyler prickled. "I plan to live."

"Suit yourself."

Skyler put the rifle back, knowing that his task ahead required subtlety. Instead he pocketed five clips of hollow-point ammunition for his submachine gun.

"This might be useful," Prumble said, offering him a small black cylinder. A holographic targeting sight, which attached to the top of his weapon. "Take a few grenades, too."

Skyler did so, pushing them carefully into his backpack. "Listen. About the second half of this plan," he said.

"What about it?"

"I was, you know, hoping you'd tell me what it is."

The fat man grinned. "The sewers do in fact lead to Nightcliff," he said, crossing the room to another cabinet. "But a series of iron gates block access. I never ventured farther, alas, as I have no key. You, however, do not need to exit the way you came."

With cautious movements, Prumble removed a brown cardboard box from the cabinet and set it on the table next to Skyler.

Inside were wrapped bars of plastic explosive. Enough to take down a small building, Skyler guessed. Prumble set another box beside it, full of blasting caps, laser initiators, and a spindle of fiber optic cable.

"They're old," Prumble said, "but should suffice." He selected one of the bars and hefted it. "Two should do the trick, so we'll bring four, yes?"

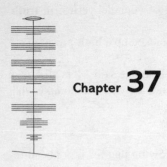

Chapter 37

THE PLAN REQUIRED waiting until the next storm hit the city. During wet season in Darwin that meant less than a day.

Thunder, Prumble hoped, would mask any noise or vibration caused by their activities. Skyler didn't cherish the idea of emerging from the sewer below Nightcliff to a circle of guns trained on his face, and readily agreed. To pass the time, he suggested they head up through the garage to the roof, where they could watch the sky.

A spectacular sunset greeted them—crimson and sapphire, broken by wide swaths of purple clouds. Wet season, for all its faults, knew how to paint a canvas.

Despite the show, the Elevator pulled at Skyler's gaze. "The subhumans are changing, I think. Mutating, or . . . something."

"Heard that, too," Prumble said. "Newsubs, right? Packs of them picking away at the edge of the city. Some say as far in as the Narrows."

Skyler let out a long sigh. The pile of problems amassed in the last few weeks felt like being buried alive. "How long do you give us?"

Prumble stared at the horizon, his leather duster whipping in the breeze. "You shall outlive me, by a good—"

"I mean all of us," Skyler said. "Humanity."

"Oh." The giant man considered the question. "I suspect we're getting our just due, for what we did to old Mother Nature."

Skyler cast his eyes downward, nodding solemnly. "She does hold a grudge, doesn't she?"

"I'd wager," Prumble said, "ten years. The population here shrinks by the day, and construction Up There could only make a snail proud."

Skyler picked up a stone and hurled it over the edge. "You never know. We're tenacious buggers."

"Perhaps. Perhaps."

Their talk turned to less depressing matters, until an angry morass of clouds loomed a few kilometers away. Lightning danced within the purple puffs.

"I think it's time," Prumble said.

Skyler agreed and led the way back to the panic room.

Two hours later they reached the barricade.

Six iron grates, spaced a half meter in succession, blocked the tunnel. The gaps between the bars in each grate were just big enough for Skyler to push his hand through.

"This is going to make a hell of a noise," he said, reaching through the first grate. With extreme care, he pushed a brick of plastic explosive against the second barricade. A loop of duct tape on the back joined it to the bars.

The process was repeated for the first grate.

"We're under Ryland Square here," Prumble said. "Not even to the wall yet. And there's a storm. It will be okay."

"I'm worried more for my own ears," Skyler said. "We should move as far back as we can."

The spindle of fiber optic cable held fifty meters of the orange wire and Skyler planned to use all of it. He poked two laser-initiated blasting caps into each brick of explosive and plugged the optical connectors into a hub on the end of the main cable.

"Let's go," he said. Prumble picked up the extra supplies and headed back the way they'd come. Skyler followed, rolling out the cable while walking backward.

Storm water swelled into the old tunnel, creating a knee-high brook of babbling rainwater in the bottom of the tube. The sound had an oddly soothing effect on Skyler, so long as he ignored the smell of excrement and urine.

When the cable ran out, Prumble handed him the trigger mechanism. A simple metal box, the size of a deck of cards, with an on-off toggle and one red button. Skyler moved the switch to "on" and set it on the ground, intending to activate the device with his foot. He plugged his ears and looked at Prumble. "Here goes—"

"Wait," Prumble said.

Skyler pulled his fingers out of his ears. "What is it?"

The big man looked like a child on the verge of tears. His lower lip quivered.

"What is it?"

"Once you blow the grate," Prumble said, "you'll need to get in there quick. In case they do hear it."

"So?" Skyler said.

"So," he said, "so this may be goodbye." Prumble stepped forward and engulfed Skyler in a crushing bear hug.

Face mashed into the faux leather of Prumble's coat, Skyler waited for the hug to end before speaking. "It's not goodbye, okay?"

"Don't underestimate the danger you're walking into, Skyler."

"It's *not* goodbye," he repeated. "It's see-you-soon, if anything. I'll get this done and bring the crew back, and we'll spend our days playing cards at your quiet little café, drinking to the good old days."

Prumble pressed his lips into a thin line, as if he'd taken a bite of lemon.

He's holding back tears, Skyler realized.

"You better, you bastard," Prumble finally said with a melancholy laugh. "Whatever happens, I'll either be there or leave word for you."

"Good."

"I'm serious, Skyler. If you leave me to rot alone in this city, I will hunt you down and sit on you."

Skyler shook his head and clapped his friend on the shoulder. "A fate worse than SUBS," he managed, laughing.

The big man grinned, nodded, and did his little jig. "Cover your ears," he sang, and danced over to the detonator. With a total lack of grace, he performed a spin and then stomped down on the switch.

The world shook.

Skyler felt, more than heard, the explosion. His clothing buffeted and a wave of hot wind slammed into him. Bits of metal and concrete splashed into the water just meters away.

"Get going," Prumble said when the shrapnel died down.

Skyler gripped the man's arm again. "Thank you. For everything. You're a true friend."

"Don't get all weepy on me, you girl. Into the mouth of hell with you."

Two bricks of plastic explosive turned out to be overkill.

All six iron grates lay in twisted ruin, skeletons of rust. The concrete around the blast area showed cracks, groundwater already dripping through.

"Can't allow shit like this in the city, eh Russell?" Skyler said, aloud, the sound echoing along the tunnel. Blackfield wasn't so paranoid after all.

The walkway along the side of the sewer tunnel had collapsed in the explosion. With no other option, Skyler grimaced and stepped into the stream of dark water. Fluid rushed his combat boots, shockingly cold.

Teeth chattering, he nevertheless took his time in navigating around the wreckage of the barricade. With all the other injuries he'd incurred, the last thing he figured he needed was a nasty gash from a rusty piece of bent iron.

Prumble had given Skyler the satchel that contained two additional bricks of explosive, plus the required blasting caps and triggers. He held the bag to his chest with one arm wrapped around it, needing his other arm free to hold his rifle, which also served as his flashlight.

Safely beyond the barricade, Skyler walked along the side of the sewer for another fifty meters before coming to a tiny alcove with an access shaft. The circular tunnel led straight up into darkness, an iron ladder along one side. Skyler put a foot on the bottom rung and stepped up, testing the ladder with his weight.

Satisfied, he slung the bag of explosives over one shoulder, then slung his rifle over that. He tightened his gun strap and arranged the gun so it pointed straight up, allowing him to climb with both hands while still able to see. On the second step he paused and triple-checked the safety, wanting to avoid shooting himself in the chin. The vision of such a comical end to his journey made him chuckle softly in the darkness and stench.

The ladder ended at a manhole cover that had been welded shut. Prumble had warned him about this. When the new sewer was built, this one had been largely sealed off.

Skyler clung to the ladder and listened for a while. Through the finger-sized holes in the steel disk, he could hear the faint sounds of Nightcliff's yard. The motors of cargo cranes turning. A loud clang as a container met asphalt. Or so he imagined.

He debated using some of the plastic to open it, but an explosion within Nightcliff's walls, at surface level, would not go unnoticed. With a sigh he climbed back down and continued along the sewer tunnel.

After another hundred meters the tunnel began to curve to the left and slope upward. Exhausted, Skyler rested for five minutes before starting to hike up the incline. A cold, clammy sweat covered his body. He mulled the irony that, after getting his leg gashed and his rib cracked and his head pummeled, the biggest ache he suffered would be from his feet. Walking, he thought, would be the death of him.

Skyler moved on when the roaches began to become curious about his boots. The insects crunched under his feet as he stalked up the tunnel. He wondered how far the ocean was now.

At the top of the slope, Skyler emerged into a cavernous underground room, built of odd angles and many sides. His light could only faintly illuminate the far side. The walls were lined with tributary tunnels. A junction, Skyler realized. Every old sewer tunnel under Nightcliff must meet here.

He counted four access ladders coming down from above, and resigned himself to try each. At that moment he wanted nothing more than to be out of the stink and darkness.

The first two proved sealed, but the third manhole gave slightly when he pushed on it.

Stifling his sense of relief, Skyler pushed the manhole up with every ounce of strength he could muster. The cover weighed at least fifty kilograms. Combined with his awkward hold on the ladder, he found it almost impossible to lift. He paused and realigned himself on the ladder, bracing one foot against a chip in the concrete on the other side of the shaft to free up his second hand.

With a grunt he pushed upward with both arms, lifting the cover a few centimeters. His foot slipped a bit against the concrete before gaining purchase again. Skyler couldn't risk holding up the cover and studying the surroundings; he'd fall if he didn't hurry. So he devoted his strength to sliding the cover aside.

Pitch darkness loomed above. Skyler flipped off his flashlight and let his eyes adjust before climbing up and looking around.

The manhole put him behind a brick building, under an awning that blocked the sky, in a wide alley that appeared to be devoted to storing broken machinery. A few tractors and old trucks were parked at the dead end, covered in years of dirt, dust, and rain. Everything that might have been useful was removed long ago.

At the alley entrance, Skyler could see only the side of another building, one story tall and lined with dark windows. Out from under the awning, he looked up and studied the night sky. Storm clouds filled it from edge to edge, but he could see the cord of the Elevator, and the tower that protected its base. The landmark gave him his bearings. He was on the western side of Nightcliff fortress, near the seaward wall. The old Platz mansion would be north and east, if he had it right.

Skyler surveyed the building in front of him. Though it was dark, he could see through the dirty windows just enough to recognize rows of bunk beds. He glanced down at his wet, filthy clothing and back at the window. A Nightcliff uniform would be a damn useful upgrade, and if not for the disguise then at least for the smell.

He walked around to the back of the barracks, intent to stay away from the central yard of the fortress. He moved casually. It would do no good to bump into someone if he was sneaking about. Better to act like he belonged there.

The back door to the building didn't budge when he turned the handle. Skyler pressed his ear to it and listened, but no sound came from within. Perhaps Blackfield had moved all his men to orbit?

Skyler waited for a thunderclap and kicked the door in. He rushed inside, gun held at the ready. He flipped the flashlight on and found the room to indeed be empty. The bunks were in disarray, vacated in a hurry. Without stopping, Skyler jogged to the front of the building and locked the front door.

From a window next to the door he could see a portion of Nightcliff's cargo yard. A water hauler sat on one of the four landing pads, its engines stirring up an angry mist even at idle speed. Workers rushed back and forth underneath the aircraft, detaching a blue water container.

The other three pads were empty. Skyler could only see one guard, standing on the far side toward the Elevator, leaning against a pylon with his arms crossed and head down.

"How vigilant," Skyler muttered.

He turned to look for a spare uniform but the howling engines of another aircraft brought his attention back to the yard. A bulky craft came into view over the eastern fortress wall.

Skyler recognized it. Kantro's ship. A fat-bellied craft with little range, often used to bring fresh soil from abandoned farms just beyond the Aura. Skyler came back to the window to watch. Kantro was a friend, and a friend would be useful.

As the craft came over the wall, a large group of Nightcliff guards poured out of the control tower. Twenty men and women, at least.

Inspection? At least I'm not the only one they pick on. The size of the force was excessive for a search, though.

Those who were armed raced toward the last landing pad in the row and began to surround it. The others streamed out toward the barracks. One turned and waved toward the control tower window, high above the yard.

Skyler followed the guard's wave up to the controller's perch. Numerous faces crowded the window there, pointing at Kantro's vehicle.

A guard burst through the door to the barracks, eyes wide as saucers. He didn't even glance at Skyler as he raced to a locker and removed a pistol. His fingers shook as he fumbled a clip of ammo into the weapon.

"What's going on?" Skyler asked as the man ran back toward the door.

"Newsubs got aboard a scavenger ship," he barked as he sped out the door toward the surrounded pad.

Skyler focused on Kantro's ship, now approaching the pad. He could see the pilot through the cockpit window. Even as Skyler watched, the pilot hefted a pistol in one hand and fired toward the back of the cockpit. The craft tilted to one side and started to drift.

Subhumans advanced into the crowded cockpit, the pilot shooting frantically, each gunshot lighting up the creatures' furious faces.

Just meters away from clipping a nearby building, the craft tilted back violently, overcompensating. It moved back in the other direction too fast, and this time its wing sliced through the corner of a scaffolding adjacent to the Elevator tower. Sparks and debris showered down.

Guards on the landing pad began to break formation, diving for cover or running for shelter.

Somewhere behind him, Skyler heard the sound of hydraulic motors followed by the deep hollow sound of a warning alarm. A missile battery, mounted on Nightcliff's wall, preparing to fire.

"Shit!" he hissed. Nightcliff would rather have flaming debris rain down on the cargo yard than let the erratic ship damage the climber tower, or worse, the cord itself.

The engine sound ramped suddenly to a high-pitched whine and the aircraft tilted forward, then back.

Skyler caught another glimpse of the cockpit, and saw no

one at the helm now. He opened the barracks door and stepped out into the mud to get a better view. The uniform could wait.

The aircraft began to spin and lose altitude. Just five meters above the asphalt now. It lurched hard to the right and the engine noise dropped to nothing.

Skyler knew then that the vehicle would crash, on the south side of the yard. It if landed on its belly the damage might not be catastrophic, but those inside would be shaken up pretty badly.

He took a few steps toward the scene, then paused. He glanced north and saw the old Platz mansion over the rooftops. The sight of it trapped him between two choices: rush to help the people on board the craft, exposing himself in the process, or use the crash as a diversion to continue his mission.

Kantro might be a friend, but Skyler didn't relish the idea of fighting a bunch of subhumans on the side of Nightcliff's goons. Sooner or later someone would realize he didn't belong in the yard, and he'd be apprehended. Mission over.

"The Aura is everything," Prumble's voice echoed in his head. *"You did what you had to do."*

The erratic vehicle tilted again and its starboard wing slapped into the ground. It fell like a stone the rest of the way, smashing into the paved surface with the torturous sound of metal scraping on stone.

People began to rush out the doors of nearby buildings. The squad of guards emerged from their cover as the doomed aircraft slid across the ground and collided with a low building south of the yard. It came to a rest there, half-embedded into the structure. A cloud of dust and debris filled the air around it.

The rear cargo hatch was open. There were people inside, lots of them, tightly packed and ragged. They swarmed down the open ramp and into the yard. Some galloped on all fours.

Skyler ran north, the sounds of shouting, screams, and gunfire at his back. He wanted no part of it, and besides, it was ten times the diversion he needed.

That an aircraft had limped in from the Clear and made it all the way to Nightcliff's yard uninvited was one thing. That it had done so with a cargo bay full of subhumans was sheer insanity. Kantro, or the pilot, must have waited until the last minute before radioing in for help; otherwise Night-cliff would have shot them down well before they reached the fortress.

"Not my problem," Skyler said to himself as he ran. He set his sights on the mansion and pumped his legs, his pains forgotten in the rush of adrenaline. A figure emerged from a building in front of him. A plump woman, in a soiled nurse's gown. Skyler shouldered his way past her and she toppled to the ground in a surprised yelp.

She shouted for him to stop. Shouted for help.

Skyler turned to yell something over his shoulder and saw a subhuman racing toward her. The once-human creature tackled the poor woman and they disappeared into the door-way she'd emerged from. A cry of surprise, then pain, came from within.

Another subhuman had followed the first. It set its gaze on Skyler and began to gallop toward him. A scrawny thing, with a face so calm, so serene, that Skyler almost tripped.

Resolute to conserve his bullets, Skyler faced forward and ran as hard as he could. The mansion came into full view. He threw himself onto a feeble chain-link fence that surrounded it and climbed.

He dropped down the other side and landed looking back-ward, directly into the face of the scrawny subhuman. The creature slapped into the fence, gripping it with white-knuckled hands, and that same, eerily serene expression on its face.

It whispered something. A woman, past middle age, he guessed, from the wisps of gray in her tangled hair. He glanced down and saw that she wore the tattered remnants of an envi-ronment suit.

Recently afflicted, then. One of Kantro's crew. He looked at her face more closely, trying to remember her.

She tilted her head to one side and whispered again, louder. "Play with me."

"Not today. A bit busy."

"Play with me," she rasped, and shook the fence. Her eyes darted up.

She began to climb.

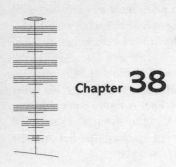

Chapter **38**

THE PLATZ FAMILY mansion, once an ultramodern architectural wonder of sharp angles and brilliant white walls, looked near collapse.

Scraps of plywood covered every window. Black mold seeped up the walls from a forest of choking weeds. The front door, two slabs of thick wood four meters tall and at least as wide, were held closed by a thick rusty chain wrapped in a figure eight around the wrought-iron handles. A padlock the size of Skyler's hand said visitors were not welcome.

Running full speed, the sound of a rattling fence behind him, Skyler angled his run to the right of the massive door. A shabby piece of plywood loomed in front of him, covering a space where a floor-to-ceiling window had once framed the entrance. Or so he hoped.

He jumped and went shoulder first into the wall of thin wood. An elbow shielding his face, Skyler crashed through the feeble barricade in a shower of splinters and fragments. A marble floor inside the foyer greeted him, cold and unyielding as he landed on his back.

Skyler's head rocked backward and cracked against the dusty stone surface. He grimaced and rolled, bringing his gun to the ready from a prone position. He aimed at the gap he'd created, and counted. The alien-created disease drove the infected to chase human prey with relentless zeal. The creature should, he thought, leap through the hole in about five seconds.

He counted to five. Then ten. Twenty.

Nothing save for dust and the distant sound of a terrible melee came through.

Skyler pursed his lips and drew himself up on one knee. Maybe the sub couldn't scale the fence after all. Experience told him otherwise, but—like it or not—things were changing. Old expectations couldn't be trusted anymore.

He took a chance and swung his rifle around the huge entry room. Marble, everywhere he looked. A series of pillars lined the walls, impressionistic takes on the classic Roman style, all square and angular.

Piles of labeled boxes and filing cabinets filled the corners of the space. Skyler vaguely recalled Neil's words from their meeting, something about the mansion being relegated to long-term storage. From the chained door to the thick coat of dust on every flat surface, Skyler guessed no one had been in here in months, maybe years.

A stairway opposite the double doors led halfway to a second floor, before splitting into two stairways that went east and west.

Upstairs didn't matter. Platz said the covert entrance to the Elevator silo was in the basement, but no more. Judging by the opulent house, Skyler imagined a vast wine cellar concealing the way in. He pictured twisting a gargoyle statue to reveal the secret entrance behind a faux wall of vintage bottles. The vision brought a laugh to his lips. "How very supervillain of you, Platz," he muttered.

At least thirty seconds passed with no sign of the subhuman. Maybe she'd found someone else to "play" with. Maybe the surprised guards in Nightcliff's yard had managed to quell the bizarre attack. Whatever the case, time was wasting.

Skyler backed into an inner room, waiting until the last second to aim his rifle away from the hole he'd made on entry. The stale air reeked of mildew. Shards of wood crunched under his boots.

He crept through a grand dining room. Chairs lay in dis-

array around a table ten meters in length. A chandelier had
fallen on the polished wood surface at some point and toppled off to one side. Skyler stepped around it and continued
into a kitchen beyond.

Big enough to service a large restaurant, the kitchen had
four rows of counters. Commercial-grade stoves, ranges,
and sinks ran the length of each. Or parts did, at least. Much
of the equipment had long ago been removed, in part or in
whole. Missing faucet heads, a stove with no door or control
panel. The scavenger in Skyler noted these on instinct. What
was missing, what was useful.

He went to the far wall, fixated on the idea of a wine cellar. But a search of the kitchen turned up nothing. He looked
through a walk-in freezer, a pantry ten times the size of his
quarters at the hangar, and lastly a small and simple dining
room where he assumed the staff used to take their meals.

Back in the main dining area, Skyler took the first hallway leading out of it. Other than the occasional hint of light
sneaking past a boarded-up window, the only illumination
came from his gun-mounted bulb.

The hall had once featured a plush carpet. Now the fabric
sluiced away under his boots like dead skin. Rectangular
patches on the walls marked where paintings once hung.

Skyler tapped each light switch he passed. None worked.
For the best, he thought. The lack of power had probably led
to the home's abandoned state, and that suited him.

Each door he passed opened to reveal simple bedrooms,
and one small recreational area with bookshelves and even
a chessboard, game frozen in mid-play.

At the end of the hall, he came to a door different from the
others. Thick and sturdy, with a large metal handle and a
key card panel on the wall beside it.

Skyler tried the handle and found it to be broken. Deliberately, from the scuff marks. The door pushed open with ease
and he stepped inside.

Stairs led below. Skyler sighed with relief and trotted
down them two at a time. At the bottom he found another
door, just like the previous, also forced open long ago.

Inside he found an office. A wide space, one side lined

with cubicles, the other with a collaborative area—couches facing a large bank of panel screens that went from floor to ceiling. Every screen had been shattered, left to rot. In his mind Skyler could see them bright and alive with news from the world's financial markets, or the faces of distant Platz employees delivering to Neil news of high-profile mergers.

A massive circular door dominated the far wall. A safe, suitable for any bank vault. Scorch marks stretched out from the main tumbler, and an electronic pad on the wall beside hung by frayed wires.

Despite the damage, the vault door was closed tight. Skyler stared at it for a long moment. He racked his mind to recall Neil's words. He'd used the word *secret* in describing the entrance. *No,* Skyler thought, *it was "hidden."* A giant vault door did not equate to hidden.

From above, a faint sound reached his ears. A light scrape, gone as quick as it had arrived. He stood very still and listened.

Dozens of times in the past he'd found himself in places like this. Pitch-black and deathly quiet. Danger lurking ahead or behind. He'd never deliberately scoured through such a place alone, though. The lack of Samantha's presence only furthered his unease.

Total silence followed. A phantom noise, perhaps. Imagination and fatigue, conspiring against him.

Moving to the center of the room, Skyler turned in place, scanning the area with his light. It *felt* right that the hidden entrance would be here. Over and over his attention returned to the massive safe door. A voice inside him said that was the point of it. The barrier was so large and tempting that any interloper would get tunnel vision the moment they saw it.

Skyler put it to his back and looked at the rest of the room.

The door through which he'd entered. Nothing interesting about it.

The cubicles. Maybe they could be concealing some small access passage? His gut said no.

Last choice, the bank of destroyed video screens. It looked like someone had taken a sledgehammer to each one. An odd thing to do in a world where such devices were always needed, especially in orbit.

Their arrangement was odd, he realized. Two-wide, running floor to ceiling. Almost like a—

Door.

Eyes locked on the monitors, Skyler swung his legs over the couch between him and the wall and stood in front of the devices. They were mounted flush to the wall. He stepped to one side and looked at them from the side, running a finger along the edge of one screen. He could just detect a ridge there. A sliver of space just before the point where the monitor connected to the wall.

I'll be damned, he thought. The monitors must have been smashed to dissuade anyone from taking them off. A clever trick, he had to admit.

He searched for a button, or lever . . . anything that might open the panel. He ran his hand along the bottoms of every table and desk, tried tapping the buttons on each monitor attached to the wall. Nothing worked.

"Fuck it," he said aloud. No time for caution and decorum. Platz could hire a crew to come back here later and fix things.

He set his rifle on a desk near the entrance, pointing its light at the bank of screens. Then he swung the bag Prumble had given him onto the floor and removed one brick of plastic explosive.

Blasting caps inserted, Skyler selected a detonator. With no more fiber cable, he couldn't use the switch, so a timed charge would have to do. He went with a twenty-second fuse, mentally planning his route. Up the stairs, through the hall, under the big table in the dining room in case any chunks of the ceiling were knocked loose.

He stood facing the bank of monitors, the explosive charge nestled between the two bottom screens. *Here goes . . .*

With a press of his thumb the twenty-second timer started.

"Play with me."

A raspy, thin whisper from the doorway. In the room. Next to his gun.

The subhuman woman stood there, crouched, coiled, her head tilted to one side like an ape. Her bloodshot eyes were as wide as saucers. "Play," she repeated.

Skyler eyed the gun. Then her.

Fifteen seconds.

He stepped toward the weapon and the woman mirrored him, jutting sideways a half meter. A grin curled the corners of her mouth.

Ten seconds.

Skyler thought of trying to fight her. No time for it. He thought of feinting for the gun and then running past her. Might work, but she could just as easily tackle him.

Five seconds.

He hesitated.

Four.

Three.

Skyler spun and ran backward, three steps to the cubicle near the giant safe door.

The subhuman laughed and gave chase.

One.

Skyler dove.

Blinding white light enveloped him. The walls shook. No, everything shook. The blast caught his legs as he tumbled like a gymnast over the half wall that fronted the cubicle.

The sound was so loud it shut his ears down. Everything went silent and slow. He had a strange awareness of his rag-doll body flipping over, his feet smacking into the far cubicle wall. To his strange delight, the wall gave way. A temporary surface standing a meter from the room's physical wall. The panel collapsed, softening the impact to his feet.

Sound returned as a high-pitched whistle, blaring at him from everywhere and nowhere. Lying on the floor under a shower of debris, he covered his ears to no effect; the whistle remained.

Shell-shocked, Skyler pushed himself up onto wobbly legs and surveyed the room. The brick-shaped bomb had done its job, and more. Half the wall had been removed along with the panel of monitors. Through the smoke he could see an adjacent room.

Not a room, he realized, but a hallway, lit from a series of soft yellow lights along its floor.

Skyler staggered through the wreckage on numb feet, tripping twice. He glanced toward where the subhuman had stood, but saw no sign of the creature in the haze. She must have taken the brunt of the blast, and been completely annihilated. *Good*.

Coughing, he entered the hall.

Skyler had descended more than a hundred steps down the spiral, scaffold staircase that lined the silo, when he realized where he was.

And that he'd left his gun behind.

He stopped and gripped the cold metal rail, taking in his surroundings.

The silo, a perfect circular tube cut from the earth itself, extended fifty meters above him. In the center of the man-made ceiling was a sphincter through which ran the cord of the space elevator, a perfect straight line of black thread so thin he had to squint to trace it. The rickety staircase wound its way around the inner wall of the silo, all the way down.

Down he looked, following the spiral of the stair, leaning over to follow its path along the pit. He estimated it descended another five hundred meters. A series of red lights, placed at regular intervals along the length of the tube, provided the only illumination.

Skyler leaned over farther and tried to see the bottom, but a thick and misty air concealed whatever lay there. An uneven humming sound drifted up, raspy and constantly shifting pitch like a failing motor.

He decided to go back for his gun, just in case. Two steps in that direction and he froze.

At the top of the stairwell, the subhuman emerged from the same tunnel Skyler entered through. It staggered to the first step and screamed, more at the sight of him than the pain she must be in. Even from this distance, Skyler could see bleeding cuts and scrapes along her entire body. Portions were charred, black skin already cracking.

She had indeed taken the brunt of the explosion. *Remarkable that she survived,* he thought. More so that she could still walk.

He'd barely finished the thought when she started to come down the steps. Running, cackling with inhuman emotion.

Pure fear gripped Skyler and held his feet firmly where he stood. Every instinct told him to run, not fight. He thought he could defeat the woman in a fight, considering her injuries compared to his own. What he feared was that she didn't want to fight, she wanted to dive on him, to "play," and in the process she'd take them both over the railing and to their deaths below.

Yet his body refused to take action. The creature raced around the spiral stairs motivated by emotions so primal and unfiltered that Skyler almost felt jealous.

At least the woman could move.

Then she fell, tumbling down a few steps before hitting the outer wall in a violent stop.

As the subhuman clawed her way back to a stand, Skyler found the will to flee. He turned and took one step, then another. Soon he jogged, then ran, clanging down the metal stairs as his initial fear receded.

Countless steps blurred together. The humming noise grew ever louder as he went. He felt dizzy from the winding path, sure he would slip as the subhuman had. If that happened he would roll a long, long way before his inertia died out. Against every instinct he had, Skyler slowed down to a manageable pace. He glanced up and saw the woman on the spiral directly above him, still chasing, and gaining ground.

She fell again. He heard her yelp and sputter, then settle into a deep moan. A worse fall than the previous one. Skyler halted his progress and took the opportunity to catch his breath.

The air here, thick and warm, made the simple task of sucking in a breath a conscious effort. His clothing dripped with sweat. More than anything in the world, he wanted a sip of cold water.

At the railing he leaned over again. The strange, jerky hum from the depths of the pit was loud enough now to make him want to cover his ears. He'd descended to roughly the halfway point and could now make out shapes in the moist air below. The Elevator cord went straight down into the heart of a dish-shaped floor. The dark material, fanned out like the iris shutter of a camera lens, looked like nothing Skyler had ever seen before. Pure matte black, with geometric patterns laced through—

Something slammed into him, lifted him. The woman.

Skyler shouted his surprise. He made a mad grasp for the rail and missed, and then he was falling. He twirled around, the warm air growing hotter, rushing past him with ferocious speed.

He heard fluttery laughter, close by. The subhuman, flailing through the air above him. They would both die, he thought, in this dark pit that no one knew about.

Then the laughter became overwhelmed by the *hum,* deep and terrifying. Sputtering and shifting all the time. It came from below, from the dish-shaped iris that now raced toward him.

Some perverse corner of Skyler's mind wanted to see the Builders' construction material close up. He spun around. Maybe he could discern some detail before splattering his brains across it.

To his shock the iris pulsed open at the last instant. He sailed right past it with a *whoosh*. The subhuman did, too.

A bright light waited below, and as he fell into it time began to slow, until he felt suspended in midair.

He felt as if every dream he'd ever had, everything he'd ever seen or smelled or tasted or touched or heard, suddenly became available for leisurely review. As if every last neuron in his brain had opened and presented its contents. He found he could focus on all of it at once, and yet any specific memory or sensation he tried to access refused to come forward.

Skyler took it all in with a serenity like none he'd ever known. He felt warm and weightless, as if in a bath. Everything glowed, electrified. Part of him knew the sensation should overwhelm him, and yet he found it merely curious.

I've died, he thought. *It's not so bad.*

Then the images fell away from him. He floated, then flew, upward, thrown by some unseen force until he shot above the glowing hole. The iris snapped shut again below him and he fell to it.

With a skull-shaking thud he collapsed onto the cold, hard surface. A corner of his mind registered the fine angular patterns seemingly etched into the surface. Interlaced lines of varying depth, like veins in a leaf if not for their perfect straight lines and right-angle corners. Then his vision blurred, mind once again wallowed in a confused swarm of pain from the impact.

Skyler rolled onto his stomach and pushed himself to his feet. Everything swam and skewed in front of him. He blinked, rubbed at his eyes. Not dead after all.

Reality began to assert itself. Slowly his vision returned to normal. He stood on the alien floor, the iris closed tight at his feet. The stairwell ended on the wall of the access shaft, a meter above him.

The humming sound had vanished.

In fact, Skyler could hear nothing but his own breathing and the occasional twang of vibration that rippled along the Elevator cord.

In a sudden panic Skyler whirled around, checking behind him, then left and right, for the subhuman. But he was utterly alone.

She'd vanished. Pulled in and consumed by the Aura generator.

But not me, he thought. *It rejected me. As if I didn't . . . fit.*

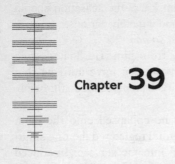

Chapter **39**

TEN MINUTES INTO Tania's jog through the quiet, curved hall of Black Level, the emergency alarm wailed.

The pulsing screech ripped her from a hard-won state of meditation. She took an awkward step, and tripped. Her palms burned on the carpet as she tried to break her fall.

"Can I get no peace?" she muttered to herself.

She saw no smoke in either direction, felt no rush of escaping air. No immediate danger, then, and the revelation only increased a sense of dread. Memories of the subhuman outbreak weeks earlier flashed through her mind.

She scanned the curving hallway and spotted an access corridor to Gray Level nearby. A quick run and she reached it, and found the connecting bulkheads still open. Interlevel access would be blocked during decompression or fire. A security situation, however, required the opposite—the guards on duty needed unfettered access.

All the official guards were locked in their quarters, except a few who had been convincing in their willingness to join the Platz side in this conflict.

Tania turned and raced back to her quarters. A few other researchers were poking their heads from darkened rooms, eyes bleary and confused. She ignored their questions and reached her door, where she found Natalie knocking on it.

"There you are," Natalie said. "What's going on?"

"I've no idea, let's find out." Tania unlocked the door and

rushed inside, leaving it open behind her. Natalie followed her in.

The terminal on the desk chirped loudly before Tania even reached it. She flicked the monitor on as she sat down, then tapped the keyboard to answer the call.

"I'm here," she said.

From the other end of the connection she heard shouting, confusion. Battle. The screen indicated the call was originating from the storage area on Red Level, all the way at the other end of the station.

". . . through the airlocks . . ." A garbled voice was full of panic. ". . . can't stop . . ."

"Slow down," Tania said. "I can't understand you."

She heard a series of shouts and rustling, then a loud click. The connection went dead.

The alarm stopped, too.

Tania tried to reestablish the connection, but it failed with an error. She tried the security desk to no avail.

"Fighting . . . my God, Nat, there's fighting."

"We're mutineers," Natalie said. "What did you expect—"

"I never wanted anyone to get hurt."

"The feeling is mutual, hon."

The room fell silent as Tania struggled to think of a plan. She felt Natalie's expectant gaze. Everyone on the station would be thinking the same thing, awaiting her orders. Watching how she handled herself. Pinning their hopes on her. For better or worse, Tania had become the leader of their little rogue nation.

Tania thought of the island of Hawaii, trees and birds and insects. Not the hell they'd landed in, but the idyllic version she'd glimpsed from above. She'd give anything to be there, far from this sterile place, this situation—

"We should get to Green Level," Natalie said. Her steady voice like the tug of gravity.

"Yes," Tania said. "You're right. The comm is dead. We should find Karl—"

"No." Natalie gripped her shoulder. "The lab. We need to suspend our program. Encrypt the data. Secure it."

"Then what?"

"Hide somewhere. Wait for this to be resolved."

Tania shook her head. "That would look great on my leadership résumé."

" 'Strong aptitude in avoidance and stealth techniques.' "

"Very funny," Tania said.

Tania led the way, creeping along the wall, eyes glued to the "horizon" of the hall, which curved up and out of view about one hundred meters ahead. They encountered nothing but silent halls along the way, a fact that made Tania all the more concerned.

Upon reaching the door to the computer lab, Natalie stepped ahead of her, key card ready. "I've got it," she said. The door clicked open and she stepped aside.

Tania pushed the door open to a dark room, allowing light from the door to spill in. A thousand blinking pin lights from the numerous terminals floated in the blackness like stars. She rushed inside and heard Natalie follow.

At the back of the lab she ducked inside the private research room, went straight to the terminal, and unlocked the screen with her passphrase.

The monitors began to come to life.

"I left the hall door open," Natalie said, and dashed back toward the front entrance. "Be right back!"

Tania started to tell her not to bother, but everything about their situation vanished from her mind when the giant displays on the wall came to life.

The day before, they'd determined that the Builders' ship would arrive imminently, and, after some difficult math and a clever bit of programming by Natalie, pinpointed where they thought it would settle into geosynchronous orbit.

Tania had worked late, long after a droopy-eyed Natalie had retired. She'd tapped into an old Platz-owned mapping satellite, overridden its routine task, and directed it to the opposite side of the planet. Borrowing some pattern recognition code from one of Natalie's brilliant scripts, Tania had instructed it to watch for the new shell ship and relay a video feed back to her.

The image brought a smile to her face. "Nat," she whispered. "We were right. We did it. . . ."

A shell ship like the first, perched high above the Earth. Tania squinted, and covered he mouth to stifle a gratified laugh.

At the tip of the shell ship, sunlight glinted off the thin thread of an Elevator cord.

Another space elevator, Tania thought. *A new one. A fresh start.* She saw no sign of the other, smaller objects, but that was a problem for another day. Clearly they'd sent no invasion fleet, no doomsday device.

She realized tears were streaming down her face.

"Come see, Nat!" Tania shouted.

Her assistant had been gone too long. Scouting the hall, maybe. Or—

"Hello, Miss Sharma," a man said, behind her. "Come see what?"

She didn't recognize the voice. It meant trouble, that much she knew. Tania's precautions for working in secret paid off as she tapped a single function key. A script she'd created immediately blanked the screens and began to encrypt and hide all the data.

"Oh," the man said, "you shouldn't have done that. Step away from there."

Tania turned to face him and took a step to her right. "It was just a simulation," she tried.

The man had a gun pointed at her and held Natalie by her elbow. Nat's eyes were firmly on the now-blank screens. She'd seen the image; she knew what the Builders had sent.

A half-dozen other people in the room all wore black uniforms and carried weapons.

"Who are you?" Tania asked. "What do you want here?"

He walked casually to stand in front of her, and she tried to muster a defiant glare. "I'm told you're in charge here," he said.

Tania's nostrils flared. She kept her jaw firm, said nothing.

"I was just about to get on the intercom," the man said, "and invite you down. Thanks for saving me the wait."

"What do you want?"

He ignored the question and shifted his attention to Natalie. "Who are you, sweetheart?"

"Natalie Ammon."

"Ah yes," he said, "Alex sends his regards."

"Tell that pig to piss off," Natalie replied.

"What—" Tania started. She stopped herself, realizing who stood in front of her. Russell Blackfield. Tania had not met him during her detention in Nightcliff, but she had no doubt he had either ordered or knowingly allowed her treatment there.

Natalie's comment flustered him for the briefest of seconds. "I'll relay your message," he said, rather lamely to Tania's ear.

"Leave her out of this," Tania said. "What do you want from me?"

He maintained eye contact with Natalie for a moment, sizing her up, then turned his focus on Tania.

"Two things," Russell said. "First, I'd like you to get on that intercom and tell the station that I am now in control. Your laughable security 'force' has been relieved."

Tania swallowed. "And second?"

Russell smiled. "You're going to tell me all about the research you've been doing for Platz. I hear it's fascinating."

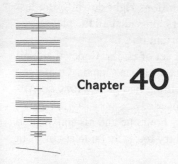

Chapter 40

NEIL TOOK A deep breath.

On the monitor in front of him, a sea of hostile soldiers rushed through the elegant hallways of Platz Station, his home.

Time would soon run out.

His gaze flicked yet again to the console at his left. Tania had not reported in, or responded to calls, for hours. The screen remained idle.

"Bloody hell," he said to no one.

A decision must be made. Never in his adult life had he struggled so hard to make one.

The soldiers were close now, past the halfway mark, cutting through closed airlock doors with reckless abandon.

If only he had more time. If only she'd called in. Silently he mouthed a prayer, hoping her control of Anchor Station remained steadfast.

Zane appeared at the door, impatience plain in his expression. "Everyone's waiting," he said. "There's no more time."

Neil weighed his options as Zane strolled over and stood behind him, leaning in to study the security feeds. Gateway soldiers swarmed through the evacuated hallways on levels three and four.

"They're nearly here, Neil," Zane said, somehow calm. Always so steady. "I don't know why you're waiting, the station is lost. . . ."

Neil Platz pushed himself to his feet. He'd done everything

he could, made all the preparations right down to the last detail. He'd given all the orders, provided all the plans.

Except one. The most important one.

Tania still needed a critical set of codes. Codes that Neil could not risk falling into Alex Warthen's hands. Or anyone else's, for that matter. If something had gone wrong on Anchor, their full plan compromised . . .

Better not to risk it. In a few hours he and his staff would arrive at Hab-8, and he could try to reach Tania again from there.

"All right. Let's go," he said.

He let Zane lead the way, watching him practically jog toward the lift. Neil allowed himself to fall behind, to walk alone through the grand hallway that led from his office all the way to the main lift on the opposite side of the ring. He soaked in the design of it, all built to his specifications. Carpet of rich burgundy contrasted by walls the color of sand.

The station, almost seventeen years old now, had become as comfortable as his old estate in Nightcliff. More so, perhaps, though he did miss the smell of salty air. The breeze, the pounding rains that cleansed everything. Days long gone.

A vision came to him, unbidden. The elder Dr. Sharma, Prathima, sitting on the sun deck between Neil and Sandeep, bouncing baby Tania on her knees. They all chuckled at the infant's delight.

Prathima. A striking woman, only to be eclipsed by her daughter. She'd gone to her early grave never knowing that her husband had died, or how. *Better that way.*

And little Tania. Her mop of black hair standing straight up, ever curious, eyes bright and wide even then. Laughing with a mixture of fear and delight as her mother bounced her ever higher, Neil and Sandeep egging her on.

Neil smiled to himself. He felt tears begin to well.

"Zane," he called out. His brother had disappeared beyond the curve of the hall. "Go on ahead, start the launch procedure."

He heard his brother's voice, distant. "What?"

"I forgot something," Neil called out. "Won't be a moment—"

A jet of steam rushed through a pair of doors ten meters ahead. The hot air screamed so loud Neil could barely hear the cutting torch underneath.

Too late, he thought. *I waited too long.*

Neil spun around and bolted toward his office. The sounds of booted feet filled the space behind him. Someone shouted. Zane? No time to find out.

He burst through the heavy oak door of his office, beating a path straight to his desk.

More shouts from outside, close. He needed time.

He moved back to the door and chanced a look into the hallway beyond. Four black-clad soldiers moved cautiously toward him, visible from foot to waist as they approached along the curved floor. Soon he saw their guns, sweeping every vantage point. He found himself transfixed, the almost alien feeling of fear gripping him.

One of the guards aimed, and Neil ducked back into the room at the same moment, sensing the action. The bullet hissed past his head, burying itself with a low *thud* in the back wall of the office.

Neil took a chance and rolled across the open doorway. The soldiers reacted too slowly, spraying gunfire after he crossed the opening. Bullets smacked into the floor, walls, and ceiling, filling the air with dust and chunks of debris. Neil grabbed the door and threw it shut.

He moved to lock it, a mistake. As he reached across and grasped the handle, another barrage tore through the thin door, poking dozens of holes in a random pattern across the surface. Two bullets ripped through his arm, leaving similar holes in his coat sleeve. Blood welled at the edges.

Neil shouted through clenched teeth and just managed to lock the door before collapsing against the wall. He tried to put pressure on the wound, only to advance his torment to a whole new level. His entire left arm felt on fire.

More bullets punched holes in the door, or thudded into the thicker wall, failing to puncture it but making no less of a racket.

The console. It's all that matters now, you fool!

Neil heard his own voice as if it were one of his teachers, shouting at him for some flub in school. The phantom voice managed to break through the pain that clouded his mind. He pushed himself to his feet, gritting his teeth every time his left arm moved. Blood soaked through his shirtsleeve and coat now, pooling on the floor below him. He ignored it. *The console.*

He could hear boots beyond the door—a lot of them. "Bring enough troops to take down an old man, Warthen?" he shouted, forcing his legs to carry him back to the safe. It seemed so far.

The response came swiftly. "We didn't start this, Mr. Platz, and you know it."

Not Warthen's voice. Neil laughed aloud. "What, Alex couldn't make it? Sent you to do his dirty work, is that it?"

"You can end this now, Neil. Give up."

"What's your name, son?"

A pause. "Jarred Larsen."

Neil reached the console and used his one good hand to type in his passphrase. The screen came alive.

"All right," Neil said in a raised voice, "I'm coming out. Hold your fire."

Forced to use just one arm, Neil accessed the information he'd been waiting to share with Tania. He selected the data and pushed it into a terse message, addressed it to her.

Then he opened a new message. He addressed it to Zane. Subject: "If I die."

"Platz?" Jarred shouted from the other side of the door. "You've got three seconds, then we're coming in."

Grunting through pain, Neil began to tap out a confession.

"You know what, Larsen?" Neil shouted. "Go fuck yourself. Anyone who enters this room is a dead man." The empty threat, he hoped, would buy a few extra seconds. He typed as rapidly as one hand would allow. A peace settled over him as he put into words the secret he'd carried for so long. He could only hope Zane would make sense of the cryptic words.

The door kicked in and a soldier dressed in black stormed inside.

Neil kept typing, his burden falling away with each letter, and the soldier reacted as he was trained: He aimed and fired.

In the same instant Neil tapped "send," the bullet entered his brain through the center of his forehead. He dropped to his knees and fell over on his side, aware but strangely at peace.

He saw their black boots sideways before they started to blur. And blur, and blur, and blur into a void . . .

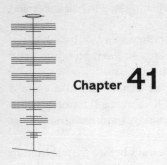

Chapter 41

DAZED AND NUMB, Skyler trudged up the silo stairs.

The memory of what had happened below already faded, and he let it. The bizarre sensations of his mind being flayed wide open, the machine pushing him back out while keeping the subhuman . . . none of it made sense. He wondered if his immunity somehow confused the device, like it had no taste for his kind.

He'd sat down there in the stark silence, looking at the black iris and its alien patterns, assuming the subhuman would reappear, too. Wondering "why not" when it didn't. He'd even drifted off for a time. A few hours, he guessed, but he had no way to be sure as his watch had stopped working.

He realized he didn't really care.

The errand Platz had given him seemed comical, in hindsight. He grinned at the idea of explaining to Platz what he'd seen.

Yes, I made it there. Yes, it sounded like a failing jet engine when I arrived, and dead silent when I left. I may have destroyed what I meant to fix, and doomed all of you. But at least I got an alien mind-fuck out of the deal.

Sorry, mate. Next time?

Destroyed the Aura. The possibility made him stop, midstep. He looked up and tried to imagine a million subhumans waiting for him. Ready to tear him to pieces for dooming them all.

Who could blame them. Skyler took another tired step, then another.

Sunlight baked the damp grounds of Nightcliff, and a stiff warm breeze came in off the ocean, carrying with it the smell of salt.

Forced to squint in the brightness, Skyler shielded his eyes with one hand and stepped through the same hole he'd created when entering the mansion.

To the south lay Kantro's plane, still embedded in the side of a low building near the landing pads. The bird listed to one side, and part of one wing lay on the tarmac, bent beyond repair. A crowd of people tugged thick chains over the fuselage, while an old tractor idled nearby, ready to try to yank the wounded aircraft free.

Skyler took in the rest of the scene; the landing pads, the climber port, and the Elevator beyond. No signs remained of the subhuman attack, and for a fleeting instant Skyler thought perhaps he'd been inside the silo for days, not hours.

But a man mopping up blood dispelled that theory. He sloshed water from an old janitor's bucket onto a red splotch on the ground, and scraped at it with a thick-bristle push broom.

Glancing up, fighting the sun, Skyler followed the cord all the way to its vanishing point in the sky above. Two climbers lazed their way up.

"You okay, mate?" someone asked.

Skyler glanced down and saw a Nightcliff guard standing at the fence, the same fence both he and the subhuman woman had scaled on the way in.

The soldier stood barely taller than a boy of perhaps seventeen, tall enough for Skyler's needs.

"Yeah," he croaked. With a cough he cleared his throat. "Yeah, I'm good."

The boy scrunched his nose. "I don't think you're supposed to be in there."

Skyler walked up to the fence. "Fled in here when the attack came, and I guess I knocked my head. Did I miss the action?"

The kid relaxed a bit. He carried only a baton for a weapon, and his uniform looked cobbled together. Camouflage pants, worn running shoes painted dark gray, and a short-sleeved black shirt. The only piece of his uniform that mattered, though, was the maroon helmet on his head. The name Nera had been stenciled on it.

Nera looked around at the landing yard and shrugged. "I missed it, too. I was on the east wall. What do you do here?"

"Fix stuff," Skyler managed. "Sinks, toilets. Speaking of, I really need to take a piss."

"There's a head in my barracks that works. Follow me?"

"Lead on," Skyler said.

The kid broke into a jog, heading west and south through the low buildings, and Skyler kept close behind him.

"Never seen you before," Skyler said, trying to sound casual.

"I just joined up."

"Really? Seem to know your way around."

Nera took it as a compliment and relaxed a bit as they entered the barracks. "I learn pretty fast," he said.

"Seems so." The barracks were empty. "Not too busy here, eh?"

"Most everyone went up."

"Why?"

The kid looked at him sideways. "Blackfield's War," he said.

A few days and already the conflict had a name. Skyler cringed.

Nera went on. "He's really taking it to Platz, they say."

"And you're stuck here?"

"I just joined up," he said again. "The vets get first crack, but I'm hoping I'll get picked. Duty roster gets posted at six-n-six."

"Ah."

"Here's the can," Nera said. He stopped in front of a door near the back.

"I'll just be a minute," Skyler said.

He went inside and found it to be empty. Skyler checked each stall anyway, confirming it. There were three windows high on the wall above a row of poorly maintained sinks. They were all closed, and too small to shimmy through anyway.

He shouted and ran to the door, pushing it open with exaggerated panic.

The young man, who had been leaning against the wall, jerked upright.

"There's . . ." Skyler pretended to catch his breath "There's a man, in the stall. Dead . . . I think. God, I'm gonna be sick."

The guard leaned in the door but made no move to enter. "Dead?"

"See for yourself," Skyler said, panting.

The boy entered the bathroom as if it brimmed with waiting subhumans; his eyes never left the row of stalls. "Which one?" he asked, his voice breaking awkwardly.

"The last," Skyler said. He moved into the bathroom behind the cautious guard and eased the door closed.

The poor boy, so fixated on the stall, never heard Skyler come up behind him. One swift blow to the back of the head and the kid collapsed.

Skyler couldn't kill him. The boy seemed innocent enough, just trying to make a better life for himself. Even so, Skyler damn well couldn't have him alerting anyone, either.

Moving quickly, Skyler swapped outfits with the unconscious kid. He kept his own shoes. Most important, he placed the maroon helmet of a Nightcliff soldier on his own head. It wore tight, but would do.

The fortress was nearly deserted. Other than the crew cleaning up the wrecked plane, Skyler spotted only a few guards. Most were on the wall, attempting to make the contingent appear status quo to outsiders, he assumed.

Skyler hoisted the unconscious kid over one shoulder and went out the back door of the barracks. Once outside he did his best to walk with confidence. Just another body being slogged through the fortress; surely not the first time, or the last.

It took a few minutes for Skyler to find the manhole cover he'd come in through. It took almost an hour of backbreaking, frustrating work to lower Nera down to the tunnel below and move him into the room where all tunnels converged.

The kid seemed pretty bright, so Skyler figured he could find a way out of the sewer when he woke. Hopefully that would be well after Skyler found his way onto a climber. A calculated risk, but he couldn't think of anything else short of suffocating the poor boy.

He had until six, according to Nera, before the next list of names would be posted. Skyler figured he'd check the list, and if Nera wasn't on it, he'd find someone who was and take their place. In the meantime, he decided to feign duty. He'd spent time in the military, and he knew that even when you had nothing to do, you had something to do.

Back at the barracks, Skyler grabbed a broom and swept the floor. The menial task cleared his mind, calmed him. He lost himself in it and almost missed the locked chest with NERA scrawled on the side at the end of a row of bunks. Skyler found the key in a pocket of his borrowed uniform.

He brushed aside a sense of guilt. Rifling through someone else's belongings never felt good, but it beat sweeping.

The objects inside reminded him of his own innocent notion of what would be important to bring to boot camp: playing cards, a few odd photos of friends snapped and printed—likely at great expense—in the main bazaar near the center of Darwin, and a worn pencil banded to some partially used graph paper.

Skyler took only a lighter and a half-full pack of foul-smelling cigarettes, leaving the rest as he found it.

Feeling more confident in his disguise, he decided to venture out and learn what he could about the situation in orbit.

He went to the wall. Along the top of that massive barricade he marched a slow patrol, nodding to other guards he passed. Eventually he came to the point that overlooked Ryland Square, just outside the southern gate, where the riots started last month. He traced the path the *Melville* had taken, coming in over the wall, belly full of spoils that would soon be seized.

An eternity had passed since that day. Part of him expected to see the *Melville* parked there, Angus in the cockpit taking that shocking sight in stride.

So odd to be up here, wearing the maroon helmet. He couldn't dream such a bizarre reversal.

He walked to the edge of the wall and ventured a look over. A crowd had formed around the fortress gate. His heart rate shot up; he was afraid he would get called to quell another riot. Then he realized they were celebrating, not rioting. Amid the sea of people, he saw container after container of food lying along the base of the wall, open to the sea of greedy hands.

Blackfield had pacified the locals, it seemed. Some were chanting his name.

Skyler frowned at that. *What a clever bastard.*

At the lookout point above the southern gate, Skyler stopped and offered a cigarette to the soaked guards who stood there, as if presiding over the assembly.

"Look at all of 'em," one guard said.

"Like pigs at the feeding trough," said the other. He'd probably been one of them just days earlier.

Skyler tried to play along. "Nothing like a meal to bring people together, eh?"

"Shit," said the second guard, popping the cigarette between his lips. "Won't last, not unless the climbers start coming back this direction."

"Nothing's coming down?" Skyler asked.

The guard shot a sidelong glance at Skyler. "Only works one direction at a time, mate."

"Oh yeah. Right."

The second guard glanced up at the sky, squinting in the bright sun. "Still, the power's finally stable again. That'll speed things up."

Skyler gave a slow nod and staggered away, his mind reeling.

Stable power. Had it bloody worked?

He thought back to the silo. Falling with the subhuman,

into that . . . energy. And the deep, irregular hum that had pounded him on the way down. The sound had disappeared when he came back out.

The reason eluded him. He had done nothing to fix the damn thing. He'd made a sloppy mess of it, if anything. Given the alien device the most cursory of inspections, and left behind a subhuman like an offering.

No point in dwelling on it now, he decided. Whatever the cause, the power had stabilized, and that meant a quicker trip to orbit, which was all that mattered. Whether he could take credit or not, the conclusion lifted his spirits a little.

He followed the wall around to the eastern gate, which had long ago been sealed. No cheering crowds here, just the daily market set up in the shadow of the wall. Skyler himself had bought and sold goods here—surplus items from speculative missions outside the city, traded for necessities produced within. The market was near empty today, due to the bountiful containers lying open in Ryland Square.

Blackfield's War. Skyler shook his head. The offer Neil Platz had made seemed nothing short of paranoid when Skyler heard it. Not anymore.

His stomach grumbled as his path along the wall reached the northern side, by the ocean. *Time to find the mess hall,* he thought. Food with a side of eavesdropping.

It proved easy enough to locate. Every guard not on duty congregated at the large building, once a warehouse by the look of it.

Skyler grabbed a tray of offered food—a variety of vegetables along with hummus and seedy crackers. The seating consisted of a series of benches, arranged in rows and spanning the gamut in terms of age and condition.

The usual cliques of such a place were nowhere to be seen. Skyler guessed this was because all the experienced soldiers had gone to orbit. Instead everyone sat together near the southern wall.

One man sat slightly apart from the rest of the crowd, and Skyler recognized him: the one who'd snuck him the memory chip full of Orbital requests. Prumble's "man inside," Kip.

Skyler took a chance and approached the man.

"Okay if I sit?"

Kip glanced up from his food, which he pushed around a tin plate with a fork. "God, don't you blokes ever give up?"

"Thanks," Skyler said, plopping his tray on the table and taking a spot on the bench. "My feet are killing me. Killing me! Patrolling the walls all morning."

"Good for you," the man said. He continued to push his meal around the dented metal plate, turning it to mush.

"What do you do here?"

He shot an annoyed glance at Skyler. Then he gathered himself and looked back at his plate. "The go-list is based on seniority, so you're wasting your time. I can't help you."

"Go-list? I'm just making friendly—"

Kip's fork stopped. "Right, right. I get put in charge of Orbital duty and suddenly everyone wants to be my chum. Bollocks."

"I'm new here," Skyler said.

"No shit."

"Any news from up top?"

The man dropped his fork and focused on Skyler. "I'm not in the mood, if you don't mind."

Skyler spread his hands and took to eating his tasteless food. After a few bites in silence, he rolled the dice. "Prumble sends his regards."

As Skyler hoped, Kip's head snapped up. "You know him?"

With a casual nod, Skyler said, "I know you, too, as a matter of fact."

Kip glanced around. The color had flushed from his face. "Who the hell are you?" he whispered.

Skyler pushed the plate of horrid food aside and stared at Kip.

"Ah, yes," Kip said, nodding. "The immune. Skyler, was it? I'll be damned."

"Call for the guards and I'll kill you before they get here," Skyler said.

Kip sat frozen for a few seconds, then shrugged and went back to drawing hummus patterns. "What is it you want?"

Skyler smiled. "Simple. Add the name Nera to your go-list, and forget you ever saw me."

"Or . . . what? You'll rat me out to Blackfield? I'm nothing now. Not without Prumble. Without you, frankly. Just a cog in this damnable machine."

"Look," Skyler said, "I've lost everything, too. My ship, my crew, the business Prumble brought me from you. The whole chain is shattered, and we're both screwed." He lowered his voice, drawing Kip closer. "All I can tell you is I *must* get to orbit. My crew was captured there, and I have to find them. I owe them that."

Kip's fork froze. He didn't look up.

"You're not nothing, Kip," Skyler added. "You're the man who can get me to orbit."

Kip fell silent. For a long time he stared at the crowd of Nightcliff guards who huddled in the corner of the mess hall. They were brash and boisterous. Making lewd jokes and laughing at one another.

"I'll see what I can do," Kip said. Then he stood and wandered from the room, his unfinished meal forgotten.

At four o'clock Skyler made his way to the cargo yard and asked where he was supposed to go for boarding. A worker gave him terse directions.

About twenty other guards, all trying to act like a ride to orbit was no big deal to them, mingled around the climber base station. Skyler stood at the edge of the pack, his maroon helmet worn low.

The chaotic situation in orbit, and the complex operation to move troops and supplies up the Elevator, made it easier than he could have hoped to blend in. In situations like that, details were missed. Things fell through the cracks.

Disguises served their purpose.

The climber car dropped into place an hour later. Skyler waited until the others had lined up before joining the queue himself. He gave the name Nera to the woman with the clipboard and was waved through without even a cursory glance.

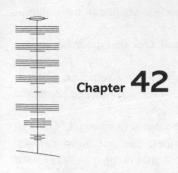

Chapter **42**

AT THE STROKE of midnight, Tania's terminal rebooted. The screen flickered through the start-up procedure, casting her small cabin in a sudden blue-green glow.

She'd been awake for hours, staring at the ceiling, thinking. In the sudden illumination, she sat up and swung her legs off the bed.

Russell Blackfield had placed her under house arrest shortly after arriving. Whatever plan he'd had to interrogate her abruptly changed after the first question he'd asked.

"Tell me about the research you've been doing for Neil Platz," he'd said.

"No," she'd replied.

Then Natalie had chimed in. Her voice so calm and collected that Tania had gone numb. "I'll tell you," Natalie had said. "I've been doing most of the work anyway."

A huge grin had spread across Russell's face. He'd instructed a pair of guards to lock Tania in her quarters until further notice. She'd been too shocked to fight them, or say anything. She could only stare at Natalie, baffled, trying to find some glimmer of explanation for her betrayal. But Natalie, her assistant and friend, would not meet her gaze. Instead she focused completely on Russell Blackfield, looking every bit the eager helper.

Tania had not been allowed to see anyone. She'd tried her computer the moment they'd closed her door, only to find it locked in station-wide "maintenance mode." The distinct beep of the reboot marked the first change in her monotonous imprisonment.

Then she heard another sound. One that made her jump.

The door unlocked.

She stared at the handle, waiting for someone to enter, wondering if she should turn off the computer or pretend to be asleep. The door remained closed.

Confused, she went to it and opened it a crack. Outside, the hallway was dark and quiet. She left the door open slightly, worried that the lock would reengage if she closed it, and went to her terminal.

Instead of the usual passphrase prompt it displayed her messages. One was new, from Neil Platz, sent eighteen hours ago.

With a rush of hope she opened it and read, *"I'm dead or captured—here's what you must do . . ."*

That hope gave way to agony at Neil's stark, abrupt words in the second half of the message.

Neil had triggered a fail-safe program, inserted into the stations' systems months ago. The door locks had been disabled, the security systems reverted to month-old backups.

She wanted to mourn, wanted to beat her fists against the wall at the madness of all this. She knew Neil would never let himself be captured. He had too much pride. He was gone and she couldn't even be there at his side. Just like when her father passed.

But Neil's amazing knack for thinking ahead gave her a sudden glimmer of confidence. The words that followed replaced her agony with an anxiety like none she'd ever known. Neil's plan, as crazy and bold as the man himself, left her breathless.

Tania read it twice, fighting tears all the while. For a moment she sat in plain awe of Neil's ability for forethought. The few simple sentences implied months, even years, of devious planning.

She memorized the instructions. Then she deleted the message and reset the terminal.

In the hall outside, people were emerging from their

rooms. She took a moment to calm herself, put on a face she hoped showed courage, and walked out into the hallway.

"What's going on?" a neighbor asked. "Why did the doors unlock?"

"I'm not sure," Tania replied. "Stay in your room. I'm going to check."

She moved at a brisk pace to Natalie's cabin and found it empty.

Flashes of her imprisonment in Nightcliff forced their way into her mind. She shuddered to think what might be happening to Nat. The poor girl had no idea what Blackfield and his thugs were capable of, regardless of her offer to help them. Yet Neil's message held a deeper grip on Tania's mind. Natalie would have to wait.

Tania headed for the observation lounge.

At one point she heard approaching soldiers, sprinting along the main hallway. She ducked into the closest cabin, pushed the door shut, and waited.

In the cramped room, a man and a woman were embracing, partially undressed, and looking at her with wide eyes. Tania recognized one of them as a low-level researcher.

"The doors opened," he said, mumbling in fear. "We hadn't seen each other—"

"Quiet," Tania said, too tersely. The man swallowed back the rest of his explanation. Tania faced the door and leaned against it. She pressed her ear to the surface and listened as the soldiers ran by. When their footsteps receded, she nodded to the amorous couple and stepped back into the hall.

The guards were headed for her room, she had no doubt of that. No time to waste, then. Tania sprinted the rest of the way.

Starlight spilling in from the giant windows provided the only light in the observation lounge. Despite everything happening around her, the view of the shell ship, and Earth beyond, still took Tania's breath away.

She shook off the feeling and went to the bench. Memories of a hundred idle conversations with the old man fought for her attention. "Your parents would be so proud of you," he had said so often, the only praise she'd ever received that mattered.

Kneeling by the bench, she looked underneath the plush cushion. In the dark she saw nothing but shadow. She reached her hand below and ran it across the cool plastic support surface. Her fingers brushed something. Paper. An envelope, glued to prevent it from falling. Try as she might, she could not pull it away, but then her fingers found a flap along one edge. She pried it open and used her nails to pinch the bundle of papers inside. They were tightly packed, but after a struggle they came free.

The overhead lights came back on. All along the curved hallway she heard the *snap snap* of doors locking. She felt glad she'd left her own door ajar. If it remained that way, she could sneak back in.

Tania stuffed the folded papers under her shirt and walked briskly to a nearby restroom. A sigh of relief escaped her lips when she tried the door and found it open. It was bright in the white-tiled room, enough to make her squint. Tania moved to the stall at the very end of the row, closed the door behind her, and sat on the water tank above the toilet, using the seat as a footrest.

Only then did she remove the papers and read them.

The information there was at once terrifying and exhilarating.

In the morning, three guards entered Tania's room without a knock. She sat bolt upright, pulling the blanket up to cover herself.

"Get dressed," the largest one said. "Blackfield wants to see you." They stood in place, waiting for an answer.

"Where's my assistant? Natalie Amm—"

"Get dressed, now."

She gripped the blanket until her knuckles turned white. "Mind waiting outside?"

The words lingered as the man in the center merely grinned. "He said not to lay a finger on you, but didn't say nothing about watching." One of his friends kicked the door closed and the three stood and waited.

She let the blanket fall as she stood up, determined not to let them see weakness in her. The soldiers were openly disappointed to see she was wearing a tank top and running shorts, but still their eyes stayed glued to her as she stepped into a jumpsuit.

"They don't make 'em like you down in Darwin," one of the guards said. Another laughed. She did her best to ignore them, cursing her hands for shaking.

"He said not to lay a finger on you." Tania considered the deeper implications. Blackfield wanted her for himself. Or he still needed something from her. In the back of her mind, a tiny voice wondered if she could use her body as a weapon. She hated herself for even thinking it.

She'd rather die.

Tania wiggled into the garment and zipped it up. "Let's go."

The tall one led the way, striding along the corridor like he owned the place, near enough to the truth. They passed only a few other researchers, each under guarded escort. Tania did everything she could to mask the embarrassment she felt. She'd become something of a leader after the mutiny, and had been wholly unprepared for the counterattack. She had let them down, and she doubted the guards had orders not to lay hands on anyone else.

She'd heard nothing from her fellow mutineers since Blackfield and his troops had arrived. They'd either fought back and failed, or melted away.

"In there," the thug in the lead said.

Tania had been lost in thought. They stood in front of the conference room on Black Level. The three guards took positions on both sides of the door, leaving Tania to open it for herself. She turned the handle and stepped inside.

"Tania!"

She felt an enormous relief to see Natalie, and ran to her. They embraced.

"No kissing now," Russell Blackfield said. "This is a family-friendly environment."

The sound of his voice made Tania's heart sink. "I was so worried," Tania whispered, holding her assistant as tightly as she could. "Why did you offer to—"

"Later," Natalie whispered.

"Enough," Russell said. "You'll make me all weepy."

"Did he hurt you?" Tania asked.

Russell threw his arms up. "I'm standing right here, dammit. Hello?"

Tania released her friend, and realized she was crying. They both were. She wiped the tears away on her sleeve and turned to Russell. "If you've hurt her . . ."

"She's fine. You're fine. Right?"

Natalie had kept hold of Tania's hand, and squeezed it. She nodded.

"There, see? Everyone's fine."

Tania stood her ground. "What do you want?"

"A thank-you would be nice."

"Thank *you*?"

He gestured toward Natalie. "Not me, her. Your lover here has earned your freedom. Strings attached, of course."

Tania glanced briefly at Natalie, who wore a sad smile and kept her eyes aimed at the table. *Lover? She must have concocted a story in a hurry.* She fixed her gaze on Russell again. "What strings?"

"I thought that would be obvious," he replied. "Your research. I want it finished, now, and I want the *results*."

Before Tania could craft a response, Russell pulled a sinister-looking pistol from a holster inside his jacket.

The room went deathly quiet as he pointed the business end at Natalie.

"You two lovebirds have twenty-four hours," he said, "to tell me where the Builder ship is going to park."

Tania's eyes grew wide at the revelation. *She really told him.* At least she had not divulged the crucial piece of information. If she'd told him that, everything would be over.

"Yes, that's right. Your girl here sang like a bird, when her mouth wasn't otherwise occupied. What a tireless little champ! Very convincing."

"You said you wouldn't tell her, you son of a bitch," Natalie said, her words startlingly loud in the closed room.

Russell kept his attention on Tania. "No more delays, no more excuses. In twenty-four hours I want the location where *my* new Builder ship has arrived, or your friend here dies."

Tania swallowed, and deep down cursed herself for doing so. "Kill me instead."

"No such luck, I'm afraid. No, if you don't give me what I want, you will spend the rest of your life servicing my soldiers. And that will only be the beginning of your misery," Russell said.

"And if we cooperate?"

He smiled. "Then you can continue here, doing whatever the hell it is you do. There's no reason that has to change in the new world order. Stay here, work, and enjoy the pleasure of each other's company."

His constant allusions to their supposed romance had a twinge of sarcasm. Tania wondered if he really believed it, or if he just found it humorous. She looked at Natalie. Their eyes met and held for a long, tense moment. Her friend then nodded to her, a nearly imperceptible motion that Tania returned.

"Fine," she said to Russell Blackfield. "Just, please, leave the rest of the crew alone."

"Agreed, for twenty-four hours. Starting now."

They walked in silence, under escort, to the computer laboratory on Green Level.

In the front room of the lab, with the guards keeping close by, Tania removed a number of bound folders from a shelf before continuing to the back room.

Two of the guards stayed with them, taking seats on each side of the door.

"It's really not necessary," Tania said. "There's nowhere to go."

"Orders," came the snapped response.

She shrugged and took a seat at the console, activating the three large monitors that spanned the back wall. A number of smaller monitors on the desk also flickered to life.

Tania turned to Natalie before she could sit. "Would you dim the lights, please?"

"I got it," the guard said. He was seated next to the switch, and ratcheted it down to quarter strength.

Natalie took the seat next to Tania, spreading out the folders Tania gave her. "Where'd you leave off?" she asked. The first words she'd spoken since they'd left Russell's presence. A genuine apology came through in the tone, unspoken but nonetheless welcome.

Tania's fingers danced across the keyboard, filling the screens with a myriad of images and data structures. She flipped the pages in one of the folders until it was open to the middle. "Here's the latest. Last week I thought it might glance off the atmosphere, aerobraking, and perhaps settle into position on its next pass, in a year or so. But look here . . ."

A quick glance at the guards proved they were not paying close attention. She picked up a pencil and circled a section of the report, and wrote next to it:

Did you tell him?

"It's braking at an incredible rate," she continued. "I didn't think it would be possible."

Natalie was nodding, slowly, and took the pencil. "I see what you mean." She added below Tania's words:

We saw the image, he knows it's a new elevator. I could convince him it's months away.

As she wrote, she said, "Have you calculated the arrival time?"

Her voice sounded false to Tania, like an amateur actress in a bad play. Tania took the pencil back and erased the words they'd written, then flipped to another page.

"Take a look at these numbers," she said, pointing out a random bit of useless info.

She wrote:

Can't let the station suffer that long. Have a plan. We need to talk alone.

She underlined the last word and said, "The deceleration rate negated all our predictions."

Natalie picked up the pencil and added:

I have an idea.

She erased the writing and turned to a random page in the folder. "How long will it take to recalculate?"

Tania had no idea what Natalie was thinking, but caught her wink and went along with it. "Eight hours, roughly."

"Let's get started, then."

Four hours later Tania paced her room, waiting anxiously for Natalie to arrive.

They had pretended to work at the data analysis for thirty minutes, to give an appearance of effort, before telling the guards that they needed to give the computer time to run simulations. The guards were willing to wait it out, but Natalie said she'd rather be returned to her quarters to rest.

When the guards pushed Tania into her own room and locked the door, she expected to hear them continue down the hall with Natalie to do the same. Instead they had gone in the other direction.

Her imagination ran wild. Had Natalie been taken to be interrogated? Could she handle something like that? Tania knew the answer was no. Natalie probably knew her limits, too, which explained why she'd decided to play the willing informant.

Her mind returned to the instructions Neil Platz had left in the envelope. A chill ran down her spine. An astonishing plan, far bolder than she could ever concoct on her own.

Footsteps outside the door. Heavy.

They were early.

Tania realized she was still fully dressed, and as the door was unlocked she abruptly flipped her light off and sat on the edge of her bed, running her hands through her hair to appear as if she'd been napping.

The door opened to the silhouette of a soldier.

"It hasn't been eight hours, has it?" Tania asked, forcing her voice to sound groggy.

"Blackfield said you can use the showers if you want," he said. Then he sniffed the stale air of the room. " 'Bout damn time, too."

"Remind you of Darwin?"

The guard actually smiled, if only for a second, and moved aside to allow her to exit the room.

She pulled a towel from her closet and stepped into the hall. The showers on this level were connected to the restrooms, and the guard followed her in.

Tania whirled on him. "You'll wait outside, or take me back to—"

"Relax," he said, walking past her, down the aisle of lockers to the large open shower. The tiled space was square in shape, with six showerheads poking out of three walls. "Just doing my job," he said, checking two corners that were hidden from view of the door.

Satisfied, he came back to the door and pushed it open. "You've got twenty minutes," he said, grinning slightly.

Something in that grin worried her. For a moment she stood in place, unsure what to do.

Before she could decide, the door opened again, and Natalie entered, carrying a towel of her own.

Tania whispered, "What's going on?"

Natalie stepped in close and gave her a quick embrace. "When the water's on," she said, so quietly that Tania barely caught it.

With that Natalie set her towel on the metal bench in front of the lockers and began to undress. Tania stood in place.

"Come on, hon," Natalie said. She smiled in an odd way as she padded down to the shower and turned on a faucet.

"When the water's on." Tania kept her head still and looked about the shower room. They were listening. Or worse, watching.

Natalie drenched herself under a fountain of steaming water, running her hands through her hair as if nothing was wrong.

Stomach aching from nervous dread, Tania shrugged off

her jumpsuit. She stood naked with her arms tight across her chest, and took a quick glance back at the door. It remained closed. Finally she walked to the shower.

Steam from the hot water already obscured Natalie's body.

Tania turned on the showerhead next to Natalie's and set it as hot as she thought she could take it. Her friend reached a hand out to her. Tania took it, expecting a friendly squeeze, but Natalie pulled her until their bodies were touching, warm water spilling over both their shoulders. Natalie's arm slipped around her waist, pressing them together.

"What are you—" Tania started to ask, before their lips met. Natalie kissed her urgently, with passion, not like a friend. Nothing like a friend.

Tania could do nothing but stand there, frozen in place, lips closed tight.

"Relax," Natalie whispered. "Russell is only allowing this because he's hoping for a good show. The mist should leave most of it to their imagination."

Tania understood, then. Natalie had been playing to Russell's perversion the moment he'd found them in the computer lab.

Her night spent in the bowels of Nightcliff filled her mind. She'd somehow convinced herself that the wall-sized mirror was just that, and that no one sat on the other side of it. A lie she had needed to make it through that night, and the weeks since. But in her heart she knew Russell had been watching.

Tania squeezed her eyes closed and forced the memory away, for Natalie's sake. To expose her ruse now would have terrible consequences for both of them.

She became aware that her arms were held out as if a Jacobite preacher groped her. Shaking with stage fright, she returned Natalie's embrace as best she could. Under the torrent of scalding hot water, she managed to relax her shoulders a bit.

Natalie pulled Tania's head to her shoulder with one hand while caressing the length of her back with the other. Then she whispered in her ear, "Russell is recording this, so speak quietly."

With nervous uncertainty Tania tried to find a place for her hands on Natalie's back. Somewhere that implied familiar affection, she hoped. "He trusts you enough to let us alone? Natalie, my God, how did you convince him? What did you have to do?"

"Shhh," Natalie whispered. She held on even tighter than before, as if Tania might slip and fall. "It's not what you think. He's just saying things to rile you."

"If they've hurt you . . . abused you—"

Natalie gripped the back of her head. "He just wants you to think that. No easy way around this, so here it is. I've been working for Alex Warthen for over a year now."

Tania tried to pull away, to fight, at the confession. But Natalie held her too tightly.

"Please listen. Alex blackmailed me. He wanted to know about the research going on here, and in exchange lifted me out of a terrible life in Darwin. It seemed harmless enough, until I mentioned that Neil met with you in private, and he wanted me to find out why. I refused, and his offer of help turned to threats. Please believe me."

For a long time Tania stood in shocked disbelief. A well of conflicting emotions churned in her mind, but the longer she stood there under the warm water, in Natalie's arms, the further they receded, until one was left.

"I forgive you," Tania said. "I forgive you. . . ."

Natalie broke into racking sobs, going to her weakened knees, pulling Tania down with her in the process. It was Tania's turn to lead the embrace. She eased her friend to the floor, sat facing her, and offered a shoulder.

Natalie buried her head there, sobbing.

Tania let her cry, and shed a few tears of her own. Neil dead or captured, and now her closest friend had admitted betrayal. Her home for so many years had become a prison, run by the man she hated most in the world. A man who, if he had his way, would soon control the new ship sent by the Builders.

Sitting there on the wet floor, wrapped tightly in her best friend's embrace, Tania had never felt more alone. She felt as if the station around them had disappeared, revealing the cold emptiness of space.

Tania had to finish Neil's plan. And, no matter what, she knew she could no longer trust Natalie. It drove a knife in her gut to admit that to herself.

Resolve building, she put her lips against Natalie's ear and whispered. "What now? Are you going to tell Russell—"

"Of course not," Natalie said. "He's a monster. I told him you were keeping me in the dark, but perhaps if I could sleep with you . . . again . . ."

"I'd give up the secret in the heat of passion?"

Natalie began to shake. "He's promised me to his guards, if I don't tell him."

Tania tensed, overwhelmed by rage. She began to stand.

"No," Natalie said, gripping her arms, "No!" She managed to bring Tania back to her sitting position. "He's watching, remember that. If he thinks we're just in here plotting . . ."

"I . . . I'll kill him. Alex, too."

"You won't, Tania. I'm sorry, but we're not fighters."

"We are when we're cornered . . ." The image of Skyler, shooting the face off a subhuman, burst into her mind. Decisive, instinctual. No second guesses. "Listen, you have to give him a false location for the Elevator."

Natalie sat very still. "He'd find out, and then kill us."

"He won't have the chance," Tania said. She wanted nothing more than to share the information Neil had provided her, but Natalie had been lying to her for months. Tania realized she forgave her, yes, but her trust was shaken. "I . . . have a plan. It's a good one, but we have to convince Blackfield to go to the wrong place."

"He'll find out! He'll get there and find no Elevator."

"Don't worry about that. It's part of the plan."

Natalie nodded, wiping her nose. She even smiled, if only slightly.

Tania remained there with her, on the cold tile floor, letting the warm water rush over her. It wasn't long before a guard entered.

"Time's up," he said.

To Tania's amazement, he waited outside while they dressed.

* * *

Precisely eight hours after the simulation had started, Tania was escorted from her room.

Anchor Station had never been quieter. Even the Nightcliff regulars were mercifully devoid of lewd comments.

Their pace remained brisk, however, and Tania could feel the emptiness in her gut grow as they drew close to the computer lab.

The stop was brief, but long enough for Tania to review the "results." She made a quick show of it, and then declared herself ready to speak with Russell.

They left the lab and the guards led her to White Level, to the station's lone luxury cabin. A room normally reserved for Neil Platz. From what Tania had overheard from the guards, Russell spent most of his time in there, using the computer terminal to scan the station's various security cameras. *For his own amusement,* Tania thought, *not anyone's security.*

When the guards knocked on the opulent double door, Tania willed herself to be calm.

"Enter," said Russell from inside.

The two guards each opened a door, leaving Tania between them to make a strangely grand entrance.

"Join us," Russell said. He sat at a small table, adjacent to a window that dominated the rear wall of the room. A half-eaten breakfast sprawled before him. Outside, the shell ship floated in partial illumination, the rest obscured in ever-moving shadows from Anchor Station's rings.

Natalie sat with him, her food untouched, looking disheveled, like she hadn't slept. She kept her eyes locked on the alien fuselage outside.

Tania approached the one remaining chair slowly. "I prefer to stand," she said.

"Nonsense, eat something."

Tania glanced at the chair. Every instinct told her to resist, to show him she could be strong, that he couldn't win *everything.*

Russell smashed his fork against the table. The flash of anger made Tania jump. "Sit. Now."

She slowly lowered herself into the chair, watching Natalie.

Her friend hadn't even blinked at the noise. She still stared out at the alien relic.

They had made a deal, hours earlier in the shower, that Natalie would avert her eyes when they next saw each other if the deception had held.

"Nat, give your woman a kiss good morning," Russell said through a mouthful of artificial egg.

Natalie turned at this, smiling sadly at Tania and giving her hand a squeeze.

Russell burped and said, "That's no kiss."

Natalie seemed to wake up, or drop out of some state of hypnosis. "Haven't you seen enough already?"

"What, the shower? That was highly disappointing." He cut off Natalie's retort before it could come. "So tell me, Tania, when will my new Elevator make landfall?"

"Don't you mean the council's new Elevator?"

He chewed a bite of food with his mouth open. "Tell me before I get angry, please."

Tania let go of Natalie and put her hands in her lap, stared down at them. "It's here already."

The room became quiet, save for the hum of the air conditioner.

"If it spins its thread at its current pace," she said in a quiet, even tone, "it should touch ground tomorrow."

Russell set his fork down gently now. His eyes were firmly locked on Tania. "Where?"

"I . . ."

"Where?"

Tania had never lied well. She practiced this one for hours, into her pillow.

Russell produced a small pistol from below the table and pointed it at Natalie. "Say it or she dies."

"Kiribati."

"Huh?"

Tania swallowed hard, still looking at her hands, which she wrung together in her lap. "Kiribati Island. About three thousand kilometers east of Darwin."

"Big place?"

"No, it's quite small."

Russell put the gun back into the holster on his hip, and Tania felt some of the tension in her dissipate. He pushed back his chair and stood, looking out the window at the first alien craft. "Guards," he called out. Within seconds the door opened and the two soldiers who had escorted Tania strode in.

Despite the hatred she kept bottled inside, Tania couldn't help but think how much Russell resembled Neil Platz just now. Confident, bordering on arrogant.

The guards stood at attention behind Tania.

"Natalie, dear," Russell said after a long time. "Is she lying?"

"Yes."

Tania turned to face her. "What are you—"

Natalie ignored her and spoke calmly to Russell. "I'm not going to tell you unless you promise to let her live."

He laughed. "I promise to let her live."

"Unless you promise not to hurt her," Natalie corrected.

"I promise to let her live."

Natalie glared at him.

"I'm joking, for fuck's sake. You have my word."

"It's worth so much."

"The best I can offer just now. *Where?*"

Natalie searched his eyes, her jaw clenched, fists balled.

"Tell me where and she won't be harmed. Tell me nothing, and I'll have the guards beat her until you do."

"Africa."

"No!" Tania rasped. The guards grabbed both her arms, this time with painful force.

Russell never took his eyes from Natalie. "Now, Africa *is* a big place."

"The Congo, near a city called Gemena. We have exact coordinates."

Tania jerked violently against the guards, a futile effort. "How could you?"

"Better," Russell said, grinning. "When does it arrive?"

"That part was the truth," Natalie said. "It's already descending and should attach in a few days."

"No!" Tania shrieked so loud that Natalie visibly flinched.

"Take her away," Russell said, calmly. "Lock her in her room until we've secured the site."

Without care for her well-being, the guards hauled Tania from the floor and dragged her from the room. For the entire way she hissed profanities at Natalie, at Russell. At everyone.

When the door slammed shut she shouted even louder. She surprised herself with the profanities that spewed forth.

All the while she kept thinking the same thing.

Well done, Nat. Well done.

Russell returned to his seat at the table, another forkful of egg in his mouth before he'd even settled. "Never seen her so feisty," he said.

"I could try to make peace," Natalie said softly. "Soothe her. You could watch, if you want."

"Enough of that. You two are about as erotic as a pair of mating sea bass," Russell said. "No, you're coming with me."

Natalie's eyes grew wide. "Where?"

"Africa, of course. To find out which of you lied."

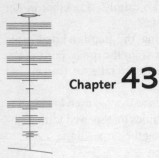

Chapter 43

SKYLER FEIGNED SLEEP on the journey up the Elevator.

A harder task than he'd hoped. More than once an anxious soldier had nudged him, wanting to talk about the experiences that awaited above. Skyler kept his eyes closed and grumbled annoyed responses. Eventually, they gave up and left him alone.

Eavesdropping proved most valuable. Much of the conversation centered on the notoriously gorgeous women of orbit, and what they planned to do with them upon arrival. By the third boast, Skyler wanted to strangle each of them. By the fourth, his thoughts shifted to Tania Sharma, so far away on Anchor Station. He wondered if distance alone could protect her from such men.

There was talk of battle against Platz and his haphazard army. This generated much more debate, and Skyler listened closely. Rumors all, but every good rumor had a kernel of truth.

"Platz built a secret army of superwarriors, armed to the teeth with exotic alien weapons," one said, drawing laughs.

"No," another said, "he's just given gun-shaped cucumbers to his cooking staff."

"Nonsense, he has no army—just a catapult to sling his bullshit!" Everyone laughed.

"Doesn't matter," another said. "Platz is dead already."

Skyler mulled the ramifications if that was true. The

conflict would be over before it really started, and he could return to a normal life.

No, he thought. Whatever happened, his normal life could never be restored, and his future would only be as good as he made it.

"What about the Ghost?" someone asked.

"A myth," came the response.

"No, it's true. The Ghost has been killing any grunt who walks Gateway Station alone." This drew nervous laughs, and Skyler fought the urge to ask what the hell they were talking about.

Much later the topic of Russell Blackfield's position on the council was discussed more soberly, after the other topics had run dry. Eyes still closed, Skyler listened as two men in particular, clearly students of current politics, appraised the situation.

"Platz still holds the power, sure, but if Russell hadn't stood up to him, to all of 'em, Darwin would be at their mercy."

"About time Platz got slapped around," the other soldier said, "Darwin's been sucking at that tit too long." A *hoo-rah* went up from the rest of the squad at this.

The talk turned to more mundane bravado after that, and Skyler drifted toward a light sleep.

Just before dozing off, he realized the climber had not suffered any power failures.

Last out of the climber, Skyler floated through the bustling cargo bay at the rear of his adopted squad. Most flailed awkwardly in the low-gravity environment, pushing off at odd angles, bumping into containers and fellow soldiers alike. As a result he found it easy to blend in.

Station personnel pushed water containers and compressed-air tanks out of the newly arrived climber with an efficiency that rarely occurred outside military operations. Random Gateway personnel hovered about, helping the soldiers who drifted into dangerous places or managed to get stuck in midair.

The Nightcliff troops far outnumbered the Gateway staff helping them.

It occurred to Skyler then that Russell was either grossly overreacting to an uprising by Neil Platz, or his ambitions were much grander.

His squad mates rallied at the entrance to an access tube, where a native Gateway Station guard awaited them. Skyler pulled his helmet low and kept his focus on the floor in front of him.

"I'm Corporal Sobchak," the Gateway guard said in a raised voice.

One of the soldiers shouted back, "When do we see some action?"

"When do we see some women?" another said, getting a few chuckles.

"That's what I meant," said the first, earning even louder laughs.

"Knock it off," Sobchak barked. "Follow me and mind yourselves. The farther we go from the hub, the heavier you'll be." With that he turned and drifted "down" the harsh metal corridor, one hand always in range of the red-painted ladder that spanned the entire length.

Skyler lagged back, following the last man into the tube. As they floated down, the man in front of him got sloppy, drifting too far from the ladder as the simulated gravity began to pull. Skyler grabbed his collar and yanked him back to safety.

"Thanks," he said.

"No worries," Skyler replied.

"Zero-g, man!"

"Yeah," Skyler said, "crazy." He kept his voice monotone, hoping to kill the conversation. It worked.

At the bottom of the shaft, at their normal weight again, the troops followed Sobchak past the decontamination area. It had been a wide hall before, but now beds and mattresses lined the walls.

The sight of wounded men, some from Nightcliff, silenced all remaining chatter from the fresh arrivals.

"Who's that?" someone asked Sobchak, nodding toward a curtained-off area at the far end of an adjacent room.

"Alex Warthen," said the corporal. "He runs security—"

"I've heard of him. What happened?"

"Took a bullet through his shoulder on Platz Station, shattered his collarbone."

"They get the son of a bitch?"

"Not on that attempt. Second time's the charm."

That caught Skyler's attention. "Neil Platz is . . . ?"

"Dead, yeah. Shot through the forehead." Sobchak motioned for the group to follow him. "They put his body out the airlock and everything."

Skyler leaned back against the wall and closed his eyes.

The end of an era. Everything would change. Neil dead, and Russell brazenly establishing himself in orbit? Whatever semblance of balance that existed before would surely evaporate.

His thoughts turned to Tania. He wondered about her fate. Would she take her orders from Blackfield now? The idea sickened him.

The council would fall apart, he suspected. None of the other members were well known to him. Platz was the face of the group, the leader by right of fame. Somehow Skyler doubted the rest of them could band together against a personality like Blackfield.

"Shit," said a grunt to Skyler's left. "There any fighting left to do?"

"Most of his staff and mercenaries fled," Sobchak said. "Platz was the last one on the station, our men said. Gotta give the old goat respect for that."

Some of the men smirked at that. Skyler did not.

"Where'd they all go then?"

"That's what everyone wants to know," the corporal said.

Odd, Skyler thought. He took a chance. "Where's Blackfield?"

"Took a squad to Anchor, in case the enemy ran there. If not, they'll work their way down and we'll work our way up. Sooner or later, we'll sandwich them."

Skyler took the information in stride, but his mind raced.

Blackfield, on Anchor, with Tania. He tasted bile and swallowed it.

Sobchak led them past Ten Backward, the bar where Skyler had last seen his crew. The place bustled with soldiers and station crew. No signs remained of the bloodshed that had occurred there.

An impressive, muscular man with sand-colored hair approached from the bar. Sobchak snapped off a salute the instant he saw the man. "Captain Larsen."

"At ease."

The man had keen eyes, and Skyler made sure to meet them as the captain's gaze swept the group. To do otherwise would only draw unwanted attention.

Satisfied, Larsen consulted a clipboard he was carrying. "This bunch is going . . . ?"

"Station patrol," Sobchak said. "Sections B and C."

One of the young Nightcliff guards spoke out. "Security? To hell with that, I want—"

"That's enough," Larsen said. He did not look up from the clipboard, and his voice, though calm, exuded absolute authority. "Security detail. All climbers are inbound right now, anyway, so there's nowhere to go at the moment. Food is more important than you guys." He paused, commanding attention. The anxious recruits settled down. "Platz may be dead, but he had a private army of unknown size. How he managed to train or arm them is anyone's guess. The problem is they are God-knows-where. When they're found, we'll have work to do. Until that time, we have a local problem to deal with."

Skyler fixated on the fact that climbers were coming down, not going up. A ride to Anchor would have to wait.

Someone asked, "Problem. You mean the Ghost?"

"Insurgents," Larsen said. "Two women, at least."

"Samantha," Skyler muttered. Aloud, he realized.

Larsen glared at him. "Come again?"

"Sounds easy," Skyler managed.

The captain held his gaze. Skyler felt his heart pounding and fought to maintain composure. Finally, mercifully, Larsen looked away.

"Brief them," Captain Larsen said to Sobchak, and marched out.

"Sir."

With a slow exhale, Skyler willed himself to be calm. *Two women. One* must *be Kelly,* he thought. The other, he could only hope.

The squad crowded around a table in the center of the tavern. A map spread out across it showed Gateway Station in every detail.

"Every hallway and room in this bloody place," Sobchak said, "is connected to a complex network of tunnels and shafts that circulate and process air, route water and waste, hide all the wiring, et cetera."

"What are the red marks?" someone asked.

Sobchak exhaled a long, frustrated breath. "Where our people have been ambushed."

Skyler glanced across the schematic. The marks were surprising in both their number and spread. He thought of Kelly and the amazing speed at which she'd led him through the maintenance shafts.

As the briefing continued, Skyler worked his way through the crowded room, moving casually, until he reached the door. Without looking back, he stepped out of the tavern.

In the hall beyond, he took a long thirty seconds to tie his boots. Sure that no one noticed his exit, or cared at least, he walked away, up the gently curved hall, looking for a ghost.

He had no plan other than to simply wander. Make himself visible, and see if the so-called Ghost would try to jump him. He just hoped she'd recognize him before inflicting any damage.

Section B proved too crowded for Skyler's needs. Weaving his way around loitering groups of station staff, some of whom eyed him with open contempt, he took the first junction tunnel that led to Section C. The bulkhead at the end of the tunnel had six guards, whom Skyler found in raucous conversation. They wore Nightcliff uniforms like his and barely acknowledged his passing. He kept his pace steady, eyes forward, and turned left to walk down the vast curved hallway. Once the junction guards passed out of view, their conversation faded and Skyler was totally alone.

He slowed to a stop and moved to the wall, kneeling next to it. The bottom half of the surface had a fine pattern of tiny holes. Placing a hand over it, Skyler felt the slightest brush of cool air.

Scanning the hall around him, he saw that every third section of wall had a similar half-height vent. He remembered his flight from the station with Kelly, and the maintenance tunnel she had led him through with all its twists and turns. Finding her now would be impossible, he knew. Best to let her come to him.

A patrol of guards approached. Skyler quickly stood and saluted.

"Nuts to be out here alone, friend," one said.

"Orders," Skyler muttered. "Sobchak said I should report to the brig and help out."

There were three of them, wearing the Gateway uniform. The one speaking was middle-aged; the others Skyler judged to be just shy of twenty.

"And he sent you to do this *alone*?" asked Thomas, according to the name on his jacket.

Skyler knew the tone of someone looking for a fight. He'd heard it often enough. He looked left and right, mocking the rhetorical question. "Apparently."

Thomas took a step closer. "Getting smart with me?"

"I'm not getting un-smart."

"What?" said the younger guard on the left.

Skyler rolled his eyes. "I *am* getting smart. It's a double negative. Never mind."

Thomas took another step toward Skyler, now within arm's length. "You know what I think, mate? I think you arrogant bastards don't know how to take orders."

"No," Skyler said, "it's just it doesn't take three of us to handle a couple of women."

All three had their weapon slung over a shoulder. Slow to bring ready, awkward to fistfight with it hanging there. Skyler felt he might have a chance, if it came to blows—

The soldier on the left lurched backward, an arm around

his neck. He cried out in surprise as he was pulled into a panel that had opened on the wall behind him.

Skyler took the opening and smashed his forehead into the nose of Thomas. Blood exploded from the man's face, and his instincts became his worst enemy as he grabbed at the shattered mess. He howled so loud, Skyler thought the whole station would hear it.

Skyler crouched, lowered his shoulder, and pushed off, throwing himself into the man's midsection, lifting him from the floor. The guard on the right, who gawked like an idiot at the space where his companion had been seconds before, had no time to react as Skyler pushed the leader straight into him. All three went down in a tangle of limbs.

A fist caught Skyler on the jaw. The blow had no weight behind it, a punch of desperation. Skyler ignored it and focused on the machine gun over the leader's shoulder.

Without warning, the second of the young guards vanished through the air vent. He screamed, a panicked, terrified sound. From inside the vent Skyler heard a dull, wet *thud,* and the noise stopped.

"Kelly, it's me, Skyler!" he yelled, finally pulling the gun away from the leader.

The man began to flail wildly as he realized death loomed. He punched and scratched at Skyler, rolling onto his back, blood streaming from his nose. Skyler kicked once, a powerful connection directly against the man's shattered nose. The man's eyes rolled back and he dropped, limp.

Skyler sat in the middle of the hall, breathing hard, clutching the gun. He saw a shape in the vent, and then a face appeared.

"Well, you idiot," Samantha said, "come on."

Seeing her familiar face made him instantly forget the melee. "You're alive," he said.

"Save it. We need to get the fuck away from here."

Skyler looked left and right. The curved hallway looked empty. *No,* Skyler realized, listening. *Footsteps, a lot of them, and close.* He pushed the gun across the floor to her and rolled into the vent.

Kelly waited deeper inside, crouched over the bodies of the two guards who had disappeared. She grinned at him.

"They heard," Sam said; "we've got to move." She pulled the vent cover back into place, as if it were second nature.

"Lead the way," Kelly said. "Hello again, Skyler."

He clasped hands with her. "Good to see you."

"So you can handle a couple of women, eh?"

Skyler grinned. "All thanks to my boyish good looks."

Samantha chortled and crawled deeper into the ventilation shaft while Kelly pushed the guards into a corner.

"The body in the hallway . . . ," Skyler said.

"His face," Kelly said, "will scare the hell out of them. Adds to our reputation, and buys us time."

He crawled as quietly as he could, struggling to keep up. Samantha's movements were fluid, familiar. She made no noise at all despite the hurry, and yet Skyler seemed to buckle every weak spot along the crawl space.

She was comfortable here, he realized.

Kelly kept right on Skyler's heels. He tried to crawl faster, his back scraping the top of the tunnel. Neither of the women said a word, so Skyler kept his silence.

After nearly two minutes of crawling, taking corners and intersections in stride, they entered a utility tunnel that seemed identical to the one Kelly had led him through during his previous escape.

Skyler's lungs ached for air, but no break was to be had. Samantha continued to lead them at a fast pace through the dark hallway. He followed her lead, ducking under obstacles he could barely see in the dim light.

"Sam," Skyler said.

"Later," she replied. She didn't break stride. Skyler realized he couldn't hear Kelly behind them, and so he chanced a look back. It was too dark to tell, but she didn't seem to be there.

"Where's Kelly?" he asked.

"She'll be along. Don't slow down."

They ran and ran, then climbed. A series of tiny panels lit the vertical shaft, and looking back Skyler saw Kelly enter the base of the tube, ten seconds behind.

The shaft extended all the way to the central ring, but Samantha stopped at the halfway point and opened a recessed access door. As Skyler followed her through, he noticed the locking mechanism had been covered with duct tape.

"They tried to track us by the locks," Samantha said.

Closer in to the center point of the station, gravity tugged at two-thirds its normal strength. Skyler had to adjust his stride to keep from bouncing into the ceiling. Thick pipes and cable conduits lined the narrow passage.

Samantha finally stopped. For the first time since Skyler had known her, she hugged him. She wrapped her arms around his shoulders and squeezed him until his arms ached.

The fierce embrace made his entire journey worthwhile.

She pulled away abruptly. "Can't believe you fucking abandoned us," she said, the words pouring out through a confused mix of laughter and crying.

"Good to see you, too."

Her hands still gripped him by the shoulders. "Takai and Angus . . ."

The look on her face finished the sentence. Tears welled into his eyes and he blinked them away. He could see the two of men, lying lifeless on the floor of that tavern, staring up at the ceiling with lifeless eyes, staring right at him. Skyler tried and failed to shake the vision, to replace it with a happy moment. Instead all he could envision was their dead stares, boring into him, accusing and sorrowful.

"So it's just you and me now," he said, numb.

Samantha bit down on her lower lip, her entire face hardening as she held back a wave of anguish.

"I'm so sorry," Skyler whispered. "I thought . . . we, Kelly and I, thought all three of you—"

"I know," Samantha replied.

"I tried to get to you, but we were too late."

"I know. Kelly told me. I'm just glad you didn't . . . what's with the goddamn Nightcliff uniform?"

Confused, Skyler glanced down at his clothing. "Oh. I hitched a ride up."

Samantha's eyebrow arched.

Kelly came through the door, finally, and closed it behind her. She gave Skyler a quick embrace. "When I saw that latch still on your bird, I thought for sure it wouldn't fly," she said.

"It didn't," Skyler said, frowning.

Samantha released his shoulders. "The *Mel* is gone?"

Skyler did not need to respond; his expression was enough. "I had to bail out, ten klicks south of the Aura."

She frowned at that. "Any trouble getting back?"

"Nothing but trouble. It's a long story," Skyler said, "and we're a bit short on time."

Kelly said, "Somewhere to be?"

"I'd hoped to find you," Skyler said, "and head to Anchor."

"Anchor?" Samantha asked. Then, "Oh. The scientist."

"Blackfield's up there, and you know what he's like. I have to help her if I can."

Grudgingly, Samantha nodded. "And here I thought you came back for me."

The remark landed like a punch to the gut. "I did. Originally just to offer myself in exchange for you and the guys," he said. "But then I heard about Blackfield heading up to Anchor, and Platz getting killed."

Kelly's face tightened. She sucked in her lower lip.

"Sorry," Skyler said. "I figured you knew."

"I knew," Kelly said. "Doesn't make it any easier."

Samantha gripped the back of her neck and gave a soldier's squeeze.

"Platz told me that Tania is the key to everything," Skyler said. "We have to get to her."

"You realize," Kelly said, "that Anchor is at the ass end of a forty-thousand-kilometer street the enemy controls."

He shrugged. "All of this started because of her research. What she knows. Platz gave his life for it, and I'm guessing he wouldn't do that in vain. So if you believe Platz had a reason for everything that's happened—"

"—then this scientist is the person who can finish it."

Skyler nodded.

Samantha folded her arms across her chest. "The climber port is crawling with Nightcliff goons, Sky."

A quiet moment passed. Then Kelly said, "I know what to do."

Kelly took the lead.

She insisted on silence as they moved along a complex path, often crossing normal station hallways. Her knowledge of the station's layout might be absolute, Skyler thought, but he wondered how long she could last now that there were so many patrols looking for her. Samantha at her side probably made the risk greater, even if their actions were more effective.

At one point she stopped them in a large, cube-shaped room with fans spanning two entire walls. The noise made for good cover, and the breeze felt good on Skyler's sweat-soaked uniform. Kelly called for a rest.

"We're close now," she said.

Skyler worked to control his breathing. "What's the plan?"

"There's a launch bay in Section E, not far, where the older utility crafts are stored. Construction and repair, that sort of thing."

"What will we do there?"

"Steal one," Kelly said, "and you'll fly us to Anchor."

Skyler moved closer to the fans, letting the constant flow of air dry the sweat on his skin. "What if I can't fly them? What if they don't have that kind of range?"

"They do," Kelly said. "We overheard some workers. This is how Russell and his men went to Anchor without passing through the other stations."

Grudgingly, Skyler nodded.

Kelly shrugged. "It's the best idea I've got."

The fact that Russell Blackfield had made use of them to get to Anchor meant they had the range. Of course, Skyler realized, they wouldn't need much fuel in space. He needed to stop thinking like an Earth-bound pilot, and soon.

"Can't hurt to have a look," he finally said.

The issue settled, Kelly took point again, her pace even

faster than before. Twice they had to crawl through tight
spaces, which renewed the aches in Skyler's healing shoulder and ribs.

Kelly had been right when she said they were close, however: A short time later she held up a hand as they reached
the end of a warm, dark corridor.

"Wait here," Kelly said. "I'll scout ahead."

Skyler half-expected Samantha to argue. *She would have
if I'd given an order like that,* he thought, but his old crew-
mate scarcely reacted. It amazed him how quickly the two
women had bonded. They worked together like veteran
partners.

Standing alone with Samantha now, Skyler found himself
unable to think of anything to say. He felt like an outsider.
The unspoken truth was that she'd left his crew and joined
Kelly's.

Not that Skyler had a crew anymore. Or a ship, for that
matter.

"What will you do when all this is over?" he asked her.

"You know I don't think that far ahead."

His gut told him to apologize, for everything that had
happened. In the end he couldn't bring himself to voice the
words.

Kelly returned with a body in tow, a Nightcliff regular.
Skyler could see a splotch of blood on the back of his head.
"The only guard. Let's go," she said.

The man could be wounded or dead, and Skyler feared
asking. A weariness grew within him from all the violence
in the last week. It reminded him of the Purge, and that was
something he preferred not to think about. The darkest
time of the darkest decade in human history, from his perspective.

An expansive bay waited for them as they exited the corridor; it was nearly half the size of the hangar at the old
airport. Strewn about the floor were a half-dozen utilitarian
vehicles in various states of disrepair. Miscellaneous parts
littered every flat surface, and the corners of the room were
stacked with old containers, barely visible in the shadows.

Kelly held her hand up and dropped into a crouch, Samantha

immediately echoing the move. Skyler took a knee as well, and let his ears adjust.

He could hear voices. Distant, casual, getting louder.

"Skyler," Kelly said, at a whisper.

He moved up to her position.

"Take the guard's place."

"What?"

She shot a glare at his helmet, and Skyler remembered he still wore Nera's uniform. He nodded once and hurried across the docking bay. At the far end he found a pair of large bulkhead doors, both open, and beyond that a standard Gateway hall running perpendicular to the room.

He guessed there were two people approaching, perhaps three. With only seconds to spare, he reached the entrance, leaned against the wall, and began to chew his fingernails.

Two men rounded the corner. One was a Gateway officer; the other wore the gray coveralls of station crew.

Skyler was thinking they might not even acknowledge him, but then the officer suddenly stopped.

"Don't get lazy," he said, analyzing Skyler's stance. "Blackfield is on his way back, and there are still the two prisoners loose."

Mind racing at the news, Skyler feigned a look of surprise. "You didn't hear?"

"Hear what?"

"They caught 'em," Skyler said. "The Ghost. Er, ghosts. Just a few minutes ago."

"Bullshit. Where?"

The station worker had stopped now, too, and was listening.

"Up at the climber port, trying to escape." Skyler gauged the man's reaction carefully and sensed indecision. He pressed. "You should go take a look."

The officer shifted on his feet, looking at the worker he'd arrived with. Then he turned to Skyler. "Can you help him out? He needs to lug some tools over to Section B."

"Sure," Skyler said. Too quickly, he thought, and added, "No point guarding this place now, eh?"

The officer had already stepped into the hall, his back to Skyler. "Thanks, mate."

Skyler turned to the worker and saw Samantha emerging from the shadows behind him, quiet as a cat.

To his surprise, she didn't kill him. Or even knock him out.

Instead Samantha positioned herself behind the man and put her gun to his back. "I sure hope you know how to launch one of these boats," she said to him.

The captive worker, it turned out, was a big admirer of the Ghost.

"I've got no love for these Nightcliff thugs," he said, and offered to help without conditions.

He led Skyler quickly to one of the repair ships. "It's the only one in any shape to fly, I'm afraid."

Skyler focused on the controls in the cockpit. There weren't many. Three flat-panel touchscreens and fewer buttons than a soda machine. At least there was a fairly standard flight stick, probably for emergencies.

Samantha and Kelly talked in hushed tones behind them.

"There's some emergency rations under the seat," the man said. "Can't help you with the controls, I'm afraid."

"I'll figure it out," Skyler replied. The little craft looked at least as old as the station. Belatedly, he realized it had a single seat. "Hang on, this one won't do. Only room for one."

"That's okay," Kelly said. Her level response came instantly.

"We're staying here," Samantha added.

Skyler stepped away from the craft. "What about Anchor?"

"Look," Kelly said. "You heard that guard. Blackfield is on his way back. Your scientist may be the solution, but *he* is the problem. This is our chance to sabotage his power grab once and for all."

"Besides," Samantha added, "Tania could be with him, for all we know. We need to cover both possibilities."

It fit Russell's reputation to take a woman like that as prisoner. The thought sobered him. "Good point."

"And if she's not, we can buy you time *and* get a crack at Blackfield."

He searched for a counterargument, some alternate plan. Nothing came to mind.

She stepped in close and gave him a soldier's embrace.

"Quickly now," she said. "We'll give this fellow an alibi after you leave, and cover your departure. No one will know."

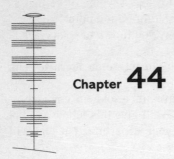

Chapter **44**

RUSSELL TAPPED HIS fingers on the armrest. He hated waiting.

Across the makeshift hospital room, Alex Warthen slept—medically induced, highly annoying. *So much to do. Wake up, you prick.*

When the nurse came in, Russell grasped her arm. More roughly than he intended. "Wake him."

"No, sir, I cannot," she said. "Remove your hand."

He tightened his grip, enough to see her wince, before letting go. "Maybe I'll wake him."

"I'd advise against that," the nurse said. "He needs rest. Could barely stand after—"

"Doesn't matter," Alex said, voice thick from the medication. "I'm up."

"Leave us, please," Russell said to the nurse.

Finally an order that she obeyed.

Alex rubbed at his shoulder. "How long have I been out?"

"The entire time I've been here," Russell said. "Ten minutes, at least." He watched as the injured director arranged pillows to prop himself into a sitting position. Alex visibly winced in pain as he turned his body to stack them.

Russell checked his wristwatch.

"Thanks for the help," Alex said.

"Hmm?"

"Nothing. What's our situation?"

Russell smiled. "Your agent inside Anchor Station proved immensely useful."

Alex closed his eyes. For an instant, Russell thought he might have drifted off to sleep again. "How is Natalie?"

"I've promoted her to Head of Backstabbing."

"She works for me," Alex said.

"On loan to me, then. I still need her."

Alex glared at him, a look Russell felt like wiping away with a swift punch to the broken collarbone. He leaned forward instead and met the man's gaze.

"Thing is, Alex, I think she went native up there. Fell for her gorgeous boss, and who can blame her. Now either she or Dr. Sharma has told me a blatant lie. Until I find out who, Natalie is not leaving my side. She's collateral."

Alex lay still for a while, gingerly probing at his wounded shoulder. "So where is she?"

"In my climber. Waiting for our departure."

"And where are you off to in such a hurry?"

Russell stood. "That information is on a need-to-know basis."

A long silence followed. "I thought we were partners in this."

Russell decided to ease off a bit. Alex needed to be an ally for a while longer, perhaps. "We are. No offense, but this place has too many ears."

"The council? Don't worry, they'll sit this out. Once things are under control—"

"Not talking about them. Fuck them; they're good as gone."

Alex Warthen stared straight into Russell's eyes for a long time. His chin kept scrunching up, then relaxing. "We never discussed disbanding the council. You're not the only person with a stake in this."

Russell walked to the end of the bed. "I said I wasn't talking about the council. Save that for later. I'm talking about the missing soldiers. Up to thirteen now."

"Thirteen. Christ . . ."

"Seven of them mine. It's getting out of control."

"I'll talk to Larsen."

"Nonsense. You rest up. I'll get Larsen and the rest of them motivated."

Russell turned and pushed through the curtain before Alex could respond. He smiled as he strode from the medical ward. A slow undermining of Alex's command structure fit well into his plans. *And with you stuck in here, friend, it's that much easier.*

"How's he doing?" Captain Larsen asked as Russell exited the infirmary.

Russell didn't break stride. "Join me for a drink."

"Sir."

The burly man fell in step beside him, along with three Nightcliff guards.

Russell thought back to his after-sex run along the parapet of the fortress, full of energy, laughing at the men trying to keep up with him. Not quite the same up here. This place felt like living in a bunker.

It hurt to admit, but he missed the feeling of wind on his face. Once he ran things, he decided he would split time between orbit and Darwin.

He willed himself to focus. "What are you doing to catch these mythical ghosts?"

Larsen cleared his throat. "I've posted men at every junction between A and C. We think we've isolated them there."

"How is it they are still loose, Larsen? It's been seven bloody days."

"Ah," Larsen said, "well. The maze of air shafts, maintenance tunnels, and equipment rooms are not well documented. And they seem to know where all the security cameras are. I ordered some repositioned, and we caught a quick glimpse. We immediately sealed off the surrounding areas."

"Good thinking."

Larsen laughed, a sad sound. "I thought so, but they're clever. That one image is all we got."

"Show me," Russell said.

"Sure," Larsen said.

"Now."

They walked straight past the tavern, deserted save for the bartender. A short distance later they entered the interdeck connection hall. Roughly twelve guards snapped to attention at the sight of the two officers and their escort. A few appeared to have been napping.

"Any sign of them?" Russell asked one bleary-eyed young man.

"No, sir!"

"Not hiding inside your eyelids, eh?"

"Uh . . ."

Russell pushed the boy into the main hallway. "Run a lap, Private."

"A . . . a lap? Alone?"

"Yes, alone, you moron. We'll call you Private Honeypot. Get to it." The kid stammered, then unslung his rifle and sprinted off down the curved hallway. "You," Russell said to the other guard, "you're Corporal Bull's-eye. Go the other way."

"Yes, sir," the man said, jogging off at a pace bordering on insubordination.

"Captain Larsen, we need to have a little chat about discipline," Russell said as they continued into Section B, toward the security office.

"Alex generally handles—"

"Alex can barely move, and he sleeps more than these blokes. You need to get this shit under control."

"I'll discuss it with Alex."

"No, you just discussed it with me. I'll make the decisions until he is up and about."

That statement bought a few seconds of hesitation from Captain Larsen, which Russell found gratifying. "Thank you, sir," the captain said.

Halfway to the security office, Russell heard a strange noise. The faintest scrape of fabric on metal. He placed it somewhere behind to the left. Casually he unholstered his pistol and placed a bullet in the chamber, covering the barrel of the gun to deaden the sound.

Larsen spoke in a low voice. "Something wrong?"

"Maybe. Have you got a wireless?"

"In the office."

"I want this hall sealed off. Ay-sap."

Larsen hesitated. "Shit," the captain said aloud. Too loud. "What?"

"Forgot to update the water distribution orders," Larsen said.

Weak acting job, Blackfield thought. "So what?"

"A real bitch to fix once the climbers leave. We'd better take care of it."

Russell sighed. "Run on ahead. I'm exhausted. Meet you there." Russell snapped at two of his guards who were close behind. "You and you, go with him." They both nodded.

Larsen jogged ahead, the two soldiers falling in with him. Russell waited until they were out of sight.

He slowed to a stop, turned to the one remaining guard on his right. "Soldier, your boot is untied." Russell gave a deliberately exaggerated nod toward the floor.

"Sorry, sir," the guard said. The man took his time, pretending to tie the shoe.

At last, competence. Russell leaned against a support beam on the wall, pushing his hands and the pistol into his jacket pockets.

He strained his ears. Beneath his own breathing, the fidgeting soldier, and the constant vibrating drone of the air processors, he heard the sound again. The barest whisper of movement from behind the kneeling guard.

Russell removed the loaded gun from his pocket and licked his lips. He would bring his wrath down upon this ghost—

He felt strong hands grab his ankles, and yank. *Hard.* At the same instant something big hit him square in the back— a shoulder. He nearly lost the gun as his hands instinctively shot out to brace his fall. Too slow. His chin cracked on the tile floor.

He caught a brief glimpse of his lone escort. The guard also lay on his stomach, a shout forming on his lips as he disappeared into an open vent behind.

Russell rolled onto his back as he felt himself yanked toward the opposite wall. He caught a glimpse of blond hair in the darkness in front of him.

Russell raised his weapon and pulled the trigger.

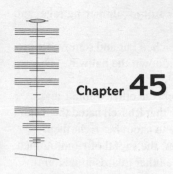

Chapter 45

THE BULLET MISSED a centimeter to the left, as he intended. A warning shot, and damn close at that.

"Enough," Russell said. "The next one is through your eye."

The woman stopped pulling his legs. Her grip relaxed.

Over his shoulder he yelled, "You, too, or your friend here dies!" The commotion behind him ended abruptly.

Russell scooted out from the ventilation shaft and rose to one knee. "Hands where I can see them," he said. "Now! Both of you!"

A pair of hands protruded from the darkness. Then another, from the opposite side.

The guard who had waited with Russell, and performed such an impressive acting job, crawled away from the opening and stood, somewhat unsteady.

Russell kept his gun trained on the blonde. He looked at the dazed guard and jerked his head toward the other vent. The man got the hint, collected his machine gun, and pointed it at the opening.

"Let's come out of there," Russell said. "Take your sweet time. I'm in a patient mood."

The woman emerged from the vent. Tall, intimidating. The recognition did not take long.

"We meet again," Russell said, craning his neck to face her. "Hardly recognized you with your clothes on."

She stared back at him, eyes full of simmering rage, and kept her mouth shut.

"Who's your friend?" He reached out and removed a pistol from her belt, then tossed it down the hallway. "Disarm her, too," he said to the guard.

"My name is Kelly Adelaide," the other woman said.

Her voice had a flippant tone that Russell hated the instant he heard it. He fought the urge to shoot her right then.

A sound caught his attention: the sound of running men. Within seconds Larsen and the other guards joined him.

"Your ghosts, Captain," Russell said.

"Nicely done." He breathed hard from the run. "What are your orders? Shall I take them to the brig?"

A thrill coursed through Russell at the word *orders*. Maybe Larsen would fall in line after all. "We all know that's not good enough," he said. "I'll bring them with me, and show them some Nightcliff hospitality."

Aboard his climber, Russell made sure the women had been properly bound. His men had been a bit too eager, perhaps— they looked like a pair of mummies.

Natalie sat alone by the far wall, strapped into a seat, as far away from the prisoners as possible. Her face bore a look of revulsion. Russell thought about chastising her for that, but he still had work to do.

He floated up to the second-level compartment, where the climber's lone terminal resided, and punched in the code for Nightcliff's control room.

"Put Osmak on the line," he said to the person who answered. "I'll wait. Be quick about it."

"Quick" left a lot to interpretation, he realized as he sat waiting. A few minutes passed before he finally felt the climber jerk and heard the hum of the grip apparatus as it began to propel itself along the Elevator cord.

Earthbound. An expedition to Africa. He smiled. He could see it already, standing there in the tall grass, arms folded across his chest and a welcoming grin on his face. Zane Platz, the bumbling fool, staggering out of his climber into the bright sun and staring straight into the muzzle of a machine gun.

"Osmak," came a voice from the terminal.

Russell had watched the fellow with some amusement over the years, allowing his little smuggling operation. As long as it didn't get too ambitious, everyone could benefit in their own way. That is, until two days ago. Russell let the hammer fall. He needed the man's contacts. "How goes the planning?"

When they'd talked the day before, Russell had given specific, ambitious orders, under threat of torturous death: "Find me ten aircraft, at least, that can travel as far as Africa with minimal cargo," he had said. "Environment suits for fifty men. Survival supplies for a few days." He told Kip that he didn't care whom he had to pull in, or what threats he had to make. "Just get it done," he had told him.

Kip Osmak cleared his throat loudly. "We'll be ready, Mr. Blackfield."

"Excellent."

"You, um . . ."

"What is it?"

"The scavenger crews aren't flying since the raid. I'm not sure how to—"

"There's no time to deal with them. Contact Grillo, he has enough planes." Planes, and ambition. The slumlord had been trying to earn Russell's favor for months. Time to see just how deep his ambition ran.

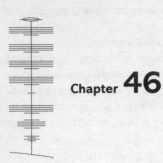

Chapter 46

SPACEFLIGHT, SKYLER DISCOVERED, was not very exciting.

After leaving Gateway he drifted a few hundred meters away from the station, aligned himself with the Elevator cord, and fired the thrusters until he'd reached a decent cruising speed. His gut wanted to push the little ship faster, but he knew he'd need fuel to slow down at the other end, and he didn't want to risk overshooting the station and spending the rest of his life drifting out into space. A life that would last a week, according to the readout that showed his air supply status.

He made only a few small course corrections during the flight, in order to avoid a collision with the much larger farm platforms clustered in groups at various intervals along the cord. He'd even slept a bit, and combined with the rations he found below the seat, he felt refreshed and alert when Anchor Station finally loomed ahead. He turned around and decelerated.

The state of affairs within the station was a total mystery. Blackfield had left, that much Skyler knew. For a time, during the trip, he had debated removing his Nightcliff uniform, in case the local station staff was back in control. He nixed the idea when he realized he had nothing else to wear. Wrinkling his nose, Skyler realized clean clothes should be near the top of his list once inside.

Feeling more confident with the controls of the tiny ship, he used the maneuvering thrusters to push out farther from the massive rotating rings. The small craft drifted toward the ring at the middle. He noticed there were large gaps between the center ring and those above and below it, and he quickly realized why.

The Darwin Elevator ended here. Surrounded by the slowly rotating central ring of the station were the remnants of the Builders' ship. He'd seen pictures, everyone had, but the sight still awed him.

He allowed himself a moment to take in the spectacular view.

The Builders' ship, resting there like a fossil, unsettled him. What purpose had been served, sending a craft across the vast emptiness to build a space elevator? Had they picked Earth specifically, or was it blind luck? He doubted anyone would ever know.

Earth loomed out his port-side window, gently spinning in all her grandeur. The sight calmed him.

He focused, scanning the station rings for docking ports or cargo bays. The ring closest to Earth had a port, of course, but Skyler guessed it would be heavily guarded.

The uppermost ring also appeared to have a cargo bay, too, but that level sat out beyond the end of the Elevator's cord, and thus probably never received traffic at all. He wondered if it even functioned as a result, and he decided to keep looking.

The level immediately below the central ring was the only other choice. He spotted a pair of cargo doors on the side of the inner hub. Skyler took a long breath, oriented his craft, and pulsed the thrusters, wondering how he would open it.

Fifty meters from the station, a panel lit up on the cockpit window, marking the door and offering docking options.

"How kind of you," Skyler said. He tapped the option for manual door override, which required a secondary confirmation. Once done, he sat back and watched as the computer handled everything.

The door slid open in silent welcome. His craft eased inside at a precise, slow pace, spinning to face out toward space at the last possible second.

A backward-view image appeared on a panel below his window. Skyler let out his breath at the sight of an empty bay.

The ship halted with perfect smoothness, in the far corner of the small bay. Skyler waited for the lights on each side of the bay door to turn green before unbuckling himself and switching off the small craft.

He gulped the last of the water and ate a Preservall packet of applesauce mixed with some kind of grain. It tasted like air. Then he sat there for a long minute, eyes closed. If anyone came to investigate the cargo door opening, he would say he'd been on the verge of a joyride but had thought better of it.

No one came. Skyler crawled out of the repair ship and smoothed the wrinkles from his clothes. He ran a hand through his hair before placing the Nightcliff helmet back on. Then he shook the lethargy from his limbs. In the back of the ship's small cockpit a sealed container held his urine and excrement from the flight, the only real evidence he'd been in there for so long. He debated finding a place to stash it, or simply venting the entire bay, to cover up his use of the ship. The idea the ship would be searched that thoroughly seemed absurd, so he left it there and exited the bay.

From the start, Anchor Station felt decidedly more modern than Gateway. Skyler guessed it had been built from a careful plan, not haphazardly like the lowest station. He floated, then climbed, down the tunnel that led to the outer section of the ring he'd entered. Gravity, at least the illusion of it, was a welcome sensation after two weightless days inside the tiny repair craft.

Skyler stepped off the ladder onto a floor of forest-green tiles.

"Who the hell are you?"

He turned at the voice, his heart racing. A Nightcliff guard stood just a few meters away.

"Nera," Skyler said. "Who the hell are *you*?"

"You with the relief squad?"

Skyler took the opening like a surprise birthday gift, and nodded. "I was told to patrol here."

The man shifted on his feet, eyes narrow now. "Who told you that?"

Careful now. "Probably just a mix-up."

"Well," the guard said, "I don't need any help. Go get a different assignment."

"Will do. Um, which way back?"

The guard sighed, and jerked his head to Skyler's right.

"You have *no* special skills?"

Skyler stood in the security office on a level with green floors, in front of the man Russell Blackfield had placed in charge. "I always complete my patrols on time," Skyler said.

"Whoop-dee-effin'-do." The man threw his pen down and ran a sweaty hand over his long face. "Some post this is, the ass end of the ladder with a bunch of idiots."

"Yes, sir."

"I wasn't talking to you."

"Yes, sir."

The man leaned back in his chair, rubbing his eyes. "Well . . . go patrol then, since you're so punctual at it. Pick a level; they're all understaffed even with you newcomers."

"Anywhere?"

"Except White Level; I don't need anyone else there. Everybody wants to see the whatever-the-fuck."

Skyler had seen a map of the station, briefly, in the hall outside, but he had no idea where Tania would be. He needed to find a local who could tell him. "Okay. Which one has the cafeteria?"

"Jesus," the man said. "I'm surrounded by lazy morons." He punched the keys of the terminal on the desk. Skyler suspected the man had no idea how to use it. "You can eat when everyone else does. Go patrol Black Level, as far away from me as possible. One rule, though. Blackfield said nobody touches the scientist named Sharma. He's got 'dibs.' Christ. Whatever, just keep away from her. You feel any *urge* that way, go to the monitoring room. They've got a vid of her in the shower."

She's here, at least there's that. Skyler didn't want to

think about the last part. He fought an urge to strangle the man. "Yes, sir."

"The next bloke who walks in here better know how to fix a goddamn terminal."

Skyler saluted, a motion that went unnoticed, and marched from the room.

The man's words rattled in Skyler's head. Blackfield had left behind a claim on Tania. The comment made his skin crawl, as did the implication they had taken some kind of lewd video of her.

At the security console outside, he stopped. A panel on the wall nearby had been left ajar.

He could hear voices in the distance, out of sight. Someone laughed. Behind, Skyler heard the administrator curse and bang a fist on the terminal keyboard.

Skyler didn't want to get caught poking around, but the security panel tempted him. He opened it and found a series of key cards hanging inside.

Moving swiftly, Skyler plucked one from its hook and stuffed it in his pocket.

He continued on, as fast as he dared, through the halls. The levels of Anchor Station were more spread out than Gateway, especially White Level, where they apparently studied the Builders' Shell. He saw only Nightcliff guards moving about, and they were few and far between. Blackfield had left only a skeleton crew behind.

After White Level, he entered the one called Wheat. The tile floor had an earthy, golden color to it.

A large mural on the entryway hall depicted a cutaway view of one of the giant agriculture platforms, carpeted with hundreds of crop sections in every shade of green and gold.

Skyler couldn't help but be impressed by the quality of the artwork, and the engineering marvel it depicted. The Platz Space-Ag logo took prominent position on the side.

He continued on, not stopping again until he entered Black Level.

He went to the nearest door in the curved hall and turned the handle. It clicked as the lock disengaged.

"Hello?" Skyler pushed the door in slightly.

A man sat on a bunk, wearing a T-shirt and underwear. He looked ill, staring at Skyler with tired eyes.

"I'm on your side," Skyler said in a quiet voice.

The man's expression turned slowly to hope, like a light turning on.

"Are you okay? Can you walk?"

His voice cracked as he spoke. "Do you have any food?"

"Sorry," Skyler said.

"Are you part of the resistance?"

Whatever that meant, it held promise, and fell near enough the mark. "Yes. I'm looking for Tania Sharma."

The man stared toward some vague point near Skyler. Dark bags hung under his unfocused eyes. "I heard Blackfield strangled her."

Skyler felt a pulse of dread rip through him and fought to control it. The words rang like rumor, and they didn't match what the administrator had said.

"Do you know where her room is?"

"Two-ten, I think. Take me with you," he said.

"How many other guards patrol this level?"

"Take me with you!"

Skyler put a hand on the man's shoulder. "I will, but not yet. I can't afford for an alert to be raised."

The feeble man searched Skyler's face. He dipped his head, and nodded slowly.

The door had "210" on a plaque next to it. Skyler swiped the card he'd stolen, and heard the lock disengage.

"Tania?" he asked. The room was dark. "It's Skyler. Remember, from Hawaii?" His voice sounded stupid to his ears.

Tania Sharma turned on a light next to the bed. Eyes like saucers, she stood on shaking legs. Her lower lip quivered as tears began to run freely down her cheeks.

Skyler caught her just as she started to collapse. She gripped his shirtsleeves fiercely and sobbed into his chest. Skyler gathered her into a fierce embrace, easing her to a sitting position on the floor in front of the bed.

"I'm so glad to see a friendly face," she said between sobs and sharp breaths.

"Likewise."

"Your uniform," she said with sudden numbness.

"I'll burn it the first chance I get," he said. "For now it's proving pretty useful."

"You're the last person I thought . . . how did you . . . ?"

"Where there's a will," he said, leaving the cliché unfinished.

"That's some will . . ."

"It's about all I have left."

She smiled. A feeble smile, but so full of gratitude that Skyler felt an instant and overwhelming love for her. "Thank you," she managed.

Skyler wiped a tear from her cheek. "We need to get out of here, Tania. Quickly. I have a ship—"

"No," she said.

Skyler frowned, puzzled.

Her face had a sudden expression of determination. "We can't leave; we need to retake the station. It's critical. Don't worry, I have a plan."

Skyler peeked into the hallway outside her cabin and saw no one. "Where to?"

"I need to use the restroom," Tania said. "It's to the left."

He moved out into the hall, taking her by the arm as if escorting her as a prisoner, hoping his guise as a Nightcliff guard would continue to hold.

"Wait," she said.

He let her go, and she jogged a short distance to a door down the hall, knocking forcefully. "Nat? Natalie?"

Skyler could hear the depth of her concern. He watched as she knocked again, then moved to stand next to her. "Let me," he said. He swiped the key card again and pushed the door open after the lock released.

The bed was made, unused. A pair of night slippers rested on the floor in perfect alignment.

"Who are we looking for?" Skyler asked.

"My assistant, Natalie. She was with Blackfield when I last saw her."

"He left, Tania. For Gateway. Took most of his men, too."

"Then our lie worked better than expected."

Skyler arched an eyebrow at that.

"I'll explain later."

He nodded and took her arm once again, gently clasping her elbow with his hand. They walked a short distance to the communal restrooms.

A minute later she emerged looking refreshed: face clean, black hair pulled into a severe bun, and no sign of tears on her cheeks.

She went straight to Skyler and kissed him.

"I'm finished crying," she said when their lips parted. "I'm finished feeling weak. Thank you, again, for finding me."

Skyler had no response. He simply smiled. "Where to?"

"First," she said, "if I don't eat something, I'm going to faint."

"Where's the cafeteria?"

She shook her head. "Too far. Too dangerous. We keep snacks in the observatory."

"Lead the way," he said.

Despite the hallway being empty, Skyler kept his voice low. "Tania, did they . . . did Russell hurt you? Or . . ."

"No," she said, "not directly."

Her choice of words filled him with dread. "What do you mean?"

"Natalie. He made allusions to mistreating her, because of my silence. Lies, I think, meant to encourage me to cooperate."

"Are you sure? Blackfield has a reputation. . . ."

Tania's face grew still, her eyes unfocused. "Lies of a different sort. Natalie was duty-bound to cooperate. Turns out she's been working for Alex Warthen for some time."

"God," Skyler whispered. He tried to imagine one of his own crew turning out to be on Blackfield's payroll. The very idea made his blood boil. "How did you find out?"

Tania grew quiet for a while. "She wanted to explain, but

they never left us alone. My imagination ran wild, of course. To be honest, I was ready to give him whatever he wanted in exchange for her safety."

"I can understand that."

The woman nodded. "Then she got the idea to tell Russell that she and I were lovers. Turned his perversion against him."

"Ah. The shower."

Tania looked at him. "How did you . . . ?"

Skyler sighed. "The rat currently in charge of the station mentioned it. Seems you've become quite famous on the local video circuit."

"Oh, wonderful."

"Think of it this way," Skyler said: "At least it's kept them away from you. Well, that and Blackfield's orders."

"Did, um, did you . . ."

"No," Skyler said. "No, I'm not like that."

She gave his arm a squeeze. "In here," she said at a double door. It led to a large circular room dominated by the viewing apparatus of a telescope. Computer terminals lined one-half of the room, and metal cabinets the other. Tania went straight to one cabinet in particular. "Hungry?"

"I could eat," Skyler said.

She popped it open and began to rummage through the contents. "See if those terminals will turn on, will you?"

Skyler tried each one, but the power button on each produced no result. "Dead."

"That's our next task." She held a plastic container, filled with nutrition bars sealed in Preservall bags. She set the container down and tore one open. The bar vanished into her mouth with astonishing speed. Then she remembered herself and tossed one to Skyler.

He caught it, then motioned to the row of blank monitors. "Can we fix these?"

Tania went back to the cabinet, emerging with two stainless steel bottles. She handed one of these to him as well. The water inside had a metallic taste, but he felt grateful for it. He gulped half the bottle down before putting the cap back on.

"They're probably locked out from the security center," Tania said.

"Why do you have a stash of food and water in here?" Skyler asked.

She crooked an eyebrow at him. "It's our shelter in the event of a solar storm. That and we're all workaholics. People do research in here all night sometimes. It's usually crowded."

They both ate in silence for a time. He spoke first. "Tania, have there been any more subhumans up here recently? Power fluctuations on the cord?"

"No," she said. "At least, none that I'm aware of. Why?"

Skyler told her about Neil's request, and what happened in the pit below Nightcliff. "I have no idea how," Skyler concluded, "but I think I fixed it. It's like the thing just needed to . . . eat."

She stared at him. Then her brow furrowed. "That might not be far from the truth. No, I mean it. Assume these subhumans had some new, rare strain of the disease. Clearly the Aura had trouble dealing with that, until your visit. Maybe all it needed was a . . ." She paused, searching for the right word. "Sample."

He gave a grudging nod. "Whatever the case, it sure didn't like how I tasted."

"Which makes sense," she said, and smiled at the objection on his face. "You're immune. What need does it have of you?"

Skyler ate the rest of his bar. The water left a metallic taste in his mouth, but he finished it all the same. "What was on those data cubes, anyway?"

The energy drained from her face. "Evidence," she said. "Neil and I thought the Builders would come back someday, and I realized if I knew where in the sky to look, I might be able to spot them early. For that I needed data from the prior events."

"And you were right, I'm guessing?"

She nodded, and yet he saw a flash of doubt in her eyes. "I thought they'd be years away, but they were right on top of us. We're lucky Neil decided to hire you when he did, or we would have missed them."

From her tone, Skyler guessed she didn't entirely believe that. The timing did seem uncanny. "They're back, then? Another care package, or did they show up in person this time?"

"As far as we can tell," Tania said, "the ship is building a new space elevator."

He almost laughed. Humankind could barely keep one of the damned things running. What good would a second do?

The answer hit him instantly: Start again. Do it right.

"So, what's our plan?"

"It's critical I get to a terminal," she said. "One that works, I mean." She walked the rest of the way around the circular room and stopped in front of Skyler. "Platz made the plan. He sent it to me before he died."

"Time to clue me in," Skyler said. "To everything."

She did. His eyes grew wider with each word.

"What in God's name is *she* doing here?"

Skyler winced at the shrill voice of the station commander. He held Tania's right arm behind her back, as if she was being moved against her will.

"You said . . . I thought you said to bring her to you?" Skyler scratched his ear.

"I never said anything of the sort, you imbecile!"

Skyler scratched his ear again. Sighed. "When I was leaving, you said 'unless she can fix a terminal.' "

The man fumed. "I wasn't talking about her, idiot, I . . . wait, can she? Can you?" he said to Tania.

"Can I what?"

"Fix a terminal."

Tania paused. Skyler gave her arm a subtle squeeze, for reassurance. "I refuse," she said.

The man leaned on his borrowed desk and absently crushed a piece of paper in his fist. "If you do not," he said, "I will have you beaten."

"You wouldn't dare," Tania said.

"Excuse me?"

"Oh," Skyler said, "I already explained we were not to lay a finger on her. Blackfield's orders, as you said."

The commander closed his eyes in frustration. "What else did you share with her?"

Skyler looked to the ceiling. "Hmm . . . Just that she was even lovelier than you described."

"Which confused me," Tania said. "Have we met before?"

Skyler spoke before the nervous man could. "He said he saw you in a video—"

"That's enough, Nera." He read the name off Skyler's uniform. "I'm going to put you to work cleaning the waste containers."

Tania coughed, politely. "I'll make you a deal," she said.

He turned his attention to her. "Go on."

"Two things. As I understand it, the station crew has not been fed or allowed to use the restrooms in nearly twenty-four hours."

"I'm understaffed. Even with the relief squad that arrived yesterday. They sent me jackasses like this bloke—"

"I understand, but my people are all locked up, so your patrols are pointless."

"Is that so?"

Tania ignored him and went on. "Release the janitorial crew so they can deliver food and perform basic services, under guard of course. Allow our people bathroom breaks, then return them to their rooms. Level by level, so you can have ample security on hand."

He blinked.

Skyler thought she'd delivered the demand with perfect intonation. Just shy of an order, slightly more than a suggestion.

The weasel ran a hand over his balding head. "And the second thing?"

"My assistant, Natalie Ammon. I'd like to see her. I want to know she is okay."

He shifted in his chair, uncomfortable. The request was impossible, and Skyler enjoyed watching the man squirm.

"Fix the terminal first," he said.

"I'll fix the terminal," Tania said with confidence, "after you feed Black Level and bring my assistant here."

Skyler watched the man, sensed his machinations. Tania's brilliant idea just might work: make two requests, one impossible so the other becomes more palatable.

"Your second request cannot be done," he said evenly.

Tania surged forward. "You goddamn monsters—"

"Hold on," the man said, raising his hands. "She's fine, she's just not here."

"Where is she?" Tania rasped.

"Blackfield took her."

A tense silence fell over the room.

"Where?" Skyler asked.

"None of your business, Nera."

"Fine," Tania said, "fine. Feed my staff then, at least. Let the janitors clean up a bit."

The man's lower lip curled into the hint of a frown. "I'll give the order now if you start immediately, and you can stay here and monitor the progress. Fair enough?"

"Deal."

"Deal," Skyler said.

"Nera, *piss off*," the man said. "Go find a hole and crawl in—"

Tania took a half step forward and stood firm between them. "He stays."

"Why?"

"He's the only one of you who has treated me with dignity."

"Oh great," he groaned. "Just the quality I look for in a jailer."

Skyler smiled proudly.

"Paul!" the commander shouted. A few seconds later another guard, whom Skyler and Tania had passed on the way in, entered and gave a vague salute. "Have we found the food storage yet?"

"It's a big station," Paul said.

"Red Level," Tania said. "Room eight."

The administrator shrank back in his seat. He rubbed his temples with his index fingers. "I need a bloody drink. All right, I want all available guards to secure their areas, then report to Red Level. Food and water are to be delivered to any occupied rooms starting with the janitorial staff, understand?"

"Yes, sir."

"Let the janitors haul food and water after that, to every level. Allow use of the restroom to the station personnel. One level at a time, under surveillance."

"Roger."

"I want regular status updates. Dismissed." The soldier named Paul saluted, turned on his heel, and left the room. The commander shot a glance at Skyler. "You see, Nera? That's called competence."

"You did handle it well, sir."

"I meant *him*—Jesus, forget it." He stepped away from the desk and held the back of the chair, motioned to Tania. "Dr. Sharma, the terminal?"

"What do I call you? Captain?"

"Edgar will do."

"Captain Edgar, then."

He grimaced. "Administrator, if you must."

Tania took a seat at the desk, while Skyler hovered near the door. He watched the administrator position himself behind Tania, watching her every keystroke.

Tania worked at the keyboard for a long time, in silence. Occasionally she would shake her head in frustration, and mumble some jargon that Edgar pretended to understand.

A handheld radio on the desk crackled to life. The guard Paul's voice came through. "Administrator?"

Edgar picked it up. "Go ahead."

"I've gathered most of the men. We'll start unpacking the food now."

"Proceed. Keep me posted." He set the radio back down.

The report marked Skyler's cue. A pulse of nervous energy coursed through him and he gave it a few seconds to subside. *Relax, here goes.*

"Hey," Skyler said, "about that shower video. Can I see—"

Edgar laughed nervously. "Nera, may I speak with you outside for a moment?"

"Of course."

The balding man stepped around the table and barreled

past Skyler without making eye contact. Skyler offered a wink to Tania, then turned and followed him out into the hallway.

"What is your problem?" he hissed at Skyler.

"Sir?"

"Do you have no filter on that stupid mouth of yours?"

Skyler feigned surprise. "Filter? What did I say?"

"The video, you idiot."

"Of her bridal shower?"

A stream of profanity gushed from Edgar's mouth as he stomped across the hall and back. "Her goddamn shower. Not a bridal shower, an actual shower."

Skyler kept his face blank.

"Water? Soap?"

Skyler slowly raised his eyebrows. "Oh . . . Oh!"

"Finally he understands! It's a fucking miracle!"

They stood facing each other. Skyler thought the man might be on the verge of a heart attack, the way his breathing came in such short bursts.

"So," Skyler said, "can I see it?"

He thought the man might try to hit him then. He might have, if an alarm had not sounded. Edgar turned to face the office, a word forming on his lips.

He never saw the punch Skyler threw. The blow landed squarely on Edgar's cheek. Completely unprepared for it, the punch spun him halfway around. Skyler moved fast, pressed the advantage. He threw an uppercut that only glanced off Edgar's neck.

On unsteady footing, Edgar lashed out. The fist caught Skyler just under the nose, splitting his upper lip.

Skyler tasted blood. He grabbed Edgar by the collar of his shirt and threw the man's head forward, simultaneously bringing up his own knee to meet it. A savage impact, the bone of Skyler's kneecap crunching into Edgar's face. The man bleated. He collapsed on the floor, moaned, and fell silent.

Tania's eyes were wide with horror when Skyler pulled the body, feetfirst, into the office.

"Your lip," she said.

"It's nothing. What's with the alarm?"

She swallowed. Skyler realized that the fear in her expression was not from Edgar's limp body. "I sealed Red Level."

"Good thinking."

She remained impassive. "I wasn't lying about the location of the stores."

"Ah." Skyler began to think through the ramifications. Basic sundries would be critical in the coming weeks. "So we scavenge, then. From the other levels. Drain the water pipes, pack whatever food people have stashed in their rooms."

"It might not be enough."

Skyler knelt by her. "People can be resourceful. Trust me."

"There's no time. The guards will find the manual override."

He thought she looked pale, exhausted. "Maybe. They're not the brightest chaps."

"Your lip looks terrible."

Skyler went back to Edgar's body and tore a chunk of the man's shirtsleeve off. He pressed it to his lip, wincing with the stab of pain. "I'll get someone to look at it later. Don't change the subject."

She smiled at that. It was something, and Skyler smiled back.

Tania said, "Now that the system hard-lock is removed, I need to restart the interstation mesh from the computer lab."

"How far?"

"This level. Not far."

He went back to Edgar's body and unholstered the man's pistol. He handed it to Tania. "Know how to use that?"

"You asked me before, on the way to Hawaii."

"Right, I forgot. And you haven't learned in the meantime?"

She frowned at the sarcasm. "It's not in my nature, Skyler."

"I know. I think it's why I like you so much."

He smiled at her as she returned the weapon.

* * *

Skyler rounded the door frame of the main computer lab, sweeping his gun across the semidark room. "Empty," he said.

Tania followed him inside. "Back there," she said, pointing toward a door at the far end of the room.

Skyler moved to and opened the door. Also empty. He let Tania in and guarded the door as she set to work on the computer systems.

"Sixty seconds," she said over angry beeps emanating from the machine.

"What's after this?"

She tapped the edge of the desk, waiting for the process to complete. "I'll unlock all the doors. Can you make an announcement on the intercom? We need everyone to get to Black Level as quickly as they can. My janitor friends can coordinate it."

"You'd better make the speech. They know you."

Tania considered this. "Second time someone told me that. I suppose you're right," she said. A slightly sinister expression crossed her face. "You'd better find something else to wear," she said, "unless you want to be mistakenly tossed out the airlock."

Skyler looked down at himself. The disheveled Nightcliff uniform had bloodstains from the split lip he had suffered. He glanced up to find that Tania had already refocused on the terminal.

He felt a growing admiration for her. The bold plan Neil provided had serious, world-changing ramifications. There would be no turning back. And yet she worked with determined efficiency, so much so that Skyler had refrained from questioning the plan.

"Watch," Tania said.

The large screen on the wall came to life. Skyler saw a schematic view of the Elevator, each station along the cord represented by icons. Having flown the entire length of it over the last few days, he recognized the layout.

"The farm platforms are clumped in groups of four," she said, tapping rapidly on the keyboard. "There's twenty in all."

Skyler focused on them, remembering how massive they were, much bigger than the other stations. They resembled snowflakes, he thought, with numerous branching arms each made up of huge tube-shaped segments.

As he watched the screen, one after another turned red.

Skyler swallowed. "Are there people on those?"

"Minimally staffed," Tania said. "I've instructed them to proceed immediately to the personnel sections."

"At least they won't have to worry about food," Skyler said.

Over the next few minutes, Skyler and Tania watched in silence as the agriculture platforms separated from the Elevator. They all drifted at the exact same speed, in the same direction.

All except one.

"I'm so sorry, Natalie," Tania whispered. A tear rolled down her cheek.

Skyler had no words to comfort her. The plan she'd concocted with her assistant did not factor Russell taking one of them to the surface.

Tania sat back and wiped her tears away with the palms of her hands. "I suppose it's our turn now."

"We still have Nightcliff guards aboard."

"I'm terrified, Skyler." Her voice distant, shaky. "We're leaving Darwin to starve. I . . . my God, I've doomed them."

He grasped her shoulder and gave it a gentle squeeze. "No, you have not. The only way Darwin will starve is if the council, or whoever is in charge, refuses to talk." The words sounded trite out of his mouth. She remained still, unconvinced. "Neil anticipated all of this," he added. "He devised this plan because it will work. Believe that, and see it through."

The statement registered. Tania began to nod, and wiped away another tear forming at the corner of her eye.

"We should hurry," Skyler said.

"Okay. You're right. Just one last thing."

Skyler watched the screen as Tania composed a broadcast message containing nothing but a set of coordinates. She encrypted the text with a key Skyler guessed Neil Platz had provided her. "So Neil's people will know where to go?" he asked.

"If they don't show up, we're dead," she said, and sent the message. Then she pushed back the chair and stood. "Let's get everyone to Black Level and seal it off."

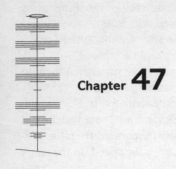

Chapter 47

THE SMALL ARMADA of aircraft rested on a blackened clearing, fanned in a rough circle. The fast, opaque waters of the Congo snaked around the spit of charred land on three sides.

Along the fourth edge of the clearing, a thick jungle canopy billowed black smoke, aglow with flames.

The explosions had been enormously satisfying. Russell had never experienced launching a missile before. Or two. Certainly not a salvo of sixteen. But his new Elevator site needed clear land, and a little barrage of Medusa rockets did just the trick.

Upon landing he'd ordered a perimeter set up. So far the soldiers had not encountered any subhumans. Not by sight, at least. Some wails and shrieks could be heard echoing through the burning trees, intermingled with the calls of an untold number of native birds.

The sound gave him a headache. Or perhaps it was the uncomfortable outfit he wore. Stale air came through the reprocessing apparatus—built by bloody Platz Industries, of course—on his back. It made Russell feel like he did in orbit: a sardine. Still, he refused to show his discomfort.

"Anything from second squad?" He knelt on the open cargo ramp of his recently commandeered aircraft. The fleet, eighteen craft in all, had been largely supplied by the slumlord Grillo, who asked for surprisingly little in return. Just a face-to-face meeting, after they returned. Russell fully expected demands would be made then, and he would be more than happy to sit and listen. As far as he was concerned, that was all he was obligated to do.

Kip Osmak looked up from the wireless. "Nothing. Second squad is still silent."

Russell did not like the man. He handled traffic control for the Elevator in Nightcliff, and until recently worked as an intermediary smuggler, a role that gave him a useful set of contacts, such as Grillo. But he also had a reputation of taking monthly trips to the nearby brothels in Darwin. Russell didn't understand why any man would pay for sex in a city where one could do anything he pleased. Russell had resigned himself to keeping Kip on a short leash until his usefulness wore out.

The thought of whores reminded him of Natalie. He looked out across the smoldering plain, seeking her. At a distance, everyone looked the same in their environment suits, but he spotted her. The wandering way she moved, and her lack of a weapon, gave her away. He didn't see the harm in letting her wander around. There was nowhere to go but into the flames, the river, or back aboard a ship.

She stood near the edge of the perimeter, facing the jungle. Transfixed by the flames, no doubt. He wondered if she'd ever seen fire before.

Russell picked up his rifle and trekked across the clearing to her.

"You're looking the wrong way," he said, startling her. "It'll come from above." For effect, he looked up at the amazing sky. A brilliant gradient, cobalt blue to the east giving way to a deep black in the west. Smoke from the fires billowed in a massive column, chasing the darkness out toward the ocean, a few thousand kilometers away.

"I've never been outside the city," Natalie said. Her voice was distant. "Never seen so many trees."

"You know what I see?" Russell asked.

She turned her head slightly, looking at him out of the corner of her eye.

"Lumber."

Natalie blinked in reaction. The rest of her face was placid. The face of someone who knew she was doomed.

"Blackfield!" The voice came from behind them, full of panic. A chorus of shouts went up with it.

Russell turned around to see what the commotion was. These men panicked at every little thing.

Next to him, Natalie began to run, straight into the burning jungle.

Russell looked back and forth, confused, unsure whether to go after the woman or find out what had spooked his troops. Had the so-called newsubs finally shown up?

The soldiers were all shouting, scattering, pointing to the sky. He looked up, hoping for a glimpse of the thin black thread of the new Elevator descending. To be present when it made landfall, that was the type of thing legends were made of. Russell wanted that perhaps more than anything.

Instead he saw a fireball.

A huge ball of flame, rolling off a dark mass at the center, growing larger by the second. It broke into a thousand glowing pieces as he watched.

Someone bumped into him, running away. The jolt interrupted his trance. Russell spun, saw Natalie heading into the trees. He raced after her.

The first explosion lit the entire area in a brilliant yellow light.

Russell dove as the second explosion hit. He landed hard on his elbow before skidding to a halt in the soil.

Stay down, a voice in his head shouted. More blasts erupted behind, buffeting him with pulses of scorching wind. Chunks of rock and dirt whooshed past him, threatening to tear his hazard suit to shreds. He knew he had to get away, get far away.

Like Natalie. She'd run the instant she could.

The bitch knew.

Russell ignored the voice in his head and willed himself to his feet. He jogged toward the tree line, swaying with the force of another explosion, only just keeping his balance. The ground heaved and fell like the chest of a frightened beast.

Whatever it is, it's not the Elevator, he thought. The crater left behind when Darwin's arrived was no bigger than a city bus.

He reached a slope that led into a narrow gully. Natalie scrambled up the far side. She turned and looked right past Russell. Even through her face mask, at this distance, he could see her eyes widen. In a calm, fluid movement, she stood, lifted her head to the sky, and spread her arms to welcome her fate.

At the same instant, the world was tinted brilliant orange. Intense heat baked his back.

Russell dove for the edge of the slope as a tremendous explosion filled the sky.

In midair his legs were lifted, causing him to somersault before landing on his back. The air in his lungs rushed out from the shock of the impact. Closing his eyes, gasping for air, he slid down a dank hill, lumpy with vines.

Through the plastic mask, Russell saw a sky filled with smoke and fire. Shrapnel from the blast rained down around him—from minute pebbles, to chunks of earth the size of a fist. The partial torso of a man landed nearby, with an arm still attached.

Russell brought up his hands, terrified that he would see the piece that would take his own life before it hit.

The shower of debris abated. A few rock-sized chunks hit him in the chest and calf, hard enough that they would leave nasty welts, but not enough to rupture the suit.

He did not know how long he remained on the slope, lying there with his face covered. A cowardly position. He sat up, ignoring the sharp pain in his back from landing on top of his own air-processing gear. That bitch Natalie was nowhere to be seen.

"I knew you were lying!" Russell shouted at the jungle, his voice echoing inside his mask. He burst into laughter, unable to contain it. Not only had Natalie lied, but Tania Sharma had tried to kill them both for it. A damn trap, and he had to tip his hat for that. It even came close to working. His laughter abated, leaving him with only a thirst for revenge.

When the smoke faded, Russell crawled to the edge of the

slope and took in the scene. A crater, filled with smoldering pieces of twisted metal, had replaced the clearing.

He checked his own condition. The hazard suit looked terrible, all scratches and burn marks. Yet it appeared to be intact. He reached behind his back, probing the air tank, felt the reassuring vibration from its tiny motor. Still working, and no alarms from it. The suit still protected him from the disease.

Russell stumbled through the debris field. He wondered what had fallen on the site. A meteor? Impossible. This had been aimed with precision. Whatever it was, it must have been massive. Wreckage filled the shallow, wide crater. The point of impact straddled the edge of the river, just beyond the circle of aircraft he had assembled in the clearing.

Not quite a bull's-eye, but damned close.

He ignored the impact zone, sure that no one could have survived. His path wound through a field of bodies, a few still moving. Russell ignored them, too. Their suits were in tatters. Good as dead. He'd shoot them himself if he could spare the bullets.

Opposite the crater, a few aircraft still remained. He walked past each one. "Anyone there?" he asked, again and again. A fear grew within him. To survive such a calamity, suit still sealed, only to be stuck out here. Left to wander the African jungle until his air ran out.

Russell could spare a bullet for himself. That much he knew.

"Here," someone said, a feeble voice that came from behind. Russell turned and saw a man emerging from the rear hatch of an aircraft.

"Are you a pilot?"

The man shook his head. He limped down the ramp, putting no weight on his left leg. "What happened?"

"Find a pilot, or we're stuck out here. Is your suit intact?" Russell walked up to him, looking for holes in the material. The man probed it frantically with his hands, moving with sudden panic. "Relax. Turn around," Russell said.

Just above the left knee, Russell saw a hole no wider than a pinky finger with a hint of blood underneath. He gritted his teeth. "You're fine. Look for a pilot, right? I'll go this way." He gestured toward the river.

The man nodded, yet his face was twisted with pain. His gaze swept across the destruction, eyes widening.

"What's your name, son?"

"Charlie."

"Relax, Charlie," Russell said. "We'll get out of here in no time."

"Find a pilot," Charlie said. "Find a . . . pilot." He staggered off, away from the river, dragging his left leg behind.

Russell loosened the pistol in his holster, eyes locked on the back of Charlie's head. The poor bastard probably already had the disease. He hesitated, then let the man walk away. There was still plenty of time, and right now Russell could use the extra set of eyes. Charlie might be good for another hour.

He continued through the maze of aircraft, toward the river. Most of the planes had been tossed around like leaves. Such an incredible waste. Russell had assembled nearly every aircraft he could for the mission. He'd ordered them pulled up the Elevator, and tapped deep into Nightcliff's power reserves to spool their ultracaps for the long flight. Most could only handle the long-range trip due to the fact that there was no cargo to bring back.

Russell wanted enough men here to secure the site, on the chance that the missing fighters loyal to Platz had a way to get down here.

The sound of an engine whirring to life interrupted his thoughts. It came from somewhere ahead, near the river. Russell ran as fast as the hazard suit would allow him.

On the bank of the Congo, he found the plane. The thrust from the engines steadily rose, bending the knee-high reeds below until they lay flat. Russell pumped his legs, drew his weapon. He came to stand in front of the cockpit, making eye contact with the pilot. Aiming his gun, Russell motioned downward with his other hand.

The pilot stared back, hovering in place, the engines howling under the strain. Russell did not know if his gun could penetrate the window, not that it mattered. His threat had the desired effect. The big craft eased back to earth.

Russell met the coward at the door. "Saving your own skin, eh?"

"I was going to circle," the pilot said. A woman, Russell realized. "Look for survivors from the air."

"Forget it, there's no one. Take me back to Darwin."

Her eyes searched the tortured landscape behind him. He could see the glistening of tears forming. Perhaps she had friends out there. A lover, maybe.

"Belay that," Russell said. "I need to use the radio. You have a look around."

"Thank you, sir."

"I want to know how many birds can still fly, and how many pilots survived."

"Understood."

"You know a guy named Charlie?"

She shook her head.

"Well, if you run into him, be wary. His suit is punctured, only matter a time before he goes all subby on us."

She saluted and ran out into the reeds.

Russell watched as she clawed her way up the embankment and stopped dead, now able to see the entire clearing. He'd give her five minutes to search.

In the copilot's seat he found a headset connector and pushed it into the jack near the waistline of his suit. The aircraft had modern controls, built after the Darwin Elevator arrived, no doubt. He slid a gloved finger over the touch-activated screen and it blinked on. The interface had a soothing amber hue. He dialed in the frequency.

The burst of static in his ears was laced with a thin voice. ". . . Alpha One this is Beta One, are you there?"

"Blackfield here," Russell said. "We had the bogus location. Secure the new elevator site and we'll join you—"

"Negative," the voice said. "There's nothing here."

The truth hit him, then. *They had both lied.* Or, he allowed, Natalie believed her story, and it was Tania who had fooled them both.

Neither location would be the site of a new Elevator. Hell,

there might not be one at all. He'd been played and could not escape that fact. "Forget it," he said. "Evacuate the area immediately, return to Darwin."

"Copy that," the voice said. "Pull out and return to base."

Russell lowered himself into the plush copilot seat and let out a long breath. He grasped the armrests and squeezed with all his strength.

Later, the pilot returned. A solemn group followed her into the plane, six in all, the weasel Kip among them. His eyes were wide and unfocused, his already pale face now bone white.

Russell looked over the sorry group with concern. "Is that all?"

She shook her head. "We split them up among the planes."

"Did you check their suits?"

"They're clean," she said. "A few weren't. They ran when they saw me, or tried to."

"What about the aircraft?"

"Seven in flying condition."

"Seven. Shit." Seven out of eighteen. The number of aircraft on Earth known to be functional just dropped considerably. Russell felt his chest constrict. Tania had dealt humanity's survival chances a major blow, whether she intended to or not.

He glanced at each of the survivors, now secured in the two rows of seats that lined the fuselage walls. "Any of you see what hit us?"

No one said a word.

And then, from the cockpit, "Nightcliff is on the wireless."

Russell felt a dark void, deep in his gut. "Don't tell me they were hit, too."

"No," the pilot said. "Something fell, but it exploded just outside the Aura, in the old downtown. They're saying— hold on. Gateway reports that all of the farm platforms have disappeared."

"What the hell does that mean, 'disappeared'?"

From the cockpit she turned to face him, holding a finger

up, listening. "They detached and drifted away. Part of An-chor Station, too."

Part of Anchor Station.

Russell felt nauseous, dizzy. His hands went cold and his vision blurred. The idea that Tania would do this, that she could orchestrate it so precisely, staggered him. He had un-derestimated her, catastrophically.

Still, she had missed. And she would suffer for it, he would make sure of that.

As the aircraft lifted away from the scorched earth, Rus-sell Blackfield smiled, despite himself.

Hat's off, Tania, he thought. *You play dirty, we have that in common. But no one,* no one, *plays dirty like me.*

Chapter **48**

Black Level, formerly part of Anchor Station
19.FEB.2283

"I EXPECTED A shell, like the other," Tania said. "This . . . flower . . . it's beautiful."

Despite the incredible sight out the small window, Skyler found himself staring at her. Her eyes were wide with open wonder, and yet they darted from one detail to the next, always analyzing. He had no doubt that the action she'd taken to thwart Russell Blackfield weighed heavily on her, but she'd not spoken of it since. Even if the bold plan worked, the collateral damage would haunt her forever.

A few kilometers away, the new Builder ship spun its elevator cord.

He disagreed with her appraisal but said nothing. Tania was beautiful. This ship, he thought, looked terrifying.

Admittedly it bore some resemblance to a flower. A conical shape of matte black petals pointing down toward Earth. The material looked exactly like the iris he'd encountered deep below Nightcliff. Even from here he could see fine patterns laced into the surface.

The shell ship nestled within, identical to the one over Darwin. Almost identical, he reminded himself. According to Tania, the ship was roughly 20 percent larger. This fact alone had sparked intense speculation from the other scientists aboard Black Level.

Tania spoke of a few smaller ships, hinted at in the telescope images, but there was no sign of them now.

For hours they watched in awe as it slowly cannibalized

itself, spinning an elevator cord out of the material in its "petals." The long oval blades visibly diminished until they could no longer be seen.

Skyler sensed a growing nervousness in the crew. Twenty hours was a lot of time for the ad hoc spacecraft to support six hundred people.

Electrical power was not the issue. A small backup thorium reactor could power the ring-shaped station for thousands of years, if needed. No, the concerned whispers were all about air and water. Recyclers would only go so far, the Platz-built stations having been designed with constant resupply in mind.

They had been under radio silence since detaching Black Level from Anchor Station, waiting to hear something from the former staff of Platz Station. Air and water were dwindling fast. If Platz's crew failed in their half of the plan, Black Level would have to drift back to the Darwin Elevator, to face whatever punishment awaited.

"It must have acted as a shield," Tania said.

Skyler soaked in her voice like the scent from some exotic spice. A slight accent, from her Indian parents, sounded at once gentle and authoritative. It made him self-conscious of his own accent, the product of a childhood spent on the streets of Amsterdam.

He knew his questions didn't help that simpleton image. They must sound stupid to her, but he asked them anyway, just to keep her talking. To keep her from worrying about the fact that no one from Neil's secret station had made contact yet. "A shield. How so?"

"The distance traveled," she said, "the speed required. It's almost impossible to comprehend. Every microscopic piece of interstellar dust would be like a missile."

Skyler considered the flower petals again with fresh eyes. "They look flawless. Well, they did, before they were converted into the thread."

"Self-healing." She shifted in her seat, leaning closer to the window. "We know they can do that. Every time we've detected a flaw in the shell ship's structure, or the Elevator cord, a second look proves it to be repaired."

He grunted in amazement.

"Imagine if we had that ability," she said. "All that decay in Darwin, replaced with buildings that healed themselves. That's what Neil was after, ultimately."

"It would put me out of a job. No spare parts to fetch."

She elbowed him, playful. "You'd still have plenty to do."

A young man floated up behind them, using the back of Skyler's seat to stop himself. "Dr. Sharma, sorry to interrupt."

"What is it, Tim?"

The young man had auburn hair and eyes to match. A spate of freckles dotted his pale cheeks and nose, and his narrow chin only served to accentuate a pair of enormous ears. He'd been dutifully manning the station controls since they'd departed. From what Tania had explained to Skyler, Tim's job before had been to program and manage subtle adjustments in the positions of the farm platforms. No one else aboard Black Level knew how to work the controls.

Tim hesitated. "Zane Platz," he finally said. "He's alive. And on the comm."

Tania spun in her seat, the view forgotten. Skyler braced for bad news and turned more slowly.

But Tim had a huge grin on his face. "Get this: He says they've got a *climber* on the way up. Full of supplies."

A chill ran the length of Skyler's spine. He closed his eyes and shivered, stress burning away like morning fog.

Tania covered her mouth with both hands, a small laugh of relief still escaping. She looked close to tears.

"They're on the ground already?" Skyler asked. "With a climber port?"

"No," Tim said, the grin on his lips growing wider. He looked at Tania. "You know Hab-Eight, the perpetually delayed station the council is always debating? Zane and the rest of the Platz Station staff moved it over here."

"Neil pulled it off," Tania said, more to herself than anyone. She shook her head in amazement.

"It's parked four hundred kilometers above the surface. The climber and supplies were stored there ahead of time. Zane is calling it New Gateway."

Needs a better name, Skyler thought.

"Come on," Tim said to Tania. "Zane wants to talk to you."

"Start the attachment process," she replied, floating up out of her chair. "We need to be ready to receive that climber."

She pushed off the wall, floating with the grace of a dancer toward the curved hallway and the makeshift command center beyond.

Skyler remained in his seat, watching her go, unsure what to do. She'd kept him at her side since Black Level's successful detachment. She had treated him like an equal as they orchestrated the flight from the cord above Darwin to the new shell ship, though Skyler could feel the eyes of her co-workers on him throughout, no doubt wondering about the stranger Tania kept so close. With everything going on, she hadn't bothered to introduce him.

News of contact from Zane changed the scenario instantly. Neil may have perished, but he'd pulled off his end of the plan, and though Skyler didn't know anything about Zane, the Platz name visibly boosted the spirits of the crew around him. Tania drifted from the room without even a glance at him. He knew it couldn't last, that his future would not consist of simply hanging around Dr. Tania Sharma. And yet he'd not dared broach the subject of his role in the new . . . new what? New nation? Whatever the case, things would change quickly now.

Survival was all anyone should be thinking about. Romantic delusions could wait for another day.

Within minutes the floating ring of Black Level, formerly attached to Anchor Station, altered course and began a slow drift toward the new Builder ship, and the new Elevator.

As news of contact from Zane spread, the mood aboard Black Level Station lifted. Worried whispers turned into animated conversations. Skyler allowed the view to envelop him, to drown the excited talk going on around him.

The Builder ship loomed just a few hundred meters above his window now. Sunlight glinted off the hair-thin cord, allowing him to track the line of it up to the nose of the Builders' ship. As he watched, the last of the material from the flower petals vanished as some unseen process converted them into cord. Black Level floated much closer now, perhaps fifty meters away.

That he sat here, taking in such a sight, bewildered him. If only he could share it with friends. Samantha would probably have rattled off a dozen lewd remarks about the phallic nature of the alien ship by now. A sudden tug of sadness stole the moment from him. Once again he'd left Sam behind. She was entirely cut off, nowhere safe to retreat to, only Kelly on her side. This time she'd at least made the decision herself, but after what Tania and Skyler had done . . . Samantha's situation could only end badly.

A man approached and gestured toward the empty chair beside Skyler. A stranger, one of the Anchor Station scientists who had packed into Black Level with them.

"This is truly amazing," the man said, enthralled by the view.

Skyler muttered something agreeable. He already missed the silence that Tania had left him with.

"Whoa," the man said, alarmed. "What is *that*?"

Skyler focused on where the man pointed, the nose of the Builder ship. An iris opened there, the cord of the Elevator at its center. It widened as Skyler watched.

A shape emerged. A dark mass, the size of a fully loaded climber, by Skyler's estimate, squeezed out of the circular opening.

It began to move down the Elevator.

Skyler realized they were still moving in toward the cord, about to attach so Zane's climber could dock.

"Oh hell," he said.

Lurching out of his seat, Skyler turned and pushed off the wall with both legs, propelling himself toward the main hallway where Tania had gone. Groups of station staff, crowded into the central hall, looked up at him in surprise.

He shouted. "Tania! Stop us! Stop attaching!"

Rebounding off the sidewall, Skyler lost his momentum and found himself adrift. One of the scientists extended an arm to him and Skyler took the woman's hand. She pulled him to the wall, where he immediately propelled himself again, this time at a better angle. He shouted again.

The station lurched. Gasps went up from the people crowded into the hall, sounds of panic.

At the door ahead of him, Tania peered out. "We've stopped. What's going on?"

Skyler grabbed her outstretched hand, bracing his leg on the doorjamb. "Something's coming out of the ship. Coming down the Elevator."

Her eyes grew wide. Not with concern, Skyler saw, but excitement. "I've got to see this!"

"Tania," he said, "the climber. The supplies. They've got to turn it around."

Apprehension washed over her. She turned back into the room, pushing inside. "Tim," she started.

"On it," the man replied. He had strapped himself into a chair in front of a console.

Tania drifted past him to a pair of monitors that had been set up on a bench by the far wall. One displayed the Builder ship. The second monitor showed Earth, far below them. As Skyler closed in on that screen, he could see a speck near the center of the display. The climber.

"Oh no," Tania said. "Tim, hurry . . ."

Behind them, Tim frantically called into a headset for the climber to be reversed.

Skyler glanced at the monitor to his left. The dark mass, oblong in shape like some sort of seed, had fully exited the Builder ship.

Another shape began to emerge, identical to the first. Skyler held his breath.

"Please, please," Tania said under her breath. "Tim!"

The man shouted into the headset.

As Skyler watched, the first mass began to accelerate, quickly moving out of the first monitor's view. He watched in horror as it came into view on the Earth-side monitor.

The pod accelerated at a phenomenal pace, careening toward Earth. The climber had no chance.

Skyler saw the explosion as a smudge on the monitor. Debris expanded in a cloud of pressurized air and water vapor.

Their chance for survival, destroyed.

Another pod sped down the cord. Then another. They continued for nearly two minutes. Skyler tried to count them, stopping at fifty. No one had said a word since the climber exploded.

As suddenly as it had begun, the stream of Builder pods ended, and a deathly silence gripped the cramped control room.

Skyler finally asked the question. "What now?"

No one replied. He only cared what Tania thought, anyway. She finally met his gaze but said nothing.

Skyler's mind raced. The climbers weren't the only problem. "Someone tell Zane they need to clear the entire cord. New Gateway, and . . . shit, all the farm platforms. Everything needs to move out of the way."

"The Ag platforms aren't attached yet," Tania said, deadpan.

The look on her face matched the Tania he'd seen in Hawaii as they fled the subhumans. Skyler tried to reassure her with a smile. "That's something, then."

Tim gave instructions into his headset. At the speed the pods were moving, Skyler wondered if it would help. Then he remembered the distance involved. It had taken him nearly two days to get from Gateway to Anchor. However fast these pods were moving, he thought, it should be at least a few hours before they reached New Gateway.

Tania grasped his hand. "Skyler, what do we do? Should we turn back?"

He heard the fear in her voice. Worse, she was looking to him for answers. Everyone else in that room had pinned their future on her leadership.

"Don't give up yet," he said to her.

"We see them now," Zane Platz said.

Tim, with the help of a few Anchor scientists, had rigged the headset into one of the terminal's speakers.

By now a number of senior Anchor staff had crowded into

the small control room. The cramped space gave Skyler a feeling of claustrophobia, but he kept it to himself.

"I counted at least fifty," Skyler said. A few of the scientists in the room gasped at that. He heard someone wonder aloud, not for the first time, what purpose the pods had. Quiet side discussions started among the researchers.

"Yes," Zane said through the speaker. "They're passing us. Speedy little buggers, aren't they?"

His voice had a light tone. No hint of concern, and Skyler felt grateful for it. Tania sighed with relief.

A long minute passed.

"I think we're clear," Zane added.

A chorus of cheers went up from the people in the room. Some hugged one another, an awkward gesture in zero-g.

Skyler watched Tania. Her face remained contorted with worry. "Let's focus, everyone," she said. "There's no time to waste. If we don't get supplies . . ."

The room grew quiet again.

"I want to hear ideas," she said.

Someone from the back asked, "Could they send another climber?"

Zane answered. "We could. Neil managed to hide the parts for six climbers aboard this station. A team has already started assembling the remaining five, but that takes time. Then we'd still have to load the supplies. I don't know if it would reach you, uh, in time."

The sobering words quieted the group.

Skyler racked his brain for something, anything, that might help. An idea formed, and he spoke up. "What about the farms?"

Tania turned to him. "What do you mean?"

"Can we descend? Dock somehow with one and—"

"Of course," Tania whispered. Others were nodding. "Of course, yes."

"But can we connect with one?" Skyler asked. "Link the air and water with our systems?"

"The docking rings are all standard," Tim said. He smiled. "Platz specifications."

"How long would it take to descend to the nearest farm?"

"A few hours," Tania said, "I'm guessing."

Not good enough, Skyler thought. He could tell from the gathered faces that everyone else had the same dark thought.

Tim rubbed at his chin. "We could raise the nearest Ag platform up," he said, "to meet us halfway."

"Perfect," Skyler said. "Do it."

Tania turned to him, a quizzical look in her eye.

"If," Skyler said, "you agree, Ms. Sharma. Tania. Dr. Sharma."

Zane's voice came over the speaker. "Who is that talking?"

"Skyler Luiken, sir."

"I'll explain later," Tania added.

"Decisive action is needed here," Zane said over the speaker. "I look forward to meeting you, Skyler."

"Likewise."

Tania winked at him. "Tim," she said, "take us lower."

Zane's voice came through the speaker again. "I'll send another climber up when we can, Tania. I think you should return on it; we have a lot to discuss."

"Agreed. See you soon, then, Zane."

"There's one last thing."

Skyler heard a tension in Zane's voice.

Tania said, "We're still here."

"Russell Blackfield is alive." Zane paused. When no one said anything, he continued. "We picked up a transmission from Gateway. A bleak situation back in Darwin, from the sound of it."

"I see," Tania said, a quiver in her voice. The room had fallen silent.

"You did what you had to," Skyler said, loud enough for just her.

"Don't . . . don't say that." She closed her eyes. "We'll discuss it when I arrive, Zane. In the meantime, perhaps you could try to arrange a comm chat with the council?"

"I'm not sure there is a council anymore," he said. "But we'll work on it."

The speaker went silent. Gradually the scientists began to exit the small control room, chatting among themselves.

"Skyler," Tania said. Her voice had a sudden tone of authority that caught his attention.

"Yes?"

"I want you to explore the ground below, where the Elevator made landfall."

The remaining people in the room stopped to listen.

"You're an expert at finding things. Resourcefulness is your job."

"*Was* my job," he said. "But, you're right. It makes sense."

"When we reach New Gateway, you can take the climber down."

He nodded. As Tania started to turn back to the monitor, he said, "Hold on . . ."

"Hmm?"

"What if this Elevator doesn't protect against SUBS?"

She frowned at that. "Why wouldn't it?"

Skyler shrugged. "I don't think we should take anything for granted, after those . . . pods . . . went down."

"Then it makes even more sense for you to go, since you're immune."

The statement drew some quizzical looks from those still in the room. Skyler ignored it. "Actually, no. Sending me won't answer the question. I think someone else needs to come."

"Someone to test the air."

He gave a single, slow nod, letting the words sink in.

"Canary in a coal mine," Tim muttered.

Tania's mouth became a hard, thin line. "I can't order anyone to do that."

"Put out the word then," Skyler said. "We need a volunteer."

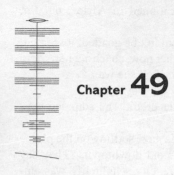

Chapter **49**

HIS OFFICE IN Nightcliff no longer felt comfortable. Russell paced it, grinding his teeth, waiting for the connection to be made. He'd been seconds away from boarding a climber for orbit when the request came.

His temper raged like a stormy sea. The damned woman had bested him. He could admit that. The idea that he would now have to beg was what churned his stomach.

Unless she simply wanted to gloat.

"I've almost got it," said Kip, sitting at Russell's terminal. "Yes. Connection established."

"About time. Will I be able to see her?"

"Audio only," Kip said, moving away from the desk.

"Figures," Russell said. He wouldn't be able to read her body language. The woman sure had a head on her shoulders. Russell vowed not to underestimate her anymore.

Taking a seat at his desk, he leaned in to the microphone. "This is Blackfield."

"Hello, Russell." Her voice sounded clear. Smooth, even. "Tania Sharma."

He'd played this conversation in his mind since the scope of her betrayal had become clear. At the moment he couldn't recall a word of it, and somehow that soothed him. He preferred to think on his feet.

"You sound good," he offered. "Well fed."

"If we could please discuss—"

"I'm fine," he said. "Thanks for asking. I do appreciate

the farm you sent while I vacationed in Africa, but I'm afraid it didn't survive reentry."

Silence from her end. She wouldn't be goaded, it seemed. Russell wondered who sat with her now, coaching her. More than that, he wondered where the hell she was.

"Your other bomb missed, by the way."

"What do you mean?" To her credit, she sounded confused.

Russell turned in his chair, his gaze settling on the plume of smoke rising from Darwin's old downtown. "They say the explosion rattled the entire city. Nightcliff was unharmed. I assume that was your target. Lucky for you it landed outside the Aura, or you'd have a lot more innocent blood on your hands."

Total silence. The damned woman had nothing to say.

"Well," Russell said. "You called me. What's on your mind, little lady?"

"I thought we might come to an arrangement."

"An arrangement?" He snorted back a laugh. "That's what's on your mind? I thought it might be all the people you're starving to death."

Another pause. The silence went on so long, Russell thought perhaps the connection had been lost.

Across the room, Kip shifted uncomfortably on his feet. Russell had forgotten he was still in the room, and he jerked his head toward the door. The man left in a hurry.

Tania spoke. "We have a proposal—"

"How about this. Send the farms back, all of them, and I won't hunt you down and strangle you."

"Please, Russell. There's no time for this." Her voice, dammit, still sounded calm.

With a concerted effort he swallowed his rage. He realized that she had said "arrangement." Knowing what she needed would tell a lot of her situation. "Fine, then, what do you want?"

"I'll be blunt, Mr. Blackfield."

"Good."

"We have food. You have people."

People. Not air, not water. Not even supplies. People.

They must have another elevator, then. At least that hadn't been a lie.

"I'm listening," he said.

"We propose a simple trade."

She kept using the word *we*. Russell found that interesting. "Go ahead." Letting her blather on, to his surprise, was proving useful.

"It's quite simple, really. We will send containers of food to Gateway, where they will be unloaded. You will then return them with people aboard."

"How much food?" he asked. "How many people?"

A pause followed. He imagined her sitting in a tin can somewhere, arguing with her fellow scientists; this was the first time any of them had tasted power. He wondered how soon it would corrupt. Perhaps it already had.

"A container holds roughly three tons of food. In exchange for each, we want forty people."

A litany of thoughts shouted for his attention. He felt a headache coming on, and wondered where the nearest bottle was. "You'd better be sending a lot of them. I've got a city to feed, not to mention the bloody Orbitals."

"If you supply empty containers, that won't be a problem," she said. "Do we have a deal?"

"Which people? Will random idiots from the outer slums do?"

"We've prepared a list."

Of course you have. "Should I send them in shackles?" The words tumbled out, and silence followed. If he'd crossed a line so be it—the words felt good.

"I'm very aware of the distasteful nature of this, Mr. Blackfield. The list is short. Beyond those, we want volunteers in good health."

He snorted. "And the males, well-endowed perhaps? You could start a harem for your little play kingdom. Or do you prefer women? I'm a little unclear on that point. I'd ask your assistant, but the last I saw her she was being annihilated—blown to smithereens—by, well, you."

Tania went quiet again. It occurred to him that she hadn't even asked about Natalie. Or anyone else, for that matter.

Russell already knew he would agree to her demands. He did need the food, after all, and the arrogant woman was offering him the perfect opportunity to send spies into her midst. Surely she must know that, but what choice did she have?

As she'd said, she needed people.

Russell would have no problem mustering an endless parade of brigands and idiots to send. He had a monopoly on that.

"Fine," he said. "Let's talk details."

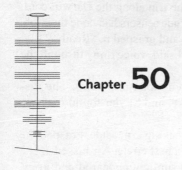

Chapter 50

FIFTY METERS ABOVE the Earth, the climber car slowed to a crawl, exactly as programmed. At twenty meters it would halt altogether and Skyler would finally be able to open the hatch. This simple climber car had no external camera, and just one small porthole window through which he could see only cloud-filled sky and endless rain forest.

He checked his equipment again, though he knew everything was ready. He'd gone over it a half-dozen times during the long trip down from New Gateway. Nervous energy coursed through him, relentless and distracting. The only thing that seemed to quell it was the tightening of straps, the adjustment of buckles. Busywork.

Skyler glanced at his volunteer companion, Karl Stromm. He wanted to inspect the man's environment suit once more. Karl had waved him off the last time, and he looked almost annoyed now. He had every right.

"Almost time," Skyler said.

Karl just nodded. Soon he would risk his life, or sanity, by opening that suit—an act of bravery he'd been quick to accept.

"He's one of the men Neil trained in secret. A former firefighter, I think. He organized the mutiny on Anchor," Tania had explained. With a grin she had added, "You'll get along fine."

The climber car lurched and came to a stop. A moment of unsettling silence passed before the small light by the hatch turned from red to green.

The bare-bones vehicle had no windows or monitors like

the ones that regularly made the trip along the Darwin cord. Skyler could only hope the altitude sensors had done their job.

Skyler moved to the handle and grasped it. "Ready?"

"Let's get it over with," Karl said, voice tinny through the speaker on his helmet.

The man carried himself with a natural calm. The disposition reminded him of Jake, and Skyler found reassurance there.

With a grunt he pulled the locking arm aside, grasped the inner handle, and turned it in a half circle. Air hissed as the pressure equalized. A line of sunlight appeared and grew, soon filling the cramped cabin.

Heavy, warm air brought with it the rich smells of wild vegetation. Skyler inhaled it deeply. In the last few weeks, between Darwin and then space, he'd forgotten the simple pleasure of breathing fresh air.

As the hatch swung away, Skyler found himself facing south. A wide and fast river rushed by, east to west. Freshwater, then, and close. *Not a bad start,* he thought.

On the far bank, a thick green marshland stretched out for miles. Farther west, lush hills gave way to mountains. To the east he saw a blanket of lush forest canopy, marred only by a smoke plume a few kilometers away. Too big to be a campfire. Fallen debris from the destroyed climber, he guessed. Skyler inched up to the opening and poked his head out to look below.

He froze, mesmerized by what he saw.

"Tell me," Karl said, behind him.

Skyler searched for words, and found none. The Elevator made landfall in the middle of what was once some sort of business park, or school. The area around the cord had been leveled by the Elevator's arrival, but it wasn't empty.

Jutting out of that land, at perfectly spaced intervals, were buildings. Alien buildings.

"There's a . . . city," Skyler finally managed to say.

"Belém. Why are you whispering?"

"Not Belém," Skyler said. "The Builders."

The surface of the matte black structures resembled the flower ship, so high above. Skyler realized they might not be buildings at all. He saw no entrances or windows. Just solid masses, arranged in concentric squares around the cord of the Elevator. The ones near the outer edge were ten meters tall, and toward the center, at least thirty meters. No two had quite the same footprint, though the shapes were similar enough that Skyler sensed they all had a shared purpose.

At the base of the cord itself, where a crater should be, Skyler saw a huge black disk with notches all around its edge. It looked like a big gear, lying on its side.

Karl moved behind Skyler, trying to look over his shoulder. His breathing came in loud, excited bursts. "Do you see any . . . any of *them*?"

Skyler shook his head. Other than birds, and swarms of insects, he saw no signs of life. "Let's drop the ladder and have a look."

For fifteen minutes they walked in silence, exploring the alien structures. The more Skyler saw, the more he thought of it as an outpost rather than a city.

It consisted of perhaps two hundred structures. More than the number of "pods" that had raced down the cord from space.

"No sign of the Builders," he said, to himself as much as Karl.

"Automated construction," the other man said. "Like the Elevator."

For what purpose, Skyler could not imagine. He stepped close to one and studied the material. The elegant, faceted walls were laced with fine, geometric patterns, all straight lines and right angles in a chaotic mix. The grooves varied in depth from the barest hint to as much as a centimeter, just like the iris he'd found below Nightcliff. "I can't wait until Tania sees this."

Karl managed a chuckle. "Not just her, the whole lot of them. They'll be tripping over each other to study this."

They surveyed the entire area. With each step, Skyler felt his sense of wonder fade. He reminded himself of the work to be done. Because of the alien structures, there would be no room to build around the base, making construction of a climber port tricky.

The human city of Belém waited beyond like an overgrown fruit tree, Skyler thought, just begging to be exploited. Supplies could be harvested from there for years before needing to explore farther out. And even then, the Americas were wholly untapped since the disease had struck the world. None of the scavengers in Darwin could range this far. His mind reeled at the possibilities.

"We're going to be busy," Karl said.

"I feel," Skyler said, "like a colonist."

The other man grunted. "Near enough the truth."

Skyler studied the edge of Belém more closely. He'd seen a hundred cities like it in his forays into the Clear and found himself noting which structures might provide valuable resources, and which could be inhabited. Hospitals, hotels, and warehouses topped his list. He wondered belatedly if there were any airports close by.

A good portion of the city fell within the Elevator's protection, assuming it offered an Aura. The thought reminded Skyler of why they had come.

"I think it's time," he said. "If you're ready."

Karl, still stoic, gave a terse nod.

Skyler slung his rifle and came to stand in front of the man. "Keep your eyes on me," he said. "Any strange thoughts, you need to tell me. We'll seal you right back up."

"If it's bad," Karl said, "you shoot me. No debate. Kill me right here."

Skyler reached out and grasped the clamps that held Karl's face mask in place. "Ever smelled fresh air?"

Karl shook his head.

"There's nothing like it," Skyler said.

He pulled the helmet from Karl's head and held it between them, ready to reattach it.

A minute passed, then two. Karl just stared at Skyler, his breathing fast at first. Gradually he got it under control, and relaxed. He inhaled deeply, once, his eyes closed. Skyler could see his nostrils flare, his eyes twitch. The man's expression turned to pleasure.

"Wonderful," he said. "The aromas . . ."

"Told you."

"It's like the first time I tasted a truly good wine."

After ten uneventful minutes, Skyler sat down and beckoned Karl to do the same. He figured an hour of exposure would do, so they killed the time by trading life stories.

The hour passed. Karl showed no sign of infection.

"I think we should head back," Skyler said. A comm capable of two-way communication with orbit had not been set up yet, and he desperately wanted to share their discovery with Tania and the others.

Karl nodded agreement and took the lead back to their ladder.

As they walked Skyler found himself looking up, watching the pillar-like shapes of the Builders' outpost pass by. It brought a childhood memory back, a vague recollection of strolling along a tree-lined avenue, his head tilted up to watch the branches overhead—

Skyler tripped.

A bare tree root caught his toes and sent him stumbling. He reached out to brace his fall, without thinking, and placed his hand upon one of the Builders' towers.

The object gave way. It moved as if weighing nothing at all, a deep creaking sound coming from the base.

Skyler watched from one knee. Karl stopped, too, his face blank.

The black tower, three meters across at the base and twenty meters high, drifted over the muddy ground as if it were in zero-g. It moved slower than Skyler's walking pace.

He stared, watched it go. Some part of him recognized that it was not slowing down, and that the shape of its base constantly shifted to match the contour of the ground.

"It's not stopping," Karl said. "Skyler! It's not stopping!"

The structure's path would take it straight into another of the massive shapes. Skyler felt his heart drop into his stomach. *What have I started?*

Seconds before impact, the second structure began to move, too. It shifted its position just enough to avoid impact, and then returned to its original position, exactly.

The tower Skyler had pushed kept going. Another structure moved out of the way, then a third.

When the tower passed the last of its kind, it continued to

move, speed never varying. A constant, straight motion in the exact direction Skyler had pushed it.

Toward the river, a few hundred meters beyond.

It moved at an angle to the wide body of water. Skyler found himself running, his feet pounding in the moist ground. He tossed Karl's helmet aside and pumped his arms.

The shape began to descend the bank of the river, its base ever shifting to match the contours of the ground, allowing the tower itself to stay perfectly upright. Skyler couldn't even begin to imagine what technology allowed any of this to occur. All he knew was that he couldn't let the thing sink into the wide river.

With a few meters to spare, he ran around the drifting object and planted his feet between it and the rushing water. The shape loomed before him, creaking all the while like a great tree in a stiff breeze.

Unsure what to do, Skyler put his hands out and grimaced. He dug his feet into the mud and leaned in as the object arrived, intending to push with all his might to try to stop it.

The pressure against his hands felt impossibly solid when it touched his skin, and yet in the span of a heartbeat it slowed and stopped.

The creaking sound faded.

Water licking at his feet, Skyler stood before the obelisk and scratched his head. On a whim he stuck out one finger and pushed against the black surface. He heard the creaking again, quieter, and the tower began to move away, so slow he didn't notice it at first.

"Unbelievable."

Karl arrived. He stopped next to Skyler and put his hands on his knees, panting. It would take him a few days to adjust to the humid air, Skyler realized. All of them.

"What does it mean?" Karl asked.

The mass continued to drift back toward the others, as if riding on an invisible pocket of air. All the while, the base of it emitted that eerie creaking noise, like an old wooden ship listing on a calm sea. Skyler could only shake his head.

They watched from the water's edge. The object crept along, back the way it had come.

"I wonder how far it would have gone had you not stopped it?" Karl said. "Assuming they can't sink."

"Good question," Skyler replied. "I don't know why, but I think it would have gone a long, long way."

Even as he said the words, the object reached its counterparts. Skyler watched in awed silence as the other towers drifted out of the way, then back as the moving object passed.

"We should go," Skyler said. Tania needed to hear about this. He could already picture the look on her face.

"Mmmph," Karl muttered. He dropped to one knee, fingers pressed against his temples.

"What's wrong?" Skyler asked. Karl was clawing at his temples now. "What is it?"

"What do you *think*?! We wandered too far!"

Skyler threw his arm around Karl without a second thought and hoisted the man to his feet. Karl fought it, moaning in agony. Every step of the way he tried to free himself from Skyler's arm. The disease's initial infection affected many this way—they were the ones who died quickly.

Four hundred meters, Skyler judged. They'd only gone four hundred meters from the base of the cord, and already they'd reached the Aura's edge. Not even close to the nine kilometers provided by Darwin's Elevator. The limited range threw their plans, and everyone's survival chances, into doubt. There would be so little room.

"Slow down," Karl said. "I'm all right. The pain's gone."

Skyler eased the man down to the ground and sat beside him. They had only moved about fifty meters toward the Elevator.

"It came on so fast," Karl muttered, still rubbing at his temples.

Skyler watched the dark obelisk as it drifted back through the others. He turned and glanced back toward the river's edge. "Stay here," he said to Karl.

Acting even as the idea formed, Skyler jogged back to the wandering tower, moved to the opposite side, and guided it back toward the river. He found he could manipulate its direction with minimal effort by pressing lightly on either side as it "floated" along. For a short span, Skyler crawled along beside it. He could see no visible gap between its base and the muddled soil beneath it, and yet somehow he knew it *was* floating. He wondered why the wind seemed to have no effect on it, yet even the gentlest touch he provided could change its direction.

He guided the tower into a position about halfway between Karl and the Elevator's base.

"What are you doing?" Karl shouted. "You've got a funny look in your eye, I can see from here."

"How bad was it, really?" Skyler yelled back.

"Bad."

"Bad enough you won't take a quick test?"

Karl arched an eyebrow. "I guess I'm game. What's your idea?"

Skyler stood next to the huge object and brought it to a reasonable stop. "Walk toward the river again."

Karl glanced behind himself. The river loomed fifty meters away.

"Shout the moment you feel the pain," Skyler said.

Dubious, Karl started back toward the water. Ten steps later he doubled over in pain.

Skyler leaned into the tower and shoved. Again he felt an initial hesitation, as if the thing were every bit the solid mass it appeared to be. Then the weight of it melted away, and the object began to move.

When it traveled the same distance Karl had walked, Skyler saw him struggle to his feet and steady himself.

"I'm okay!" Karl shouted. "Holy shit, I'm okay!"

My God, we can shape it, Skyler thought.

Two hundred towers, each capable of creating pockets of protected area. Smaller than Darwin's, yes, but *mobile* . . .

Possibilities unfolded in his mind. Aura "roads" extending from the Elevator into the most useful areas of Belém. Pockets of safe, defensible ground. Teams venturing out into the wilds, a tower always at their center, exploring as far as they wished to go.

It was a scavenger's dream.

He grinned, broad and unabashed. A smile born of pure joy. A smile born of discovery.

Acknowledgments

This novel would not have been possible without the help and support of the following:

My endlessly patient wife, Nancy.

Sara Megibow, my agent and champion.

My observant editor, Mike Braff.

All my family and friends. Notably: the Brotherhood and the Cosmonicans.

Kip Williams, who encouraged me to pursue this story above all others when he heard the pitch.

Heartfelt thanks also go to:

My cousins Paul, Daniel, and Sean. They asked a million questions and forced me to get my story straight.

Mike Kalmbach, who helped me find the myriad of flaws in the first draft.

Xavier Burrow, for his insights into "life on the ground" in Darwin.

I offer sincere apologies to the wonderful people of Darwin, Australia, for turning their beautiful town into a fictional postapocalyptic slum. It's nothing personal, I promise.

Read on for an excerpt from

The Exodus Towers

The Dire Earth Cycle: Two

Coming from Del Rey Books

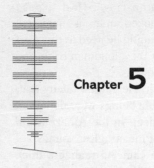

Chapter **5**

TEN STEPS INTO the rain forest, Skyler came to a steep embankment that dropped two meters down to a narrow stream. Rivulets of water traced miniature caves and waterfalls into the earthen wall. He hopped down and crouched by the water. The rhythmic sound of subhuman humming danced at the edge of his senses, as the dense foliage confused and baffled the noise. He forced himself to pause in order to ascertain the source's direction.

Satisfied he had the right vector, Skyler moved ahead. As the sound grew ever louder, he took care to step over any twig or leaf in his path that might otherwise crack beneath his boot.

The trees here were tall, forming a cathedral-like canopy that blocked much of the gray clouds above. Raindrops fell in irregular places as they percolated through the maze of broad leaves and smooth branches. Insects small and large buzzed around his face, an annoyance he'd grown accustomed to since arriving in Belém.

A chill swept over him. With so little sunlight, the air here had a sharp bite. Skyler zipped his vest all the way to the top, and did his best to ignore the tingle from his earlobes and nose.

After fifty meters, the chorus of crooning subhumans became unmistakable. The farther Skyler crept, the more voices he estimated were part of the inhuman choir. They came from left, right, and center. After a dozen more steps, a growing fear slowed his pace to a crawl. He'd stepped over countless roots and vines, ducked under as many low branches. Retreat would be slow, should he need to run. Part of him said to go back now, report the subhuman tribe, and come back with twenty armed colonists.

Yet the strange noise pulled him. He couldn't deny that, and had to know what the miserable beings were doing out here, in the middle of nowhere, deep in the Amazon rain forest, singing softly in a babble of meaningless sounds.

Skyler slowed further when he came to realize a thick mist enveloped the forest ahead. He thought it might be smoke at first, but no odor accompanied the haze. Against every instinct save curiosity, he took another step. Then another. Before long the still mist surrounded him, and visibility fell to five meters or less.

"Stupid, stupid," he whispered, even as he took another step.

Individual subhuman voices stood out against the thrum now. Here the sounds came from the left and right, but not from ahead, he realized. It was as if the beings were formed in a line, and he'd just crossed it.

Only then did it occur to him that there were no trees here. None upright, anyway. Fallen trunks of shattered wood littered the ground around him, some still tucked in the embrace of strangler figs. He stepped around the huge stump of a kapok tree. The smooth, fleshy base ended in a violent mess of splinters. Another nearby had been uprooted completely. The chill he'd felt before vanished, replaced by humid warmth that grew with each step.

The mist cleared slightly, if only for an instant, and Skyler realized he'd walked into a wide ravine with curved walls. The ground beneath him sloped gradually downward.

Not ten steps later a wall of earth loomed ahead of him, and then he saw the mouth of the cave. Or, more aptly, the tunnel, for this huge circular opening was clearly not a natural formation.

Skyler knew then, with sudden certainty, where he was.

Something had crashed here. It didn't take much imagination to guess what. The proximity to the Elevator, the ring of chanting subhumans lining the site . . .

He'd found one of Tania's five mystery shell ships. Of this he had no doubt. The objects had trailed in behind the Belém Elevator's construction vessel, and then she'd lost track of them. In truth, no one had given the objects much thought since then. Not that he was aware of, anyway.

Swallowing a growing dread, Skyler crept forward, gun constantly sweeping the fog ahead of him until he reached the mouth of the tunnel.

Faced with that black opening, tall as a two-story home, and no backup, Skyler finally stopped. He stood there, caught between the sane choice of returning to get help and the intoxicating urge to see what lay within.

A vision hit him. The colonists, huddled around the comm, a dozen people speaking at once and as many more coming through the speaker, as they debated the proper course of action to explore the crash site. If it even was a crash site. A slew of other theories were offered. Fair or not, the mental image resonated.

"Yeah," Skyler said to himself, "enough of debate and consensus."

He set to work on his gun again, taking care to keep noise to a minimum. The grenade launcher came off, the flashlight taking its place once again. Backpack re-slung over his shoulders, he took a few tentative steps into the darkness. He glanced back with each step, waiting until he could see little of the ground outside before turning on the flashlight. The last thing he needed right now was for fifty subhumans to spot him and come charging in.

Root systems from the trees above the tunnel dangled from the ceiling, charred and gnarled. The air had an overpowering smoke scent to it. Exposed rocks dotted the curved wall of the circular passage, some cleaved in half, signs of slag from the heat of whatever had forged this cavity. Water trailed down the center of the floor, eroding a jagged path into the darkness.

When the trickle of runoff began to widen into a pool, Skyler knew the back of the tunnel loomed. The diameter of the cavity began to shrink as well, and the heat became stifling. Without taking his eyes off the dark passage, he reached and unzipped his vest. Moisture and sweat trickled down his neck and sides.

Two steps later he caught the first hints of a shape in the gloom. The light from his weapon struggled to illuminate the form at first, as if it were somehow absorbing the beam. Each step brought more clarity, and Skyler was up to his knees in water when he finally had a clear view.

A shell ship, just as he thought. Perhaps ten meters long, miniature compared to those above Belém and Darwin. It rested on the bottom of the tunnel, a portion of it submerged in the pool of runoff. How the Builders' vessel had forged this cave so much wider than its own girth, Skyler had no idea.

The tapered end wasn't quite circular, he realized, but oval. The very tip of it folded inward on itself in a sharp beveled edge, not unlike the corners of the Aura towers. He stepped to one side, staying behind the hulking black form, to study the length of it. Much of the fuselage lay submerged in the rainwater, obscured by steam where the cold pool met balmy air.

His beam caught a gap in the center of the vessel, as if part of the shell had torn off. The gap spanned three meters left to right, and went clear over the top of the vessel.

Knee-high in cold water, Skyler froze up. He dared not draw a breath.

Something lurked within.